D1070337

Three Victorian Detective Novels

The Unknown Weapon
by
ANDREW FORRESTER

My Lady's Money
by
WILKIE COLLINS

The Big Bow Mystery
by
ISRAEL ZANGWILL

Edited and with an Introduction by
E. F. BLEILER

DOVER PUBLICATIONS, INC.
NEW YORK

Published in Canada by General Publishing Company, Ltd., 30 Lesmill Road, Don Mills, Toronto, Ontario.

Published in the United Kingdom by Constable and Company, Ltd.

Three Victorian Detective Novels is a new selection of three unabridged works, first published in collected form by Dover Publications, Inc., in 1978. The novels were originally published as follows:

The Unknown Weapon, by Andrew Forrester, in *The Female Detective*, Ward & Lock, London, 1864.

My Lady's Money, by Wilkie Collins, in the *Illustrated London News*, Christmas Issue, 1877.

The Big Bow Mystery, by Israel Zangwill, in the London *Star*, 1891.

International Standard Book Number: 0-486-23668-4
Library of Congress Catalog Card Number: 77-91266

Manufactured in the United States of America
Dover Publications, Inc.
180 Varick Street
New York, N.Y. 10014

CONTENTS

INTRODUCTION

The early history of the detective story is complex, partly because it was a form of multiple origins and many anticipatory moments, and partly because the question of definition enters into any discussion. What constitutes a detective story, and is it different from a crime story or a mystery story? As may be guessed, there are many answers to these questions.

It is safe to say, however, that despite a few prehistoric works, the modern detective story began in 1841 with Edgar Allan Poe's "Murders in the Rue Morgue." After this the chain of development becomes complex, for in addition to works that were modeled after Poe's stories there were soon other detective stories that grew from other roots. Sometimes these roots were fictional forms, like the early sensation novels; sometimes these roots were historical or social matters, in which fiction simply reflected or enhanced local developments that were important.

The policing of London served as one such focus of interests. Up through the 1820s Metropolitan London had no official police force; crime was contained or not contained by a system of magistrates and court runners, the most famous being the Bow Street Runners, supplemented by various chains of watchmen. In 1829, after decades of squabbling and debate, the Metropolitan police force was formed, and for the next twenty or thirty years the doings of the new Peelers or Bobbies were controversial and received enormous attention in Parliament, in the newspapers and journals, and, in the 1850s and 1860s, in fiction.

The first school of detective fiction in Great Britain did not evolve from the pattern established by Poe; indeed, it peaked before individual authors seem to have become aware of Poe's work. Nor was this first school of British detective fiction connected with the concept of ratiocination (the so-called Zadig or Sherlock Holmes trick of logically basing large conclusions on minutiae of evidence). The stories concerned were narratives of detective work, usually told by a professional detective, reasonably factual in subject matter, but usually melodramatic and sensational in presentation.

The first to have the wit to recognize that the exploits of the London police were interesting as fiction was one "Waters," who authored the story "Recollections of a Police-officer" in *Chambers's Edinburgh Review* in July 1849. Waters may have been aware of the earlier *Richmond; or, Scenes in the Life of a Bow Street Officer* (1827)* which narrated some cases of the fictional Bow Street Runner Thomas Richmond, or, more likely, he may simply have recognized the potential of a police story. "Recollections of a Police-officer" was followed by a sequel, then another, and eventually, in 1852 these stories were published in book form in America as *Recollections of a Detective Police-Officer*. An English edition followed in 1856, and after this came a flood of casebooks based on the exploits of various detective-figures: London detectives, private detectives, sheriffs, customs officers, French detectives, New York detectives, and so on, by Waters and others.

Who was this Waters who set off the first detective story boom in Great Britain in the 1850s and 1860s? Nothing is known of him. His name may have been William Russell (not to be confused with the *Times* correspondent of the same name) but even this is uncertain. A worthy task for a British researcher would be tracking down William Russell in the various public records offices.

Much the same mystery surrounds the most important member of Waters's school, Andrew Forrester, Jr. Forrester's name is to be found on the title pages of five books, but beyond this there is no record of his existence. The name may have been that of a person who dropped out of sight for one reason or another, or it may be a pseudonym. The most that can be said of him is that he seems to have been a well-educated man, that he followed French and American literature, that he was a conscious experimenter in both style and form, and that he may have been a Scot with some legal training.

If I were to make a guess about the identity of Andrew Forrester, Jr., I would consider the probabilities strong that Forrester was a

---

* Reprinted in 1976 by Dover Publications, with introductory material by E. F. Bleiler.

pseudonym chosen to capitalize on the fame of the historical Forrester brothers, who served as detectives for the City of London and
were pioneers in the application of scientific methods to detection.

Andrew Forrester, Jr. wrote three books of crime and detection
stories whose contents may have been assembled from somewhat
earlier periodicals. These books are *The Revelations of a Private
Detective* (1863), *Secret Service* (1864) and *The Female Detective*
(1864). Two other books, *The Private Detective* and *Tales by a
Female Detective*, are partial reissues of the corresponding earlier
books. In these books Forrester seems to have been the first British
detective story writer to reveal an acquaintance with Poe's work, and
to incorporate Poe's techniques into the British form. It should be
noted that this is some fourteen years after Waters wrote the first
casebook stories.

Since these three books are so rare as to be almost unobtainable,
it might be well to describe their contents. *Secret Service,* which is
the weakest of the three books, consists of reminiscences, narratives
and semi-essays about matters criminal and legal. *The Revelations
of a Private Detective* is in much the same vein; indeed, several of
the stories in this book are not concerned with the Private Detective,
but are simple crime stories. Yet there are two stories in this collection that show advances beyond the form established by Waters.
"The Forger's Escape" involves a consultation between the detective and a friend whose hobby is working out the codes and ciphers
in the agony columns of newspapers, a pastime which also delighted
Sherlock Holmes. Even more significant is "Arrested on Suspicion"
in which a young man confesses his admiration for Edgar Allan Poe
and plays detective to save his sister from a false charge of shoplift-
ing. By solving a cipher message and applying ratiocination he de-
tects the true criminals.

The most important of the three books published as by Andrew
Forrester, Jr., however, is *The Female Detective*. This chronicles
seven adventures of the first professional female detective in the
literature, Mrs. G—— of the Metropolitan Police. Five of her cases
deserve mention. "The Tenant for Life" is concerned with a complex inheritance fraud, while "The Unravelled Mystery" follows the
pattern of Poe's "Mystery of Marie Roget" in attempting to solve by
ratiocination the circumstances surrounding a corpse found floating
in the Thames. (There are also echoes of *The Woman in White.*)
"A Child Found Dead, Murder or No Murder" is based on the case
of Constance Kent, a factual murder case which is still remembered

and disputed today. "The Mystery," the final story in the book, is a short sealed room mystery with a touch of humor.

The most significant story in *The Female Detective* is *The Unknown Weapon*, which is reprinted in this volume. Remarkable for its period, it offers the germs of scientific detection in its use of the microscope to analyze dust, and it centers on a very original, colorful crime, considerably more advanced thematically than the exploits of Forrester's contemporaries. Forrester, however, for some reason that will never be known, chose to present this case in the style of a French feuilleton episode, with short paragraphing and short declarative sentences. Since it is the only story in the volume written in this style—the others being smooth and unexperimental—one may wonder whether this is not a suggestion for separate periodical publication of the individual stories at an earlier date.

The Unknown Weapon is also interesting as one of the small group of pioneer works that have some reason to be called the first modern detective novel, much depending on how one defines modern, detective and novel. Its fellows are *The Dead Letter* (1864), a very bad novel by Metta C. Victor, under the pseudonym of Seeley Regester, and *L'Affaire Lerouge* by Emile Gaboriau, which was first serialized in 1865–66, and is, of course, the most important. *The Female Detective* was officially published in May 1864, and would seem to be the earliest of the three, the exact date of Mrs. Victor's novel being unclear.

Andrew Forrester's better work was in advance of his colleagues'; he developed his material into true short stories in the modern sense, with character analysis, action, conflict and dramatic structure, and he seems to have been the first author to recognize that he was writing in a tradition, that of Poe, and was not simply creating ersatz police blotters. Yet it cannot be said that Forrester was important historically, for casebooks continued to be written in the old manner long after Forrester had stopped writing.

II

Andrew Forrester, Jr.'s most important creation was the female detective Mrs. G——, but it is not generally known that Wilkie Collins's first "detective" was also a woman, Anne Rodway, who appeared in the short story "The Diary of Anne Rodway" in *Household Words*, July 1856. In this story, which is generally accessible in the collection *The Queen of Hearts*, Anne Rodway and her friend Mary Mallenson are impoverished seamstresses in London. Mary dies as the result of a concussion which the coroner's inquest rules to be accidental, caused by a fainting spell and fall. Anne Rodway does not accept this decision and, tracing a torn cravat which has been found in Mary's clenched hand, locates the true criminal. The detection that Anne Rodway accomplished, however, was rudimentary, and Collins was really more interested in social matters and the action of fate than in detection. Collins seldom wrote detective stories in the strictest sense.

One of the few exceptions to this last statement is *My Lady's Money*, which first appeared in the Christmas Number of the *Illustrated London News* for 1877. It contains a crime, an informal detective, a formal detective, a rational methodology for solving the crime, and a puzzle for the reader. A short novel, too long for inclusion in collections, too short for saleable separate publication, it has not been reprinted very often and is now almost forgotten. In the nineteenth century it was often doubled with another short novel by Collins from the same period, *The Haunted Hotel.**

The year that *My Lady's Money* was written, 1877, was a bad year for Wilkie Collins (1824–89). He was now 53 years old, and his best work was behind him, although he was still popular and had no difficulty in placing his fiction. But the days of the great mystery novels were gone, and *The Woman in White* (1859–60), *Armadale* (1866) and *The Moonstone* (1868) were memories on a shelf. Collins could still manipulate complex plots, create mystery and discovery situations (not strong enough to be called detective fiction), but his focus was on the novel of social problem and this area, of course, was not his forte.

Collins was in bad health in 1877. His gout, which had settled in his eyes, was bothering him badly, and was to become worse the next year. At times he was blind in one eye, and had to remain in a darkened room. Some of his work during this period was dictated, since he could not write. His drug habit, too, was at a peak. To tolerate the severe ocular pain, he consumed unbelievable quantities of laudanum, his tolerance having become so great that he could

---

* Reprinted in 1975 by Dover Publications in *Three Supernatural Novels of the Victorian Period*, edited by E. F. Bleiler.

consume as much in a single sitting as would kill an ordinary man. (Indeed, one of his servants took half of one of Collins's doses, and died!)

During the fall of 1877, just before the composition of *My Lady's Money*, Collins had been traveling in Switzerland with his friend Frank Lehmann. One day Lehmann suddenly saw Collins transformed into a shocking travesty of himself: his supply of laudanum had run out and he was having withdrawal symptoms. Collins declared that he could not survive until they returned to Paris, unless he obtained a large quantity of his drug. The two men thereupon posed as English physicians and, going to various apothecaries and writing themselves prescriptions for the maximum amount allowed by law, barely managed to get enough laudanum to bring Collins home.

On his return to London Collins received a commission to prepare a short novel for the Christmas issue of the *Illustrated London News*. It was customary in Christmas issues, which were usually out of series, to feature thrillers, ghost stories or mysteries, and Collins prepared a mystery which demonstrates much of his old skill at revivifying old themes by imaginative development.

The basic themes in *My Lady's Money* are theft and deception, types of criminality that interested Collins much more than the murders which have since become accepted as standard themes. His ultimate plot is by no means original, being a fairly common one for Victorian mysteries—"The Ebony Box" and "The Stolen Necklace" by Mrs. Henry Wood come to mind—but Collins still offers his usual good characterizations and painterly detail.

Collins also conformed to the contemporary method for pointing a mystery story. One of the ways in which the typical Victorian mystery or detective story differed from the modern is that the puzzle element for the reader lay not so much in identities as in means. That is to say, in the modern classical detective story the author's aim is to conceal the criminal from the reader; there are even severe rules, according to some, as to how "fair" the author should be with the reader. In the typical Victorian situation, on the other hand, the identity of the criminal must have been obvious to the dullest reader at an early stage, and the focus of the story was on resolving the problem that the criminal had created. All this, of course, may be a Gothic hangover. In Collins's earlier *Moonstone*, for example, after a short time it was obvious that Ablewhite had stolen the gem; the question that occupied most of the novel there-after was how the lost nexus around the stone could be rewoven.

In his concept of a detective, however, Collins is not entirely typical. Old Sharon is quite different from most of the fictional professional detectives of his day, who were desperately anxious to achieve the respectability that had so long evaded their profession. In part Old Sharon is probably emergent from Gaboriau's Père Tabaret; indeed, Sharon, on first appearance, waves a French novel which he praises and states that in it there is a detective much like himself. It must be admitted, however, that the demonic aspect of Sharon is not present in Tabaret, and is more reminiscent of the half-monstrous figures that appear in the lower-level popular literature of the day. America, too, may play a part in the formation of Old Sharon. Four or five years before *My Lady's Money* appeared, the American detective Old Sleuth started the detective rage in dime-novel publishing, with a series of exploits published by George Munro. Old Sleuth is old, retired, and one of his favorite disguises is that of a particularly repulsive tramp. There is no record, how-ever, that Collins was aware of Old Sleuth and this resemblance should not be pushed too far.

It is also possible that still another element emerges in Old Sharon, not fictional, but a projection of the humiliation that Collins had suffered not long before, when he ran out of his drug. Collins was not reticent or apologetic about taking laudanum, which he often did in company, but at no other time, that I have been able to discover, did he break down as he did in Switzerland. Did Old Sharon's love-me-or-leave-me attitude carry wider implications than Collins himself realized?

III

Wilkie Collins, to state a truism, was obviously the Victorian mystery novelist par excellence (Doyle being a short-story writer primarily), and he is now remembered for three great mysteries.

Just the opposite is true, however, of Israel Zangwill (1864–1926), who wrote one of the landmark novels in the history of the detective novel, *The Big Bow Mystery*. *The Big Bow Mystery* does not align itself with Zangwill's life interests, and Zangwill is now remembered for his role in Judaism at the turn of the century.

Zangwill, whose name means spice or ginger in Hebrew, was born in London of immigrant parents; his father came from Latvia, his mother from Poland. His father was a peddler who was away from the household for long periods of time, wandering about the West Country, and the family was very poor. Religion permeated the household in much the same radical ambiguity that appeared in Zangwill's own life: his father was a very pious man, and eventually migrated to Palestine, while his mother was almost irreligious. Although in later life Zangwill was an active Zionist, the right-hand man of Herzl, he married a Christian girl and felt himself as much Hellenic Christian as Jewish.

After early childhood in Bristol, attendance at the Jews' Free School in London, and a Triple First at the University of London, Zangwill turned to journalism for a livelihood. He worked on various papers and journals for several years, with reportage, essays, humor and short stories.

Fame came to Zangwill as the result of an essay entitled "Judaism," which appeared in the *Jewish Quarterly Review* in England. The essay was called to the attention of the Jewish Publication Society of America, which had just been founded, and was looking for a suitable author to write a *"Robert Elsmere* of Judaism." The Jewish Publication Society of America sponsored Zangwill, and the result was *Children of the Ghetto* (1892), a novel about aspirations in the then London ghetto. This work established Zangwill as a writer of international reputation. It was followed by similar works: *Ghetto Tragedies* (1893), *The King of Schnorrers* (1894), *They That Walk in Darkness* (1899) and others. After a time, however, Zangwill felt that his bent was drama, and he wrote many plays for the London and New York stages, the best-known being *Merely Mary Ann* (based on his novel of the same name) and *The Melting Pot* (1908), which was very popular in America.

More important to Zangwill than his literary work, however, was his activity as a Zionist. He had become acquainted with Herzl around 1895, and for many years worked with Herzl attempting to found Jewish national homes in Uganda, or Mexico, or Australia or elsewhere. After Herzl's death Zangwill and his followers clashed with Weizmann, and eventually a schism took place within the Zionist movement, as Zangwill walked out. Zangwill, although amiable, generous, humorous and kindly, was always something of a stormy petrel, and his last adventure in the world of Judaism cost him much. Under the auspices of the American Jewish Congress Zangwill delivered the now famous address, "Watchman, What of the Night?" in which he attacked political Zionism, American Judaism and many other things. His action was bitterly resented, and he returned to England discredited and disgruntled.

All this public life, the ghetto novels, involvement with the stage, dedication to his own blend of Hellenism and Judaism, however, have little to do with *The Big Bow Mystery*, which is best seen as one of a group of works with which Zangwill experimented before achieving his individuality.

The Big Bow Mystery first appeared serially in 1891 in the London *Star*, a daily on which Zangwill was working at the time. According to some biographical accounts, he wrote the story in a single sitting; his own account, in the introduction to the novel, is more credible. Apart from its mystery aspect, which is properly Zangwill's, it is greatly indebted to the periodical literature of the time, and a reader can find in it traces of F. Anstey and Jerome K. Jerome. Despite the divagations of a young, undisciplined, ebullient author, however, *The Big Bow Mystery* occupies a prominent place in the development of the detective story. It was the first significant story to be based solidly and solely on the concept of the locked room. This storeme, which is one of the central situations in the modern detective story, involves a seemingly impossible crime, committed in a room so secured that neither entry nor exit is possible.

Before Zangwill there had been several isolated stories that involved the sealed room situation. The earliest known at this moment (though earlier may well turn up) is J. S. LeFanu's "Passage in the Secret History of an Irish Countess" (1838), where the mystery is explained by a trick window frame. LeFanu later used the same concept in his masterly *Uncle Silas*, which is an expanded version of the short story. Much more important historically, however, is Poe's "Murders in the Rue Morgue" (1841), which involves the now familiar situation of an ape's transcendence of human limitations as a criminal. Those readers who read Poe avidly, and there were some on both sides of the Atlantic, often lighted upon the sealed room situation and made use of it. In all these stories, however, the idea of the sealed room was not recognized for its total power, and it remained for Zangwill to strike the heart situation in fullest clarity.

Since Zangwill's day sealed room mysteries have become quite common, and much ingenuity has been expended on working out mechanisms. There have been sealed rooms that involve elaborate devices for closing doors or windows, pulling latches, turning keys or slamming bolts. There have been sealed rooms that are elaborately invaded by unsuspected means—more sophisticated versions of secret passages; sealed rooms that necessitate the paraphernalia of professional magicians; sealed rooms that turn out to be fraudulent, sealed rooms that are constructed after the event, and many more. In all probability more imagination has been devoted to sealing rooms than to any other motif in the form. And behind practically all this stand two early classics, *The Mystery of the Yellow Room* by Gaston Leroux* and *The Big Bow Mystery* by Israel Zangwill.

IV

These three novels have been chosen to fit two criteria. First, they are eminently readable. Secondly, each exemplifies a moment in the history of the detective story. The story by Andrew Forrester, Jr. shows development within the early casebooks, the first stirrings away from narrative into a more imaginative form. Wilkie Collins's *My Lady's Money* shows a typical detective story of the 1860s or 1870s, within a different stream of development, the domestic novel enlivened by sensation. Zangwill's *Big Bow Mystery* shows the first stirrings of something new, a sophisticated idea and a successful desire to deceive the reader. After *The Big Bow Mystery* the way was open to the new Edwardian detective novel.

New York, 1977   E. F. Bleiler

---

* Reprinted in 1977 by Dover Publications.

The Unknown Weapon

by

ANDREW FORRESTER

I am about to set out here one of the most remarkable cases which have come under my actual observation.

I will give the particulars, as far as I can, in the form of a narrative.

The scene of the affair lay in a midland county, and on the outskirts of a very rustic and retired village, which has at no time come before the attention of the world.

Here are the exact preliminary facts of the case. Of course I alter names, for as this case is now to become public, and as the inquiries which took place at the time not only ended in disappointment, but by some inexplicable means did not arrest the public curiosity, there can be no wisdom in covering the names and places with such a thin veil of fiction as will allow of the truth being seen below that literary gauze. The names and places here used are wholly fictitious, and in no degree represent or shadow out the actual personages or localities.

The mansion at which the mystery which I am about to analyse took place was the manor-house, while its occupant, the squire of the district, was also the lord of the manor. I will call him Petleigh.

I may at once state here, though the fact did not come to my knowledge till after the catastrophe, that the squire was a thoroughly mean man, with but one other passion than the love of money, and that was a greed for plate.

Every man who has lived with his eyes open has come across human beings who concentrate within themselves the most wonderful contradictions. Here is a man who lives so scampishly that it is a question if ever he earnt an honest shilling, and yet he would firmly believe his moral character would be lost did he enter a theatre; there is an individual who never sent away a creditor or took more than a just commercial discount, while any day in the week he may be arrested upon a charge which would make him a scandal to his family.

So with Squire Petleigh. That he was extremely avaricious there can be no doubt, while his desire for the possession and display of plate was almost a mania.

His silver was quite a tradition in the county. At every meal—and I have heard the meals at Petleighcote were neither abundant nor succulent—enough plate stood upon the table to pay for the feeding of the poor of the whole county for a month. He would eat a mutton chop off silver.

Mr. Petleigh was in parliament, and in the season came up to town, where he had the smallest and most miserable house ever rented by a wealthy county member.

Avaricious, and therefore illiberal, Petleigh would not keep up two establishments; and so, when he came to town for the parliamentary season, he brought with him his country establishment, all the servants composing which were paid but third-class fares up to town.

The domestics I am quite sure, from what I learnt, were far from satisfactory people; a condition of things which was quite natural, seeing that they were not treated well, and were taken on at the lowest possible rate of wages.

The only servitor who remained permanently on the establishment was the housekeeper at the manor-house, Mrs. Quinion.

It was whispered in the neighbourhood that she had been the foster-sister ("and perhaps more") of the late Mrs. Petleigh; and it was stated wih sufficient openness, and I am afraid also with some general amount of chuckling satisfaction, that the squire had been bitten with his lady.

The truth stood that Petleigh had married the daughter of a Liverpool merchant in the great hope of an alliance with her fortune, which at the date of her marriage promised to be large. But cotton commerce, even twenty-five years ago, was a risky business, and to curtail here particulars which are only remotely essential to the absolute comprehension of this narrative, he never had a penny with her, and his wife's father, who had led a deplorably irregular life, started for America and died there.

Mrs. Petleigh had but one child, Graham Petleigh, and she died when he was about twelve years of age.

During Mrs. Petleigh's life, the housekeeper at Petleighcote was the foster-sister to whom reference has been made. I myself believe that it would have been more truthful to call Mrs. Quinion the natural sister of the squire's wife.

Be that as it may, after the lady's death Mrs. Quinion, in a half-conceded, and after an uncomfortable fashion, became in a measure the actual mistress of Petleighcote.

Possibly the squire was aware of a relationship to his wife at which I have hinted, and was therefore not unready in recognising that it was better she should be in the house than any other woman. For, apart from his avariciousness and his mania for the display of plate, I found beyond all dispute that he was a man of very estimable judgment.

Again, Mrs. Quinion fell in with his avaricious humour. She shaved down his household expenses, and was herself contented with a very moderate remuneration.

From all I learnt, I came to the conclusion that Petleighcote had long been the most uncomfortable house in the county, the display of plate only tending to intensify the general barrenness.

Very few visitors came to the house, and hospitality was unknown; yet, notwithstanding these drawbacks, Petleigh stood very well in the county, and indeed, on the occasion of one or two charitable collections, he had appeared in print with sufficient success.

Those of my readers who live in the country will comprehend the style of the squire's household when I say that he grudged permission to shoot rabbits on his ground. Whenever possible, all the year round, specimens of that rather tiring food were to be found in Squire Petleigh's larder. In fact, I learnt that a young curate who remained a short time at Tram (the village), in gentle satire of this cheap system of rations, called Petleighcote the "Warren."

The son, Graham Petleigh, was brought up in a deplorable style, the father being willing to persuade himself, perhaps, that as he had been disappointed in his hopes of a fortune with the mother, the son did not call for that consideration to which he would have been entitled had the mother brought her husband increased riches. It is certain that the boy roughed life. All the schooling he got was that which could be afforded by a foundation grammar school, which happened fortunately to exist at Tram.

To this establishment he went sometimes, while at others he was off with lads miserably below him in station, upon some expedition which was not perhaps, as a rule, so respectable an employment as studying the humanities.

Evidently the boy was shamefully ill-used; for he was neglected.

By the time he was nineteen or twenty (all these particulars I learnt readily after the catastrophe, for the townsfolk were only too eager to talk of the unfortunate young man)—by the time he was nineteen or twenty, a score of years of neglect bore their fruit. He was ready, beyond any question, for any mad performance. Poaching especially was his delight, perhaps in a great measure because he found it profitable; because, to state the truth, he was kept totally without money, and to this disadvantage he added a second, that of being unable to spread what money he did obtain over any expanse of time.

I have no doubt myself that the depredations on his father's estate might have with justice been put to his account, and, from the inquiries I made, I am equally free to believe that when any small article of the mass of plate about the premises was missing, that the son knew a good deal more than was satisfactory of the lost valuables.

That Mrs. Quinion, the housekeeper, was extremely devoted to the young man is certain; but the money she received as wages, and whatever private or other means she had, could not cover the demands made upon them by young Graham Petleigh, who certainly spent money, though where it came from was a matter of very great uncertainty.

From the portrait I saw of him, he must have been of a daring, roving, jovial disposition—a youngster not inclined to let duty come between him and his inclinations; one, in short, who would get more out of the world than he would give it.

The plate was carried up to town each year with the establishment, the boxes being under the special guardianship of the butler, who never let them out of his sight between the country and town houses. The man, I have heard, looked forward to those journeys with absolute fear.

From what I learnt, I suppose the convoy of plate boxes numbered well on towards a score.

Graham Petleigh sometimes accompanied his father to town, and at other times was sent to a relative in Cornwall. I believe it suited father and son better that the latter should be packed off to Cornwall in the parliamentary season, for in town the lad necessarily became comparatively expensive—an objection in the eyes of the father, while the son found himself in a world to which, thanks to the education he had received, he was totally unfitted.

Young Petleigh's passion was horses, and there was not a farmer on the father's estate, or in the neighbourhood of Tram, who was not plagued for the loan of this or that horse—for the young man had none of his own.

On my part, I believe if the youth had no self-respect, the want was in a great measure owing to the father having had not any for his son.

I know I need scarcely add, that when a man is passionately fond of horses generally he bets on those quadrupeds.

It did not call for many inquiries to ascertain that young Petleigh had "put" a good deal of money upon horses, and that, as a rule, he had been lucky with them. The young man wanted some excitement, some occupation, and he found it in betting. Have I said that after the young heir was taken from the school he was allowed to run loose? This was the case. I presume the father could not bring his mind to incurring the expense of entering his son at some profession.

Things then at Petleighcote were in this condition; the father neglectful and avaricious; the son careless, neglected, and daily slipping down the ladder of life; and the housekeeper, Mrs. Quinion, saying nothing, doing nothing, but existing, and perhaps showing that she was attached to her foster-sister's son. She was a woman of much sound and discriminating sense, and it is certain that she expressed herself to the effect that she foresaw the young man was being silently, steadfastly, unceasingly ruined.

All these preliminaries comprehended, I may proceed to the action of this narrative.

It was the 19th of May (the year is unimportant), and early in the morning when the discovery was made, by the gardener to Squire Petleigh—one Tom Brown.

Outside the great hall-door, and huddled together in an extraordinary fashion, the gardener, at half-past five in the morning (a Tuesday), found lying a human form. And when he came to make an examination, he discovered that it was the dead body of the young squire.

Seizing the handle of the great bell, he quickly sounded an alarm, and within a minute the housekeeper herself and the one servant, who together numbered the household which slept at Petleighcote when the squire was in town, stood on the threshold of the open door.

The housekeeper was half-dressed, the servant wench was huddled up in a petticoat and a blanket.

The news spread very rapidly, by means of the gardener's boy, who, wondering where his master was stopping, came loafing about the house, quickly to find the use of his legs.

"He must have had a fit," said the housekeeper; and it was a flying message to that effect carried by the boy into the village, which brought the village doctor to the spot in the quickest possible time.

It was then found that the catastrophe was due to no *fit*.

A very slight examination showed that the young squire had died from a stab caused by a rough iron barb, the metal shaft of which was six inches long, and which still remained in the body.

At the inquest, the medical man deposed that very great force must have been used in thrusting the barb into the body, for one of the ribs had been half severed by the act. The stab given, the barb had evidently been drawn back with the view of extracting it—a purpose which had failed, the flanges of the barb having fixed themselves firmly in the cartilage and tissue about it. It was impossible the deceased could have turned the barb against himself in the manner in which it had been used.

Asked what this barb appeared like, the surgeon was unable to reply. He had never seen such a weapon before. He supposed it had been fixed in a shaft of wood, from which it had been wrenched by the strength with which the barb, after the thrust, had been held by the parts surrounding the wound.

The barb was handed round to the jury, and every man cordially agreed with his neighbour that he had never seen anything of the kind before; it was equally strange to all of them.

The squire, who took the catastrophe with great coolness, gave evidence to the effect that he had seen his son on the morning previous to the discovery of the murder, and about noon—seventeen and a half hours before the catastrophe was discovered. He did not know his son was about to leave town, where he had been staying. He added that he had not missed the young man; his son was in the habit of being his own master, and going where he liked. He could offer no explanation as to why his son had returned to the country, or why the materials found upon him were there. He could offer no explanation in any way about anything connected with the matter.

It was said, as a scandal in Tram, that the squire exhibited no emotion upon giving his evidence, and that when he sat down after his examination he appeared relieved.

Furthermore, it was intimated that upon being called upon to submit to a kind of cross-examination, he appeared to be anxious, and answered the few questions guardedly.

These questions were put by one of the jurymen—a solicitor's clerk (of some acuteness it was evident), who was the Tram oracle.

It is perhaps necessary for the right understanding of this case, that these questions should be here reported, and their answers also.

They ran as follows:

"Do you think your son died where he was found?"

"I have formed no opinion."

"Do you think he had been in your house?"

"Certainly not."

"Why are you so certain?"

"Because had he entered the house, my housekeeper would have known of his coming."

"Is your housekeeper here?"

"Yes."

"Has it been intended that she should be called as a witness?"

"Yes."

"Do you think your son attempted to break into your house?"

[The reason for this question I will make apparent shortly. By the way, I should, perhaps, here at once explain that I obtained all these particulars of the evidence from the county paper.]

"Do you think your son attempted to break into your house?"

"Why should he?"

"That is not my question. Do you think he attempted to break into your house?"

"No, I do not."

"You swear that, Mr. Petleigh?"

[By the way, there was no love lost between the squire and the

Tram oracle, for the simple reason that not any existed that could be spilt.]

"I do swear it."

"Do you think there was anybody in the house he wished to visit clandestinely?"

"No."

"Who were in the house?"

"Mrs. Quinion, my housekeeper, and one servant woman."

"Is the servant here?"

"Yes."

"What kind of a woman is she?"

"Really Mr. Mortoun you can see her and judge for yourself."

"So we can. I am only going to ask one question more."

"I reserve to myself the decision whether I shall or shall not answer it."

"I think you will answer it, Mr. Petleigh."

"It remains, sir, to be seen. Put your question."

"It is very simple—do you intend to offer a reward for the discovery of the murderer of your son?"

The squire made no reply.

"You have heard my question, Mr. Petleigh."

"I have."

"And what is your answer?"

The squire paused for some moments. I should state that I am adding the particulars of the inquest I picked up, or detected if you like better, to the information afforded by the county paper to which I have already referred.

"I refuse to reply," said the squire.

Mortoun thereupon applied to the coroner for his ruling.

Now it appears evident to me that this juryman had some hidden motive in thus questioning the squire. If this were so, I am free to confess I never discovered it beyond any question of doubt. I may or I may not have hit on his motive. I believe I did.

It is clear that the question Mr. Mortoun urged was badly put, for how could the father decide whether he would offer a reward for the discovery of a murderer who did not legally exist till after the finding of the jury? And indeed it may furthermore be added that this question had no bearing upon the elucidation of the mystery, or at all events it had no apparent bearing upon the facts of the catastrophe.

It is evident that Mr. Mortoun was actuated in all probability by one of two motives, both of which were obscure. One might have been an attempt really to obtain a clue to the murder, the other might have been the endeavour to bring the squire, with whom it has been said he lived bad friends, into disrespect with the county.

The oracle-juryman immediately applied to the coroner, who at once admitted that the question was not pertinent, but nevertheless urged the squire as the question had been put to answer it.

It is evident that the coroner saw the awkward position in which the squire was placed, and spoke as he did in order to enable the squire to come out of the difficulty in the least objectionable manner.

But as I have said, Mr. Petleigh, all his incongruities and faults apart, was a clear-seeing man of a good and clear mind. As I saw the want of consistency in the question, as I read it, so he must have remarked the same failure when it was addressed to him.

For after patiently hearing the coroner to the end of his remarks, Petleigh said, quietly,——

"How can I say I will offer a reward for the discovery of certain murderers when the jury have not yet returned a verdict of murder?"

"But supposing the jury do return such a verdict?" asked Mortoun.

"Why then it will be time for you to ask your question."

I learnt that the juryman smiled as he bowed and said he was satisfied.

It appears to me that at that point Mr. Mortoun must have either gained that information which fitted in with his theory, or, accepting the lower motive for his question, that he felt he had now sufficiently damaged the squire in the opinion of the county. For the reporters were at work, and every soul present knew that not a word said would escape publication in the county paper.

Mr. Mortoun however was to be worsted within the space of a minute.

"Have you ceased questioning me, gentlemen?" asked the squire.

The coroner bowed, it appeared.

"Then," continued the squire, "before I sit down—and you will allow me to remain in the room until the inquiry is terminated—I will state that of my own free will which I would not submit to make public upon an illegal and a totally uncalled for attempt at compulsion. Should the jury bring in a verdict of murder against unknown persons, I shall *not* offer a reward for the discovery of those alleged murderers."

"Why not?" asked the coroner, who I learnt afterwards admitted that the question was utterly unpardonable.

"Because," said Squire Petleigh, "it is quite my opinion that no *murder* has been committed."

According to the newspaper report these words were followed by "sensation."

"No murder?" said the coroner.

"No; the death of the deceased was, I am sure, an accident."

"What makes you think that, Mr. Petleigh?"

"The nature of the death. Murders are not committed, I should think, in any such extraordinary manner as that by which my son came to his end. I have no more to say."

"Here," says the report, "the squire took his seat."

The next witness called—the gardener who had discovered the body had already been heard, and simply testified to the finding of the body—was Margaret Quinion, the housekeeper.

Her depositions were totally valueless from my point of view, that of the death of the young squire. She stated simply that she had gone to bed at the usual time (about ten) on the previous night, and that Dinah Yarton retired just previously, and to the same room. She heard no noise during the night, was disturbed in no way whatever until the alarm was given by the gardener.

In her turn Mrs. Quinion was now questioned by the solicitor's clerk, Mr. Mortoun.

"Do you and this—what is her name?—Dinah Yarton; do you and she sleep alone at Petleighcote?"

"Yes—when the family is away."

"Are you not afraid to do so?"

"No."

"Why?"

"Why should I be?"

"Well—most women are afraid to sleep in large lonely houses by themselves. Are you not afraid of burglars?"

"No."

"Why not?"

"Simply because burglars would find so little at Petleighcote to steal that they would be very foolish to break into the house."

"But there is a good deal of plate in the house—isn't there?"

"It all goes up to town with Mr. Petleigh."

"All, ma'am?"

"Every ounce—as a rule."

"You say the girl sleeps in your room?"

"In my room."

"Is she an attractive girl?"

"No."

"Is she unattractive?"

"You will have an opportunity of judging, for she will be called as a witness, sir."

"Oh; you don't think, do you, that there was anything between this young person and your young master?"

"Between Dinah and young Mr. Petleigh?"

"Yes."

"I think there could hardly be any affair between them, for [here she smiled] they have never seen each other—the girl having come to Petleighcote from the next county only three weeks since, and three months after the family had gone to town."

"Oh; pray have you not expected your master's son home recently?"

"I have not expected young Mr. Petleigh home recently—he never comes home when the family is away."

"Was he not in the habit of coming to Petleighcote unexpectedly?"

"No."

"You know that for a fact?"

"I know that for a fact."

"Was the deceased kept without money?"

"I know nothing of the money arrangements between the father and son."

"Well—do you know that often he wanted money?"

"Really—I decline to answer that question."

"Well—did he borrow money habitually from you?"

"I decline also to answer that question."

"You say you heard nothing in the night?"

"Not anything."

"What did you do when you were alarmed by the gardener in the morning?"

"I am at a loss to understand your question."

"It is very plain, nevertheless. What was your first act after hearing the catastrophe?"

[After some consideration.] "It is really almost impossible, I should say, upon such terrible occasions as was that, to be able distinctly to say what is one's first act or words, but I believe the first thing I did, or the first I remember, was to look after Dinah."

"And why could she not look after herself?"

"Simply because she had fallen into a sort of epileptic fit—to which she is subject—upon seeing the body."

"Then you can throw no light upon this mysterious affair?"

"No light: all I know of it was the recognition of the body of Mr. Petleigh, junior, in the morning."

The girl Dinah Yarton was now called, but no sooner did the unfortunate young woman, waiting in the hall of the publichouse at which the inquest was held, hear her name, than she swooped into a fit which totally precluded her from giving any evidence "except," as the county paper facetiously remarked, "the proof by her screams that her lungs were in a very enviable condition."

"She will soon recover," said Mrs. Quinion, "and will be able to give what evidence she can."

"And what will that be, Mrs. Quinion?" asked the solicitor's clerk.

"I am not able to say, Mr. Mortoun," she replied.

The next witness called (and here as an old police-constable I may remark upon the unbusiness-like way in which the witnesses were arranged)—the next witness called was the doctor.

His evidence was as follows, omitting the purely professional points. "I was called to the deceased on Tuesday morning, at near upon six in the morning. I recognized the body as that of Mr. Petleigh junior. Life was quite extinct. He had been dead about seven or eight hours, as well as I could judge. That would bring his death about ten or eleven on the previous night. Death had been caused by a stab, which had penetrated the left lung. The deceased had bled inwardly. The instrument which had caused death had remained in the wound, and stopped what little effusion of blood there would otherwise have been. Deceased literally died from suffocation, the blood leaking into the lungs and filling them. All the other organs of the body were in a healthy condition. The instrument by which death was produced is one with which I have no acquaintance. It is a kind of iron arrow, very roughly made, and with a shaft. It must have been fixed in some kind of handle when it was used, and which must have yielded and loosed the barb when an attempt was made to withdraw it—an attempt which had been made, because I found that one of the flanges of the arrow had caught behind a rib. I repeat that I am totaly unacquainted with the instrument with which death was effected. It is remarkably coarse and rough. The deceased might have lived a quarter of a minute after the wound had been inflicted. He would not in all probability have called out. There is no evidence of the least struggle having taken place—not a particle of evidence can I find to show that the deceased had exhibited even any knowledge of danger. And yet, nevertheless, supposing the deceased not to have been asleep at the time of the murder, for murder it undoubtedly was, or manslaughter, he must have seen his assailant, who, from the position of the weapon, must have been more before than behind him. Assuredly the death was the result of either murder or accident, and not the result of suicide, because I will stake my professional reputation that it would be quite impossible for any man to thrust such an instrument into his body with such a force as in this case has been used, as is proved by the cutting of a true bone-formed rib. Nor could a suicide, under such circumstances as those of the present catastrophe, have thrust the dart in the direction which this took. To sum up, it is my opinion that the deceased was murdered without, on his part, any knowledge of the murderer."

Mr. Mortoun cross-examined the doctor:

To this gentleman's inquiries he answered willingly.

"Do you think, Dr. Pitcherley, that no blood flowed externally?"

"Of that I am quite sure."

"How?"

"There were no marks of blood on the clothes."

"Then the inference stands that no blood stained the place of the murder?"

"Certainly."

"Then the body may have been brought an immense way, and no spots of blood would form a clue to the road?"

"Not one."

"Is it your impression that the murder was committed far away from the spot, or near the place where the body was found?"

"This question is one which it is quite out of my power to answer, Mr. Mortoun, my duty here being to give evidence as to my being called to the deceased, and as to the cause of death. But I need not tell you that I have formed my own theory of the catastrophe, and if the jury desire to have it, I am ready to offer it for their consideration."

Here there was a consultation, from which it resulted that the jury expressed themselves very desirous of obtaining the doctor's impression.

[I have no doubt the following words led the jury to their decision.]

The medical gentleman said:

"It is my impression that this death resulted out of a poaching—I will not say affray—but accident. It is thoroughly well-known in these districts, and at such a juncture as the present I need feel no false delicacy, Mr. Petleigh, in making this statement, that young Petleigh was much given to poaching. I believe that he and his companions were out poaching—I myself on two separate occasions, being called out to nightcases, saw the young gentleman under very suspicious circumstances—and that one of the party was armed with the weapon which caused the death, and which may have been carried at the end of such a heavy stick as is frequently used for flinging at rabbits. I suppose that by some frightful accident —we all know how dreadful are the surgical accidents which frequently arise when weapons are in use—the young man was wounded mortally, and so died, after the frightened companion had hurriedly attempted to withdraw the arrow, only to leave the barb sticking in the body and hooked behind a rib, while the force used in the resistance of the bone caused the weapon to part company from the haft. The discovery of the body outside the father's house can then readily be accounted for. His companions knowing who he was, and dreading their identification with an act which could but result in their own condemnation of character, carried the body to the threshold of his father's house, and there left it. This," the doctor concluded, "appears to me the most rational mode I can find of accounting for the circumstances of this remarkable and deplorable case. I apologize to Mr. Petleigh for the slur to which I may have committed myself in referring to the character of that gentleman's son, the deceased, but my excuse must rest in this fact, that where a crime or catastrophe is so obscure that the criminal, or guilty person, may be in one of many directions, it is but just to narrow the circle of inquiry as much as possible, in order to avoid the resting of suspicion upon the greater number of individuals. If, however, any one can suggest a more lucid explanation of the catastrophe than mine, I shall indeed be glad to admit I was wrong."

[There can be little question, I repeat, that Dr. Pitcherley's analysis fitted in very satisfactorily and plausibly with the facts of the case.]

Mr. Mortoun asked Dr. Pitcherley no more questions.

The next witness called was the police-constable of Tram, a stupid, hopeless dolt, as I found to my cost, who was good at a rustic publichouse row, but who as a detective was not worth my dog Dart.

It appeared that he gave his flat evidence with a stupidity which called even for the rebuke of the coroner.

All he could say was, that he was called, and that he went, and that he saw whose body it "be'd." That was "arl" he could say.

Mr. Mortoun took him in hand, but even he could do nothing with the man.

"Had many persons been on the spot where the body was found before he arrived?"

"Noa."

"How was that?"

"Whoy, 'cos Toom Broown, the gard'ner, coomed t'him at wun-cet, and 'cos Toom Broown coomed t'him furst, 'cas he's cot wur furst coomed too."

This was so, as I found when I went down to Tram. The gardener, Brown, panic-stricken, after calling to, and obtaining the attention of the housekeeper, had rushed off to the village for that needless help which all panic-stricken people will seek, and the constable's cottage happening to be the first dwelling he reached, the constable obtained the first alarm. Now, had the case been conducted properly, the constable being the first man to get the alarm, would have obtained such evidence as would at once have put the detectives on the right scent.

The first two questions put by the lawyerlike juryman showed that he saw how important the evidence might have been which this witness, Joseph Higgins by name, should have given had he but known his business.

The first question was——

"It had rained, hadn't it, on the Monday night?"

[That previous to the catastrophe.]

"Ye-es t'had rained," Higgins replied.

Then followed this important question:

"You were on the spot one of the very first. Did you notice if there were any footsteps about?"

It appears to me very clear that Mr. Mortoun was here following up the theory of the catastrophe offered by the doctor. It would be clear that if several poaching companions had carried the young squire, after death, to the hall-door, that, as rain had fallen during the night, there would inevitably be many boot-marks on the soft ground.

This question put, the witness asked, "Wh-a-at?"

The question was repeated.

"Noa," he replied; "ah didn't see noa foot ma-arks."

"Did you look for any?"

"Noa; ah didn't look for any."

"Then you don't know your business," said Mr. Mortoun.

And the juryman was right; for I may tell the reader that boot-marks have sent more men to the gallows, as parts of circumstantial evidence, than any other proof whatever; indeed, the evidence of the boot-mark is terrible. A nail fallen out, or two or three put very close together, a broken nail, or all the nails perfect, have, times out of number, identified the boot of the suspected man with the boot-mark near the murdered, and has been the first link of the chain of evidence which has dragged a murderer to the gallows, or a minor felon to the hulks.

Indeed, if I were advising evil-doers on the best means of avoiding detection, I would say by all means take a second pair of boots in your pocket, and when you near the scene of your work change those you have on for those you have in your pocket, and do your wickedness in these latter; flee from the scene in these latter, and when you have "made" some distance, why return to your other boots, and carefully hide the tell-tale pair. Then the boots you wear will rather be a proof of your innocence than presumable evidence of your guilt.

Nor let any one be shocked at this public advice to rascals; for I flatter myself I have a counter-mode of foiling such a felonious arrangement as this one of two pairs of boots. And as I have disseminated the mode amongst the police, any attempt to put the suggestions I have offered actually into action, would be attended with greater chances of detection than would be incurred by running the ordinary risk.

To return to the subject in hand.

The constable of Tram, the only human being in the town, Mortoun apart perhaps, who should have known, in the ordinary course of his duty, the value of every foot-mark near the dead body, had totally neglected a precaution which, had he observed it, must have led to a discovery (and an immediate one), which in consequence of his dullness was never publicly made.

Nothing could be more certain than this, that what is called foot-mark evidence was totally wanting.

The constable taking no observations, not the cutest detective in existence could have obtained any evidence of this character, for the news of the catastrophe spreading, as news only spreads in villages, the rustics tramped up in scores, and so obliterated what foot-marks might have existed.

To be brief, Mr. Josh. Higgins could give no evidence worth hearing.

And now the only depositions which remained to be given were those of Dinah Yarton.

She came into court "much reduced," said the paper from which I gain these particulars, "from the effects of the succession of fits which she had fallen into and struggled out of."

She was so stupid that every question had to be repeated in half-a-dozen shapes before she could offer a single reply. It took four inquiries to get at her name, three to know where she lived, five to know what she was; while the coroner and the jury, after a score of questions, gave over trying to ascertain whether she knew the nature of an oath. However, as she stated that she was quite sure she would go to a "bad place" if she did not speak the truth, she was declared to be a perfectly competent witness, and I have no doubt she was badgered accordingly.

And as Mr. Mortoun got more particulars out of her than all the rest of the questioners put together, perhaps it will not be amiss, as upon her evidence turned the whole of my actions so far as I was concerned, to give that gentleman's questions and her answers in full, precisely as they were quoted in the greedy county paper, which doubtless looked upon the whole case as a publishing godsend, the proprietors heartily wishing that the inquest might be adjourned a score of times for further evidence.

"Well now, Dinah," said Mr. Mortoun, "what time did you go to bed on Monday?"

[The answers were generally got after much hammering in on the part of the inquirist. I will simply return them at once as ultimately given.]

"Ten."

"Did you go to sleep?"

"Noa—Ise didunt goa to sleep."

"Why not?"

"Caize Ise couldn't."

"But why?"

"Ise wur thinkin'."

"What of?"

"Arl manner o' thing'."

"Tell us one of them?"

[No answer—except symptoms of another fit.]

"Tut—tut! Well, did you go to sleep at last?"

"Ise did."

"Well, when did you wake?"

"Ise woke when missus ca'd I."

"What time?"

"Doant know clock."

"Was it daylight?"

"E-es, it wur day."

"Did you wake during the night?"

"E-es, wuncet."

"How did that happen?"

"Doant knaw."

"Did you hear anything?"

"Noa."

"Did you think you heard anything?"

"E-es."

"What?"

"Whoy, it movin'."

"What was moving?"

"Whoy, the box."

"Box—tut, tut," said the lawyer, "answer me properly."

Now here he raised his voice, and I have no doubt Dinah had to thank the juryman for the return of her fits.

"Do you hear?—answer me properly."

"E-es."

"When you woke up did you hear any noise?"

"Noa."

"But you thought you heard a noise?"

"E-es, in the——"

"Tut, tut. Never mind the box—where was it?"

"Ter box? In t' hall!"

"No—no, the noise."

"In t' hall, zur!"

"What—the noise was?"

"Noa, zur, ter box."

"There, my good girl," says the Tram oracle, "never mind the box, I want you to think of this—did you hear any noise *outside the house?*"

"Noa."

"But you said you heard a noise?"

"No, zur, I didunt."

"Well, but you said you thought you heard a noise?"

"E-es."

"Well—where?"

"In ter box——"

Here, said the county paper, the lawyer, striking his hand on the table before him, continued—

"Speak of the box once more, my girl, and to prison you go."

"Prizun!" says the luckless witness.

"Yes, jail and bread and water!"

And thereupon the unhappy witness without any further remarks plunged into a fit, and had to be carried out, battling with that strength which convulsions appear to bring with them, and in the arms of three men, who had quite their work to do to keep her moderately quiet.

"I don't think, gentlemen," said the coroner, "that this witness is material. In the first place, it seems doubtful to me whether she is capable of giving evidence; and, in the second, I believe she has little evidence to give—so little that I doubt the policy of adjourning the inquest till her recovery. It appears to me that it would be cruelty to force this poor young woman again into the position she has just endured, unless you are satisfied that she is a material witness. I think she has said enough to show that she is not. It appears certain, from her own statement, that she retired to rest with Mrs. Quinion, and knows nothing more of what occurred till the housekeeper awoke her in the morning, after she herself had received the alarm. I suggest, therefore, that what evidence she could give is included in that already before the jury, and given by the housekeeper."

The jury coincided in the remarks made by the coroner, Mr. Mortoun, however, adding that he was at a loss to comprehend the girl's frequent reference to the box. Perhaps Mrs. Quinion could help to elucidate the mystery.

The housekeeper immediately rose.

"Mrs. Quinion," said Mr. Mortoun, "can you give any explanation as to what the young person meant by referring to a box?"

"No."

"There are of course boxes at Petleighcote?"

"Beyond all question."

"Any box in particular?"

"No box in particular."

"No box which is spoken of as *the* box?"

"Not any."

"The girl said it was in the hall. Is there a box in the hall?"

"Yes, several."

"What are they?"

"There is a clog and boot box, a box on the table in which letters for the post are placed when the family is at home, and from which they are removed every day at four; and also a box fixed to the wall, the use of which I have never been able to discover, and of the removal of which I have several times spoken to Mr. Petleigh."

"How large is it?"

"About a foot-and-a-half square and three feet deep."

"Locked?"

"No, the flap is always open."

"Has the young woman ever betrayed any fear of this box?"

"Never."

"You have no idea to what box in the hall she referred in her evidence?"

"Not the least idea."

"Do you consider the young woman weak in her head?"

"She is decidedly not of strong intellect."

"And you suppose this box idea a mere fancy?"

"Of course."

"And a recent one?"

"I never heard her refer to a box before."

"That will do."

The paper whence I take my evidence describes Mrs. Quinion as a woman of very great self-possession, who gave what she had to say with perfect calmness and slowness of speech.

This being all the evidence, the coroner was about to sum up, when the Constable Higgins remembered that he had forgotten something, and came forward in a great hurry to repair his error.

He had not produced the articles found on the deceased.

These articles were a key and a *black crape mask*.

The squire being recalled, and the key shown to him, he identified the key as (he believed) one of his "household keys." It was of no particular value, and it did not matter if it remained in the hands of the police.

The report continued: "The key is now in the custody of the constable."

With regard to the crape mask the squire could offer no explanation concerning it.

The coroner then proceeded to sum up, and in doing so he paid many well-termed compliments to the doctor for that gentleman's view of the matter (which I have no doubt threw off all interest in the matter on the part of the public, and slackened the watchfulness of the detective force, many of whom, though very clever, are equally simple, and accept a plain and straightforward statement with extreme willingness)—and urged that the discovery of the black crape mask appeared to be very much like corroborative proof of the doctor's suggestion. "The young man," said the coroner, "would, if poaching, be exceedingly desirous of hiding his face, considering his position in the county, and then the finding of this black crape mask upon the body would, if the poaching explanation were accepted, be a very natural discovery. But——"

And then the coroner proceeded to explain to the jury that they had to decide not upon suppositions but facts. They might all be convinced that Dr. Pitcherley's explanation was the true one, but in law it could not be accepted. Their verdict must be in accordance with facts, and the simple facts of the case were these:—A man was found dead, and the causes of his death were such that it was impossible to believe that the deceased had been guilty of suicide. They would therefore under the circumstances feel it was their duty to return an open verdict of murder.

The jury did not retire, but at the expiration of a consultation of three minutes, in which (I learnt) the foreman, Mr. Mortoun, had all the talking to himself, the jury gave in a verdict of wilful murder against some person or persons unknown.

Thus ended the inquest.

And I have little hesitation in saying it was one of the weakest inquiries of that kind which had ever taken place. It was characterized by no order, no comprehension, no common sense.

The facts of the case made some little stir, but the plausible explanations offered by the doctor, and the several coinciding circumstances, deprived the affair of much of its interest, both to the public and the detective force; to the former, because they had little room for ordinary conjecture; to the latter, because I need not say the general, the chief motive power in the detective is gain, and here the probabilities of profit were almost annihilated by the possibility that a true explanation of the facts of this affair had been offered, while it was such as promised little hope of substantial reward.

But the mere fact of my here writing this narrative will be sufficient to show that *I* did not coincide with the general view taken of the business.

That I was right the following pages will I think prove.

Of course the Government offered the usual reward, £100, of which proclamation is published in all cases of death where presumably foul play has taken place.

But it was not the ordinary reward which tempted me to choose this case for investigation. It was several peculiar circumstances which attracted me.

They were as follows:

1. Why did the father refuse to offer a reward?

2. Why did the deceased have one of the household keys with him at the time of his death, and how came he to have it at all?

3. What did the box mean?

1. It seemed to me that the refusal by the father to offer a reward must arise from one of three sources. Either he did not believe a murder had been committed, and therefore felt the offer was needless; or he knew murder was committed, and did not wish to accelerate the action of the police; or, thirdly, whether he believed or disbelieved in the murder, knew or did not know it to be a murder, that he was too sordid to offer a reward by the payment of which he would lose without gaining any corresponding benefit.

2. How came the deceased to have one of the keys of his father's establishment in his pocket? Such a possession was extremely un-

usual, and more inexplicable. How came he to possess it? Why did he possess it? What was he going to do with it?

3. What did the box mean? Did the unhappy girl Dinah Yarton refer to any ordinary or extraordinary box? It appeared to me that if she referred to any ordinary box it must be an ordinary box under extraordinary circumstances. But fools have very rarely any imagination, and knowing this I was not disposed to accredit Dinah with any ability to invest the box ordinary with any extraordinary attributes. And then remembering that there was nobody in the house to play tricks with her but a grave housekeeper who would not be given to that kind of thing, I came to the conclusion that the box in question was an extraordinary box. *"It was in the hall."* Now if the box were no familiar box, and it was in the hall, the inference stood that it had just arrived there. Did I at this time associate the box intimately with the case? I think not.

At all events I determined to go down to Tram and investigate the case, and as with us detectives action is as nearly simultaneous with determination to act as it can be, I need not say that, making up my mind to visit Tram, I was soon nearing that station by the first train which started after I had so determined.

Going down I arranged mentally the process with which I was to go through.

Firstly, I must see the constable.

Secondly, I must talk to the girl Dinah.

Thirdly, I must examine the place of the murder.

All this would be easy work.

But what followed would be more difficult.

This was to apply what I should discover to any persons whom my discoveries might implicate, and see what I could make of it all.

Arrived at Tram at once I found out the constable, and I am constrained to say—a greater fool I never indeed did meet.

He was too stupid to be anything else than utterly, though idiotically, honest.

Under my corkscrew-like qualities as a detective he had no more chance than a tender young cork with a corkscrew proper. I believe that to the end of the chapter he never comprehended that I was a detective. His mind could not grasp the idea of a police officer in petticoats.

I questioned him as the shortest way of managing him, smoothing his suspicions and his English with shillings of the coin of this realm.

Directly I came face to face with him I knew what I had to do. I had simply to question him. And here I set out my questions and his answers as closely as I can recollect them, together with a narrative of the actions which resulted out of both.

I told him at once I was curious to know all I could about the affair; and as I illustrated this statement with the exhibition of the first shilling, in a moment I had the opportunity of seeing every tooth he had in his head—thirty-two. Not one was missing.

"There was found on the body a key and a mask—where are they?"

"War be they—why, in my box, sin' I be coonstubble!"

"Will you show them me?"

"Oh, Ise show they ye!"

And thereupon he went to a box in the corner of the room, and unlocked it solemnly.

As the constable of Tram it was perfectly natural that he should keep possession of these objects, since a verdict of wilful murder had been given, and at any time, therefore, inquiries might have to be made.

From this box he took out a bundle; this opened, a suit of clothes came to view, and from the middle of these he produced a key and a mask.

I examined the key first. It was a well-made—a beautifully-made key, and very complicated. We constables learn in the course of our experience a good deal about keys, and therefore I saw at a glance that it was the key to a complicated and more than ordinarily valuable lock.

On the highly-polished loop of the key a carefully-cut number was engraved—No. 13.

Beyond all question this key was no ordinary key to an ordinary lock.

Now, extraordinary locks and keys guard extraordinary treasures.

The first inference I arrived at, therefore, from my interview with the Tram constable was this—that the key found upon the body opened a lock put upon something valuable.

Then I examined the mask.

It was of black crape, stretched upon silver wire. I had never seen anything like it before, although as a detective I had been much mixed up with people who wore masks, both at masquerades and on other occasions even less satisfactory.

I therefore inferred that the mask was of foreign manufacture.

[I learnt ultimately that I was right, and no great credit to me either, for that which is not white may fairly be guessed to be of some other colour. The mask was what is called abroad a *masque de luxe*, a mask which, while it changes the countenance sufficiently to prevent recognition, is made so delicately that the material, crape, admits of free perspiration—a condition which inferior masks will not admit.]

"Anything else found on the body?"

"Noa."

"No skeleton keys?"

"Noa; on'y wan key."

So, if the constable were right, and if *the body had remained as it fell*, when found by the gardener, Brown, the only materials found were a key and mask.

But, surely, there was something else in the pockets.

"Was there no purse found?" I asked.

"Noa; noa poorse."

"No handkerchief?"

"Ooh, 'ees; thar war a kerchiefer."

"Where is it?"

He went immediately to the bundle.

"Are these the clothes in which he was found?"

"Ees, they be."

So far, so good, I felt.

The constable, stupid and honest as he appeared, and as he existed, was very suspicious, and therefore I felt that he had to be managed most carefully.

Having hooked the handkerchief out from some recess in the bundle with the flattest forefinger I think I ever remarked, he handed it to me.

It was a woman's handkerchief.

It was new; had apparently never been used; there was no crease nor dirt upon it, as there would have been had it been carried long in the pocket; and it was marked in the corner "Freddy"—undoubtedly the diminutive of Frederica.

"Was the 'kerchiefer,'" I asked, using the word the constable had used—"was it wrapped in anything?"

"Noa."

"What pocket was it in?"

"Noa poockut."

"Where was it, then?"

"In 's weskit, agin 's hart, an' joost aboove th' ole made in 'um."

Now, what was the inference of the handkerchief?

It was a woman's; it was not soiled; it had not been worn long; it was thrust in his breast; it was marked.

The inference stood thus:

This handkerchief belonged to a woman, in all probability young, whose Christian name was Frederica; as it was not soiled, and as it was not blackened by wear, it had recently been given to, or taken, by him; and as the handkerchief was found in the breast of his shirt, it appeared to have been looked upon with favour. Suppose then we say that it was a gift by a young woman to the deceased about the time when he was setting out on his expedition?

Now, the deceased had left London within eighteen hours of his death; had the handkerchief been given him in London or after he left town?

Again, had the mask anything to do with this woman?

Taking it up again and re-examining it, the delicacy of the fabric struck me more than before, and raising it close to my eyes to make a still narrower examination I found that it was scented.

The inference stood, upon the whole, that this mask had belonged to a woman.

Again I began to question Joseph Higgins, constable.

"I should be glad to look at the clothes," I said.

"Lard, thee may look," said the constable.

They were an ordinary suit of clothes, such as a middle-class man would wear of a morning, but not so good or fashionable as one might have expected to find in wear by the son of a wealthy squire. [This apparent incongruity was soon explained away by my learning, as I did in the evening of my arrival, that the squire was mean and even parsimonious.]

There was nothing in the pockets, but my attention was called to the *fluffy* state of the cloth, which was a dark grey, and which therefore in a great measure hid this fluffiness.

"You have not been taking care of these clothes, I am afraid."

"They be joost as they coomed arf him!"

"What, was all this fluff about the cloth?"

"Yoa."

[Yoa was a new version of "e-es," and both meant "yes."]

"They look as though they had been rolled about a bed."

"Noa."

The clothes in question were stained on their underside with gravel-marks, and they were still damp on these parts.

The remarking of this fact, recalled to my mind something which came out at the inquest, and which now I remembered and kept in mind while examining the state of the clothes.

On the Monday night, as the body was discovered on the Tuesday morning, it had rained.

Now the clothes were not damp all over, for the fluff was quite wavy, and flew about in the air. It was necessary to know what time it left off raining on the Monday night, or Tuesday morning.

It was very evident that the clothes had not been exposed to rain between the time of their obtaining the fluffiness and the discovery of the body. Therefore ascertain at what hour the rain ceased, and I had the space of time (the hour at which the body was discovered being half-past five) within which the body had been deposited.

The constable knew nothing about the rain, and I believe it was at this point, in spite of the shillings, that the officer began to show rustic signs of impatience.

I may add here that I found the rain had only ceased at three o'clock on the Tuesday morning. It was therefore clear that the body had been deposited between three and half-past five—*two hours and a-half.*

This discovery I made that same evening of my landlady, a most useful person.

Now, does it not strike the reader that three o'clock on a May morning, and when the morning had almost come, was an extraordinarily late hour at which to be poaching?

This indisputable fact, taken into consideration with the needlessness of the mask (for poachers do not wear masks), and the state of the clothes, to say nothing of the kind of clothes found on the deceased, led me to throw over Mr. Mortoun's theory that the young squire had met his death in a poaching affray, or rather while out on a poaching expedition.

I took a little of the fluff from the clothes and carefully put it away in my pocket-book.

The last thing I examined was the barb which had caused the death.

And here I admit I was utterly foiled—completely, positively foiled. I had never seen anything of the kind before—never.

It was a very coarse iron barb, shaped something like a queen's broad arrow, only that the flanges widened from their point, so that each appeared in shape like the blade of a much-worn penknife. The shaft was irregular and perhaps even coarser than the rest of the work. The weapon was made of very poor iron, for I turned its point by driving it, not by any means heavily, against the frame of the window—to the intense disgust of the constable, whose exclamation, I remember thoroughly well, was "Woa."

Now what did I gain by my visit to the constable? This series of suppositions:

That the deceased was placed where he was found between three and half-past five A.M. on the Tuesday; that he was not killed from any result of a poaching expedition; and that he had visited a youngish woman named Frederica a few hours before death, and of whom he had received a handkerchief and possibly a mask.

The only troublesome point was the key, which, by the way, had been found in a small fob-pocket in the waist of the coat.

While taking my tea at the inn at which I had set down, I need not say I asked plenty of questions, and hearing a Mrs. Green frequently referred to, I surmised she was a busybody, and getting her address, as that of a pleasant body who let lodgings, I may at once add that that night I slept in the best room of the pleasant body's house.

She was the most incorrigible talker ever I encountered. Nor was she devoid of sharpness; indeed, with more circumspection than she possessed, or let me say, with ordinary circumspection, she would have made a good ordinary police officer, and had she possessed that qualification I might have done something for her. As it was the idea could not be entertained for any part of a moment.

She was wonderful, this Mrs. Green.

You only had to put a question on any point, and she abandoned the subject in which she had been indulging, and sped away on a totally new tack.

She was ravenous to talk of the murder; for it was her foregone conclusion that murder had been committed.

In a few words, all the information afforded to this point, which has not arisen out of my own seeking, or came by copy from the county newspaper (and much of that information which is to follow) all proceeded from the same gushing source—Mrs. Green.

All I had to do was to put another question when I thought we had exhausted the previous one, and away she went again at score, and so we continued from seven to eleven. It was half-past eight or nine before she cleared away the long-since cold and sloppy tea-things.

"And what has become of Mrs. Quinion?" I asked, in the course of this to me valuable entertainment on the part of Mrs. Green, throughout the whole of which she never asked me my business in these parts (though I felt quite sure so perfect a busybody was dying to know my affairs), because any inquiry would have called for a reply, and this was what she could not endure while I was willing to listen to her. Hence she chose the less of two evils.

"And what became of the girl?"

"What gal?"

"Dinah."

"Dinah Yarton?"

"Yes. I believe that *was* her name."

"Lor' bless 'ee! it's as good and as long as a blessed big book to tell 'ee all about Dinah Yarton. She left two days after, and they not having a bed for she at the Lamb and Flag, and I having a bed, her came here—the Lamb and Flag people always sending me their over beds, bless 'em, bless 'ee! and that's how I comes to know arl about it, bless 'ee, and the big box!"

[The box—now this was certainly what I did want Mrs. Green to come to. The reader will remember that I laid some stress upon the girl's frequent reference to the trunk.]

"Bless 'ee! the big box caused arl the row, because Mrs. Quinion said she were a fool to have been frightened by a big box; but so Dinah would be, and so her did, being probable in the nex' county at this time, at Little Pocklington, where her mother lives making lace, and her father a farmer, and where her was born—Dinah, and not her mother—on the 1st o'April, 1835, being now twenty years old. What art thee doing? bless 'ee!"

[I was making a note of Little Pocklington.]

Nor will I here make any further verbatim notes of Mrs. Green's remarks, but use them as they are required in my own way, and as in actuality really I did turn them to account.

I determined to see the girl at once; that is, after I had had a night's rest. And therefore next morning, after carefully seeing my box and bag were locked, I made a quick breakfast, and sallied out. Reaching the station, there was Mrs. Green. She had obviously got the start of me by crossing Goose Green fields, as in fact she told me.

She said she thought I must have dropped that, and had come to see.

"That" was a purse so old that it was a curiosity.

"Bless 'ee!" she says, "isn't yourn? Odd, beant it? But, bless 'ee! ye'll have to wait an hour for a train. There beant a train to anywhere for arl an hour."

"Then I'll take a walk," said I.

"Shall I come, and tark pleasant to 'ee?" asked Mrs. Green.

"No," I replied; "I've some business to transact."

I had an hour to spare, and remembering that I had seen the things at Higgins's by a failing evening light, I thought I would again visit that worthy, and make a second inspection.

It was perhaps well I did so.

Not that I discovered anything of further importance, but the atom of novelty of which I made myself master, helped to confirm me in my belief that the deceased had visited a young woman, probably a lady, a very short time before his death.

Higgins, a saddler by trade, was not at all delighted at my reappearance, and really I was afraid I should have to state what I was in order to get my way, and then civilly bully him into secrecy. But happily his belief in me as a mild mad woman overcame his surliness, and so with the help of a few more shillings I examined once more the clothes found on the unfortunate young squire.

And now, in the full blazing spring morning sunlight, I saw what had missed my view on the previous evening. This was nothing less than a bright crimson scrap of silk braid, such as ladies use in prosecuting their embroidery studies.

This bit of braid had been wound round and round a breast button, and then tied in a natty bow at the top.

"She is a lady," I thought; "and she was resting her head against his breast when she tied that bit of braid there. She is innocent, I should think, or she never would have done such a childish action as that."

Higgins put away the dead youth's clothes with a discontented air.

"Look ye yere—do 'ee think ye'l want 'em wuncet more?"

"No."

"Wull, if 'ee do, 'ee wunt have 'un."

"Oh, very well," I said, and went back to the station.

Of course there was Mrs. Green on the watch, though in the morning I had seen about the house symptoms of the day being devoted to what I have heard comic Londoners describe as "a water party"—in other words, a grand wash.

That wash Mrs. Green had deserted.

"Bless 'ee, I'm waitin' for a dear fren'!"

"Oh, indeed, Mrs. Green."

"Shall I take ticket for 'ee, dear?"

"Yes, if you like. Take it for Stokeley," said I.

"Four mile away," says Mrs. Green. "*I've* got a fren' at Stokeley. I wounds if your fren' be *my* fren'! Who *be* your fren', bless 'ee?"

"Mrs. Blotchley."

"What, her as lives near th' peump?" (pump)

"Yes."

"Oh, I don't know *she*."

It seemed to me Mrs. Green was awed—I never learnt by what, because as I never knew Mrs. Blotchley, and dropped upon her name by chance, and indeed never visited Stokeley, why Green had all the benefit of the discovery.

"And, Mrs. Green, if I am not home by nine, do not sit up for me."

"*Oh!*—goin' maybe to sleep at *her* hoose?"

"Very likely."

"*Oh!*"

And as Mrs. Green here dropped me a curtsey I have remained under the impression that Mrs. B. was a lady of consequence whose grandeur Mrs. Green saw reflected upon me.

I have no doubt the information she put at once in circulation helped to screen the actual purpose for which I had arrived at Tram from leaking out.

When the train reached Stokeley I procured another ticket on to Little Pocklington, and reached that town about two in the afternoon. It was not more than sixty miles from Tram.

The father of this Dinah Yarton was one of those small few-acre farmers who throughout the country are gradually but as certainly vanishing.

I may perhaps at once say that the poor girl Dinah had no less than three fits over the cross-examination to which I submitted her, and here (to the honour of rustic human nature) let it be recorded that actually I had to use my last resource, and show myself to be a police officer, by the production of my warrant in the presence of the Little Pocklington constable, who was brought into the affair, before I could overcome the objections of the girl's father. He with much justifiable reason urged that the "darned" business had already half-killed his wench, and he would be "darned" if I should altogether send her out of the "warld."

As I have said, the unhappy girl had three fits, and I have no doubt the family were heartily glad when I had turned my back upon the premises.

The unhappy young woman had to make twenty struggles before she could find one reply.

Here I need not repeat her evidence to that point past which it was not carried when she stood before the coroner and jury, but I will commence from that point.

"Dinah," I inquired in a quiet tone, and I believe the fussiness betrayed by the girl's mother tended as much to the fits as the girl's own nervousness—"Dinah, what was all that about the big box?"

"Darn the box," said the mother.

And here it was that the unfortunate girl took her second fit.

"There, she's killed my Dinah now," said the old woman, and it must be confessed Dinah was horribly convulsed, and indeed looked frightful in the extreme. The poor creature was quite an hour fighting with the fit, and when she came to and opened her eyes, the first object they met made her shut them again, for that object was myself.

However, I had my duty to perform, and therein lies the excuse for my torture.

"What—oh—o-o-oh wha-at did thee say?"

"What about the big box?"

"Doa noa." [This was the mode in those part of saying "I do not know."]

"Where was it?"

"In th' hall."

"Where did it come from?"

"Doa noa."

"How long had it been there?"

"Sin' the day afore."

"Who brought it?"

"Doa noa."

"Was it a man?"

"Noa."

"What then?"

"Two men."

"How did they come?"

"They coomed in a great big waggoon."

"And did they bring the box in the waggon?"

"Yoa." [This already I knew meant "Yes."]

"And they left the box at the hall?"

"Yoa."

"What then?"

"Whoa?" [This I guessed meant "What."]

"What did they say?"

"Zed box wur for squoire."

"Did they both carry it?"

"Yoa."

"How?"

"Carefool loike." [Here there were symptoms of another convulsion.]

"What became of the big box?"

"Doa noa."

"Did they come for it again?"

"Doa noa."

"Is it there now?"

"Noa."

"Then it went away again?"

"Yoa."

"You did not see it taken away?"

"Noa."

"Then how do you know it is not there now?"

"Doa noa."

"But you say it is not at the hall—how do you know that?"

"Mrs. Quanyan (Quinion) told I men had been for it."

"When was that?"

"After I'd been garne to bed."

"Was it there the next morning?"

"Whoa?"

"Was it there the morning when they found the young squire dead outside the door?"

And now "Diney," as her mother called her, plunged into the

third fit, and in the early throes of that convulsion I was forced to leave her, for her father, an honest fellow, told me to leave his house, "arficer or no arficer," and that if I did not do so he would give me what he called a "sta-a-art."

Under the circumstances I thought that perhaps it was wise to go, and did depart accordingly.

That night I remained in Little Pocklington in the hope, in which I was so grievously disappointed, of discovering further particulars which the girl might have divulged to her companions. But in the first place Diney had no companions, and in the second all attempts to draw people out, for the case had been copied into that county paper which held sway at Little Pocklington, all attempts signally failed.

Upon my return to Tram, Mrs. Green received me with all the honours, clearly as a person who had visited Mrs. Blotchley, and I noticed that the parlour fire-place was decorated with a new stove-ornament in paper of a fiery and flaring description.

I thanked Mrs. Green, and in answer to that lady's inquiries I was happy to say Mrs. Blotchley was well—except a slight cold. Yes, I had slept there. What did I have for dinner at Mrs. Blotchley's? Well, really I had forgotten. "Dear heart," said Mrs. Green, " 'ow unfortnet."

After seeing "Diney," and in coming home by the train (and indeed I can always think well while travelling), I turned over all that I had pinched out of Dinah Yarton in reference to the big box.

Did that box, or did it not, in any way relate to the death?

It was large; it had been carried by two men; and according to Dinah's information it had been removed again from the hall.

At all events I must find out what the box meant.

The whole affair was still so warm—not much more than a fortnight had passed since the occurrence—that I still felt sure all particulars about that date which had been noticed would be remembered.

I set Mrs. Green to work, for nobody could better suit my purpose.

"Mrs. Green, can you find out whether any strange carrier's cart or waggon, containing a very big box, was seen in Tram on the Monday, and the day before young Mr. Petleigh's body was found?"

I saw happiness in Mrs. Green's face; and having thus set her to work, I put myself in the best order, and went up to Petleighcote Hall.

The door was opened (with suspicious slowness) by a servant-woman, who closed it again before she took my message and a card to Mrs. Quinion. The message consisted of a statement that I had come after the character of a servant.

A few moments passed, and I was introduced into the house-keeper's presence.

I found her a calm-looking, fine, portly woman, with much quiet determination in her countenance. She was by no means badly featured.

She was quite self-possessed.

The following conversation took place between us. The reader will see that not the least reference was made by me to the real object of my visit—the prosecution of an inquiry as to the mode by which young Mr. Petleigh had met his death. And if the reader complains that there is much falsity in what I state, I would urge that as evil-doing is a kind of lie levelled at society, if it is to be conquered it must be met on the side of society, through its employés, by similar false action.

Here is the conversation.

"Mrs. Quinion, I believe?"

"Yes, as I am usually termed—but let that pass. You wish to see me?"

"Yes; I have called about the character of a servant."

"Indeed—who?"

"I was passing through Tram, where I shall remain some days, on my way from town to York, and I thought it would be wise to make a personal inquiry, which I find much the best plan in all affairs relating to my servants."

"A capital plan; but as you came from town, why did you not apply to the town housekeeper, since I have no doubt you take the young person from the town house?"

"There is the difficulty. I should take the young person, if her character were to answer, from a sort of charity. She has never been in town, and here's my doubt. However, if you give me any hope of the young person——"

"What is her name?"

"Dinah—Dinah—you will allow me to refer to my pocket-book."

"Don't take that trouble," said she, and I thought she looked pale; but her pallor might have been owing, I thought at the time, to the deep mourning she was wearing; "you mean Dinah Yarton."

"Yarton—that is the name. Do you think she will suit?"

"Much depends upon what she is wanted for."

"An under nurserymaid."

"Your own family?"

"Oh, dear no—a sister's."

"In town?"

[She asked this question most calmly.]

"No—abroad."

"Abroad?" and I remarked that she uttered the word with an energy which, though faint in itself, spoke volumes when compared with her previous serenity.

"Yes," I said, "my sister's family are about leaving England for Italy, where they will remain for years. Do you think this girl would do?"

"Well—yes. She is not very bright, it is true, but she is wonderfully clean, honest, and extremely fond of children."

Now, it struck me then and there that the experience of the housekeeper at childless Petleighcote as to Dinah's love of children must have been extremely limited.

"What I most liked in Dinah," continued Mrs. Quinion, "was her frankness and trustworthiness. There can be no doubt of her gentleness with children."

"May I ask why you parted with her?"

"She left me of her own free will. We had, two or three weeks since, a very sad affair here. It operated much upon her; she wished to get away from the place; and indeed I was glad she determined to go."

"Has she good health?"

"Very fair health."

Not a word about the fits.

It struck me Mrs. Qunion relished the idea of Dinah Yarton's going abroad.

"I think I will recommend her to my sister. She tells me she would have no objection to go abroad."

"Oh! you have seen her?"

"Yes—the day before yesterday, and before leaving for town, whence I came here. I will recommend the girl. Good morning."

"Good morning, ma'am; but before you go, will you allow me to take the liberty of asking you, since you are from London, if you can recommend me a town servant, or at all events a young person who comes from a distance. When the family is away I require only one servant here, and I am not able to obtain this one now that the hall has got amongst the scandal-mongers, owing to the catastrophe to which I have already referred. The young person I have with me is intolerable; she has only been here four days, and I am quite sure she must not remain fourteen."

"Well, I think I can recommend you a young person, strong and willing to please, and who only left my sister's household on the score of followers. Shall I write to my sister's housekeeper and see what is to be done?"

"I should be most obliged," said Mrs. Quinion; "but where may I address a letter to you in event of my having to write?"

"Oh!" I replied, "I shall remain at Tram quite a week. I have received a telegraphic message which makes my journey to the north needless; and as I have met here in Tram with a person who is a friend of an humble friend of mine, I am in no hurry to quit the place."

"Indeed! may I ask who?"

"Old Mrs. Green, at the corner of the Market Place, and her friend is Mrs. Blotchley of Stokeley."

"Oh, thank you. I know neither party."

"I may possibly see you again," I continued.

"Most obliged," continued Mrs. Quinion; "shall be most happy."

"Good morning."

She returned the salute, and there was an end of the visit.

And then it came about that upon returning to the house of old Mrs. Green, I said in the most innocent manner in the world, and in order to make all my acts and words in the place as consistent as possible, for in a small country town if you do not do your falsehood deftly you will very quickly be discovered—I said to that willing gossip——

"Why, Mrs. Green, I find you are a friend of Mrs. Blotchley of Stokeley!"

"E-es," she said in a startled manner, "Ise her fren', bless 'ee."

"And I'm gratified to hear it, for as her friend you are mine, Mrs. Green."

And here I took her hand.

No wonder after our interview was over that she went out in her best bonnet, though it was only Wednesday. I felt sure it was quite out of honour to Mrs. Blotchley and her friend, who had claimed her friendship, and the history of which she was taking out to tea with her.

Of the interview with Mrs. Green I must say a few words, and in her own expressions.

"Well, Mrs. Green, have you heard of any unusual cart having been seen in Tram on the day before Mr. Petleigh was found dead?"

"Lardy, lardy, e-es," said Mrs. Green; "but bless 'ee, whaty want to know for?"

"I want to know if it was Mrs. Blotchley's brother's cart, that's all."

"Des say it war. I've been arl over toon speering aboot that waggoon. I went to Jones the baker, and Willmott, who married Mary Sprinters—which wur on'y fair; the grocer, an' him knowed nought about it; an' the bootcher in froont street, and bootcher in back street; and Mrs. Macnab, her as mangles, and no noos, bless 'ee, not even of Tom Hatt the milkman, but, lardy, lardy! when Ise tarking for a fren' o' my fren's Ise tark till never. 'Twur draper told I arl aboot the ca-art."

"What?" I said, I am afraid too eagerly for a detective who knew her business thoroughly.

"Why, draper White wur oot for stroll loike, an' looking about past turning to the harl (hall), and then he sees coming aloong a cart him guessed wur coming to him's shop; but, bless 'ee, 'twarnt comin' to his shop at ARL!"

"Where was it going?"

"Why the cart turned right arf to harl, and that moost ha' been wher they cart went to; and, bless 'ee, that's arl."

Then Mrs. Green, talking like machinery to the very threshold, went, and I guess put on her new bonnet instanter, for she wore it before she went out, and when she brought in my chop and potatoes.

Meanwhile I was ruminating the news of the box, if I may be allowed the figure, and piecing it together.

It was pretty clear to me that a box had been taken to the hall, for the evidence of the girl Dinah and that which Mrs. Green brought together coincided in supporting a supposition to that effect.

The girl said a big box (which must have been large, seeing it took two men to carry it) had been brought to the hall in a large cart on the day previous to the finding of the body.

It was on that day the draper, presumably, had seen a large cart turn out of the main road towards Petleighcote.

Did that cart contain the box the girl Dinah referred to?

If so, had it anything to do with the death?

If so, where was it?

If hidden, who had hidden it?

These were the questions which flooded my mind, and which the reader will see were sufficiently important and equally embarrassing.

The first question to be decided was this,——

Had the big box anything to do with the matter?

I first wrote my letter to headquarters putting things in train to plant one of our people as serving woman at Petleighcote, and then I sallied out to visit Mr. White, the draper.

He was what men would call a "jolly" man, one who took a good deal of gin-and-water, and the world as it came. He was a man to be hail met with the world, but to find it rather a thirsty sphere, and diligently to spirit-and-water that portion of it contained within his own suit of clothes.

He was a man to be rushed at and tilted over with confidence.

"Mr. White," said I, "I want an umbrella, and also a few words with you."

"Both, mum," said he; and I would have bet, for though a woman I am fond of a little wager now and then,—yes, I would have bet that before his fourth sentence he would drop the "mum."

"Here are what we have in umberellers, mum."

"Thank you. Do you remember meeting a strange cart on the day, a Monday, before Mr. Petleigh—Petleigh—what was his name?— was found dead outside the hall? I mention that horrid circumstance to recall the day to your mind."

"Well, yes, I do, mum. I've been hearing of this from Mary Green."

"What kind of cart was it?"

"Well, mum, it was a wholesale fancy article manufacturer's van."

"Ah, such as travel from drapers to drapers with samples, and sometimes things for sale."

"Yes; that were it."

[He dropped the mum at the fourth sentence.]

"A very large van, in which a man could almost stand upright?"

"A man, my dear!' He was just the kind of man to "my dear" a customer, though by so doing he should offend her for life. "Half-a-dozen of 'em, and filled with boxes of samples, in each of which you might stow away a long—what's the matter, eh? What do you want to find out about the van for, eh?"

"Oh, pray don't ask me, White," said I, knowing the way to such a man's confidence is the road of familiarity. "Don't, don't inquire what. But tell me, how many men were there on the van?"

"Two, my dear."

"What were they like?"

"Well, I didn't notice."

"Did you know them, or either of them?"

"Ha! *I* see," said White; and I am afraid I allowed him to infer that he had surprised a personal secret. "No; I knew neither of 'em, if *I* know it. Strangers to me. Of course *I* thought they were coming with samples to *my* shop; for I am the only one in the village. But they DIDN'T."

"No; they went to the hall, I believe?"

"Yes. *I* thought they had turned wrong, and I hollered after them, but it was no use. I wish I could describe them for you, my dear, but I can't. However, I believe they looked like gentlemen. Do you think *that* description will answer?"

"Did they afterwards come into the town, Mr. White?"

"Well, my dear, they did, and baited at the White Horse, and then it was I was so surprised they did not call. And then—in fact, my dear, if you would like to know all——"

"Oh, don't keep anything from me, White."

"Well, then, my dear, I went over as they were making ready to go, and I asked them if they were looking for a party of the name of White? And then——"

"Oh, pray, pray continue."

"Well, then, one of them told me to go to a place, to repeat which before you, my dear, I would not; from which it seemed to me that they did *not* want a person of the name of White."

"And, Mr. White, did they quit Tram by the same road as that by which they entered it?"

"No, they did *not*; they drove out at the other end of the town."

"Is it possible? And tell me, Mr. White, if they wanted to get back to the hall, could they have done so by any other means than by returning through the village?"

"No, not without—let me see, me dear—not without going thirty miles round by the heath, which," added Mr. White, "and no offence, my dear, I am bound to submit they were not men who seemed likely to take any unnecessary trouble; or why—why in fact did they tell me to go to where in fact they told me to go to?"

"True; but they may have returned, and you not know anything about it, Mr. White."

"There you have it, my dear. You go to the gateman, and as it's only three weeks since, you take his word, for Tom remembers every vehicle that passes his 'pike—there are not many of them, for business is woundily slack. Tom remembers 'em all for a good quarter."

"Oh, thank you, Mr. White. I think I'll take the green umbrella. How much is it?"

"Now look here, my dear," the draper continued, leaning over the counter, and dropping his voice; "I know the umbereller is the excuse, and though business *is* bad, I'm sure I don't want you to take it; unless, indeed, you want it," he added, the commercial spirit struggling with the spirit proper of the man.

"Thank you," said I. "I'll take the green—you will kindly let me call upon you again?"

"With pleasure, my dear; as often as you like; the more the better. And look here, you need not buy any more umberellers or things. You just drop in in a friendly way, you know. *I* see it all."

"Thank you," I said; and making an escape I was rather desirous of obtaining, I left the shop, which, I regret to say, I was ungrateful enough not to revisit. But, on the other hand, I met White several and at most inconvenient times.

Tom the 'pikeman's memory for vehicles was, I found, a proverb in the place; and when I went to him, he remembered the vehicle almost before I could explain its appearance to him.

As for the question—"Did the van return?"—he treated the "Are you sure of it?" with which I met his shake of the head—he treated my doubt with such violent decision that I became confident he was right.

Unless he was bribed to secrecy?

But the doubt was ridiculous; for could all the town be bribed to secrecy?

I determined that doubt at once. And indeed it is the great gain and drawback to our profession that we have to doubt so imperiously. To believe every man to be honest till he is found out to be a thief, is a motto most self-respecting men cling to; but we detectives on the contrary would not gain salt to our bread, much less the bread itself, if we adopted such a belief. We have to believe every man a rogue till, after turning all sorts of evidence inside out, we can only discover that he is an honest man. And even then I am much afraid we are not quite sure of him.

I am aware this is a very dismal way of looking upon society, but the more thinking amongst my profession console themselves with the knowledge that our system is a necessary one (under the present condition of society), and that therefore in conforming to the melancholy rules of this system, however repulsive we may feel them, we are really doing good to our brother men.

Returning home after I left the 'pikeman—from whom I ascertained that the van had passed his gate at half-past eight in the evening, I turned over all my new information in my mind.

The girl Dinah must have seen the box in the hall as she went to bed. Say this was half-past nine; at half-past five, at the time the alarm was given, the box was gone.

This made eight hours.

Now, the van had left Tram at half-past eight, and to get round to the hall it had to go thirty miles by night over a heath. (By a reference to my almanack I found there was no moon that night.) Now, take it that a heavy van travelling by night-time could not go more than five miles an hour, and allowing the horse an hour's rest when half the journey was accomplished, we find that seven hours would be required to accomplish that distance.

This would bring the earliest time at which the van could arrive at the hall at half-past three, assuming no impediments to arise.

There would be then just two hours before the body was discovered, and actually as the dawn was breaking.

Such a venture was preposterous even in the contemplation.

In the first place, why should the box be left if it were to be called for again?

In the second, why should it be called for so early in the morning as half-past three?

And yet at half-past five it had vanished, and Mrs. Quinion had said to the girl (I assumed the girl's evidence to be true) that the box had been taken away again.

From my investigation of these facts I inferred—firstly:

That the van which brought the box had not taken it away.

Secondly: That Mrs. Quinion, for some as yet unexplained purpose, had wished the girl to suppose the box had been removed.

Thirdly: That the box was still in the house.

Fourthly: That as Mrs. Quinion had stated the box was gone, while it was still on the premises, she had some purpose (surely important) in stating that it had been taken away.

It was late, but I wanted to complete my day's work as far as it lay in my power.

I had two things to do.

Firstly, to send the "fluff" which I had gathered from the clothes to a microscopic chemist; and secondly, to make some inquiry at the inn where the van-attendants had baited, and ascertain what they were.

Therefore I put the "fluff" in a tin box, and directed it to the gentleman who is good enough to control these kind of investigations for me, and going out I posted my communication. Then I made for the tavern, with the name of which Mrs. Green had readily furnished me, and asked for the landlady.

The interest she exhibited showed me in a moment that Mrs. Green's little remarks and Mr. White's frank observations had got round to that quarter.

And here let me break off for a moment to show how nicely people will gull themselves. I had plainly made no admission which personally identified me with the van, and yet people had already got up a very sentimental feeling in my favour in reference to that vehicle.

For this arrangement I was unfeignedly glad. It furnished a motive for my remaining in Tram, which was just what I wanted.

And furthermore, the tale I told Mrs. Quinion about my remaining in Tram because I had found a friend of my own friend, would, if it spread (which it did not, from which I inferred that Mrs. Quinion had no confidences with the Tram maiden at that hour with her, and that this latter did not habitually listen) do me no harm, as I might ostensibly be supposed to invent a fib which might cover my supposed tribulation. Here is a condensation of the conversation I had with the landlady.

"Ah! I know; I'm glad to see you. Pray sit down. Take that chair—it's the easiest. And how are you, my poor dear?"

"Not strong," I had to say.

"Ah! and well you may not be."

"I came to ask, did two persons, driving a van—a large black van, picked out with pale blue (this description I had got from the 'pikeman)—stop here on the day before Mr.——I've forgotten his name—the young squire's death?"

"Yes, my poor dear, an' a tall gentleman with auburn whiskers, and the other shorter, without whiskers."

"Dear me; did you notice anything peculiar in the tall gentleman?"

"Well, my poor dear, I noticed that every now and then his upper lip flitched a bit, like a dog's asleep will sometimes go."

Here I sighed.

"And the other?" I continued.

"Oh! all that seemed odd in him was that he broke out into bits of song, something like birds more nor English Christian singing; which the words, if words there were, I could not understand."

"Italian scraps," I thought; and immediately I associated this evidence of the man with the foreign mask.

If they were commercial travellers, one of them was certainly an unusual one, operatic accomplishments not being usually one of the tendencies of commercial men.

"Were they nice people?"

"Oh!" says the landlady, concessively and hurriedly; "they were every inch gentlemen; and I said to mine, said I—'they aint like most o' the commercial travellers that stop here;' and mine answers me back, 'No,' says he, 'for commercials prefers beers to sherries, and whiskies after dinner to both!' "

"Oh! did they only drink wine?"

"Nothing but sherry, my dear; and says they to mine—'Very good wine,'—those were their very words—'whatever you do, bring it dry;' and said mine—I saying his very words—'Gents, I will.' "

Some more conversation ensued, with which I need not trouble the reader, though I elicited several points which were of minor importance.

I was not permitted to leave the hotel without "partaking,"—I use the landlady's own verb—without partaking of a warmer and stronger comfort than is to be found in mere words.

And the last inference I drew, before satisfactorily I went to bed that night, was to the effect that the apparent commercial travellers were not commercial travellers, but men leading the lives of gentlemen.

And now as I have set out a dozen inferences which rest upon very good evidence, before I go to the history of the work of the following days, I must recapitulate these inferences—if I may use so pompous a word.

They are as follow:

1. That the key found on the body opened a receptacle containing treasure.

2. That the mask found on the body was of foreign manufacture.

3. That the handkerchief found on the body had very recently belonged to a young lady named Frederica, and to whom the deceased was probably deeply attached.

4. That the circumstances surrounding the deceased showed that he had been engaged in no poaching expedition, nor in any housebreaking attempt, notwithstanding the presence of the mask, because no house-breaking implements were found upon him.

5. [Omitted by the author. E.F.B.]

6. That the young lady was innocent of participation in whatever evil work the deceased may have been engaged upon. [This inference, however, was solely based upon the discovery of the embroidery braid round the button of the deceased's coat. This inference is the least supported by evidence of the whole dozen.]

7. That a big box had been taken to the hall on the day previous to that on which the deceased was found dead outside the hall.

8. That the box was not removed again in the van in which it had been brought to the house.

9. That whatever the box contained that something was heavy, as it took the two men to carry it into the house.

10. That Mrs. Quinion, for some so far unexplainable reason, had endeavoured to make the witness Dinah Yarton believe that the box had been removed; while, in fact, the box was still in the house.

11. That as Mrs. Quinion had stated the box was gone while it was still on the premises, she had some important motive for saying it had been taken away.

12. That the van-attendants, who were apparent commercial travellers, were not commercial travellers, and were in the habit of living the lives of gentlemen.

And what was the condensed inference of all these inferences?

Why—THAT THE FIRST PROBABLE MEANS BY WHICH THE SOLUTION OF THE MYSTERY WAS TO BE ARRIVED AT WAS THE FINDING OF THE BOX.

To hunt for this box it was necessary that I should obtain free admission to Petleighcote, and by the most extraordinary chance Mrs. Quinion had herself thrown the opportunity in my way by asking me to recommend her a town servant.

Of course, beyond any question, she had made this request with the idea of obtaining a servant who, being a stranger to the district, would have little or not any of that interest in the catastrophe of the young squire's death which all felt who, by belonging to the neighbourhood, had more or less known him.

I had now to wait two days before I could move in the matter—those two days being consumed in the arrival of the woman police officer who was to play the part of servant up at the hall, and in her being accepted and installed at that place.

On the morning of that second day the report came from my microscopic chemist.

He stated that the fluff forwarded him for inspection consisted of two different substances; one, fragments of feathers, the other, atoms of nap from some linen material, made of black and white stuff, and which, from its connexion with the atoms of feather, he should take to be the fluff of a bed-tick.

For a time this report convinced me that the clothes had been covered with this substance, in consequence of the deceased having lain down in his clothes to sleep at a very recent time before he was found dead.

And now came the time to consider the question—"What was my own impression regarding the conduct of the deceased immediately preceding the death?"

My impression was this—that he was about to commit some illegal action, but that he had met with his death before he could put his intention into execution.

This impression arose from the fact that the mask showed a secret intention, while the sound state of the clothes suggested that no struggle had preceded the bloody death—struggle, however brief, generally resulting in clothes more or less damaged, as any soldier who has been in action will tell you (and perhaps tell you wonderingly), to the effect that though he himself may have come out of the fight without a scratch, his clothes were one vast rip.

The question that chiefly referred to the body was, who placed it where it was found between three o'clock (the time when the rain ceased, before which hour the body could not have been deposited, since the clothes, where they did not touch the ground, were dry) and half-past five?

Had it been brought from a distance?

Had it been brought from a vicinity?

The argument against distance was this one, which bears in all cases of the removal of dead bodies—that if it is dangerous to move them a yard, it is a hundred times more dangerous to move them a hundred yards.

Granted the removal of young Petleigh's body, in a state which would at once excite suspicion, and it is clear that a great risk was run by those who carried that burden.

But was there any apparent advantage to compensate that risk?

No, there was not.

The only rational way of accounting for the deposition of the body where it was found, lay in the supposition that those who were mixed up with his death were just enough to carry the body to a spot where it would at once be recognised and cared for.

But against this argument it might be held, the risk was so great that the ordinary instinct of self-preservation natural to man would prevent such a risk being encountered. And this impression becomes all the deeper when it is remembered that the identification of the body could have been secured by the slipping of a piece of paper in the pocket bearing his address.

Then, when it is remembered that it must have been quite dawn at the time of the assumed conveyance, the improbability becomes the greater that the body was brought any great distance.

Then this probability became the greater, that the young man had died in the vicinity of the spot where he was found.

Then followed the question, how close?

And in considering this point, it must not be forgotten that if it were dangerous to bring the body to the hall, it would be equally dangerous to remove the body *from the hall*; *supposing* the murder (if murder it were) had been committed within the hall.

Could this be the case?

Beyond all question, the only people known to be at the hall on the night of the death were Mrs. Quinion and Dinah.

Now we have closed in the space within which the murder (as we will call it) had been done, as narrowly circumscribing the hall. Now was the place any other than the hall, and yet near it?

The only buildings near the hall, within a quarter of a mile, were the gardener's cottage, and the cottage of the keeper.

The keeper was ill at the time, and it was the gardener who had discovered the body. To consider the keeper as implicated in the affair, was quite out of the question; while as to the gardener, an old man, and older servant of the family (for he had entered the service of the family as a boy), it must be remembered that he was the discoverer of the dead body.

Now is it likely that if he was implicated in the affair that he would have identified himself with the discovery? Such a supposition is hardly holdable.

Very well; then, as the doctor at six A.M. declared death had taken place from six to eight hours; and as the body, from the dry state of the clothes, had *not* been exposed during the night's rain, which ceased at three, it was clear either that the murder had been committed within doors, or that the body had been sheltered for some hours after death beneath a roof of some kind.

Where was that roof?

Apart from the gardener's cottage and the keeper's, there was no building nearer than a quarter of a mile; and if therefore the body had been carried after three to where it was found, it was evident that those cognizant of the affair had carried it a furlong at or after dawn.

To suppose such an amount of moral courage in evil-doers was to suppose an improbability, against which a detective, man or woman, cannot too thoroughly be on his or her guard.

But what of the supposition that the body had been removed from the hall, and placed where it was found?

So far, all the external evidences of the case leant in favour of this theory.

But the theory was at total variance with the ordinary experience of life.

In the first place, what apparent motive could Mrs. Quinion have for taking the young heir's life? Not any apparently.

What motive had the girl?

She had not sufficient strength of mind to hold a fierce motive. I doubt if the poor creature could ever have imagined active evil.

I may here add I depended very much upon what that girl said, because it was consistent, was told under great distress of mind, and was in many particulars borne out by other evidence.

I left Dinah Yarton quite out of my list of suspects.

But in accepting her evidence I committed myself to the belief that no one had been at Petleighcote on the night of the catastrophe beyond the girl and the housekeeper.

Then how could I support the supposition that the young man had passed the night and met his death at the hall?

Very easily.

Because a weak-headed woman like Dinah did not know of the presence of the heir at Petleighcote, it did not follow he could not be there—his presence being known only to the housekeeper.

But was there any need for such secrecy?

Yes.

I found out that fact before the town servant arrived.

Mrs. Quinion's express orders were not to allow the heir to remain at the hall while the family were in town.

Then here was a good reason why the housekeeper should maintain his presence a secret from a stupid blurting servant maid.

But I have said motive for murder on the part of the housekeeper could scarcely be present.

Then suppose the death was accidental (though certainly no circumstance of the catastrophe justified such a supposition), and suppose Mrs. Quinion the perpetratress, what was the object in exposing the body outside the house?

Such an action was most unwomanly, especially where an accident had happened.

I confess that at this point of the case (and up to the time when my confederate arrived) I was completely foiled. All the material evidence was in favour of the murder or manslaughter having been committed under the roof of Petleighcote Hall, while the mass of the evidence of probability opposed any such belief.

Up to this time I had in no way identified the death with the "big box," although I identified that box with the clearing up of the mystery. This identification was the result of an ordinary detective law.

The law in question is as follows:

In all cases which are being followed up by the profession, a lie is a suspicious act, whether it has relation or no relation, apparent or beyond question, with the matter in hand. As a lie it must be followed to its source, its meaning cleared up, and its value or want of value decided upon. The probability stands good always that a lie is part of a plot.

So as Mrs. Quinion had in all probability lied in reference to the removal of the box, it became necessary to find out all about it, and hence my first directions to Martha—as she was always called (she is now in Australia and doing well) at our office, and I doubt if her surname was known to any of us—hence my first instruction to Martha was to look about for a big box.

"What kind of box?"

"That I don't know," said I.

"Well there will be plenty of boxes in a big house—is it a new box?"

"I can't tell; but keep an eye upon boxes, and tell me if you find one that is more like a new one than the rest."

Martha nodded.

But by the date of our first interview after her induction at Pet-leighcote, and when Quinion sent her down upon a message to a tradesman, I had learnt from the polished Mr. White that boxes such as drapers' travellers travelled with were invariably painted black.

This information I gave her. Martha had not any for me in return —that is of any importance. I heard, what I had already inferred, that Quinion was a very calm, self-possessed woman, "whom it would take," said Martha, "one or two good collisions to drive off the rails."

"You mark my words," said Matty, "she'd face a judge as cool as she faces herself in a looking-glass, and that I can tell you she does face cool, for I've seen her do it twice."

Martha's opinion was, that the housekeeper was all right, and I am bound to say that I was unable to suppose that she was all wrong, for the suspicion against her was of the faintest character.

She visited me the day after Martha's arrival, thanked me coolly enough for what I had done, said she believed the young person would do, and respectfully asked me up to the hall.

Three days passed, and in that time I had heard nothing of value from my aide-de-camp, who used to put her written reports twice a day in a hollow tree upon which we had decided.

It was on the fourth day that I got a fresh clue to feel my way by.

Mrs. Lamb, the publican's wife, who had shown such a tender interest in my welfare on the night when I had inquired as to the appearance of the two persons who baited the van-horses at their stables on the night of the death—Mrs. Lamb in reluctantly letting me leave her (she was a most sentimental woman, who I much fear increased her tendencies by a too ready patronage of her own liquors) intreated me to return, "like a poor dear as I was"—for I had said I should remain at Tram—"and come and take a nice cup of tea" with her.

In all probability I never should have taken that nice cup of tea, had I not learnt from my Mrs. Green that young Petleigh had been in the habit of smoking and drinking at Lamb's house.

That information decided me.

I "dropped in" at Mrs. Lamb's that same afternoon, and I am bound to say it was a nice cup of tea.

During that refreshment I brought the conversation round to young Petleigh, and thus I heard much of him told to his credit from a publican's point of view, but which did not say much for him from a social standing-place.

"And this, my poor dear, is the very book he would sit in this very parlour and read from for an hour together, and—coming!"

For here there was a tap-tap on the metal counter with a couple of halfpence.

Not thinking much of the book, for it was a volume of a very ordinary publication, which has been in vogue for many years amongst cheap literature devotees, I let it fall open, rather than opened it, and I have no doubt that I did not once cast my eyes upon the page during the spirting of the beer-engine and the return of Mrs. Lamb.

"Bless me!" said she, in a moved voice, for she was one of the most sentimental persons ever I encountered. "Now that's very odd! —poor dear."

"What's odd, Mrs. Lamb?" I asked.

"Why if you haven't got the book open at his fav'rite tale!"

"Whose, Mrs. Lamb?"

"Why that poor dear young Graham Petleigh."

I need not say I became interested directly.

"Oh! did he read this tale?"

"Often; and very odd it is, my own dear, as you should be about to read it too; though true it is that that there book do always open at that same place, which I take to be his reading it so often the place is worn and—coming!"

Here Mrs. Lamb shot away once more, while I, it need not be said, looked upon the pages before me.

And if I say that, before Mrs. Lamb had done smacking at the beer-engine, and ending her long gossip with the customer, I had got the case by the throat—I suppose I should astonish most of my readers.

And yet there is nothing extraordinary in the matter.

Examine most of the great detected cases on record, and you will find a little accident has generally been the clue to success.

So with great discoveries. One of the greatest improvements in the grinding of flour, and by which the patentee has made many thousands of pounds, was discovered by seeing a miller blow some flour out of a nook; and all the world knows that the cause which led the great Newton to discover the great laws of the universe was the fall of an apple.

So it frequently happens in these days of numberless newspapers that a chance view of a man will identify him with the description of a murderer.

Chance!

In the history of crime and its detection chance plays the chief character.

Why, as I am writing a newspaper is near me, in which there is the report of a trial for attempt to murder, where the woman who was shot at was only saved by the intervention of a piece of a ploughshare, which was under her shawl, and which she had *stolen* only a few minutes before the bullet struck the iron!

Why, compared with that instance of chance, what was mine when, by reading a tale which had been pointed out to me as one frequently read by the dead young man, I discovered the mystery which was puzzling me?

The tale told of how, in the north of England, a pedlar had left a pack at a house, and how a boy saw the top of it rise up and down; how they supposed a man must be *in* it who intended to rob the house; and how the boy shot at the pack, and killed a man.*

I say, before Mrs. Lamb returned to her "poor dear" I had the mystery by heart.

The young man had been attracted by the tale, remembered it, and put it in form for some purpose. What?

In a moment I recalled the mania of the squire for plate, and, remembering how niggardly he was to the boy, it flashed upon me

---

* This story was probably "The Long Pack" by James Hogg. E.F.B.

that the youth had in all probability formed a plan for robbing his father of a portion of his plate.

It stood true that it was understood the plate went up to town with the family. But was this so?

Now see how well the probabilities of the case would tell in with such a theory.

The youth was venturesome and daring, as his poaching affrays proved.

He was kept poor.

He knew his father to possess plate.

He was not allowed to be at Petleighcote when the father was away.

He had read a tale which coincided with my theory.

A large box had been left by strangers at the hall.

The young squire's body had been found under such circumstances, that the most probable way of accounting for its presence where it was found was by supposing that it had been removed there from the hall itself.

Such a plot explained the presence of the mask.

Finally, there was the key, a key opening, beyond all question, an important receptacle—a supposition very clear, seeing the character of the key.

Indeed, by this key might be traced the belief of treasure in the house.

Could this treasure really exist?

Before Mrs. Lamb had said "Good night, dear," to a female customer who had come for a pint of small beer and a gallon of more strongly brewed scandal, I had come to the conclusion that plate might be in the house.

For miserly men are notoriously suspicious and greedy. What if there were some of the family plate which was not required at the town house then at Petleighcote, and which the squire, relying for its security upon the habitual report of his taking all his plate to town, had not lodged at the county bank, because of that natural suspiciousness which might lead him to believe more in his own strong room than a banker's?

Accept this supposition, and the youth's motive was evident.

Accept young Petleigh's presence in the house under these circumstances, and then we have to account for the death.

Here, of course, I was still at fault.

If Mrs. Quinion and the girl only were in the house, and the girl was innocent, then the housekeeper alone was guilty.

Guilty—what of? Murder or manslaughter?

Had the tale young Petleigh used to read been carried out to the end?

Had he been killed without any knowledge of who he was?

That I should have discovered the real state of the case without Mrs. Lamb's aid I have little doubt, for even that very evening, after leaving Mrs. Lamb, and promising to bear in mind the entreaty to "come again, you *dear* dear," my confederate brought me a piece of information which must have put me on the track.

It appeared that morning Mrs. Quinion had received a letter which much discomposed her. She went out directly after breakfast, came down to the village, and returned in about an hour. My confederate had picked the pocket (for, alas! we police officers have sometimes to turn thieves—for the good of society of course) of the housekeeper while she slept that afternoon, and while the new maid was supposed to be putting Mrs. Quinion's stockings in wearable order, and she had made a mental copy of that communication. It was from a Joseph Spencer, and ran as follows:

"MY DEAR MARGARET,—For God's sake look all over the place for key 13. There's such a lot of 'em I never missed it; and if the governor finds it out I'm as good as ruined. It must be somewhere about. I can't tell how it ever come orf the ring. So no more at present. It's post time. With dear love, from your own
"JOSEPH SPENCER"

Key 13!

Why, it was the same number as that on the key found on the dead man.

A letter was despatched that night to town, directing the police to find out who Joseph Spencer was, and giving the address heading the letter—a printed one.

Mrs. Green then came into operation.

No, she could not tell who lived at the address I mentioned. Thank the blessed stars *she* knowed nought o' Lunnon. What! Where had Mrs. Quinion been that morning? Why, to Joe Higgins's. What for? Why, to look at the young squire's clothes and things. What did she want with them? Why, she "actially" wanted to take " 'em arl oop" to the Hall. No, Joe Higgins wouldn't.

Of course I now surmised that Joseph Spencer was the butler.

And my information from town showed I was right.

Now, certain as to my preliminaries, I knew that my work lay within the walls of the Hall.

But how was I to reach that place?

Alas! the tricks of detective police officers are infinite. I am afraid many a kindly-disposed advertisement hides the hoof of detection. At all events I know mine did.

It appeared in the second column of the *Times*, and here is an exact copy of it. By the way, I had received the *Times* daily, as do most detectives, during the time I had been in Tram:

"Wanted, to hear of Margaret Quinion, or her heirs-at-law. She was known to have left the South of England (that she was a Southerner I had learnt by her accent) about the year 1830 to become housekeeper to a married foster-sister, who settled in a midland county (this information, and especially the date, Mrs. Green had to answer for). Address,——" Here followed that of my own solicitors, who had their instructions to keep the lady hanging about the office several days, and until they heard from me.

I am very much afraid I intended that should the case appear as black against her as I feared it would, she was to be arrested at the offices of the gentlemen to whom she was to apply in order to hear of something to her advantage. And furthermore, I am quite sure that many an unfortunate has been arrested who has been enticed to an office under the promise of something to his or her special benefit.

For of such misrepresentations is this deplorable world.

When this advertisement came out, the least acute reader is already aware of the use I made of it.

I pointed out the news to Mrs. Green, and I have no doubt she digited the intelligence to every soul she met, or rather overtook, in the course of the day. And indeed before evening (when I was honoured with a visit from Mrs. Quinion herself), it was stated with absolute assurance that Mrs. Quinion had come in for a good twenty-two thousand pounds, and a house in Dyot Street, Blooms-bury Square, Lunnun.

It was odd, and yet natural, that Mrs. Quinion should seek me out. I was the only stranger with whom she was possibly acquainted in the district, and my strangeness to the neighbourhood she had already, from her point of view, turned to account. Therefore (human nature considered) I did not wonder that she tried to turn me to account again. My space is getting contracted, but as the following is the last conversation I had with Mrs. Quinion, I may perhaps be pardoned for here quoting it. Of course I abridge it very considerably. After the usual salutations, and an assurance that Martha suited very fairly, she said,——

"I have a favour to ask you."

"Indeed; pray what is it?"

"I have received some news which necessarily takes me from home."

"I think," said I, smiling, "I know what that news is," and I related how I had myself seen the advertisement in the morning.

I am afraid I adopted this course the more readily to attract her confidence.

I succeeded.

"Indeed," said she, "then since you have identified yourself with that news, I can the more readily ask you the favour I am about to——"

"And what is that?"

"I am desirous of going up to town—to London—for a few hours, to see what this affair of the advertisement means, but I hesitate to leave Martha alone in the house. You have started, and perhaps you feel offended that I should ask a stranger such a favour, but the fact is, I do not care to let anyone belonging to the neighbourhood know that I have left the Hall—it will be for only twenty-four hours. The news might reach Mr. Petleigh's ears, and I desire that he should hear nothing about it. You see the position in which I am placed. If, my dear lady, you can oblige me I shall be most grateful; and, as you are staying here, it seemed—to—me——"

Here she trailed off into silence.

The cunning creature! How well she hid her real motive—the desire to keep those who knew of the catastrophe out of the Hall, because she feared their curiosity.

Started! Yes, indeed I had started. At best I had expected that I should have to divulge who I was to the person whom she would leave in the place did the advertisement take, and here by the act of what she thought was her forethought, she was actually placing herself at my mercy, while I still remained screened in all my actions referring to her. For I need not say that had I had to declare who I was, and had I failed, all further slow-trapping in this affair would have been at an end—the "game" would have taken the alarm, and there would have been an end to the business.

To curtail here needless particulars, that same evening at nine I was installed in the housekeeper's parlour, and she had set out for the first station past Tram, to which she was going to walk across the fields in order to avoid all suspicion.

She had not got a hundred yards away from the house, before I had turned up my cuffs, and I and Martha (a couple of detectives) were hard at work, trying to find that box.

Her keys we soon found, in a work-basket, and lightly covered with a handkerchief.

Now, this mode of hiding should have given me a clue.

But it did not.

For three hours—from nine till midnight, we hunted for that box, and unsuccessfully.

In every room that, from the absence of certain dusty evidences, we knew must have been recently opened—in every passage, cellar, corridor, and hall we hunted.

No box.

I am afraid that we even looked in places where it could not have gone—such as under beds.

But we found it at last, and then the turret-clock had gone twelve about a quarter of an hour.

It was in her bedroom; and what is more, it formed her dressing-table.

And I have no doubt I should have missed it had it not been that she had been imperfect in her concealment.

Apparently she comprehended the value of what I may call "audacity hiding"—that is, such concealment that an ordinary person searching would never dream of looking for the object where it was to be found.

For instance, the safest hiding-place in a drawing-room for a bank note, would be the bottom of a loosely-filled card-basket. Nobody would dream of looking for it in such a place.

The great enigma-novelist, Edgar Poe, illustrates this style of concealment where he makes the holder of a letter place it in a card-rack over the mantelpiece, when he knows his house will be ransacked, and every inch of it gone over to find the document.

Mrs. Quinion was evidently acquainted with this mode of concealment.

Indeed, I believe I should not have found the box had it not been that she had overdone her unconcealed-concealment. For she had used a bright pink slip with a white flounce over it to complete the appearance of a dressing-table, having set the box up on one side.

And therefore the table attracted my notice each time I passed and saw it. As it was Martha, in passing between me and the box, swept the drapery away with her petticoats, and showed a *black corner*.

The next moment the box was discovered.

I have no doubt that being a strong-minded woman she could not endure to have the box out of her sight while waiting for an opportunity to get rid of it.

It was now evident that my explanation of the case, to the effect that young Petleigh had been imitating the action of the tale, was correct.

The box was quite large enough to contain a man lying with his legs somewhat up; there was room to turn in the box; and, finally, there were about two dozen holes round the box, about the size of a crown piece, and which were hidden by the coarse black canvas with which the box was covered.

Furthermore, the box was closeable from within by means of a bolt, and therefore openable from within by the same means.

Furthermore, if any further evidence were wanting, there was a pillow at the bottom of the box (obviously for the head to rest on), and from a hole the feathers had escaped over the bottom of the box, which was lined with black and white striped linen bed-tick, this material being cut away from the holes.

I was now at no loss to comprehend the fluff upon the unhappy young man's coat.

And, finally, there was the most damnifying evidence of all.

For in the black canvas over one of the holes *there was a jagged cut.*

"Lie down, Martha," said I, "in the box, with your head at this end."

"Why, whatever——"

"Tut—tut,—girl; do as I tell you."

She did; and using the stick of a parasol which lay on the dressing-table, I found that by passing it through the hole its end reached the officer in exactly the region by a wound in which young Mr. Petleigh had been killed.

Of course the case was now clear.

After the young woman, Dinah, had gone to bed, the housekeeper must have had her doubts about the chest, and have inspected it.

Beyond all question, the young man knew the hour at which the housekeeper retired, and was waiting perhaps for eleven o'clock to strike by the old turret-clock before he ventured out—to commit what?

It appeared to me clear, bearing in mind the butler's letter, to rob the plate-chest No. 13, which I inferred had been left behind, a fact of which the young fellow might naturally be aware.

The plan doubtless was to secure the plate without any alarm, to let himself out of the Hall by some mode long-since well-known to him, and then to meet his confederates, and share with them the plunder, leaving the chest to tell the tale of the robbery, and to exculpate the housekeeper.

It struck me as a well-executed scheme, and one far beyond the ordinary run of robbery plots.

What had caused that scheme to fail?

I could readily comprehend that a strong-minded woman like Quinion would rely rather upon her own than any other assistance.

I could comprehend her discovery; perhaps a low-muttered blasphemy on the part of the young man; or maybe she may have heard his breathing.

Then, following out her action, I could readily suppose that once aware of the danger near her she would prepare to meet it.

I could follow her, silent and self-possessed, in the hall, asking herself what she should do.

I could mark her coming to the conclusion that there must be holes in the box through which the evil-doer could breathe, and I apprehended readily enough that she had little need to persuade herself that she had a right to kill one who might be there to kill her.

Then in my mind's eye I could follow her seeking the weapon, and feeling all about the box for a hole.

She finds it.

She fixes the point for a thrust.

A movement—and the manslaughter is committed.

That the unhappy wretch had time to open the box is certain, and doubtless it was at that moment the fierce woman, still clutching the shaft of the arrow, or barb—call it what you will—leant back, and so withdrew the shaft from the rankling iron.

Did the youth recognise her? Had he tried to do so?

From the peacefulness of the face, as described at the inquest, I imagined that he had, after naturally unbolting the lid, fallen back, and in a few moments died.

Then must have followed her awful discovery, succeeded by her equally awful determination to hide the fault of her master's, and perhaps of her own sister's son.

And so it came to pass that she dragged the youth's dead body out into the cold morning atmosphere, as the bleak dawn was filling the air, and the birds were fretfully awaking.

No doubt, had a sharp detective been at once employed, she would not have escaped detection.

As it was she had so far avoided discovery.

And I could easily comprehend that a powerfully-brained woman like herself would feel no compunction and little grief for what she had done—no compunction, because the act was an accident; little grief, because she must have felt she had saved the youth from a life of misery—for a son who at twenty robs a father, however bad, is rarely at forty, if he lives so long, an honest man.

But though I had made this discovery I could do nothing so far against the housekeeper, whom of course it was my duty to arrest, if I could convince myself she had committed manslaughter. I was not to be ruled by any feeling of screening the family—the motive indirectly which had actuated Quinion, for, strong-minded as she was, it appeared to me that she would not have hesitated to admit the commission of the act which she had completed had the burglar, as I may call the young man, been an ordinary felon, and unknown to her.

No, the box had no identification with the death, because it exhibited no unanswerable signs of its connexion with that catastrophe.

So far, how was it identifiable (beyond my own circumstantial evidence, known only to myself) with the murder?

The only particle of evidence was that given by the girl, who could or could not swear to the box having been brought on the previous day, and to the housekeeper saying that it had been taken away again—a suspicious circumstance certainly, but one which, without corroborative evidence, was of little or indeed no value.

As to the jagged cut in the air-hole, in the absence of all blood-stain it was not mentionable.

Corroborative evidence I must have, and that corroborative evidence would best take the shape of the discovery of the shaft of the weapon which had caused death, or a weapon of similar character.

This, the box being found, was now my work.

"Is there any armoury in the house, Martha?"

"No; but there's lots of arms in the library."

We had not searched in the library for the box, because I had taken Martha's assurance that no boxes were there.

When we reached the place, I remarked immediately—"What a damp place."

As I said so I observed that there were windows on each side of the room, and that the end of the chamber was circular.

"Well it may be," said Martha, "for there's water all round it—a kind of fountain-pond, with gold fish in it. The library," continued Martha, who was more sharp than educated, "butts out of the house."

Between each couple of book-cases there was fixed a handsome stand of arms, very picturesque and taking to the eyes.

There were modern arms, antique armour, and foreign arms of many kinds; but I saw no arrows, though in the eagerness of my search I had the chandelier, which still held some old yellow wax-candles, lighted up.

No arrow.

But my guardian angel, if there be such good creatures, held tight on to my shoulder that night, and by a strange chance, yet not a tithe so wonderful as that accident by which the woman was saved from a bullet by a piece of just stolen iron, the origin of the weapon used by Quinion came to light.

We had been searching amongst the stands of arms for some minutes, when I had occasion suddenly to cry——

"Hu-u-sh! what are you about?"

For my confederate had knocked off its hook a large drum, which I had noticed very coquettishly finished off a group of flags, and cymbals, and pikes.

"I'm very sorry," she said, as I ran to pick up the still reverberating drum with that caution which, even when useless, generally stands by the detective, when——

There, sticking through the drum, and hooked by its barbs, was the point of such a weapon—the exact counterpart—as had been used to kill young Petleigh.

Had a ghost, were there such a thing, appeared I had not been more astounded.

The drum was ripped open in a moment, and there came to light an iron arrow with a wooden shaft about eighteen inches long, this shaft being gaily covered with bits of tinsel and coloured paper.

[I may here at once state, what I ultimately found out—for in spite of our danger I kept hold of my prize and brought it out of battle with me—that this barb was one of such as are used by picadors in Spanish bull-fights for exciting the bull. The barbs cause the darts to stick in the flesh and skin. The cause of the decoration of the haft can now readily be comprehended. Beyond all doubt the arrow used by Quinion and the one found by me were a couple placed as curiosities amongst the other arms. The remaining one the determined housekeeper had used as suiting best her purpose, the other (which I found) had doubtless at some past time been used by an amateur picador, perhaps the poor dead youth himself, with the drum for an imaginary bull, and within it the dart had remained till it was to reappear as a witness against the guilty and yet guiltless housekeeper.

I had barely grasped my prize when Martha said—"What a smell of burning!"

"Good God!" I cried, "we have set the house on fire!"

The house was on fire, but we were not to blame.

We ran to the door.

We were locked in!

What brought her back I never learnt, for I never saw or heard of her again. I guess that the motion of the train quickened her thought (it does mine), that she suspected—that she got out at the station some distance from Tram, and that she took a post-chaise back to Petleighcote.

All this, however, is conjecture.

But if not she, who locked us in? We could not have done it ourselves.

We were locked in, and I attribute the act to her—though how she entered the house I never learnt.

The house was on fire, and we were surrounded by water.

This tale is the story of the "Unknown Weapon," and therefore I cannot logically here go into any full explanation of our escape. Suffice it to our honour as detectives to say, that we did not lose our presence of mind, and that by the aid of the library tables, chairs, big books, &c., we made a point of support on one side the narrow pond for the library ladder to rest on, while the other end reached shallow water.

Having made known the history of the "Unknown Weapon," my tale is done; but my reader might fancy my work incomplete did I not add a few more words.

I have no doubt that Quinion returning, her quick mind in but a few moments came to the conclusion that the only way to save her master's honour was the burning of the box by the incendiarism of the Hall.

The Petleighs were an old family, I learnt, with almost Spanish notions of family honour.

Effectually did she complete her work.

I acknowledge she conquered me. She might have burnt the same person to a cinder into the bargain; and, upon my word, I think she would have grieved little had she achieved that purpose.

For my part in the matter—I carried it no further.

At the inquiry, I appeared as the lady who had taken care of the house while Mrs. Quinion went to look after her good fortune; and I have no doubt her disappearance was unendingly connected with my advertisement in the *Times*.

I need not say that had I found Quinion I would have done my best to make her tremble.

I have only one more fact to relate—and it is an important one. It is this——

The squire had the ruins carefully examined, and two thousand ounces of gold and silver plate, melted into shapelessness of course, were taken out of the rubbish.

From this fact it is pretty evident that the key No. 13, found upon the poor, unhappy, ill-bred, and neglected boy, was the "Open Sesamè" to the treasure which was afterwards taken from the ruins —perhaps worth £4000, gold and silver together.

Beyond question he had stolen the key from the butler, gone into a plot with his confederates—and the whole had resulted in his death and the conflagration of Petleighcote, one of the oldest, most picturesque, and it must be admitted dampest seats in the midland counties.

And, indeed, I may add that I found out who was the "tall gentleman with the auburn whiskers and the twitching of the face;" I discovered who was the short gentleman with no whiskers at all; and finally I have seen the young lady (she was very beautiful) called Frederica, and for whose innocent sake I have no doubt the unhappy young man acted as he did.

As for me, I carried the case no further.

I had no desire to do so—had I had, I doubt if I possessed any further evidence than would have sufficed to bring me into ridicule.

I left the case where it stood.

My Lady's Money

by

WILKIE COLLINS

PERSONS OF THE STORY

WOMEN

LADY LYDIARD (*Widow of Lord Lydiard*).
ISABEL MILLER (*her adopted Daughter*).
MISS PINK (*of South Morden*).
THE HON. MRS. DRUMBLADE (*Sister of the Hon. Alfred Hardyman*).

MEN

THE HON. ALFRED HARDYMAN (*of the Stud Farm*).
MR. FELIX SWEETSIR (*Lady Lydiard's Nephew*).
ROBERT MOODY (*Lady Lydiard's Factotum*).
MR. TROY (*Lady Lydiard's Lawyer*).
OLD SHARON (*in the By-ways of Legal Bohemia*).

ANIMAL

TOMMIE (*Lady Lydiard's Dog*).

PART THE FIRST

The Disappearance

I

Old Lady Lydiard sat meditating by the fireside, with three letters lying open on her lap.

Time had discolored the paper and had turned the ink to a brownish hue. The letters were all addressed to the same person— "THE RIGHT HON. LORD LYDIARD"—and were all signed in the same way—"Your affectionate cousin, James Tollmidge." Judged by these specimens of his correspondence, Mr. Tollmidge must have possessed one great merit as a letter-writer—the merit of brevity. He will weary nobody's patience, if he is allowed to have a hearing. Let him, therefore, be permitted, in his own high-flown way, to speak for himself:

First letter: "My statement, as your lordship requests, shall be short and to the point. I was doing very well as a portrait painter in the country, and I had a wife and children to consider. Under these circumstances, if I had been left to decide for myself, I should certainly have waited until I had saved a little money before I ventured on the serious expense of taking a house and studio at the west end of London. Your lordship, I positively declare, encouraged me to try the experiment without waiting. And here I am, unknown and unemployed, a helpless artist, lost in London, with a sick wife and hungry children, and bankruptcy staring me in the face. On whose shoulders does this dreadful responsibility rest? On your lordship's!"

Second letter: "After a week's delay, you favor me, my lord, with a curt reply. I can be equally curt on my side. I indignantly deny that I or my wife have ever presumed to use your lordship's name as a means of recommendation to sitters without your permission. Some enemy has slandered us. I claim, as my right, to know the name of that enemy."

Third (and last) letter: "Another week has passed, and not a word of answer has reached me from your lordship. It matters little. I have employed the interval in making inquiries, and I have at last discovered the hostile influence which has estranged you from me. I have been, it seems, so unfortunate as to offend Lady Lydiard (how, I can not imagine); and the all-powerful influence of this noble lady is now used against the struggling artist who is united to you by the sacred ties of kindred. Be it so. I can fight my way upward, my lord, as other men have done before me. A day may yet come when the throng of carriages waiting at the door of the fashionable portrait painter will include her ladyship's vehicle, and bring me the tardy expression of her ladyship's regret. I refer you, my Lord Lydiard, to that day!"

Having read Mr. Tollmidge's formidable assertions relating to herself for the second time, Lady Lydiard's meditations came to an abrupt end. She rose, took the letters in both hands to tear them up, hesitated, and threw them back into the cabinet drawer in which she had discovered them, among other papers that had not been arranged since Lord Lydiard's death.

"The idiot!" said her ladyship, thinking of Mr. Tollmidge. "I never even heard of him in my husband's life-time; I never even knew that he was really related to Lord Lydiard, till I found his letters. What is to be done next?"

She looked, as she put that question to herself, at an open newspaper thrown on the table, which announced the death of "that accomplished artist, Mr. Tollmidge, related, it is said, to the late well-known connoisseur, Lord Lydiard." In the next sentence the writer of the obituary notice deplored the destitute condition of Mrs. Tollmidge and her children, "thrown helpless on the mercy of the world." Lady Lydiard stood by the table, with her eyes on those lines, and saw but too plainly the direction in which they pointed— the direction of her check-book.

Turning toward the fire-place, she rang the bell. "I can do nothing in this matter," she thought to herself, "until I know whether the report about Mrs. Tollmidge and her family is to be depended on.

Has Moody come back?" she asked, when the servant appeared at the door. "Moody" (otherwise her ladyship's steward) had not come back. Lady Lydiard dismissed the subject of the artist's widow from further consideration until the steward returned, and gave her mind to a question of domestic interest which lay nearer to her heart. Her favorite dog had been ailing for some time past, and no report of him had reached her that morning. She opened a door near the fire-place, which led, through a little corridor hung with rare prints, to her own boudoir. "Isabel!" she called out, "how is Tommie?"

A fresh young voice answered from behind the curtain which closed the further end of the corridor, "No better, my lady."

A low growl followed the fresh young voice, and added (in dog's language), "Much worse, my lady—much worse!"

Lady Lydiard closed the door again, with a compassionate sigh for Tommie, and walked slowly to and fro in her spacious drawing-room, waiting for the steward's return.

Accurately described, Lord Lydiard's widow was short and fat, and perilously near her sixtieth birthday. But it may be said, without paying a compliment, that she looked younger than her age by ten years at least. Her complexion was of that delicate pink tinge which is sometimes seen in old women with well-preserved constitutions. Her eyes (equally well-preserved) were of that hard light-blue color which wears well, and does not wash out when tried by the test of tears. Add to this her short nose, her plump cheeks that set wrinkles at defiance, her white hair dressed in stiff little curls, and if a doll could grow old, Lady Lydiard at sixty would have been the living image of that doll, taking life easily on its journey downward to the prettiest of tombs, in a burial-ground where the myrtles and roses grew all the year round.

These being her ladyship's personal merits, impartial history must acknowledge, on the list of her defects, a total want of tact and taste in her attire. The lapse of time since Lord Lydiard's death had left her at liberty to dress as she pleased. She arranged her short, clumsy figure in colors that were far too bright for a woman of her age. Her dresses, badly chosen as to their hues, were perhaps not badly made, but were certainly badly worn. Morally as well as physically, it must be said of Lady Lydiard that her outward side was her worst side. The anomalies of her dress were matched by the anomalies of her character.

There were moments when she felt and spoke as became a lady of rank, and there were other moments when she felt and spoke as might have become the cook in the kitchen. Beneath these superficial inconsistencies the great heart, the essentially true and generous nature of the woman, only waited the sufficient occasion to assert themselves. In the trivial intercourse of society she was open to ridicule on every side of her. But when a serious emergency tried the metal of which she was really made, the people who were loudest in laughing at her stood aghast, and wondered what had become of the familiar companion of their every-day lives.

Her ladyship's promenade had lasted but a little while, when a man in black clothing presented himself noiselessly at the great door which opened on the staircase. Lady Lydiard signed to him impatiently to enter the room.

"I have been expecting you for some time, Moody," she said. "You look tired. Take a chair."

The man in black bowed respectfully, and took his seat.

II

Robert Moody was at this time nearly forty years of age. He was a shy, quiet, dark person, with a pale, closely shaven face, agreeably animated by large black eyes set deep in their orbits. His mouth was perhaps his best feature; he had firm, well-shaped lips, which softened on rare occasions into a particularly winning smile. The whole look of the man, in spite of his habitual reserve, declared him to be eminently trustworthy. His position in Lady Lydiard's household was in no sense of the menial sort. He acted as her almoner and secretary as well as her steward—distributed her charities, wrote her letters on business, paid her bills, engaged her servants, stocked her wine-cellar, was authorized to borrow books from her library, and was served with his meals in his own room. His parentage gave him claims to these special favors; he was by birth entitled to rank as a gentleman. His father had failed at a time of commercial panic as a country banker, had paid a good dividend, and had died in exile abroad, a broken-hearted man. Robert had tried to hold his place in the world, but adverse fortune kept him down. Undeserved disaster followed him from one employment to another, until he abandoned the struggle, bade a last farewell to the pride of other days, and accepted the position considerately and delicately offered to him in Lady Lydiard's house. He had now no near relations living, and he had never made many friends. In the intervals of occupation he led a lonely life in his little room. It was a matter of secret wonder among the women in the servants' hall, considering his personal advantages and the opportunities which must surely have been thrown in his way, that he had never tempted fortune in the character of a married man. Robert Moody entered into no explanations on that subject. In his own sad and quiet way he continued to lead his own sad and quiet life. The women all failing, from the handsome housekeeper downward, to make the smallest impression on him, consoled themselves by prophetic visions of his future relations with the sex, and predicted vindictively that "his time would come."

"Well," said Lady Lydiard, "and what have you done?"

"Your ladyship seemed to be anxious about the dog," Moody answered, in the low tone which was habitual to him. "I went first to the veterinary surgeon. He has been called away into the country; and——"

Lady Lydiard waved away the conclusion of the sentence with her hand. "Never mind the surgeon. We must find somebody else. Where did you go next?"

"To your ladyship's lawyer. Mr. Troy wished me to say that he will have the pleasure of waiting on you——"

"Pass over the lawyer, Moody. I want to know about the painter's widow. Is it true that Mrs. Tollmidge and her family are left in helpless poverty?"

"Not quite true, my lady. I have seen the clergyman of the parish, who takes an interest in the case——"

Lady Lydiard interrupted her steward for the third time. "You have not mentioned my name?" she asked, sharply.

"Certainly not, my lady. I followed my instructions, and described you as a benevolent person in search of real distress. It is quite true that Mr. Tollmidge has died, leaving nothing to his family. But the widow has a little income of seventy pounds in her own right."

"Is that enough to live on, Moody?" her ladyship asked.

"Enough in this case, for the widow and her daughter," Moody answered. "The difficulty is to pay the few debts left standing, and to start the two sons in life. They are reported to be steady lads; and the family is much respected in the neighborhood. The clergyman proposes to get a few influential names to begin with, and to start a subscription."

"No subscription!" protested Lady Lydiard. "Mr. Tollmidge was Lord Lydiard's cousin, and Mrs. Tollmidge is related to his lordship by marriage. It would be degrading to my husband's memory to have the begging-box sent around for his relations, no matter how distant they may be. Cousins!" exclaimed her ladyship, suddenly descending from the lofty ranges of sentiment to the low. "I hate the very name of them! A person who is near enough to me to be my relation and far enough off from me to be my sweetheart, is a double-faced sort of person that I don't like. Let's get back to the widow and her sons. How much do they want?"

"A subscription of five hundred pounds, my lady, would provide for everything—if it could only be collected."

"It *shall* be collected, Moody! I will pay the subscription out of my own purse." Having asserted herself in those noble terms, she spoiled the effect of her own outburst of generosity by dropping to the sordid view of the subject in her next sentence. "Five hundred pounds is a good bit of money, though; isn't it, Moody?"

"It is indeed, my lady." Rich and generous as he knew his mistress to be, her proposal to pay the whole subscription took the steward by surprise. Lady Lydiard's quick perception instantly detected what was passing in his mind.

"You don't quite understand my position in this matter," she said. "When I read the newspaper notice of Mr. Tollmidge's death, I searched among his lordship's papers to see if they really were related. I discovered some letters from Mr. Tollmidge, which showed me that he and Lord Lydiard were cousins. One of those letters contains some very painful statements, reflecting most untruly and unjustly on my conduct—lies, in short," her ladyship burst out, losing her dignity, as usual. "Lies, Moody, for which Mr. Tollmidge deserved to be horsewhipped. I would have done it myself if his lordship had told me at the time. No matter; it's useless to dwell on the thing now," she continued, ascending again to the forms of expression which became a lady of rank. "This unhappy man has done me a gross injustice; my motives may be seriously misjudged if I appear personally in communicating with his family. If I relieve them anonymously in their present trouble, I spare them the exposure of a public subscription, and I do what I believe his lordship would have done himself if he had lived. My desk is on the other table. Bring it here, Moody, and let me return good for evil, while I'm in the humor for it."

Moody obeyed in silence. Lady Lydiard wrote a check.

"Take that to the banker's, and bring back a five-hundred-pound note," she said. "I'll inclose it to the clergyman as coming from 'an unknown friend.' And be quick about it. I am only a fallible mortal, Moody. Don't leave me time enough to take the stingy view of five hundred pounds."

Moody went out with the check. No delay was to be apprehended in obtaining the money; the banking-house was hard by, in St. James's Street. Left alone, Lady Lydiard decided on occupying her mind in the generous direction by composing her anonymous letter to the clergyman. She had just taken a sheet of notepaper from her desk when a servant appeared at the door, announcing a visitor——

"Mr. Felix Sweetsir."

III

"My nephew!" Lady Lydiard exclaimed, in a tone which expressed astonishment, but certainly not pleasure as well. "How many years is it since you and I last met?" she asked, in her abruptly straightforward way, as Mr. Felix Sweetsir approached her writing-table.

The visitor was not a person easily discouraged. He took Lady Lydiard's hand, and kissed it with easy grace. A shade of irony was in his manner, agreeably relieved by a playful flash of tenderness.

"Years, my dear aunt?" he said. "Look in your glass, and you will see that time has stood still since we met last. How wonderfully well you wear! When shall we celebrate the appearance of your first wrinkle? I am too old; I shall never live to see it."

He took an easy chair, uninvited, placed himself close at his aunt's side, and ran his eye over her ill-chosen dress with an air of satirical admiration. "How perfectly successful!" he said, with his well-bred insolence. "What a chaste gayety of color!"

"What do you want?" asked her ladyship, not in the least softened by the compliment.

"I want to pay my respects to my dear aunt," Felix answered, perfectly impenetrable to his ungracious reception, and perfectly comfortable in a spacious armchair.

No pen-and-ink portrait need surely be drawn of Felix Sweetsir, he is too well-known a picture in society. The little lithe man, with his bright, restless eyes, and his long iron-gray hair falling in curls to his shoulders; his airy step and his cordial manner; his uncertain age, his innumerable accomplishments, and his unbounded popularity—is he not familiar everywhere and welcome everywhere? How gratefully he receives, how prodigally he repays, the cordial appreciation of an admiring world! Every man he knows "is a charming fellow." Every woman he sees is "sweetly pretty." What picnics he gives on the banks of the Thames in the summer season! What a well-earned little income he derives from the whist table! What an inestimable actor he is at private theatricals of all sorts (weddings included)! Did you never read Sweetsir's novel, dashed off in the intervals of curative perspiration at a German bath? Then you don't know what brilliant fiction really is. He has never written a second work; he does everything, and only does it once. One song—the despair of professional composers. One picture—just to show how easily a gentleman can take up an art and drop it again. A really multiform man, with all the graces and all the accomplishments scintillating perpetually at his fingers' ends. If these poor pages have achieved nothing less, they have done a service to persons not in society by presenting them to Sweetsir. In his gracious company the narrative brightens; and writer and reader (catching reflected brilliancy) understand each other at last, thanks to Sweetsir.

"Well," said Lady Lydiard, "now you are here, what have you got to say for yourself? You have been abroad, of course? Where?"

"Principally at Paris, my dear aunt. The only place that is fit to live in—for this excellent reason, that the French are the only people who know how to make the most of life. One has relations and friends in England; and every now and then one returns to London——"

"When one has spent all one's money in Paris," her ladyship interposed. "That's what you were going to say, isn't it?"

Felix submitted to the interruption with his delightful good-humor.

"What a bright creature you are!" he exclaimed. "What would I not give for your flow of spirits! Yes; one does spend money in Paris, as you say. The clubs, the stock exchange, the race-course: you try your luck here, there and everywhere; and you lose and win,

win and lose, and you haven't a dull day to complain of." He paused, his smile died away, he looked inquiringly at Lady Lydiard. "What a wonderful existence yours must be!" he resumed. "The everlasting question with your needy fellow-creatures, 'Where am I to get money?' is a question that has never passed your lips. Enviable woman!" He paused once more, surprised and puzzled this time. "What is the matter, my dear aunt? You seem to be suffering under some uneasiness."

"I am suffering under your conversation," her ladyship answered, sharply. "Money is a sore object with me just now," she went on, with her eyes on her nephew, watching the effect of what she said. "I have spent five hundred pounds this morning with a scrape of my pen. And, only a week since, I yielded to temptation, and made an addition to my picture-gallery." She looked, as she said those words, toward an archway at the further end of the room, closed by curtains of purple velvet. "I really tremble when I think of what that one picture cost me before I could call it mine. A landscape by Hobbema; and the national gallery bidding against me. Never mind!" she concluded, consoling herself, as usual, with considerations that were beneath her. "Hobbema will sell at my death for a bigger price than I gave for him—that's one comfort!" She looked again at Felix; a smile of mischievous satisfaction began to show itself in her face. "Anything wrong with your watch-chain?" she asked.

Felix, absently playing with his watch-chain, started as if his aunt had suddenly awakened him. While Lady Lydiard had been speaking, his vivacity had subsided little by little, and had left him looking so serious and so old that his most intimate friend would hardly have known him again. Roused by the sudden question that had been put to him, he seemed to be casting about in his mind in search of the first excuse for his silence that might turn up. "I was wondering," he began, "why I miss something when I look round this beautiful room; something familiar, you know, that I fully expected to find here."

"Tommie?" suggested Lady Lydiard, still watching her nephew as maliciously as ever.

"That's it!" cried Felix, seizing his excuse, and rallying his spirits. "Why don't I hear Tommie snarling behind me? why don't I feel Tommie's teeth in my trousers?"

The smile vanished from Lady Lydiard's face; the tone taken by her nephew in speaking of her dog was disrespectful in the extreme. She showed him plainly that she disapproved of it. Felix went on, nevertheless, impenetrable to reproof of the silent sort. "Dear little Tommie! So delightfully fat; and such an infernal temper! I don't know whether I hate him or love him. Where is he?"

"Ill in bed," answered her ladyship, with a gravity which startled even Felix himself. "I wish to speak to you about Tommie. You know everybody. Do you know of a good dog-doctor? The person I have employed so far doesn't at all satisfy me."

"Professional person?" inquired Felix.

"Yes."

"All humbugs, my dear aunt. The worse the dog gets the bigger the bill grows, don't you see? I have got the man for you—a gentleman. Knows more about horses and dogs than all the veterinary surgeons put together. We met in the boat yesterday crossing the Channel. You know him by name, of course. Lord Rotherfield's youngest son, Alfred Hardyman."

"The owner of the stud farm? The man who has bred the famous race-horse?" cried Lady Lydiard. "My dear Felix, how can I presume to trouble such a great personage about my dog?"

Felix burst into his genial laugh. "Never was modesty more wofully out of place," he rejoined. "Hardyman is dying to be presented to your ladyship. He had heard, like everybody, of the magnificent decorations of this house, and he is longing to see them. His chambers are close by, in Pall Mall. If he is at home we will have him here in five minutes. Perhaps I had better see the dog first?"

Lady Lydiard shook her head. "Isabel says he had better not be disturbed," she answered. "Isabel understands him better than anybody."

Felix lifted his lively eyebrows with a mixed expression of curiosity and surprise. "Who is Isabel?"

Lady Lydiard was vexed with herself for carelessly mentioning Isabel's name in her nephew's presence. Felix was not the sort of person whom she was desirous of admitting to her confidence in domestic matters. "Isabel is an addition to my household since you were here last," she answered, shortly.

"Young and pretty?" inquired Felix. "Ah! you look serious, and you don't answer me. Young and pretty evidently. Which may I see first, the addition to your household or the addition to your picture-gallery? You look at the picture-gallery—I am answered again." He rose to approach the archway, and stopped at his first step forward.

"A sweet girl is a dreadful responsibility, aunt," he resumed, with an ironical assumption of gravity. "Do you know, I shouldn't be surprised if Isabel, in the long run, cost you more than Hobbema. Who is this at the door?"

The person at the door was Robert Moody, returned from the bank. Mr. Felix Sweetsir, being near-sighted, was obliged to fit his eyeglass in position before he could recognize the prime-minister of Lady Lydiard's household.

"Ha! our worthy Moody. How well he wears! Not a gray hair on his head—and look at mine! What do you use, Moody? If he had my open disposition he would tell. As it is, he looks unutterable things, and holds his tongue. Ah! if I could only have held *my* tongue—when I was in the diplomatic service, you know—what a position I might have occupied by this time! Don't let me interrupt you, Moody, if you have anything to say to Lady Lydiard."

Having acknowledged Mr. Sweetsir's lively greeting by a formal bow, and a grave look of wonder which respectfully repelled that vivacious gentleman's flow of humor, Moody turned toward his mistress.

"Have you got the bank-note?" asked her ladyship.

Moody laid the bank-note on the table.

"Am I in the way?" inquired Felix.

"No," said his aunt. "I have a letter to write; it won't occupy me for more than a few minutes. You can stay here, or go and look at the Hobbema: which you please."

Felix made a second sauntering attempt to reach the picture-gallery. Arrived within a few steps of the entrance, he stopped again, attracted by an open cabinet of Italian workmanship filled with rare old china. Being nothing if not a cultivated amateur, Mr. Sweetsir paused to pay his passing tribute of admiration before the contents of the cabinet. "Charming! charming!" he said to himself, with his head twisted appreciatively a little on one side. Lady Lydiard and Moody left him in undisturbed enjoyment of the china, and went on with the business of the bank-note.

"Ought we to take the number of the note, in case of accident?" asked her ladyship.

Moody produced a slip of paper from his waistcoat pocket. "I took the number, my lady, at the bank."

"Very well. You keep it. While I am writing my letter, suppose you direct the envelope. What is the clergyman's name?"

Moody mentioned the name and directed the envelope. Felix,

happening to look round at Lady Lydiard and the steward, while they were both engaged in writing, returned suddenly to the table as if he had been struck by a new idea.

"Is there a third pen?" he asked. "Why shouldn't I write a line at once to Hardyman, aunt? The sooner you have his opinion about Tommie, the better—don't you think so?"

Lady Lydiard pointed to the pen-tray, with a smile. To show consideration for her dog was to seize irresistibly on the high-road to her favor. Felix set to work on his letter, in a large, scrambling handwriting, with plenty of ink and a noisy pen. "I declare we are like clerks in an office," he remarked, in his cheery way. "All with our noses to the paper, writing as if we lived by it! Here, Moody, let one of the servants take this at once to Mr. Hardyman's."

The messenger was dispatched. Robert returned, and waited near his mistress, with the directed envelope in his hand. Felix sauntered back slowly toward the picture-gallery for the third time. In a moment more Lady Lydiard finished her letter, and folded up the bank-note in it. She had just taken the directed envelope from Moody, and had just placed the letter inside it, when a scream from the inner room, in which Isabel was nursing the sick dog, startled everybody. "My lady! my lady!" cried the girl, distractedly, "Tommie is in a fit! Tommy is dying!"

Lady Lydiard dropped the unclosed envelope on the table, and ran—yes, short as she was and fat as she was, ran—into the inner room. The two men, left together, looked at each other.

"Moody," said Felix, in his lazy, cynical way, "do you think if you or I were in a fit that her ladyship would run? Bah! these are the things that shake one's faith in human nature. I feel infernally seedy. That cursed Channel passage—I tremble in my inmost stomach when I think of it. Get me something, Moody."

"What shall I send you, sir?" Moody asked coldly.

"Some dry Curaçoa and a biscuit. And let it be brought to me in the picture-gallery. Damn the dog! I'll go and look at Hobbema."

This time he succeeded in reaching the archway, and disappeared behind the curtains of the picture-gallery.

IV

Left alone in the drawing-room, Moody looked at the unfastened envelope on the table.

Considering the value of the inclosure, might he feel justified in wetting the gum and securing the envelope for safety's sake. After thinking it over, Moody decided that he was not justified in meddling with the letter. On reflection, her ladyship might have changes to make in it, or might have a postscript to add to what she had already written. Apart, too, from these considerations, was it reasonable to act as if Lady Lydiard's house was a hotel, perpetually open to the intrusion of strangers? Objects worth twice five hundred pounds in the aggregate were scattered around on the tables and in the unlocked cabinets all round him. Moody withdrew, without further hesitation, to order the light restoratives prescribed for himself by Mr. Sweetsir. The unclosed letter reposed in its place on the table.

The footman who took the Curaçoa into the picture-gallery found Felix recumbent on a sofa—to all appearance so completely absorbed in the Hobbema that he was quite unable to look at anything else.

He took the Curaçoa mechanically, drained the glass at a draught, and held it out to be filled for the second time. "Don't interrupt me," he said, peevishly, catching the servant in the act of staring at him. "Put down the bottle and go!" Forbidden to look at Mr. Sweetsir, the man's eyes, as he left the gallery, turned wonderingly toward the famous landscape. And what did he see? He saw one towering big cloud in the sky that threatened rain, two withered, mahogany-colored trees sorely in want of rain, a muddy road greatly the worse for rain, and a vagabond boy running home who was afraid of the rain. That was the picture to the footman's eye. He took a gloomy view of the state of Mr. Sweetsir's brains on his return to the servants' hall. "A slate loose, poor devil!" That was the footman's report of the brilliant Felix.

An interval of some minutes elapsed, and at last the silence in the picture-gallery was broken by voices penetrating into it from the drawing-room. Felix rose to a sitting position on the sofa. He had recognized the voice of Alfred Hardyman saying, "Don't disturb Lady Lydiard," and the voice of Moody answering, "I will just knock at the door of her ladyship's room, sir; you will find Mr. Sweetsir in the picture-gallery."

The curtains over the archway parted, and disclosed the figure of a tall, lean man, with a closely cropped head set a little stiffly on his shoulders. The immovable gravity of face and manner which every Englishman seems to acquire who lives constantly in the society of horses, was the gravity which this gentleman displayed as he entered the picture-gallery. He was a finely made, sinewy man, with clearly cut, regular features. If he had not been affected with horses on the brain, he would doubtless have been personally popular with the women. As it was, the serene and hippic gloom of the handsome horse-breeder daunted the daughters of Eve, and they failed to make up their minds about the exact value of him, socially considered. Alfred Hardyman was, nevertheless, a remarkable man in his way. He had been offered the customary alternatives submitted to the younger sons of the nobility—the Church or the diplomatic service —and had refused the one and the other. "I like horses," he said, "and I mean to get my living out of them. Don't talk to me about my position in the world. Talk to my eldest brother, who gets the money and the title." Starting in life with these sensible views, and with a small capital of five thousand pounds, Hardyman took his own place in the sphere that was fitted for him. At the period of this narrative he was already a rich man, and one of the greatest author-ities on horse-breeding in England. His prosperity made no change in him. He was always the same grave, quiet, obstinately resolute man, true to the few friends whom he admitted to his intimacy, and sincere to a fault in the expression of his feelings among persons whom he distrusted or disliked. As he entered the picture-gallery and paused for a moment looking at Felix on the sofa, his large, cold, steady gray eyes rested on the little man with an indifference that just verged on contempt. Felix, on the other hand, sprung to his feet with alert politeness, and greeted his friend with exuberant cordiality.

"Dear old boy! This is so good of you," he began. "I feel it; I do assure you I feel it!"

"You needn't trouble yourself to feel it," was the quietly un-gracious answer. "Lady Lydiard brings me here. I come to see the house—and the dog." He looked round the gallery in his gravely attentive way. "I don't understand pictures," he remarked, re-signedly.

"I shall go back to the drawing-room."

After a moment's consideration Felix followed him into the drawing-room, with the air of a man who was determined not to be repelled.

"Well?" asked Hardyman. "What is it?"

"About that matter?" Felix said, inquiringly.

"What matter?"

"Oh, you know. Will next week do?"

"Next week *won't* do."

Mr. Felix Sweetsir cast one look at his friend. His friend was too intently occupied with the decorations of the drawing-room to notice the look.

"Will to-morrow do?" Felix resumed, after an interval.

"Yes."

"At what time?"

"Between twelve and one in the afternoon."

"Between twelve and one in the afternoon," Felix repeated. He looked again at Hardyman, and took his hat. "Make my apologies to my aunt," he said. "You must introduce yourself to her ladyship. I can't wait here any longer." He walked out of the room, having deliberately returned the contemptuous indifference of Hardyman by a similar indifference on his own side at parting.

Left by himself, Hardyman took a chair and glanced at the door which led into the boudoir. The steward had knocked at that door, had disappeared through it, and had not appeared again. How much longer was Lady Lydiard's visitor to be left unnoticed in Lady Lydiard's house?

As the question passed through his mind the boudoir door opened. For once in his life Alfred Hardyman's composure deserted him. He started to his feet, like an ordinary mortal taken completely by surprise.

Instead of Mr. Moody, instead of Lady Lydiard, there appeared in the open door-way a young woman in a state of embarrassment, who actually quickened the beat of Mr. Hardyman's heart the moment he set eyes on her. Was the person who produced this amazing impression at first sight a person of importance? Nothing of the sort. She was only "Isabel," surnamed "Miller." Even her name had nothing in it. Only "Isabel Miller!"

Had she any pretensions to distinction in virtue of her personal appearance?

It is not easy to answer the question. The women (let us put the worst judges first) had long since discovered that she wanted that indispensable elegance of figure which is derived from slimness of waist and length of limb. The men (who were better acquainted with the subject) looked at her figure from their point of view, and finding it essentially embraceable, asked for nothing more. It might have been her bright complexion, or it might have been the bold luster of her eyes (as the women considered it), that dazzled the lords of creation generally, and made them all alike incompetent to discover her faults. Still, she had compensating attractions which no severity of criticism could dispute. Her smile, beginning at her lips, flowed brightly and instantly over her whole face. A delicious atmosphere of health, freshness, and good-humor seemed to radiate from her wherever she went and whatever she did. For the rest, her brown hair grew low over her broad, white forehead, and was topped by a neat little lace cap with ribbons of a violet color. A plain collar and plain cuffs encircled her smooth, round neck and her plump, dimpled hands. Her merino dress, covering but not hiding the charming outline of her bosom, matched the color of her cap ribbons, and was brightened by a white muslin apron coquettishly trimmed about the pockets, a gift from Lady Lydiard. Blushing and smiling, she let the door fall to behind her, and, shyly approaching the stranger, said to him, in her small, clear voice, "If you please, sir, are you Mr. Hardyman?"

The gravity of the great horse-breeder deserted him at her first question. He smiled as he acknowledged that he was "Mr. Hardyman"—he smiled as he offered her a chair.

"No, thank you, sir," she said, with a quaintly pretty inclination of her head. "I am only sent here to make her ladyship's apologies. She has put the poor, dear dog into a warm bath, and she can't leave him. And Mr. Moody can't come instead of me, because I was too frightened to be of any use, and so he had to hold the dog. That's all. We are very anxious, sir, to know if the warm bath is the right thing. Please come into the room and tell us."

She led the way back to the door. Hardyman, naturally enough, was slow to follow her. When a man is fascinated by the charm of youth and beauty, he is in no hurry to transfer his attention to a sick animal in a bath. Hardyman seized on the first excuse that he could devise for keeping Isabel to himself—that is to say, for keeping her in the drawing-room.

"I think I shall be better able to help you," he said, "if you will tell me something about the dog first."

Even his accent in speaking had altered to a certain degree. The quiet, dreary monotone in which he habitually spoke quickened a little under his present excitement. As for Isabel she was too deeply interested in Tommie's welfare to suspect that she was being made the victim of a stratagem. She left the door and turned to Hardyman with eager eyes. "What can I tell you, sir?" she asked, innocently.

Hardyman pressed his advantage without mercy.

"You can tell me what sort of dog he is?"

"Yes, sir."

"How old he is?"

"Yes, sir."

"What his name is?—what his temper is?—what his illness is?— what disease his father and mother?—what——"

Isabel's head began to turn giddy. "One thing at a time, sir?" she interposed, with a gesture of entreaty. "The dog sleeps on my bed, and I had a bad night with him, he disturbed me so, and I am afraid I am very stupid this morning. His name is Tommie. We are obliged to call him by it, because he won't answer to any other than the name he had when my lady bought him. But we spell it with an 'i e' at the end, which makes it less vulgar than Tommy with a 'y.' I am very sorry, sir, I forget what else you wanted to know. Please to come in here, and my lady will tell you everything."

She tried to get back to the door of the boudoir. Hardyman, feasting his eyes on the pretty, changeful face that looked up at him with such innocent confidence in his authority, drew her away again from the door by the one means at his disposal. He returned to his questions about Tommie.

"Wait a little, please. What sort of a dog is he?"

Isabel turned back again from the door. To describe Tommie was a labor of love. "He is the most beautiful dog in the world!" the girl began, with kindling eyes. "He has the most exquisite white curly hair and two light-brown patches on his back, and, oh! *such* lovely dark eyes! They call him a Scotch terrier. When he is well his appetite is truly wonderful—nothing comes amiss to him, sir, from *pâté de foie gras* to potatoes. He has his enemies, poor dear, though you wouldn't think it. People who won't put up with being bitten by him (what shocking tempers one does meet with, to be sure!) call him a mongrel. Isn't it a shame? Please come in and see him, sir; my

lady will be tired of waiting." Another journey to the door followed
those words, checked instantly by a serious objection.

"Stop a minute! You must tell me what his temper is or I can do
nothing for him."

Isabel returned once more, feeling that it was really serious this
time. Her gravity was even more charming than her gayety. As she
lifted her face to him, with large, solemn eyes, expressive of her
sense of responsibility, Hardyman would have given every horse in
his stables to have had the privilege of taking her in his arms and
kissing her.

"Tommie has the temper of an angel with the people he likes,"
she said. "When he bites, it generally means that he objects to
strangers. He loves my lady, and he loves Mr. Moody, and he loves
me, and—and I think that's all. This way, sir, if you please; I am
sure I heard my lady call."

"No," said Hardyman, in his immovably obstinate way. "Nobody
called. About this dog's temper? Doesn't he take to any strangers?
What sort of people does he bite in general?"

Isabel's pretty lips began to curl upwards at the corners in a quiet
smile. Hardyman's last imbecile question had opened her eyes to the
true state of the case. Still, Tommie's future was in this strange
gentleman's hands; she felt bound to consider that. And, moreover, it
was no every-day event in Isabel's experience to fascinate a famous
personage, who was also a magnificent and perfectly dressed man.
She ran the risk of wasting another minute or two and went on with
the memoirs of Tommie.

"I must own, sir," she resumed, "that he behaves a little
ungratefully—even to strangers who take an interest in him. When
he gets lost in the street (which is very often), he sits down on the
pavement and howls till he collects a pitying crowd round him; and
when they try to read his name and address on his collar he snaps at
them. The servants generally find him and bring him back; and as
soon as he gets home he turns round on the door-steps and snaps at
the servants. I think it must be his fun. You should see him sitting
up in his chair at dinner-time, waiting to be helped, with his fore-
paws on the edge of the table, like the hands of a gentleman at a
public dinner making a speech. But, oh!" cried Isabel, checking
herself, with the tears in her eyes, "how can I talk of him in this way
when he is so dreadfully ill? Some of them say its bronchitis, and
some say it's his liver. Only yesterday I took him to the front door

to give him a little air, and he stood still on the pavement, quite stupefied. For the first time in his life he snapped at nobody who went by; and oh, dear, he hadn't even the heart to smell a lamp-post!"

Isabel had barely stated this last afflicting circumstance when the memoirs of Tommie were suddenly cut short by the voice of Lady Lydiard—really calling this time—from the inner room.

"Isabel! Isabel!" cried her ladyship, "what are you about?"

Isabel ran to the door of the boudoir and threw it open. "Go in, sir. Pray go in!" she said.

"Without you?" Hardyman asked.

"I will follow you, sir. I have something to do for her ladyship first."

She still held the door open, and pointed entreatingly to the passage which led to the boudoir. "I shall be blamed, sir," she said, "if you don't go in."

This statement of the case left Hardyman no alternative. He presented himself to Lady Lydiard without another moment of delay.

Having closed the drawing-room door on him, Isabel waited a little, absorbed in her own thoughts.

She was now perfectly well aware of the effect which she had produced on Hardyman. Her vanity, it is not to be denied, was flattered by his admiration—he was so grand and so tall, and he had such fine large eyes. The girl looked prettier than ever as she stood with her head down and her color heightened, smiling to herself. A clock on the chimney-piece striking the half-hour roused her. She cast one look at the glass as she passed it, and went to the table at which Lady Lydiard had been writing.

Methodical Mr. Moody, in submitting to be employed as bath attendant upon Tommie, had not forgotten the interests of his mistress. He reminded her ladyship that she had left her letter, with a bank-note inclosed in it, unsealed. Absorbed in the dog, Lady Lydiard answered, "Isabel is doing nothing, let Isabel seal it. Show Mr. Hardyman in here," she continued, turning to Isabel, "and then seal a letter of mine which you will find on the table." "And when you have sealed it," careful Mr. Moody added, "put it back on the table; I will take charge of it when her ladyship has done with me."

Such were the special instructions which now detained Isabel in the drawing-room. She lit the taper, and closed and sealed the open envelope, without feeling curiosity enough even to look at the address. Mr. Hardyman was the uppermost subject in her thoughts. Leaving the sealed letter on the table, she returned to the fire-place, and studied her own charming face attentively in the looking-glass. The time passed, and Isabel's reflection was still the subject of Isabel's contemplation. "He must see many beautiful ladies," she thought, veering backward and forward between pride and humility. "I wonder what he sees in me?"

The clock struck the hour. Almost at the same moment the boudoir door opened, and Robert Moody, released at last from attendance on Tommie entered the drawing-room.

V

"Well," asked Isabel, eagerly, "what does Mr. Hardyman say? Does he think he can cure Tommie?"

Moody answered a little coldly and stiffly. His dark, deeply set eyes rested on Isabel with an uneasy look.

"Mr. Hardyman seems to understand animals," he said. "He lifted the dog's eyelid and looked at his eye, and then he told us the bath was useless."

"Go on," said Isabel, impatiently. "He did something, I suppose, besides telling you that the bath was useless."

"He took a knife out of his pocket, with a lancet in it."

Isabel clasped her hands with a faint cry of horror. "Oh, Mr. Moody, did he hurt Tommie?"

"Hurt him?" Moody repeated, indignant at the interest which she felt in the animal and the indifference which she exhibited toward the man (as represented by himself). "Hurt him, indeed! Mr. Hardyman bled the brute——"

"Brute?" Isabel reiterated, with flashing eyes. "I know some people, Mr. Moody, who really deserve to be called by that horrid word. If you can't say, 'Tommie,' when you speak of him in my presence, be so good as to say 'the dog.' "

Moody yielded with the worst possible grace. "Oh, very well! Mr. Hardyman bled the dog, and brought him to his senses directly. I am charged to tell you——" He stopped as if the message which he was instructed to deliver was in the last degree distasteful to him.

"Well, what were you charged to tell me?"

"I was to say that Mr. Hardyman will give you instructions how to treat the dog for the future."

Isabel hastened to the door, eager to receive her instructions. Moody stopped her before she could open it.

"You are in a great hurry to get to Mr. Hardyman," he remarked.

Isabel looked back at him in surprise. "You said just now that Mr. Hardyman was waiting to tell me how to nurse Tommie."

"Let him wait," Moody rejoined, sternly. "When I left him, he was sufficiently occupied in expressing his favorable opinion of you to her ladyship."

The steward's pale face turned paler still as he said those words. With the arrival of Isabel in Lady Lydiard's house "his time had come"—exactly as the women in the servants' hall had predicted. At last the impenetrable man felt the influence of the sex; at last he knew the passion of love—misplaced, ill-starred, hopeless love, for a woman who was young enough to be his child. He had already spoken to Isabel more than once in terms which told his secret plainly enough. But the smoldering fire of jealousy in the man, fanned into flame by Hardyman, now showed itself for the first time. His looks, even more than his words, would have warned a woman with any knowledge of the natures of men to be careful how she answered him. Young, giddy, and inexperienced, Isabel followed the flippant impulse of the moment, without a thought of the consequences. "I'm sure it's very kind of Mr. Hardyman to speak favorably of me," she said, with a pert little laugh. "I hope you are not jealous of him, Mr. Moody?"

Moody was in no humor to make allowances for the unbridled gayety of youth and good spirits. "I hate any man who admires you," he burst out, passionately, "let him be who he may!"

Isabel looked at her strange lover with unaffected astonishment. How unlike Mr. Hardyman, who had treated her as a lady from first to last. "What an odd man you are!" she said. "You can't take a joke. I'm sure I didn't mean to offend you."

"You don't offend me—you do worse, you distress me."

Isabel's color began to rise. The merriment died out of her face; she looked at Moody gravely. "I don't like to be accused of distressing people when I don't deserve it," she said. "I had better leave you. Let me by, if you please."

Having committed one error in offending her, Moody committed another in attempting to make his peace with her. Acting under the fear that she would really leave him, he took her roughly by the arm.

"You are always trying to get away from me," he said. "I wish I knew how to make you like me, Isabel."

"I don't allow you to call me Isabel!" she retorted, struggling to free herself from his hold. "Let go of my àrm. You hurt me."

Moody dropped her arm with a bitter sigh. "I don't know how to deal with you," he said, simply. "Have some pity on me!"

If the steward had known anything of women (at Isabel's age) he would never have appealed to her mercy in those plain terms and at that unpropitious moment. "Pity you?" she repeated, contemptuously. "Is that all you have to say to me after hurting my arm? What a bear you are!" She shrugged her shoulders and put her hands coquettishly into the pockets of her apron. That was how she pitied him! His face turned paler and paler—he writhed under it.

"For God's sake, don't turn everything I say to you into ridicule!" he cried. "You know I love you with all my heart and soul. Again and again I have asked you to be my wife, and you laugh at me as if it was a joke. I haven't deserved to be treated in that cruel way. It maddens me—I can't endure it!"

Isabel looked down at the floor, and followed the lines in the pattern of the carpet with the end of her smart little shoe. She could hardly have been further away from really understanding Moody if he had spoken in Hebrew. She was partly startled, partly puzzled, by the strong emotions which she had unconsciously called into being. "Oh, dear me!" she said, "why can't you talk of something else? why can't we be friends? Excuse me for mentioning it," she went on, looking up at him with a saucy smile, "you are old enough to be my father."

Moody's head sunk on his breast. "I own it," he answered, humbly. "But there is something to be said for me. Men as old as I am have made good husbands before now. I would devote my whole life to make you happy. There isn't a wish you could form which I wouldn't be proud to obey. You mustn't reckon me by years. My youth has not been wasted in a profligate life. I can be truer to you and fonder of you than many a younger man. Surely my heart is not quite unworthy of you, when it is all yours. I have lived such a lonely, miserable life; and you might so easily brighten it! You are kind to everybody else, Isabel. Tell me, dear, why are you so hard on *me?*"

His voice trembled as he appealed to her in those simple words. He had taken the right way at last to produce an impression on her. She really felt for him. All that was true and tender in her nature began to rise in her and take his part. Unhappily, he felt too deeply and too strongly to be patient and to give her time. He completely misinterpreted her silence—completely mistook the motive that made her turn aside for a moment to gather composure enough to speak to him. "Ah!" he burst out, bitterly, turning away on his side, "you have no heart!"

She instantly resented those unjust words. At that moment they wounded her to the quick.

"You know best," she said. "I have no doubt you are right. Remember one thing, however: though I have no heart, I have never encouraged you, Mr. Moody. I have declared over and over again that I could only be your friend. Understand that for the future, if you please. There are plenty of nice women who will be glad to marry you, I have no doubt. You will always have my best wishes for your welfare. Good-morning. Her ladyship will wonder what has become of me. Be so kind as to let me pass."

Tortured by the passion that consumed him, Moody obstinately kept his place between Isabel and the door. The unworthy suspicion of her, which had been in his mind all through the interview, now forced its way outward to expression at last.

"No woman ever used a man as you use me without some reason for it," he said. "You have kept your secret wonderfully well; but sooner or later all secrets get found out. I know what is in your mind as well as you know it yourself. You are in love with some other man."

Isabel's face flushed deeply; the defensive pride of her sex was up in arms in an instant. She cast one disdainful look at Moody, without troubling herself to express her contempt in words. "Stand out of my way, sir!" that was all she said to him.

"You are in love with some other man," he reiterated, passionately. "Deny it if you can!"

"Deny it?" she repeated, with flashing eyes. "What right have you to ask the question? Am I not free to do as I please?"

He stood looking at her, meditating his next words, with a sudden and sinister change to self-restraint. Suppressed rage was in his rigidly set eyes, suppressed rage was in his trembling hand as he raised it emphatically while he spoke his next words.

"I have one thing more to say," he answered, "and then I have done. If I am not your husband, no other man shall be. Look well to it, Isabel Miller. If there *is* another man between us, I can tell him this—he shall find it no easy matter to rob me of you!"

She started, and turned pale; but it was only for a moment. The high spirit that was in her rose brightly in her eyes, and faced him without shrinking.

"Threats?" she said, with quiet contempt. "When you make love, Mr. Moody, you take strange ways of doing it. My conscience is easy. You may try to frighten me, but you will not succeed. When you have recovered your temper I will accept your excuses." She paused, and pointed to the table. "There is the letter that you told me to leave for you when I had sealed it," she went on. "I suppose you have her ladyship's orders. Isn't it time you began to think of obeying them?"

The contemptuous composure of her tone and manner seemed to act on Moody with crushing effect. Without a word of answer the unfortunate steward took up the letter from the table. Without a word of answer he walked mechanically to the great door which opened on the stair-case, turned on the threshold to look at Isabel, waited a moment, pale and still, and suddenly left the room.

That silent departure, that hopeless submission, impressed Isabel in spite of herself. That sustaining sense of injury and insult sunk, as it were, from under her the moment she was alone. He had not been gone a minute before she began to be sorry for him once more. The interview had taught her nothing. She was neither old enough nor experienced enough to understand the overwhelming revolution produced in a man's character when he feels the passion of love for the first time in the maturity of his life. If Moody had stolen a kiss at the first opportunity, she would have resented the liberty that he had taken with her; but she would have thoroughly understood him. His terrible earnestness, his overpowering agitation, his abrupt violence —all these evidences of a passion that was a mystery to himself— simply puzzled her. "I'm sure I didn't wish to hurt his feelings" (such was the form that her reflections took in her present penitent frame of mind); "but why did he provoke me? It is a shame to tell me that I love some other man, when there is no other man. I declare I begin to hate the men, if they are all like Mr. Moody. I wonder whether he will forgive me when he sees me again? I'm sure I'm willing to forget and forgive on my side, especially if he won't insist on my being fond of him because he is fond of me. Oh! dear, I wish he would come back and shake hands. It's enough to try the patience of a saint to be treated in this way. I wish I was ugly! The ugly ones have a quiet time of it—the men let them be. Mr. Moody! Mr. Moody!" She went out to the landing and called to him softly. There was no answer. He was no longer in the house. She stood still for a moment in silent vexation. "I'll go to Tommie," she decided. "I'm sure he's the more agreeable company of the two. And—oh, good gracious!—there's Mr. Hardyman waiting to give me my instructions! How do I look, I wonder?"

She consulted the glass once more, gave one or two corrective touches to her hair and cap, and hastened into the boudoir.

VI

For a quarter of an hour the drawing-room remained empty. At the end of that time the council in the boudoir broke up. Lady Lydiard led the way back to the drawing-room, followed by Hardyman, Isabel being left to look after the dog. Before the door closed behind him, Hardyman turned round to reiterate his last medical directions, or, in plainer words, to take a last look at Isabel.

"Plenty of water, Miss Isabel, for the dog to lap, and a little bread or biscuit if he wants something to eat. Nothing more, if you please, till I see him to-morrow."

"Thank you, sir. I will take the greatest care——"

At that point Lady Lydiard cut short the interchange of instructions and civilities. "Shut the door, if you please, Mr. Hardyman. I feel the draught. Many thanks! I am really at a loss to tell you how gratefully I feel your kindness. But for you my poor little dog might have been dead by this time."

Hardyman answered, in the quiet, melancholy monotone which was habitual with him, "Your ladyship need feel no further anxiety about the dog. Only be careful not to overfeed him. He will do very well under Miss Isabel's care. By the bye, her family name is Miller, is it not? Is she related to the Warwickshire Millers, of Duxborough House?"

Lady Lydiard looked at him with an expression of satirical surprise. "Mr. Hardyman," she said, "this makes the fourth time you have questioned me about Isabel. You seem to take a great interest in my little companion. Don't make any apologies, pray. You pay Isabel a compliment; and as I am very fond of her, I am naturally gratified when I find her admired. At the same time," she added, with one of her abrupt transitions of language, "I had my eye on you and I had my eye on her when you were talking in the next room, and I don't mean to let you make a fool of the girl. She is not in your line of life, and the sooner you know it the better. You make me laugh when you ask if she is related to gentlefolks. She is the orphan daughter of a chemist in the country. Her relations haven't a penny to bless themselves with, except an old aunt, who lives in a village on two or three hundred a year. I heard of the girl by accident. When she lost her father and mother, her aunt offered to take her. Isabel said, 'No, thank you; I will not be a burden on a relation who has only enough for herself. A girl can earn an honest living if she tries, and I mean to try'—that's what she said. I admired her independence," her ladyship proceeded, ascending again to the higher regions of thought and expression. "My niece's marriage, just at that time, had left me alone in this great house. I proposed to Isabel to come to me as companion and reader for a few weeks, and to decide for herself whether she liked the life or not. We have never been separated since that time. I could hardly be fonder of her if she were my own daughter, and she returns my affection with all her heart. She has excellent qualities—prudent, cheerful, sweet-tempered; with good sense enough to understand what her place is in the world, as distinguished from her place in my regard. I have taken care, for her own sake, never to leave that part of the question in any doubt. It would be cruel kindness to deceive her as to her future position when she marries. I shall take good care that the man who pays his addresses to her is a man in her rank of life. I know but too well, in the case of one of my own relatives, what miseries unequal marriages bring with them. Excuse me for troubling you at this length on domestic matters. I am very fond of Isabel, and a girl's head is so easily turned. Now you know what her position really is, you will also know what limits there must be to the expression of your interest in her. I am sure we understand each other; and I say no more."

Hardyman listened to this long harangue with the immovable gravity which was part of his character—except when Isabel had taken him by surprise. When her ladyship gave him the opportunity of speaking on his side he had very little to say, and that little did not suggest that he had greatly profited by what he had heard. His mind had been full of Isabel when Lady Lydiard began, and it remained just as full of her, in just the same way, when Lady Lydiard had done.

"Yes," he remarked, quietly, "Miss Isabel is an uncommonly nice girl, as you say. Very pretty, and such frank, unaffected manners. I don't deny that I feel an interest in her. The young ladies one meets in society are not much to my taste. Miss Isabel is my taste."

Lady Lydiard's face assumed a look of blank dismay. "I am afraid I have failed to convey my exact meaning to you," she said.

Hardyman gravely declared that he understood her perfectly. "Perfectly," he repeated, with his impenetrable obstinacy. "Your ladyship exactly expresses my opinion of Miss Isabel. Prudent and cheerful and sweet-tempered, as you say—all the qualities in a woman that I admire. With good looks, too—of course with good looks. She will be a perfect treasure (as you remarked just now) to the man who marries her. I may claim to know something about it. I have twice narrowly escaped being married myself; and though I can't exactly explain it, I'm all the harder to please in consequence. Miss Isabel pleases me. I think I have said that before. Pardon me for saying it again. I'll call to-morrow morning and look at the dog, as early as eleven o'clock, if you will allow me. Later in the day I must be off to France to attend a sale of horses. Glad to have been of any use to your ladyship, I am sure. Good-morning."

Lady Lydiard let him go, wisely resigning any further attempt to establish an understanding between her visitor and herself.

"He is either a person of very limited intelligence when he is away from his stables," she thought, "or he deliberately declines to take a plain hint when it is given to him. I can't drop his acquaintance, on Tommie's account. The only other alternative is to keep Isabel out of his way. My good little girl shall not drift into a false position while I am living to look after her. When Mr. Hardyman calls to-morrow, she shall be out on an errand. When he calls, on his return, she shall be upstairs with a headache. And, if he tries it again, she shall be away at my house in the country. If he makes any remarks on her absence—well, he will find that I can be just as dull of understanding as he is when the occasion calls for it."

Having arrived at this satisfactory solution of the difficulty, Lady Lydiard became conscious of an irresistible impulse to summon

Isabel to her presence and caress her. In the nature of a warm-hearted woman, this was only the inevitable reaction which followed the subsidence of anxiety about the girl, after her own resolution had set that anxiety at rest. She threw open the door, and made one of her sudden appearances in the boudoir. Even in the fervent out-pouring of her affection there was still the inherent abruptness of manner which so strongly marked Lady Lydiard's character in all the relations of life.

"Did I give you a kiss this morning?" she asked, when Isabel rose to receive her.

"Yes, my lady," said the girl, with her charming smile.

"Come, then, and give me a kiss in return. Do you love me? Very well, then, treat me like your mother. Never mind 'my lady' this time. Give me a good hug."

Something in those homely words, or something perhaps in the look that accompanied them, touched sympathies in Isabel which seldom showed themselves on the surface. Her smiling lips trembled, the bright tears rose in her eyes. "You are too good to me," she murmured, with her head on Lady Lydiard's bosom. "How can I ever love you enough in return?"

Lady Lydiard patted the pretty head that rested on her with such filial tenderness. "There! there!" she said. "Go back and play with Tommie, my dear. We may be as fond of each other as we like, but we mustn't cry. God bless you! Go away!—go away!"

She turned aside quickly; her own eyes were moistening, and it was part of her character to be reluctant to let Isabel see it. "Why have I made a fool of myself?" she wondered, as she approached the drawing-room door. "It doesn't matter. I am all the better for it. Odd, that Mr. Hardyman should have made me feel fonder of Isabel than ever!"

With these reflections she re-entered the drawing-room, and suddenly checked herself with a start. "Good heavens!" she exclaimed, irritably, "how you frightened me! Why was I not told you were here?"

Having left the drawing-room in a state of solitude, Lady Lydiard, on her return, found herself suddenly confronted with a gentleman mysteriously planted on the hearth-rug in her absence. The new visitor may be rightly described as a gray man. He had gray hair, eyebrows and whiskers; he wore a gray coat, waistcoat, and trousers, and gray gloves. For the rest, his appearance was eminently suggestive of wealth and respectability, and in this case appearances were really to be trusted. The gray man was no other than Lady Lydiard's legal adviser, Mr. Troy.

"I regret, my lady, that I should have been so unfortunate as to startle you," he said, with a certain underlying embarrassment in his manner. "I had the honor of sending word by Mr. Moody that I would call at this hour on some matters of business connected with your ladyship's house property. I presumed that you expected to find me here, waiting your pleasure——"

Thus far Lady Lydiard had listened to her legal adviser, fixing her eyes on his face in her usually frank, straightforward way. She now stopped him in the middle of a sentence, with a change of expression on her own face, which was undisguisedly a change to alarm.

"Don't apologize, Mr. Troy," she said. "I am to blame for forgetting your appointment, and for not keeping my nerves under proper control." She paused for a moment, and took a seat before she said her next words. "May I ask," she resumed, "if there is something unpleasant in the business that brings you here?"

"Nothing whatever, my lady, mere formalities, which can wait till to-morrow or next day, if you wish it."

Lady Lydiard's fingers drummed impatiently on the table. "You have known me long enough, Mr. Troy, to know that I can not endure suspense. You *have* something unpleasant to tell me."

The lawyer respectfully remonstrated. "Really, Lady Lydiard," he began.

"It won't do, Mr. Troy. I know how you look at me on ordinary occasions, and I see how you look at me now. You are a very clever lawyer; but, happily for the interests that I commit to your charge, you are also a thoroughly honest man. After twenty years' experience of you, you can't deceive *me*. You bring me bad news. Speak at once, sir, and speak plainly."

Mr. Troy yielded, inch by inch, as it were. "I bring news which, I fear, may annoy your ladyship." He paused, and advanced another inch. "It is news which I only became acquainted with myself on entering this house." He waited again, and made another advance. "I happened to meet your ladyship's steward, Mr. Moody, in the hall——"

"Where is he?" Lady Lydiard interposed, angrily. "I can make *him* speak out, and I will. Send him here instantly."

The lawyer made a last effort to hold off the coming disclosure a

little longer. "Mr. Moody will be here directly," he said. "Mr.
Moody requested me to prepare your ladyship—"

"Will you ring the bell, Mr. Troy, or must I?"

Moody had evidently been waiting outside while the lawyer spoke
for him. He saved Mr. Troy the trouble of ringing the bell by
presenting himself in the drawing-room. Lady Lydiard's eyes
searched his face as he approached. Her bright complexion faded
suddenly. Not a word passed her lips. She looked and waited.

In silence on his side, Moody laid an open sheet of paper on the
table. The paper quivered in his trembling hand.

Lady Lydiard recovered herself first. "Is that for me?" she asked.

"Yes, my lady."

She took up the paper without an instant's hesitation. Both the
men watched her anxiously as she read it.

The handwriting was strange to her. The words were these:

"I hereby certify that the bearer of these lines, Robert Moody by
name, has presented to me the letter with which he was charged,
addressed to myself, with the seal intact. I regret to add that there
is, to say the least of it, some mistake. The inclosure referred to by
the anonymous writer of the letter, who signs 'A Friend in Need,'
has not reached me. No five-hundred-pound bank-note was in the
letter when I opened it. My wife was present when I broke the seal,
and can certify to this statement if necessary. Not knowing who my
charitable correspondent is (Mr. Moody being forbidden to give me
any information), I can only take this means of stating the case
exactly as it stands, and hold myself at the disposal of the writer of
the letter. My private address is at the head of the page.

SAMUEL BRADSTOCK
Rector St. Anne's, Deansbury, London."

Lady Lydiard dropped the paper on the table. For the moment,
plainly as the rector's statement was expressed, she appeared to be
incapable of understanding it. "What, in God's name, does this
mean?" she asked.

The lawyer and the steward looked at each other. Which of the
two was entitled to speak first? Lady Lydiard gave them no time to
decide. "Moody," she said, sternly, "you take charge of the letter; I
look to you for an explanation."

Moody's dark eyes flashed. He answered Lady Lydiard, without caring to conceal that he resented the tone in which she had spoken to him.

"I undertook to deliver the letter at its address," he said. "I found it, sealed, on the table. Your ladyship has the clergyman's written testimony that I handed it to him with the seal unbroken. I have done my duty, and I have no explanation to offer."

Before Lady Lydiard could speak again, Mr. Troy discreetly interfered. He saw plainly that his experience was required to lead the investigation in the right direction.

"Pardon me, my lady," he said, with that happy mixture of the positive and the polite in his manner of which lawyers alone possess the secret. "There is only one way of arriving at the truth in painful matters of this sort. We must begin at the beginning. May I venture to ask your ladyship a question?"

Lady Lydiard felt the composing influence of Mr. Troy. "I am at your disposal, sir," she said, quietly.

"Are you absolutely certain that you inclosed the bank-note in the letter?" the lawyer asked.

"I certainly believe I inclosed it," Lady Lydiard answered. "But I was so alarmed at the time by the sudden illness of my dog that I do not feel justified in speaking positively."

"Was anybody in the room with your ladyship when you put the inclosure in the letter, as you believe?"

"*I* was in the room," said Moody. "I can swear that I saw her ladyship put the bank-note in the letter, and the letter in the envelope."

"And seal the envelope?" asked Mr. Troy.

"No, sir. Her ladyship was called away into the next room to the dog before she could seal the envelope."

Mr. Troy addressed himself once more to Lady Lydiard. "Did your ladyship take the letter into the next room with you?"

"I was too much alarmed to think of it, Mr. Troy. I left it here on the table."

"With the envelope open?"

"Yes."

"How long were you absent in the other room?"

"Half an hour or more."

"Ha!" said Mr. Troy to himself, "this complicates it a little." He reflected for a while, and then turned again to Moody. "Did any of the servants know of this bank-note being in her ladyship's possession?"

"Not one of them," Moody answered.

"Do you suspect any of the servants?"

"Certainly not, sir."

"Are there any workmen employed in the house?"

"No, sir."

"Do you know of any persons who had access to the room while Lady Lydiard was absent from it?"

"Two visitors called, sir."

"Who were they?"

"Her ladyship's nephew, Mr. Felix Sweetsir, and the Honorable Alfred Hardyman."

Mr. Troy shook his head irritably. "I am not speaking of gentlemen of high position and repute," he said. "It's absurd even to mention Mr. Sweetsir and Mr. Hardyman. My question related to strangers who might have obtained access to the drawing-room— people calling, with her ladyship's sanction, for subscriptions, for instance, or people calling with articles of dress or ornament to be submitted to her ladyship's inspection."

"No such persons came to the house, to my knowledge," Moody answered.

Mr. Troy suspended the investigation, and took a turn thoughtfully in the room. The theory on which his inquiries had proceeded thus far had failed to produce any results. His experience warned him to waste no more time on it, and return to the starting-point of the investigation—in other words, to the letter. Shifting his point of view, he turned again to Lady Lydiard, and tried his questions in a new direction.

"Mr. Moody mentioned just now," he said, "that your ladyship was called into the next room before you could seal your letter. On your return to this room did you seal the letter?"

"I was busy with the dog," Lady Lydiard answered. "Isabel Miller was of no use in the boudoir, and I told her to seal it for me."

Mr. Troy started. The new direction in which he was pushing his inquiries began to look like the right direction already. "Miss Isabel Miller," he proceeded, "has been a resident under your ladyship's roof for some little time, I believe?"

"For nearly two years, Mr. Troy."

"As your ladyship's companion and reader?"

"As my adopted daughter," her ladyship answered, with marked emphasis.

Wise Mr. Troy rightly interpreted the emphasis as a warning to him to suspend the examination of her ladyship, and to address to Mr. Moody the far more serious questions which were now to come.

"Did any one give you the letter before you left the house with it," he said to the steward, "or did you take it yourself?"

"I took it myself, from the table here."

"Was it sealed?"

"Yes."

"Was anybody present when you took the letter from the table?"

"Miss Isabel was present."

"Did you find her alone in the room?"

"Yes, sir."

Lady Lydiard opened her lips to speak, and checked herself. Mr. Troy, having cleared the ground before him, put the fatal question.

"Mr. Moody," he said, "when Miss Isabel was instructed to seal the letter, did she know that a bank-note was inclosed in it?"

Instead of replying, Robert drew back from the lawyer with a look of horror. Lady Lydiard started to her feet, and checked herself again on the point of speaking.

"Answer him, Moody," she said, putting a strong constraint on herself.

Robert answered very unwillingly. "I took the liberty of reminding her ladyship that she had left her letter unsealed," he said. "And I mentioned as my excuse for speaking"—he stopped and corrected himself—"I *believe* I mentioned that a valuable inclosure was in the letter."

"You believe?" Mr. Troy repeated. "Can't you speak more positively than that?"

"*I* can speak positively," said Lady Lydiard, with her eyes on the lawyer. "Moody did mention the inclosure in the letter, in Isabel Miller's hearing as well as in mine." She paused, steadily controlling herself. "And what of that, Mr. Troy?" she added, very quietly and firmly.

Mr. Troy answered quietly and firmly on his side. "I am surprised that your ladyship should ask the question," he said.

"I persist in repeating the question," Lady Lydiard rejoined. "I say that Isabel Miller knew of the inclosure in my letter, and I ask, What of that?"

"And I answer," retorted the impenetrable lawyer, "that the suspicion of theft rests on your ladyship's adopted daughter, and on nobody else."

"It's false!" cried Robert, with a burst of honest indignation. "I wish to God I had never said a word to you about the loss of the bank-note! Oh, my lady! my lady! don't let him distress you! What does *he* know about it?"

"Hush!" said Lady Lydiard. "Control yourself and hear what he has to say." She rested her hand on Moody's shoulder, partly to encourage him, partly to support herself, and fixing her eyes again on Mr. Troy, repeated his last words, " 'Suspicion rests on my adopted daughter, and on nobody else.' Why on nobody else?"

"Is your ladyship prepared to suspect the rector of St. Anne's of embezzlement, or your own relatives and equals of theft?" Mr. Troy asked. "Does a shadow of doubt rest on the servants? Not if Mr. Moody's evidence is to be believed. Who, to our own certain knowledge, had access to the letter while it was unsealed? Who was alone in the room with it? And who knew of the inclosure in it? I leave the answer to your ladyship."

"Isabel Miller is as incapable of an act of theft as I am. There is my answer, Mr. Troy!"

The lawyer bowed resignedly, and advanced to the door.

"Am I to take your ladyship's generous assertions as finally disposing of the question of the lost bank-note?" he inquired.

Lady Lydiard met the challenge without shrinking from it.

"No!" she said. "The loss of the bank-note is known out of my house. Other persons may suspect this innocent girl as you suspect her. It is due to Isabel's reputation—her unstained reputation, Mr. Troy—that she should know what has happened, and should have an opportunity of defending herself. She is in the next room, Moody. Bring her here."

Robert's courage failed him; he trembled at the bare idea of exposing Isabel to the terrible ordeal that awaited her. "Oh, my lady!" he pleaded, "think again before you tell the poor girl that she is suspected of theft. Keep it a secret from her; the shame of it will break her heart."

"Keep it a secret," said Lady Lydiard, "when the rector and the rector's wife both know of it! Do you think they will let the matter rest where it is, even if I could consent to hush it up? I must write to them, and I can't write anonymously after what has happened. Put yourself in Isabel's place, and tell me if you would thank the person who knew you to be innocently exposed to a disgraceful suspicion, and who concealed it from you? Go, Moody! The longer you delay, the harder it will be."

With his head sunk on his breast, with anguish written in every line of his face, Moody obeyed. Passing slowly down the short passage which connected the two rooms, and still shrinking from the duty that had been imposed on him, he paused, looking through the curtains which hung over the entrance to the boudoir.

VII

The sight that met Moody's view wrung him to the heart.

Isabel and the dog were at play together. Among the varied accomplishments possessed by Tommie, the capacity to take his part at a game of hide-and-seek was one. His playfellow for the time being put a shawl or a handkerchief over his head, so as to prevent him from seeing, and then hid among the furniture a pocket-book, or a cigar-case, or a purse, or anything else that happened to be at hand, leaving the dog to find it, with his keen sense of smell to guide him. Doubly relieved by the fit and the bleeding, Tommie's spirits had revived, and he and Isabel had just begun their game when Moody looked into the room, charged with his terrible errand.

"You're burning, Tommie, you're burning!" cried the girl, laughing and clapping her hands. The next moment she happened to look round, and saw Moody through the parted curtains. His face warned her instantly that something serious had happened. She advanced a few steps, her eyes resting on him in silent alarm. He was himself too painfully agitated to speak. Not a word was exchanged between Lady Lydiard and Mr. Troy in the next room. In the complete stillness that prevailed the dog was heard sniffing and fidgeting about the furniture. Robert took Isabel by the hand and led her into the drawing-room. "For God's sake, spare her, my lady!" he whispered. The lawyer heard him.

"No," said Mr. Troy, "Be merciful, and tell her the truth."

He spoke to a woman who stood in no need of his advice. The inherent nobility in Lady Lydiard's nature was roused; her great heart offered itself patiently to any sorrow, to any sacrifice.

Putting her arm round Isabel—half caressing her, half supporting her—Lady Lydiard accepted the whole responsibility and told the whole truth.

Reeling under the first shock, the poor girl recovered herself with admirable courage. She raised her head and eyed the lawyer without uttering a word. In its artless consciousness of innocence the look was nothing less than sublime. Addressing herself to Mr. Troy, Lady Lydiard pointed to Isabel. "Do you see guilt there?" she asked.

Mr. Troy made no answer. In the melancholy experience of humanity to which his profession condemned him, he had seen conscious guilt assume the face of innocence, and helpless innocence admit the disguise of guilt; the keenest observation in either case failing completely to detect the truth. Lady Lydiard misinterpreted his silence as expressing the sullen self-assertion of a heartless man. She turned from him in contempt, and held out her hand to Isabel.

"Mr. Troy is not satisfied yet," she said, bitterly. "My love, take my hand, and look me in the face as your equal: I know no difference of rank at such a time as this. Before God, who hears you, are you innocent of the theft of the bank-note?"

"Before God, who hears me," Isabel answered, "I am innocent."

Lady Lydiard looked once more at the lawyer, and waited to hear if he believed *that*.

Mr. Troy took refuge in dumb diplomacy—he made a low bow. It might have meant that he believed Isabel, or it might have meant that he modestly withdrew his own opinion into the background. Lady Lydiard did not condescend to inquire what it meant.

"The sooner we bring this painful scene to an end the better," she said. "I shall be glad to avail myself of your professional assistance, Mr. Troy, within certain limits. Outside of my house, I beg that you will spare no trouble in tracing the lost money to the person who has really stolen it. Inside of my house, I must positively request that the disappearance of the note may never be alluded to, in any way whatever, until your inquiries have been successful in discovering the thief. In the meanwhile Mrs. Tollmidge and her family must not be sufferers by my loss; I shall pay the money again." She paused, and pressed Isabel's hand with affectionate fervor. "My child," she said, "one last word to you, and I have done. You remain here, with my trust in you and my love for you absolutely unshaken. You are dearer to me than ever. Never forget that."

Isabel bent her head, and kissed the kind hand that still held hers.

The high spirit that was in her, inspired by Lady Lydiard's example, rose equal to the dreadful situation in which she was placed.

"No, my lady," she said, calmly and sadly, "it can not be. What this gentleman has said of me is not to be denied—the appearances are against me. The letter was open, and I was alone in the room with it, and Mr. Moody told me that a valuable inclosure was inside it. Dear and kind mistress, I am not fit to be a member of your household, I am not worthy to live with the honest people who serve you, while my innocence is in doubt. It is enough for me now that *you* don't doubt it. I can wait patiently, after that, for the day that gives me back my good name. Oh, my lady, don't cry about it! Pray, pray, don't cry!"

Lady Lydiard's self-control failed her for the first time. Isabel's courage had made Isabel dearer to her than ever. She sunk into a chair, and covered her face with her handkerchief. Mr. Troy turned aside abruptly, and examined a Japanese vase, without any idea in his mind of what he was looking at. Lady Lydiard had gravely misjudged him in believing him to be a heartless man.

Isabel followed the lawyer, and touched him gently on the arm to rouse his attention.

"I have one relation living, sir—an aunt—who will receive me if I go to her," she said, simply. "Is there any harm in my going? Lady Lydiard will give you the address when you want me. Spare her ladyship, sir, all the pain and trouble that you can."

At last the heart that was in Mr. Troy asserted itself. "You are a fine creature!" he said, with a burst of enthusiasm. "I agree with Lady Lydiard; I believe you are innocent, too; and I will leave no effort untried to find the proof of it." He turned aside again, and had another look at the Japanese vase.

As the lawyer withdrew himself from observation, Moody approached Isabel.

Thus far he had stood apart, watching her and listening to her in silence. Not a look that had crossed her face, not a word that had fallen from her, had escaped him. Unconsciously on her side, unconsciously on his side, she now wrought on his nature with a purifying and ennobling influence which animated it with a new life. All that had been selfish and violent in his passion for her left him to return no more. The immeasurable devotion which he laid at her feet in the days that were yet to come—the unyielding courage which cheerfully accepted the sacrifice of himself when events de-

manded it at a later period of his life—struck root in him now.
Without attempting to conceal the tears that were falling fast over
his cheeks, striving vainly to express those new thoughts in him that
were beyond the reach of words, he stood before her the truest
friend and servant that ever woman had. "Oh, my dear! my heart is
heavy for you. Take me to serve you and help you. Her ladyship's
kindness will permit it, I am sure."

He could say no more. In those simple words the cry of his heart
reached her. "Forgive me, Robert," she answered, gratefully, "if I
said anything to pain you when we spoke together a little while
since. I didn't mean it." She gave him her hand, and looked timidly
over her shoulder at Lady Lydiard. "Let me go!" she said, in low,
broken tones; "let me go!"

Mr. Troy heard her, and stepped forward to interfere before Lady
Lydiard could speak. The man had recovered his self-control; the
lawyer took his place again on the scene.

"You must not leave us, my dear," he said to Isabel, "until I have
put a question to Mr. Moody in which you are interested. Do you
happen to have the number of the lost bank-note?" he asked, turning to the steward.

Moody produced his slip of paper with the number on it. Mr.
Troy made two copies of it before he returned the paper. One copy
he put in his pocket, the other he handed to Isabel.

"Keep it carefully," he said. "Neither you nor I know how soon it
may be of use to you."

Receiving her copy from him, she felt mechanically in her apron
for her pocket-book. She had used it in playing with the dog, as an
object to hide from him; but she had suffered and was still suffering
too keenly to be capable of the effort of remembrance. Moody,
eager to help her even in the most trifling thing, guessed what had
happened. "You were playing with Tommie," he said; "is it in the
next room?"

The dog heard his name pronounced, through the open door. The
next moment he trotted into the drawing-room with Isabel's pocket-
book in his mouth. He was a strong, well-grown Scotch terrier of the
largest size, with bright, intelligent eyes, and a coat of thick curling
white hair, diversified by two light-brown patches on his back. As he
reached the middle of the room, and looked from one to another of
the persons present, the fine sympathy of his race told him that there
was trouble among his human friends. His tail dropped; he whined

softly as he approached Isabel, and laid her pocket-book at her feet.

She knelt as she picked up the pocket-book, and raised her play-fellow of happier days to take her leave of him. As the dog put his paws on her shoulders, returning her caress, her first tears fell. "Foolish of me," she said, faintly, "to cry over a dog. I can't help it. Good-bye, Tommie!"

Putting him away from her gently, she walked toward the door. The dog instantly followed. She put him away from her, for the second time, and left him. He was not to be denied; he followed her again, and took the skirt of her dress in his teeth, as if to hold her back. Robert forced the dog, growling and resisting with all his might, to let go of the dress. "Don't be rough with him," said Isabel. "Put him on her ladyship's lap; he will be quieter there." Robert obeyed. He whispered to Lady Lydiard as she received the dog; she seemed to be still incapable of speaking—she bowed her head in silent assent. Robert hurried back to Isabel before she had passed the door. "Not alone!" he said, entreatingly. "Her ladyship permits it, Isabel. Let me see you safe to your aunt's house."

Isabel looked at him, felt for him, and yielded.

"Yes," she answered, softly; "to make amends for what I said to you when I was thoughtless and happy." She waited a little to compose herself before she spoke her few farewell words to Lady Lydiard. "Good-bye, my lady. Your kindness has not been thrown away on an ungrateful girl. I love you, and thank you, with all my heart."

Lady Lydiard rose, placing the dog on the chair as she left it. She seemed to have grown older by years, instead of by minutes, in the short interval that had passed since she had hidden her face from view. "I can't bear it!" she cried, in husky, broken tones. "Isabel! Isabel! I forbid you to leave me!"

But one person present could venture to resist her. That person was Mr. Troy—and Mr. Troy knew it.

"Control yourself," he said to her in a whisper. "The girl is doing what is best and most becoming in her position, and is doing it with a patience and courage wonderful to see. She places herself under the protection of her nearest relative until her character is vindi-cated and her position in your house is once more beyond a doubt. Is this a time to throw obstacles in her way? Be worthy of yourself,

Lady Lydiard, and think of the day when she will return to you without the breath of a suspicion to rest on her."

There was no disputing with him—he was too plainly in the right. Lady Lydiard submitted; she concealed the torture that her own resolution inflicted on her with an endurance which was indeed worthy of herself. Taking Isabel in her arms, she kissed her, in a passion of sorrow and love. "My poor dear! My own sweet girl! don't suppose that this is a parting kiss! I shall see you again—often and often I shall see you again at your aunt's." At a sign from Mr. Troy, Robert took Isabel's arm in his and led her away. Tommie, watching her from his chair, lifted his little white muzzle as his play-fellow looked back on passing the doorway. The long, melancholy farewell howl of the dog was the last sound Isabel Miller heard as she left the house.

PART THE SECOND

The Discovery

VIII

On the day after Isabel left Lady Lydiard's house, Mr. Troy set forth for the head office in Whitehall to consult the police on the question of the missing money. He had previously sent information of the robbery to the Bank of England, and had also advertised the loss in the daily newspapers.

The air was so pleasant and the sun was so bright that he determined on proceeding to his destination on foot. He was hardly out of sight of his own offices when he was overtaken by a friend, who was also walking in the direction of Whitehall. This gentleman was a person of considerable worldly wisdom and experience; he had been officially associated with cases of striking and notorious crime, in which government had lent its assistance to discover and punish the criminals. The opinion of a person in this position might be of the greatest value to Mr. Troy, whose practice as a solicitor had thus far never brought him into collision with thieves and mysteries. He accordingly decided, in Isabel's interests, on confiding to his friend the nature of his errand to the police. Concealing the names, but concealing nothing else, he described what had happened on the previous day at Lady Lydiard's house, and then put the question plainly to his companion:

"What would you do in my place?"

"In your place," his friend answered, quietly, "I should not waste time and money in consulting the police."

"Not consult the police!" exclaimed Mr. Troy, in amazement. "Surely I have not made myself understood? I am going to the head office, and I have got a letter of introduction to the chief inspector in the detective department. I am afraid I omitted to mention that."

"It doesn't make any difference," proceeded the other, as coolly as ever. "You have asked for my advice, and I give you my advice. Tear up your letter of introduction, and don't stir a step further in the direction of Whitehall."

Mr. Troy began to understand. "You don't believe in the detective police?" he said.

"Who *can* believe in them, who reads the newspapers and remembers what he reads?" his friend rejoined. "Fortunately for the detective department, the public in general forgets what it reads. Go to your club and look at the criminal history of our own time recorded in the newspapers. Every crime is more or less a mystery. You will see that the mysteries which the police discover are, almost without exception, mysteries made penetrable by the commonest capacity, through the extraordinary stupidity exhibited in the means taken to hide the crime. On the other hand, let the guilty man or woman be a resolute and intelligent person, capable of setting his (or her) wits fairly against the wits of the police—in other words, let the mystery really *be* a mystery—and cite me a case if you can (a really difficult and perplexing case) in which the criminal has not escaped. Mind, I don't charge the police with neglecting their work. No doubt they do their best, and take the greatest pains in following the routine to which they have been trained. It is their misfortune, not their fault, that there is no man of superior intelligence among them—I mean no man who is capable, in great emergencies, of placing himself above conventional methods, and following a new way of his own. There have been such men in the police—men naturally endowed with that faculty of mental analysis which can decompose a mystery, resolve it into its component parts, and find the clew at the bottom, no matter how remote from ordinary observation it may be. But those men have died or have retired. One of them would have been invaluable to you in the case you have just mentioned to me. As things are, unless you are wrong in believing in the young lady's innocence, the person who has stolen that bank-note will be no easy person to find. In my opinion, there is only one man now in London who is likely to be of the slightest assistance to you, and he is not in the police."

"Who is he?" asked Mr. Troy.

"An old rogue, who was once in your branch of the legal profession," the friend answered. "You may, perhaps, remember the man; they call him 'Old Sharon.'"

"What! the scoundrel who was struck off the roll of attorneys years since? Is he still alive?"

"Alive and prospering. He lives in a court or a lane running out of Long-acre, and he offers advice to persons interested in recovering missing objects of any sort. Whether you have lost your wife or lost your cigar-case, Old Sharon is equally useful to you. He has an inbred capacity for reading the riddle the right way in cases of mystery, great or small. In short, he possesses exactly that analytical faculty to which I alluded just now. I have his address at my office, if you think it worth while to try him."

"Who can trust such a man?" Mr. Troy objected. "He would be sure to deceive me."

"You are entirely mistaken. Since he was struck off the rolls Old Sharon has discovered that the straight way is, on the whole, the best way, even in a man's own interest. His consultation fee is a guinea; and he gives a signed estimate beforehand for any supplementary expenses that may follow. I can tell you (this is, of course, strictly between ourselves) that the authorities at my office took his advice in a government case that puzzled the police. We approached him, of course, through persons who were to be trusted to represent us without betraying the source from which their instructions were derived, and we found the old rascal's advice well worth paying for. It is quite likely that he may not succeed so well in your case. Try the police, by all means, and if they fail, why, there is Sharon as a last resource."

This arrangement commended itself to Mr. Troy's professional caution. He went on to Whitehall, and he tried the detective police. They at once adopted the obvious conclusion, to persons of ordinary capacity—the conclusion that Isabel was the thief.

Acting on this conviction, the authorities sent an experienced woman from the office to Lady Lydiard's house to examine the poor girl's clothes and ornaments before they were packed up and sent after her to her aunt's. The search led to nothing. The only objects of any value that were discovered had been presents from Lady Lydiard. No jewelers' or milliners' bills were among the papers found in her desk. Not a sign of secret extravagance in dress was to be seen anywhere. Defeated so far, the police proposed next to have Isabel privately watched. There might be a prodigal lover somewhere in the back-ground, with ruin staring him in the face unless he could raise five hundred pounds. Lady Lydiard (who had only consented to the search under the stress of persuasive argument from Mr. Troy) resented this ingenious idea as an insult. She declared that if Isabel was watched, the girl should know of it instantly from her own lips. The police listened with perfect resignation and decorum, and politely shifted their ground. A certain suspicion (they remarked) always rested in cases of this sort on the servants. Would her ladyship object to private inquiries into the characters and proceedings of the servants? Her ladyship instantly objected in the most positive terms. Thereupon the "inspector" asked for a minute's private conversation with Mr. Troy. "The thief is certainly a member of Lady Lydiard's household," this functionary remarked in his politely positive way. "If her ladyship persists in refusing to let us make the necessary inquiries, our hands are tied, and the case comes to an end through no fault of ours. If her ladyship changes her mind, perhaps you will drop me a line, sir, to that effect. Good-morning."

So the experiment of consulting the police came to an untimely end. The only result obtained was the expression of purblind opinion by the authorities of the detective department, which pointed at Isabel, or at one of the servants, as the undiscovered thief. Thinking the matter over in the retirement of his own office, and not forgetting his promise to Isabel to leave no means untried of establishing her innocence, Mr. Troy could see but one alternative left to him. He took up his pen and wrote to his friend at the government office. There was nothing for it now but to run the risk and try Old Sharon.

IX

The next day Mr. Troy (taking Robert Moody with him as a valuable witness) rang the bell at the mean and dirty lodging-house in which Old Sharon received the clients who stood in need of his advice.

They were led up-stairs to a back room on the second floor of the house. Entering the room, they discovered, through a thick cloud of tobacco-smoke, a small, fat, bald-headed, dirty old man in an arm-chair, robed in a tattered flannel dressing-gown, with a short pipe in his mouth, a pug-dog on his lap, and a French novel in his hands.

"Is it business?" asked Old Sharon, speaking in a hoarse, asthmatical voice, and fixing a pair of bright, shameless black eyes attentively on the two visitors.

"It *is* business," Mr. Troy answered, looking at the old rogue who had disgraced an honorable profession, as he might have looked at a reptile which had just risen rampant at his feet. "What is your fee for a consultation?"

"You give me a guinea and I'll give you a half an hour." With this reply Old Sharon held out his unwashed hand across the rickety, ink-splashed table at which he was sitting.

Mr. Troy would not have touched him with the tips of his own fingers for a thousand pounds. He laid the guinea on the table.

Old Sharon burst into a fierce laugh—a laugh strangely accompanied by a frowning contraction of his eyebrows, and a frightful exhibition of the whole inside of his mouth. "I am not clean enough for you, eh?" he said, with an appearance of being very much amused. "There is a dirty old man described in this book that is a little like me." He held up his French novel. "Have you read it? A capital story—well put together. Ah, you haven't read it? You have got a pleasure to come. I say, do you mind tobacco-smoke? I think faster while I smoke—that's all."

Mr. Troy's respectable hand waved a silent permission to smoke, given under dignified protest.

"All right," said Old Sharon. "Now, get on."

He laid himself back in his chair and puffed out his smoke, with eyes lazily half closed, like the eyes of the pug-dog on his lap. At that moment, indeed, there was a curious resemblance between the two. They both seemed to be preparing themselves, in the same idle way, for the same comfortable nap.

Mr. Troy stated the circumstances under which the five-hundred-pound note had disappeared in clear and consecutive narrative. When he had done, Old Sharon suddenly opened his eyes. The pug-dog suddenly opened his eyes. Old Sharon looked hard at Mr. Troy. The pug-dog looked hard at Mr. Troy. Old Sharon spoke. The pug growled.

"I know who you are—you're a lawyer. Don't be alarmed, I never saw you before, and I don't know your name. What I do know is a lawyer's statement of facts when I hear it. Who's this?" Old Sharon looked inquisitively at Moody as he put the question.

Mr. Troy introduced Moody as a competent witness, thoroughly acquainted with the circumstances, and ready and willing to answer any questions relating to them. Old Sharon waited a little, smoking hard and thinking hard. "Now, then!" he burst out, in his fiercely sudden way, "I'm going to get to the root of the matter."

He leaned forward, with his elbows on the table, and began his examination of Moody. Heartily as Mr. Troy despised and disliked the old rogue, he listened with astonishment and admiration, literally extorted from him by the marvelous ability with which the questions were adapted to the end in view. In a quarter of an hour Old Sharon had extracted from the witness everything, literally everything, down to the smallest detail, that Moody could tell him. Having now, in his own phrase, "got to the root of the matter," he relit his pipe with a grunt of satisfaction, and laid himself back again in his old arm-chair.

"Well," said Mr. Troy, "have you formed your opinion?"

"Yes; I've formed my opinion."

"What is it?"

Instead of replying, Old Sharon winked confidentially at Mr. Troy, and put a question on his side.

"I say! is a ten-pound note much of an object to you?"

"It depends," answered Mr. Troy, "on what the money is wanted for."

"Look here," said Old Sharon; "I can give you an opinion for your guinea; but, mind this, it's an opinion founded on hearsay—and you know as a lawyer what that is worth. Venture your ten pounds—in plain English, pay me for my time and trouble in a baffling and difficult case—and I'll give you an opinion founded on my own experience."

"Explain yourself a little more clearly," said Mr. Troy. "What do you guarantee to tell us if we venture the ten pounds?"

"I guarantee to name the person, or the persons, on whom the suspicion really rests. And if you employ me after that, I guarantee (before you pay me a half-penny more), to prove that I am right by laying my hand on the thief."

"Let us have the guinea opinion first," said Mr. Troy.

Old Sharon made another frightful exhibition of the whole inside of his mouth; his laugh was louder and fiercer than ever. "I like you," he said to Mr. Troy, "you are so devilish fond of your money. Lord! how rich you must be! Now listen. Here's the guinea opinion: suspect, in this case, the very last person on whom suspicion could possibly fall."

Moody, listening attentively, started and changed color at these last words. Mr. Troy looked thoroughly disappointed, and made no attempt to conceal it. "Is that all?" he asked.

"All?" retorted the cynical vagabond. "You're a pretty lawyer! What more can I say, when I don't know for certain whether the witness who has given me my information has misled me or not? Have I spoken to the girl, and formed my own opinion? No! Have I been introduced among the servants (as errand-boy, or to clean the boots and shoes, or what not), and have I formed my own judgment of *them?* No! I take your opinions for granted, and I tell you how I should set to work myself if they were *my* opinions too; and that's a guinea's worth—a devilish good guinea's worth to a rich man like you!"

Old Sharon's logic produced a certain effect on Mr. Troy, in spite of himself. It was smartly put, from his point of view—there was no denying that.

"Even if I consented to your proposal," he said, "I should object to your annoying the young lady with impertinent questions, or to your being introduced as a spy into a respectable house."

Old Sharon doubled his dirty fists and drummed with them on the rickety table in a comical frenzy of impatience while Mr. Troy was speaking.

"What the devil do you know about my way of doing my business?" he burst out, when the lawyer had done. "One of us two is talking like a born idiot, and (mind this) it isn't me. Look here! Your young lady goes out for a walk, and she meets with a dirty, shabby old beggar—I look like a shabby old beggar already, don't I? Very good. This dirty old wretch whines and whimpers and tells a long story, and gets sixpence out of the girl, and knows her by that time, inside and out, as well as if he had made her—and, mark! hasn't asked her a single question, and, instead of annoying her, has made her happy in the performance of a charitable action. Stop a bit. I haven't done with you yet. Who blacks your boots and shoes? Look here!" He pushed his pug-dog off his lap, dived under the table, appeared again with an old boot and a bottle of blacking, and set to work with tigerish activity. "I'm going out for a walk, you know, and I may as well make myself smart." With that announcement he began to sing over his work—a song of sentiment, popular in England, in the early part of the present century—" 'She's all my fancy painted her, she's lovely, she's divine; but her heart it is another's, and it never can be mine! Too-ral-loo-ral-loo.' I like a love-song. Brush away! brush away! till I see my own pretty face in the blacking. Hey! Here's a nice, harmless, jolly old man! sings and jokes over his work, and makes the kitchen quite cheerful. What's that you say? He's a stranger and don't talk to him too freely. You ought to be ashamed of yourself to speak in that way of a poor old fellow with one foot in the grave. Mrs. Cook will give him a nice bit of dinner in the scullery, and John Footman will look out an old coat for him. And when he's heard everything he wants to hear, and doesn't come back again the next day to his work, what do they think of it in the servants' hall? Do they say, 'We've had a spy among us?' Yah! you know better than that by this time. The cheerful old man has been run over in the street, or is down with the fever, or has turned up his toes in the parish dead-house—that's what they say in the servants' hall. Try me in your kitchen, and see if your servants take me for a spy. Come, come, Mr. Lawyer! out with your ten pounds, and don't waste any more precious time about it!"

"I will consider, and let you know," said Mr. Troy.

Old Sharon laughed more ferociously than ever, and hobbled round the table in a great hurry to the place at which Moody was sitting. He laid one hand on the steward's shoulder, and pointed derisively with the other to Mr. Troy.

"I say, Mr. Silent-man! Bet you five pounds I never hear of that lawyer again!"

Silently attentive all through the interview (except when he was answering questions), Moody only replied in the fewest possible words. "I don't bet," was all he said. He showed no resentment at Sharon's familiarity, and he appeared to find no amusement in Sharon's extraordinary talk. The old vagabond seemed actually to produce a serious impression on him. When Mr. Troy set the example of rising to go, he still kept his seat, and looked at the lawyer as if he regretted leaving the atmosphere of tobacco-smoke reeking in the dirty room.

"Have you anything to say before we go?" Mr. Troy asked.

Moody rose slowly, and looked at old Sharon. "Not just now, sir," he replied, looking away again, after a moment's reflection.

Old Sharon interpreted Moody's look and Moody's reply from his own peculiar point of view. He suddenly drew the steward away into a corner of the room.

"I say!" he began in a whisper. "Upon your solemn word of honor, you know—are you as rich as the lawyer there?"

"Certainly not."

"Look here! It's half price to a poor man. If you feel like coming back, on your own account, five pounds will do from *you*. There! there! Think of it—think of it."

"Now, then?" said Mr. Troy, waiting for his companion, with the door open in his hand. He looked back at Sharon when Moody joined him. The old vagabond was settled again in his arm-chair, with his dog in his lap, his pipe in his mouth, and his French novel in his hand, exhibiting exactly the picture of frowzy comfort which he had presented when his visitors first entered the room.

"Good-day," said Mr. Troy, with haughty condescension.

"Don't interrupt me," rejoined Old Sharon, absorbed in his novel. "You've had your guinea's worth. Lord! what a lovely book this is! Don't interrupt me."

"Impudent scoundrel!" said Mr. Troy, when he and Moody were in the street again. "What could my friend mean by recommending him? Fancy his expecting me to trust him with ten pounds! I consider even the guinea completely thrown away."

"Begging your pardon, sir," said Moody, "I don't quite agree with you there."

"What! you don't mean to tell me you understand that oracular sentence of his—'Suspect the very last person on whom suspicion could possibly fall'? Rubbish!"

"I don't say I understand it, sir. I only say it has set me thinking."

"Thinking of what? Do your suspicions point to the thief?"

"If you will please to excuse me, Mr. Troy, I should like to wait a while before I answer that."

Mr. Troy suddenly stood still, and eyed his companion a little distrustfully.

"Are you going to turn detective policeman on your own account?" he asked.

"There's nothing I won't turn to, and try, to help Miss Isabel in this matter," Moody answered, firmly.

"I have saved a few hundred pounds in Lady Lydiard's service, and I am ready to spend every farthing of it if I can only discover the thief."

Mr. Troy walked on again. "Miss Isabel seems to have a good friend in you," he said. He was (perhaps unconsciously) a little

offended by the independent tone in which the steward spoke, after
he had himself engaged to take the vindication of the girl's innocence into his own hands.

"Miss Isabel has a devoted servant and slave in me," Moody
answered, with passionate enthusiasm.

"Very creditable; I haven't a word to say against it," Mr. Troy
rejoined. "But don't forget that the young lady has other devoted
friends, besides you. I am her devoted friend, for instance; I have
promised to serve her, and I mean to keep my word. You will
excuse me for adding that my experience and discretion are quite as
likely to be useful to her as your enthusiasm. I know the world well
enough to be careful in trusting strangers. It will do you no harm
Mr. Moody, to follow my example."

Moody accepted his reproof with becoming patience and resignation. "If you have anything to propose, sir, that will be of service to
Miss Isabel," he said, "I shall be happy if I can assist you in the
humblest capacity."

"And if not?" Mr. Troy inquired, conscious of having nothing to
propose as he asked the question.

"In that case, sir, I must take my own course, and blame nobody
but myself if it leads me astray."

Mr. Troy said no more; he parted from Moody at the next turning.

Pursuing the subject privately in his own mind, he decided on
taking the earliest opportunity of visiting Isabel at her aunt's house,
and on warning her, in her future intercourse with Moody, not to
trust too much to the steward's discretion. "I haven't a doubt,"
thought the lawyer, "of what he means to do next. The infatuated
fool is going back to old Sharon!"

X

Returning to his office, Mr. Troy discovered, among the correspondence that was waiting for him, a letter from the very person
whose welfare was still the uppermost subject in his mind. Isabel
Miller wrote in these terms:

"DEAR SIR,—My aunt, Miss Pink, is very desirous of consulting
you professionally at the earliest opportunity. Although South

Morden is within little more than half an hour's railway ride from London, Miss Pink does not presume to ask you to visit her, being well aware of the value of your time. Will you, therefore, be so kind as to let me know when it will be convenient to you to receive my aunt at your office in London? Believe me, dear sir,

Respectfully yours, ISABEL MILLER.

P. S.—I am further instructed to say that the regrettable event at Lady Lydiard's house is the proposed subject of the consultation.

THE LAWN, SOUTH MORDEN. THURSDAY."

Mr. Troy smiled as he read the letter. "Too formal for a young girl," he said to himself. "Every word of it has been dictated by Miss Pink." He was not long in deciding what course he should take. There was a pressing necessity for cautioning Isabel, and here was his opportunity. He sent for his head clerk, and looked at his list of engagements for the day. There was nothing set down in the book which the clerk was not quite as well able to manage as the master. Mr. Troy consulted his railway-guide, ordered his cab, and caught the next train to South Morden.

South Morden was then (and remains to this day) one of those primitive agricultural villages, passed over by the march of modern progress, which are still to be found in the near neighborhood of London. Only the slow trains stopped at the station; and there was so little to do that the station master and his porter grew flowers on the embankment, and trained creepers over the waiting-room window. Turning your back on the railway, and walking along the one street of South Morden, you found yourself in the old England of two centuries since. Gabled cottages, with fast-closed windows; pigs and poultry in quiet possession of the road; the venerable church surrounded by its shady burial-ground; the grocer's shop which sold everything, and the butcher's shop which sold nothing; the scarce inhabitants who liked a good look at a stranger, and the unwashed children who were pictures of dirty health; the clash of the iron-chained bucket in the public well, and the thump of the falling ninepins in the skittle-ground behind the public-house; the horse-pond on one bit of open ground, and the old elm-tree with the wooden seat round it on the other—these were some of the objects that you saw and some of the noises that you heard in South Morden, as you passed from one end of the village to the other.

About half a mile beyond the last of the old cottages modern

England met you again under the form of a row of little villas, set
up by an adventurous London builder who had bought the land at a
bargain. Each villa stood in its own little garden, and looked across
a stony road at the meadow lands and softly rising wooded hills
beyond. Each villa faced you in the sunshine with the horrid glare of
new red brick, and forced its nonsensical name on your attention,
traced in bright paint on the posts of its entrance gate. Consulting
the posts as he advanced, Mr. Troy arrived in due course of time at
the villa called The Lawn, which derived its name apparently from a
circular patch of grass in front of the house. The gate resisting his
efforts to open it, he rang the bell.

Admitted by a trim, clean, shy little maid-servant, Mr. Troy
looked about him in silent amazement. Turn which way he might,
he found himself silently confronted by posted and painted instructions to visitors, which forbade him to do this, and commanded him
to do that, at every step of his progress from the gate to the house.
On one side of the lawn a label informed him that he was not to
walk on the grass. On the other side a painted hand pointed along a
boundary wall to an inscription which warned him to go that way if
he had business in the kitchen. On the gravel walk at the foot of the
house-steps words, neatly traced in little white shells, reminded him
not to "forget the scraper." On the door-step he was informed, in
letters of lead, that he was "Welcome." On the mat in the passage
bristly black words burst on his attention, commanding him to
"wipe his shoes." Even the hat-stand in the hall was not allowed to
speak for itself; it had "Hats and Cloaks" inscribed on it, and it
issued its directions imperatively in the matter of your wet umbrella
—"Put it here!"

Giving the trim little servant his card Mr. Troy was introduced to
a reception-room on the lower floor. Before he had time to look
round him the door was opened again from without, and Isabel stole
into the room on tiptoe. She looked worn and anxious. When she
shook hands with the old lawyer the charming smile that he remembered so well was gone.

"Don't say you have seen me," she whispered. "I am not to come
into the room till my aunt sends for me. Tell me two things before I
run away again. How is Lady Lydiard? And have you discovered
the thief?"

"Lady Lydiard was well when I last saw her, and we have not yet
succeeded in discovering the thief." Having answered the questions

in those terms Mr. Troy decided on cautioning Isabel on the subject of the steward while he had the chance. "One question on my side," he said, holding her back from the door by the arm. "Do you expect Moody to visit you here?"

"I am *sure* he will visit me," Isabel answered, warmly. "He has promised to come here, at my request. I never knew what a kind heart Robert Moody had till this misfortune fell on me. My aunt, who is not easily taken with strangers, respects and admires him. I can't tell you how good he was to me on the journey here, and how kindly, how nobly, he spoke to me when we parted." She paused and turned her head away. The tears were rising in her eyes. "In my situation," she said, faintly, "kindness is very keenly felt. Don't notice me, Mr. Troy."

The lawyer waited a moment to let her recover herself.

"I agree entirely, my dear, in your opinion of Moody," he said. "At the same time, I think it right to warn you that his zeal in your service may possibly outrun his discretion. He may feel too confidently about penetrating the mystery of the missing money, and, unless you are on your guard, he may raise false hopes in you when you next see him. Listen to any advice that he may give you by all means; but before you decide on being guided by his opinion, consult my older experience, and hear what I have to say on the subject. Don't suppose that I am attempting to make you distrust this good friend," he added, noticing the look of uneasy surprise which Isabel fixed on him. "No such idea is in my mind. I only warn you that Moody's eagerness to be of service to you may mislead him. You understand me?"

"Yes, sir," replied Isabel, coldly; "I understand you. Please let me go now. My aunt will be down directly, and she must not find me here." She courtesied with distant respect, and left the room.

"So much for trying to put two ideas together into a girl's mind," thought Mr. Troy, when he was alone again. "The little fool evidently thinks I am jealous of Moody's place in her estimation. Well, I have done my duty, and I can do no more."

He looked round the room. Not a chair was out of its place, not a speck of dust was to be seen. The brightly perfect polish of the table made your eyes ache; the ornaments on it looked as if they had never been touched by mortal hand; the piano was an object for distant admiration, not an instrument to be played on; the carpet made Mr. Troy look nervously at the soles of his shoes; and the sofa (protected by layers of white crochet-work) said as plainly as if in words, "Sit on me if you dare!" Mr. Troy retreated to a book-case at the further end of the room. The books fitted the shelves to such absolute perfection that he had some difficulty in taking one of them out. When he had succeeded, he found himself in possession of a volume of the "History of England." On the fly-leaf he encoun-tered another written warning: "This book belongs to Miss Pink's Academy for Young Ladies, and is not to be removed from the library." The date, which was added, referred to a period of ten years since. Miss Pink now stood revealed as a retired school-mistress; and Mr. Troy began to understand some of the characteris-tic peculiarities of that lady's establishment which had puzzled him up to the present time.

He had just succeeded in putting the book back again when the door opened once more, and Isabel's aunt entered the room.

If Miss Pink could, by any possible conjuncture of circumstances, have disappeared mysteriously from her house and her friends, the police would have found the greatest difficulty in composing the necessary description of the missing lady. The acutest observer could have discovered nothing that was noticeable or characteristic in her personal appearance. The pen of the present writer portrays her in despair by a series of negatives. She was not young, she was not old, she was neither tall nor short, nor stout nor thin; nobody could call her features attractive, and nobody could call them ugly; there was nothing in her voice, her expression, her manner, or her dress that differed in any appreciable degree from the voice, expres-sion, manner, and dress of five hundred thousand other single ladies of her age and position in the world. If you had asked her to describe herself, she would have answered, "I am a gentlewoman;" and if you had further inquired which of her numerous accomplish-ments took highest rank in her own esteem, she would have replied, "My powers of conversation." For the rest, she was Miss Pink, of South Morden; and when that has been said, all has been said.

"Pray be seated, sir. We have had a beautiful day, after the late long-continued wet weather. I am told that the season is very un-favorable for wall-fruit. May I offer you some refreshment after your journey?" In these terms, and in the smoothest of voices, Miss Pink opened the interview.

Mr. Troy made a polite reply, and added a few strictly conven-tional remarks on the beauty of the neighborhood. Not even a lawyer could sit in Miss Pink's presence, and hear Miss Pink's conversation, without feeling himself called upon (in the nursery phrase) to "be on his best behavior."

"It is extremely kind of you, Mr. Troy, to favor me with this visit," Miss Pink resumed. "I am well aware that the time of professional gentlemen is of especial value to them, and I will therefore ask you to excuse me if I proceed abruptly to the subject on which I desire to consult your experience."

Here the lady modestly smoothed out her dress over her knees, and the lawyer made a bow. Miss Pink's highly trained conversation had perhaps one fault—it was not, strictly speaking, conversation at all. In its effect on her hearers it rather resembled the contents of a fluently conventional letter, read aloud.

"The circumstances under which my niece Isabel has left Lady Lydiard's house," Miss Pink proceeded, "are so indescribably painful—I will go further, I will say so deeply humiliating—that I have forbidden her to refer to them again in my presence, or to mention them in the future to any living creature besides myself. You are acquainted with those circumstances, Mr. Troy, and you will understand my indignation when I first learned that my sister's child had been suspected of theft. I have not the honor of being acquainted with Lady Lydiard. She is not a countess, I believe? Just so! her husband was only a baron. I am not acquainted with Lady Lydiard, and I will not trust myself to say what I think of her conduct to my niece."

"Pardon me, madam," Mr. Troy interposed. "Before you say any more about Lady Lydiard, I must really beg leave to observe——"

"Pardon *me*," Miss Pink rejoined, "I never form a hasty judgment. Lady Lydiard's conduct is beyond the reach of any defense, no matter how ingenious it may be. You may not be aware, sir, that in receiving my niece under her roof her ladyship was receiving a gentlewoman by birth as well as by education. My late lamented sister was the daughter of a clergyman of the Church of England. I need hardly remind you that, as such, she was a born lady. Under favoring circumstances, Isabel's maternal grandfather might have been Archbishop of Canterbury, and have taken precedence of the whole House of Peers, the princes of the blood royal alone excepted. I am not prepared to say that my niece is equally well connected on her father's side. My sister surprised—I will not add shocked—us when she married a chemist. At the same time, a chemist is not a tradesman. He is a gentleman at one end of the profession of medicine, and a titled physician is a gentleman at the other end. That is all. In inviting Isabel to reside with her, Lady Lydiard, I repeat, was bound to remember that she was associating herself with a young gentlewoman. She has *not* remembered this, which is one insult; and she has suspected my niece of theft, which is another."

Miss Pink paused to take breath. Mr. Troy made a second attempt to get a hearing.

"Will you kindly permit me, madam, to say two words?"

"No!" said Miss Pink, asserting the most immovable obstinacy under the blandest politeness of manner. "Your time, Mr. Troy, is really too valuable. Not even your trained intellect can excuse conduct which is manifestly *in*excusable on the face of it. Now you know my opinion of Lady Lydiard, you will not be surprised to hear that I decline to trust her ladyship. She may, or she may not, cause the necessary inquiries to be made for the vindication of my niece's character. In a matter so serious as this—I may say, in a duty which I owe to the memories of my sister and my parents—I will not leave the responsibility to Lady Lydiard. I will take it on myself. Let me add that I am able to pay the necessary expenses. The earlier years of my life, Mr. Troy, have been passed in the tuition of young ladies. I have been happy in meriting the confidence of parents, and I have been strict in observing the golden rules of economy. On my retirement, I have been able to invest a modest, a very modest, little fortune in the Funds. A portion of it is at the service of my niece for the recovery of her good name; and I desire to place the necessary investigation, confidentially, in your hands. You are acquainted with the case, and the case naturally goes to you. I could not prevail on myself—I really could not prevail on myself—to mention it to a stranger. That is the business on which I wished to consult you. Please say nothing more about Lady Lydiard; the subject is inexpressibly disagreeable to me. I will only trespass on your kindness to tell me if I have succeeded in making myself understood."

Miss Pink leaned back in her chair at the exact angle permitted by the laws of propriety, rested her left elbow on the palm of her right hand, and lightly supported her cheek with her forefinger and thumb. In this position she waited Mr. Troy's answer—the living picture of human obstinacy in its most respectable form.

If Mr. Troy had not been a lawyer—in other words, if he had not been professionally capable of persisting in his own course in the face of every conceivable difficulty and discouragement—Miss Pink might have remained in undisturbed possession of her own opinions. As it was, Mr. Troy had got his hearing at last; and no matter how obstinately she might close her eyes to it, Miss Pink was now destined to have the other side of the case presented to her view.

"I am sincerely obliged to you, madam, for the expression of your confidence in me," Mr. Troy began; "at the same time, I must beg you to excuse me if I decline to accept your proposal."

Miss Pink had not expected to receive such an answer as this. The lawyer's brief refusal surprised and annoyed her.

"Why do you decline to assist me?" she asked.

"Because," answered Mr. Troy, "my services are already engaged in Miss Isabel's interest by a client whom I have served for more than twenty years. My client is——"

Miss Pink anticipated the coming disclosure. "You need not trouble yourself, sir, to mention your client's name," she said.

"My client," persisted Mr. Troy, "loves Miss Isabel dearly——"

"That is a matter of opinion," Miss Pink interposed.

"And believes in Miss Isabel's innocence," proceeded the irrepressible lawyer, "as firmly as you believe in it yourself."

Miss Pink (being human) had a temper, and Mr. Troy had found his way to it.

"If Lady Lydiard believes in my niece's innocence," said Miss Pink, suddenly sitting bolt-upright in her chair, "why has my niece been compelled, in justice to herself, to leave Lady Lydiard's house?"

"You will admit, madam," Mr. Troy answered cautiously, "that we are all of us liable, in this wicked world, to be the victim of appearances. Your niece is a victim—an innocent victim. She wisely withdraws from Lady Lydiard's house until appearances are proved to be false, and her position is cleared up."

Miss Pink had her reply ready. "That is simply acknowledging, in other words, that my niece is suspected. I am only a woman, Mr. Troy, but it is not quite so easy to mislead me as you seem to suppose."

Mr. Troy's temper was admirably trained, but it began to acknowledge that Miss Pink's powers of irritation could sting to some purpose.

"No intention of misleading you, madam, has ever crossed my

mind," he rejoined, warmly. "As for your niece, I can tell you this. In all my experience of Lady Lydiard I never saw her so distressed as she was when Miss Isabel left the house."

"Indeed?" said Miss Pink, with an incredulous smile. "In my rank of life, when we feel distressed about a person, we do our best to comfort that person by a kind letter or an early visit. But then I am not a lady of title."

"Lady Lydiard engaged herself to call on Miss Isabel in my hearing," said Mr. Troy. "Lady Lydiard is the most generous woman living."

"Lady Lydiard is here!" cried a joyful voice on the other side of the door.

At the same moment Isabel burst into the room in a state of excitement which actually ignored the formidable presence of Miss Pink. "I beg your pardon, aunt. I was up-stairs at the window, and I saw the carriage stop at the gate. And Tommie has come, too! The darling saw me at the window!" cried the poor girl, her eyes sparkling with delight, as a perfect explosion of barking made itself heard over the tramp of horses' feet and the crash of carriage-wheels outside.

Miss Pink rose slowly, with a dignity that looked capable of adequately receiving, not one noble lady only, but the whole peerage of England.

"Control yourself, dear Isabel," she said. "No well-bred young lady permits herself to become unduly excited. Stand by my side—a little behind me."

Isabel obeyed. Mr. Troy kept his place and privately enjoyed his triumph over Miss Pink. If Lady Lydiard had been actually in league with him, she could not have chosen a more opportune time for her visit. A momentary interval passed; the carriage drew up at the door; the horses trampled on the gravel; the bell rang madly; the uproar of Tommie released from the carriage and clamoring to be let in, redoubled its fury. Never before had such an unruly burst of noises invaded the tranquility of Miss Pink's villa.

XI

The trim little maid-servant ran upstairs from her modest little kitchen, trembling at the terrible prospect of having to open the door. Miss Pink, deafened by the barking, had just time to say, "What a very ill-behaved dog!" when a sound of small objects overthrown in the hall, and a scurrying of furious claws across the oilcloth, announced that Tommie had invaded the house. As the servant appeared, introducing Lady Lydiard, the dog ran in. He made a frantic leap at Isabel, which would certainly have knocked her down but for the chair that happened to be standing behind her. Received on her lap, the faithful creature half smothered her with his caresses. He barked, he shrieked, in his joy at seeing her again. He jumped off her lap and tore round and round the room at the top of his speed, and every time he passed Miss Pink he showed the whole range of his teeth, and snarled ferociously at her ankles. Having at last exhausted his superfluous energy, he leaped back again on Isabel's lap, with his tongue quivering in his open mouth, his tail wagging softly, and his eye on Miss Pink, inquiring how she liked a dog in her drawing-room.

"I hope my dog has not disturbed you, ma'am?" said Lady Lydiard, advancing from the mat at the door-way, on which she had patiently waited until the raptures of Tommie subsided into repose.

Miss Pink, trembling between terror and indignation, acknowledged Lady Lydiard's polite inquiry by a ceremonious bow, and an answer which administered by implication a dignified reproof. "Your ladyship's dog does not appear to be a very well-trained animal," the ex-school-mistress remarked.

"Well-trained?" Lady Lydiard repeated, as if the expression were perfectly unintelligible to her; "I don't think you have had much experience of dogs, ma'am." She turned to Isabel, and embraced her tenderly. "Give me a kiss, my dear. You don't know how wretched I have been since you left me." She looked back again at Miss Pink. "You are not, perhaps, aware, ma'am, that my dog is devotedly attached to your niece. A dog's love has been considered by many great men (whose names at the moment escape me) as the most touching and disinterested of all earthly affections." She looked the other way, and discovered the lawyer. "How do you do, Mr. Troy?

It's a pleasant surprise to find you here. The house was so dull
without Isabel that I really couldn't put off seeing her any longer.
When you are more used to Tommie, Miss Pink, you will understand and admire him. *You* understand and admire him, Isabel,
don't you? My child, you are not looking well. I shall take you back
with me when the horses have had their rest. We shall never be
happy away from each other."

Having expressed her sentiments, distributed her greetings, and
defended her dog—all, as is were, in one breath—Lady Lydiard sat
down by Isabel's side, and opened a large green fan that hung at her
girdle. "You have no idea, Miss Pink, how fat people suffer in hot
weather," said the old lady, using her fan vigorously.

Miss Pink's eyes dropped modestly to the ground—"fat" was
such a coarse word to use, if a lady *must* speak of her own superfluous flesh! "May I offer some refreshment?" Miss Pink asked,
mincingly. "A cup of tea?"

Lady Lydiard shook her head.

"A glass of water?"

Lady Lydiard declined this last hospitable proposal with an exclamation of disgust. "Have you got any beer?" she inquired.

"I beg your ladyship's pardon," said Miss Pink, doubting the
evidence of her own ears. "Did you say—beer?"

Lady Lydiard gesticulated vehemently with her fan. "Yes, to be
sure! Beer! beer!"

Miss Pink rose, with a countenance expressive of genteel disgust,
and rang the bell. "I think you have beer down-stairs, Susan?" she
said, when the maid appeared at the door.

"Yes, miss."

"A glass of beer for Lady Lydiard," said Miss Pink, under protest.

"Bring it in a jug," shouted her ladyship, as the maid left the
room. "I like to froth it for myself," she continued, addressing Miss
Pink. "Isabel sometimes does it for me, when she is at home; don't
you, my dear?"

Miss Pink had been waiting her opportunity to assert her own
claim to the possession of her own niece from the time when Lady
Lydiard had coolly declared her intention of taking Isabel back with
her. The opportunity now presented itself.

"Your ladyship will pardon me," she said, "if I remark that my
niece's home is under my humble roof. I am properly sensible, I

hope, of your kindness to Isabel; but, while she remains the object
of a disgraceful suspicion, she remains with *me*."

Lady Lydiard closed her fan with an angry snap.

"You are completely mistaken, Miss Pink. You may not mean it,
but you speak most unjustly if you say that your niece is an object
of suspicion to me or to anybody in my house."

Mr. Troy, quietly listening up to this point, now interposed to
stop the discussion before it could degenerate into a personal quarrel. His keen observation, aided by his accurate knowledge of his
client's character, had plainly revealed to him what was passing in
Lady Lydiard's mind. She had entered the house, feeling (perhaps
unconsciously) a jealousy of Miss Pink as her predecessor in Isabel's affections, and as the natural protectress of the girl under
existing circumstances. Miss Pink's reception of her dog had addi-
tionally irritated the old lady. She had taken a malicious pleasure in
shocking the school-mistress's sense of propriety, and she was now
only too ready to proceed to further extremities on the delicate
question of Isabel's justification for leaving her house. For Isabel's
own sake, therefore—to say nothing of other reasons—it was ur-
gently desirable to keep the peace between the two ladies. With this
excellent object in view, Mr. Troy seized his opportunity of striking
into the conversation for the first time.

"Pardon me, Lady Lydiard," he said, "you are speaking of a
subject which has been already sufficiently discussed between Miss
Pink and myself. I think we shall do better not to dwell uselessly on
past events, but to direct our attention to the future. We are all
equally satisfied of the complete rectitude of Miss Isabel's conduct,
and we are all equally interested in the vindication of her good
name."

Whether these temperate words would of themselves have exercised the pacifying influence at which Mr. Troy aimed may be
doubtful. But, as he ceased speaking, a powerful auxiliary appeared
in the shape of the beer. Lady Lydiard seized on the jug, and filled
the tumbler for herself with an unsteady hand. Miss Pink, trembling
for the integrity of her carpet, and scandalized at seeing a peeress
drinking beer like a washer-woman, forgot the sharp answer that
was just rising to her lips when the lawyer interfered. "Small!" said
Lady Lydiard, setting down the empty tumbler, and referring to the
quality of the beer. "But very pleasant and refreshing. What's the
servant's name? Susan? Well, Susan, I was dying of thirst, and you

have saved my life. You can leave the jug; I dare say I shall empty it before I go."

Mr. Troy, watching Miss Pink's face, saw that it was time to change the subject again.

"Did you notice the old village, Lady Lydiard, on your way here?" he asked. "The artists consider it one of the most picturesque places in England."

"I noticed that it was a very dirty village," Lady Lydiard answered, still bent on making herself disagreeable to Miss Pink. "The artists may say what they please; I see nothing to admire in rotten cottages and bad drainage and ignorant people. I suppose the neighborhood has its advantages. It looks dull enough, to my mind."

Isabel had hitherto modestly restricted her exertions to keeping Tommie quiet on her lap. Like Mr. Troy, she occasionally looked at her aunt, and she now made a timid attempt to defend the neighborhood, as a duty that she owed to Miss Pink.

"Oh, my lady! don't say it's a dull neighborhood," she pleaded. "There are such pretty walks all round us. And when you get to the hills the view is beautiful."

Lady Lydiard's answer to this was a little masterpiece of good-humored contempt. She patted Isabel's cheek, and said, "Pooh! pooh!"

"Your ladyship does not admire the beauties of nature," Miss Pink remarked, with a compassionate smile. "As we get older, no doubt our sight begins to fail——"

"And we leave off canting about the beauties of nature," added Lady Lydiard. "I hate the country. Give me London, and the pleasures of society."

"Come! come! Do the country justice, Lady Lydiard!" put in peace-making Mr. Troy. "There is plenty of society to be found out of London—as good society as the world can show."

"The sort of society," added Miss Pink, "which is to be found, for example, in this neighborhood. Her ladyship is evidently not aware that persons of distinction surround us whichever way we turn. I may instance, among others, the Honorable Mr. Hardyman——"

Lady Lydiard, in the act of pouring out a second glassful of beer, suddenly set down the jug.

"Who is that you're talking of, Miss Pink?"

"I am talking of our neighbor, Lady Lydiard, the Honorable Mr. Hardyman."

"Do you mean Alfred Hardyman, the man who breeds the horses?"

"The distinguished gentleman who owns the famous stud-farm," said Miss Pink, correcting the bluntly direct form in which Lady Lydiard had put her question.

"Is he in the habit of visiting here?" the old lady inquired, with a sudden appearance of anxiety. "Do you know him?"

"I had the honor of being introduced to Mr. Hardyman at our last flower-show," Miss Pink replied. "He has not yet favored me with a visit."

Lady Lydiard's anxiety appeared to be to some extent relieved.

"I knew that Hardyman's farm was in this county," she said, "but I had no notion that it was in the neighborhood of South Morden. How far away is he—ten or a dozen miles, eh?"

"Not more than three miles," answered Miss Pink. "We consider him quite a near neighbor of ours."

Renewed anxiety showed itself in Lady Lydiard. She looked round sharply at Isabel. The girl's head was bent so low over the rough head of the dog that her face was almost entirely concealed from view. So far as appearances went, she seemed to be entirely absorbed in fondling Tommie. Lady Lydiard roused her with a tap of the green fan.

"Take Tommie out, Isabel, for a run in the garden," she said. "He won't sit still much longer, and he may annoy Miss Pink. Mr. Troy, will you kindly help Isabel to keep my ill-trained dog in order?"

Mr. Troy got on his feet, and, not very willingly, followed Isabel out of the room. "They will quarrel now, to a dead certainty," he thought to himself, as he closed the door. "Have you any idea of what this means?" he said to his companion, as he joined her in the hall. "What has Mr. Hardyman done to excite all this interest in him?"

Isabel's guilty color rose. She knew perfectly well that Hardyman's unconcealed admiration of her was the guiding motive of Lady Lydiard's inquiries. If she had told the truth, Mr. Troy would have unquestionably returned to the drawing-room, with or without an acceptable excuse for intruding himself. But Isabel was a woman; and her answer, it is needless to say, was, "I don't know, I'm sure."

In the meantime the interview between the two ladies began in a manner which would have astonished Mr. Troy—they were both silent. For once in her life, Lady Lydiard was considering what she should say, before she said it. Miss Pink, on her side, naturally waited to hear what objects her ladyship had in view—waited until her small reserves of patience gave way. Urged by irresistible curiosity, she spoke first.

"Have you anything to say to me in private?" she asked.

Lady Lydiard had not got to the end of her reflections. She said "Yes," and she said no more.

"Is it anything relating to my niece?" persisted Miss Pink.

Still immersed in her reflections, Lady Lydiard suddenly rose to the surface, and spoke her mind, as usual.

"About your niece, ma'am. The other day Mr. Hardyman called at my house, and saw Isabel."

"Yes," said Miss Pink, politely attentive, but not in the least interested, so far.

"That's not all, ma'am. Mr. Hardyman admires Isabel; he owned it to me himself in so many words."

Miss Pink listened, with a courteous inclination of her head. She looked mildly gratified, nothing more. Lady Lydiard proceeded:

"You and I think differently on many matters," she said; "but we are both agreed, I am sure, in feeling the sincerest interest in Isabel's welfare. I beg to suggest to you, Miss Pink, that Mr. Hardyman, as a near neighbor of yours, is a very undesirable neighbor while Isabel remains in your house."

Saying those words, under a strong conviction of the serious importance of the subject, Lady Lydiard insensibly recovered the manner and resumed the language which befitted a lady of her rank. Miss Pink, noticing the change, set it down to an expression of pride on the part of her visitor, which, in referring to Isabel, assailed indirectly the social position of Isabel's aunt.

"I fail entirely to understand what your ladyship means," she said, coldly.

Lady Lydiard, on her side, looked in undisguised amazement at Miss Pink.

"Haven't I told you already that Mr. Hardyman admires your niece?" she asked.

"Naturally," said Miss Pink. "Isabel inherits her lamented mother's personal advantages. If Mr. Hardyman admires her, Mr. Hardyman shows his good taste."

Lady Lydiard's eyes opened wider and wider in wonder. "My

good lady," she exclaimed, "is it possible you don't know that when a man admires a woman he doesn't stop there? He falls in love with her (as the saying is) next."

"So I have heard," said Miss Pink.

"So you have *heard?*" repeated Lady Lydiard. "If Mr. Hardyman finds his way to Isabel, I can tell you what you will *see.* Catch the two together, ma'am, and you will see Mr. Hardyman making love to your niece."

"Under due restrictions, Lady Lydiard, and with my permission first obtained, of course, I see no objection to Mr. Hardyman paying his addresses to Isabel."

"The woman is mad!" cried Lady Lydiard. "Do you actually suppose, Miss Pink, that Alfred Hardyman could by any earthly possibility marry your niece?"

Not even Miss Pink's politeness could submit to such a question as this. She rose indignantly from her chair. "Are you aware, Lady Lydiard, that the doubt you have just expressed is an insult to my niece and an insult to Me?"

"Are *you* aware of who Mr. Hardyman really is?" retorted her ladyship. "Or do you judge of his position by the vocation in life which he has perversely chosen to adopt? I can tell you, if you do, that Alfred Hardyman is the younger son of one of the oldest barons in the English peerage, and that his mother is related by marriage to the royal family of Würtemberg."

Miss Pink received the full shock of this information without receding from her position by a hair's-breadth.

"An English gentlewoman offers a fit alliance to any man living who seeks her hand in marriage," said Miss Pink. "Isabel's mother (you may not be aware of it) was the daughter of an English clergyman——"

"And Isabel's father was a chemist in a country town," added Lady Lydiard.

"Isabel's father," rejoined Miss Pink, "was attached in a most responsible capacity to the useful and honorable profession of Medicine. Isabel is, in the strictest sense of the word, a young gentlewoman. If you contradict that for a single instant, Lady Lydiard, you will oblige me to leave the room."

Those last words produced a result which Miss Pink had not anticipated—they roused Lady Lydiard to assert herself. As usual in such cases, she rose superior to her own eccentricity. Confronting

Miss Pink, she now spoke and looked with the gracious courtesy and the unpresuming self-confidence of the order to which she belonged.

"For Isabel's own sake, and for the quieting of my conscience," she answered, "I will say one word more, Miss Pink, before I relieve you of my presence. Considering my age and my opportunities, I may claim to know quite as much as you do of the laws and customs which regulate society in our time. Without contesting your niece's social position, and without the slightest intention of insulting you, I repeat that the rank which Mr. Hardyman inherits makes it simply impossible even for him to think of marrying Isabel. You will do well not to give him any opportunities of meeting with her alone. And you will do better still (seeing that he is so near a neighbor of yours) if you permit Isabel to return to my protection, for a time at least. I will wait to hear from you when you have thought the matter over at your leisure. In the meantime, if I have inadvertently offended you, I ask your pardon—and I wish you good-evening."

She bowed and walked to the door. Miss Pink, as resolute as ever in maintaining her pretensions, made an effort to match the great lady on her own ground.

"Before you go, Lady Lydiard, I beg to apologize if I have spoken too warmly on my side," she said. "Permit me to send for your carriage."

"Thank you, Miss Pink. My carriage is only at the village inn. I shall enjoy a little walk in the cool evening air. Mr. Troy, I have no doubt, will give me his arm." She bowed once more, and quietly left the room.

Reaching the little back garden of the villa through an open door at the further end of the hall, Lady Lydiard found Tommie rolling luxuriously on Miss Pink's flower-beds, and Isabel and Mr. Troy in close consultation on the gravel-walk. She spoke to the lawyer first.

"They are baiting the horses at the inn," she said. "I want your arm, Mr. Troy, as far as the village, and, in return, I will take you back to London with me. I have to ask your advice about one or two little matters, and this is a good opportunity."

"With the greatest pleasure, Lady Lydiard. I suppose I must say good-bye to Miss Pink?"

"A word of advice to you, Mr. Troy. Take care how you ruffle Miss Pink's sense of her own importance. Another word for your private ear—Miss Pink is a fool!"

On the lawyer's withdrawal, Lady Lydiard put her arm fondly round Isabel's waist. "What were you and Mr. Troy so busy in talking about?" she asked.

"We were talking, my lady, about tracing the person who stole the money," Isabel answered, rather sadly. "It seems a far more difficult matter than I supposed it to be. I try not to lose patience and hope, but it is a little hard to feel that the appearances are against me, and to wait day after day in vain for the discovery that is to set me right."

"You are a dear good child," said Lady Lydiard, "and you are more precious to me than ever. Don't despair, Isabel. With Mr. Troy's means of inquiring, and with my means of paying, the discovery of the thief can not be much longer delayed. If you don't return to me soon, I shall come back and see you again. Your aunt hates the sight of me; but I don't care two straws for that," remarked her ladyship, showing the undignified side of her character once more. "Listen to me, Isabel. I have no wish to lower your aunt in your estimation, but I feel far more confidence in your good sense than in hers. Mr. Hardyman's business has taken him to France for the present. It is at least possible that you may meet with him on his return. If you do, keep him at a distance, my dear—politely, of course. There! there! you needn't turn red; I am not blaming you; I am only giving you a little good advice. In your position you can not possibly be too careful. Here is Mr. Troy. You must come to the gate with us, Isabel, or we shall never get Tommie away from you. I am only his second favorite; you have the first place in his affections. God bless and prosper you, my child! I wish to Heaven you were going back to London with me! Well, Mr. Troy, how have you done with Miss Pink? Have you offended that terrible 'gentlewoman' (hateful word), or has it been all the other way, and has she given you a kiss at parting?"

Mr. Troy smiled mysteriously, and changed the subject. His brief parting interview with the lady of the house was not of a nature to be rashly related. Miss Pink had not only positively assured him that her visitor was the most-ill-bred woman she had ever met with, but had further accused Lady Lydiard of shaking her confidence in the aristocracy of her native country. "For the first time in my life," said Miss Pink, "I feel that something is to be said for the republican point of view; and I am not indisposed to admit that the Constitution of the United States *has* its advantages."

XII

The conference between Lady Lydiard and Mr. Troy, on the way back to London, led to some practical results.

Hearing from her legal adviser that the inquiry after the missing money was for the moment at a standstill, Lady Lydiard made one of those bold suggestions with which she was accustomed to startle her friends in cases of emergency. She had heard favorable reports of the extraordinary ingenuity of the French police, and she now proposed sending to Paris for assistance, after first consulting her nephew, Mr. Felix Sweetsir. "Felix knows Paris as well as he knows London," she remarked. "He is an idle man, and it is quite likely that he will relieve us of all trouble by taking the matter into his own hands. In any case, he is sure to know who are the right people to address in our present necessity. What do you say?"

Mr. Troy, in reply, expressed his doubts as to the wisdom of employing foreigners in a delicate investigation which required an accurate knowledge of English customs and English character. Waiving this objection, he approved of the idea of consulting her ladyship's nephew. "Mr. Sweetsir is a man of the world," he said. "In putting the case before him, we are sure to have it presented to us from a new point of view." Acting on this favorable expression of opinion, Lady Lydiard wrote to her nephew. On the day after the visit to Miss Pink the proposed council of three was held at Lady Lydiard's house.

Felix, never punctual in keeping an appointment, was even later than usual on this occasion. He made his apologies with his hand pressed on his forehead, and his voice expressive of the languor and discouragement of a suffering man.

"The beastly English climate is telling on my nerves," said Mr. Sweetsir; "the horrid weight of the atmosphere, after the exhilarating air of Paris; the intolerable dirt and dullness of London, you know. I was in bed, my dear aunt, when I received your letter. You may imagine the completely demoralized state I was in when I tell you of the effect which the news of the robbery produced on me. I fell back on my pillow as if I had been shot. Your ladyship should really be a little more careful in communicating these disagreeable surprises to a sensitively organized man. Never mind, my valet is a perfect treasure; he brought me some drops of ether on a lump of sugar. I said 'Alfred' (his name is Alfred), 'put me into my clothes.' Alfred put me in. I assure you, it reminded me of my young days, when I was put into my first pair of trousers. Has Alfred forgotten anything? Have I got my braces on? Have I come out in my shirt-sleeves? Well, dear aunt! well, Mr. Troy! what can I say? what can I do?"

Lady Lydiard, entirely without sympathy for nervous suffering, nodded to the lawyer. "You tell him," she said.

"I believe I speak for her ladyship," Mr. Troy began, "when I say that we should like to hear, in the first place, how the whole case strikes you, Mr. Sweetsir."

"Tell it me all over again," said Felix.

Patient Mr. Troy told it all over again, and waited for the result.

"Well?" said Felix.

"Well?" said Mr. Troy. "Where does the suspicion of robbery rest, in your opinion? You look at the theft of the bank-note with a fresh eye."

"You mentioned a clergyman just now," said Felix. "The man, you know, to whom the money was sent. What was his name?"

"The Reverend Samuel Bradstock."

"You want me to name the person whom I suspect?"

"Yes, if you please," said Mr. Troy.

"I suspect the Reverend Samuel Bradstock," said Felix.

"If you have come here to make stupid jokes," interposed Lady Lydiard, "you had better go back to your bed again. We want a serious opinion."

"You *have* a serious opinion," Felix coolly rejoined. "I never was more in earnest in my life. Your ladyship is not aware of the first principle to be adopted in cases of suspicion. One proceeds on what I call the exhaustive system of reasoning. Thus: Does suspicion point to the honest servants down-stairs? No. To your ladyship's adopted daughter? Appearances are against the poor girl; but you know her better than to trust to appearances. Are you suspicious of Moody? No. Of Hardyman, who was in the house at the time? Ridiculous! But I was in the house at the time too. Do you suspect me? Just so! That idea is ridiculous too. Now let us sum up. Servants, adopted daughter, Moody, Hardyman, Sweetsir—all beyond suspicion. Who is left? The Reverend Samuel Bradstock!"

This ingenious exposition of "the exhaustive system of reasoning" failed to produce any effect on Lady Lydiard. "You are wasting our time," she said, sharply. "You know as well as I do that you are talking nonsense."

"I don't," said Felix. "Taking the gentlemanly professions all around, I know of no men who are so eager to get money, and who have so few scruples about how they get it, as the parsons. Where is there a man in any other profession who perpetually worries you for money? who holds the bag under your nose for money? who sends his clerk round from door to door to beg a few shillings of you, and calls it an 'Easter offering?' The parson does all this. Bradstock is a parson. I put it logically. Bowl me over if you can."

Mr. Troy attempted to "bowl him over," nevertheless. Lady Lydiard wisely interposed.

"When a man persists in talking nonsense," she said, "silence is the best answer; anything else only encourages him." She turned to Felix. "I have a question to ask you," she went on. "You will either give me a serious reply, or wish me good-morning." With this brief preface, she made her inquiry as to the wisdom and possibility of engaging the services of the French police.

Felix took exactly the view of the matter which had been already expressed by Mr. Troy. "Superior in intelligence," he said, "but not superior in courage, to the English police. Capable of performing wonders on their own ground and among their own people. But, my dear aunt, the two most dissimilar nations on the face of the earth are the English and the French. The French police may speak our language, but they are incapable of understanding our national character and our national manners. Set them to work on a private inquiry in the city of Pekin, and they would get on in time with the Chinese people. Set them to work in the city of London, and the English people would remain, from first to last, the same impenetrable mystery to them. In my belief, the London Sunday would be enough of itself to drive them back to Paris in despair. No balls, no concerts, no theaters, not even a museum or a picture-gallery open; every shop shut up but the gin-shop, and nothing moving but the church-bells and the men who sell the penny ices. Hundreds of Frenchmen come to see me on their first arrival in England. Every man of them rushes back to Paris on the second Saturday of his visit, rather than confront the horrors of a second Sunday in London. However, you can try it, if you like. Send me a written abstract of the case, and I will forward it to one of the official people in the

Rue Jérusalem, who will do anything he can to oblige me. Of course," said Felix, turning to Mr. Troy, "some of you have got the number of the lost bank-note. If the thief has tried to pass it in Paris, my man may be of some use to you."

"Three of us have got the number of the note," answered Mr. Troy, "Miss Isabel Miller, Mr. Moody and myself."

"Very good," said Felix. "Send me the number, with the abstract of the case. Is there anything else I can do toward recovering the money?" he asked, turning to his aunt. "There is one lucky circumstance in connection with this loss, isn't there? It has fallen on a person who is rich enough to take it easy. Good heavens! suppose it had been *my* loss!"

"It has fallen doubly on me," said Lady Lydiard; "and I am certainly not rich enough to take *that* easy. The money was destined to a charitable purpose, and I have felt it my duty to pay it again."

Felix rose and approached his aunt's chair with faltering steps, as became a suffering man. He took Lady Lydiard's hand and kissed it with enthusiastic admiration.

"You excellent creature!" he said. "You may not think of it, but you reconcile me to human nature. How generous! how noble! I think I'll go to bed again, Mr. Troy, if you really don't want any more of me. My head feels giddy, and my legs tremble under me. It doesn't matter; I shall feel easier when Alfred has taken me out of my clothes again. God bless you, my dear aunt! I never felt so proud of being related to you as I do to-day. Good-morning, Mr. Troy. Don't forget the abstract of the case, and don't trouble yourself to see me to the door. I dare say I sha'n't tumble down-stairs, and if I do, there's the porter in the hall to pick me up again. Enviable porter! as fat as butter, and as idle as a pig. *Au revoir! au revoir!*" He kissed his hand, and drifted feebly out of the room. Sweetsir, one might say, in a state of eclipse; but still the serviceable Sweetsir, who was never consulted in vain by the fortunate people privileged to call him friend.

"Is he really ill, do you think?" Mr. Troy asked.

"My nephew has turned fifty," Lady Lydiard answered, "and he persists in living as if he were a young man. Every now and then Nature says to him. 'Felix, you are old!' And Felix goes to bed, and says it's his nerves."

"I suppose he is to be trusted to keep his word about writing to Paris?" pursued the lawyer.

"Oh, yes. He may delay doing it, but he will do it. In spite of his lackadaisical manner, he has moments of energy that would surprise you. Talking of surprises, I have something to tell you about Moody. Within the last day or two there has been a marked change in him—a change for the worst."

"You astonish me, Lady Lydiard. In what way has Moody deteriorated?"

"You shall hear. Yesterday was Friday. You took him out with you, on business, early in the morning?"

Mr. Troy bowed, and said nothing. He had not thought it desirable to mention the interview at which Old Sharon had cheated him of his guinea.

"In the course of the afternoon," pursued Lady Lydiard, "I happened to want him, and I was informed that Moody had gone out again. Where had he gone? Nobody knew. Had he left word when he would be back? He had left no message of any sort. Of course he is not in the position of an ordinary servant. I don't expect him to ask permission to go out, but I do expect him to leave word down-stairs of the time at which he is likely to return. When he did come back, after an absence of some hours, I naturally asked for an explanation. Would you believe it? he simply informed me that he had been away on business of his own, expressed no regret, and offered no explanation—in short, spoke as if he were an independent gentleman. You may not think it, but I kept my temper. I merely remarked that I hoped it would not happen again. He made me a bow, and he said, 'My business is not completed yet, my lady. I can not guarantee that it may not call me away again at a moment's notice.' What do you think of that? Nine people out of ten would have given him warning to leave their service. I begin to think I am a wonderful woman: I only pointed to the door. One does hear sometimes of men's brains softening in the most unexpected manner. I have my suspicions of Moody's brains, I can tell you."

Mr. Troy's suspicions took a different direction; they pointed along the line of streets which led to Old Sharon's lodgings. Discreetly silent as to the turn which his thoughts had taken, he merely expressed himself as feeling too much surprised to offer any opinion at all.

"Wait a little," said Lady Lydiard, "I haven't done surprising you yet. You have seen a boy here in a page's livery, I think. Well, he is a good boy, and he has gone home for a week's holiday with his friends. The proper person to supply his place with the boots and shoes and other small employments is, of course, the youngest footman, a lad of only a few years older than himself. What do you think Moody does? Engages a stranger, with the house full of idle men-servants already, to fill the page's place. At intervals this morning I heard them wonderfully merry in the servants' hall—*so* merry that the noise and laughter found its way up-stairs to the breakfast-room. I like my servants to be in good spirits, but it certainly did strike me that they were getting beyond reasonable limits. I questioned my maid, and was informed that the noise was all due to the jokes of the strangest old man that ever was seen. In other words, the person whom my steward had taken it on himself to engage in the page's absence. I spoke to Moody on the subject. He answered in an odd, confused way, that he had exercised his discretion to the best of his judgment, and that (if I wished it) he would tell the old man to keep his good spirits under better control. I asked him how he came to hear of the man. He only answered, 'By accident, my lady;' and not one word more could I get out of him, good or bad. Moody engages the servants, as you know; but on every other occasion he has invariably consulted me before an engagement was settled. I really don't feel at all sure about this person who has been so strangely introduced into the house; he may be a drunkard or a thief. I wish you would speak to Moody yourself, Mr. Troy. Do you mind ringing the bell?"

Mr. Troy rose, as a matter of course, and rang the bell.

He was by this time, it is needless to say, convinced that Moody had not only gone back to consult Old Sharon on his own responsibility, but, worse still, had taken the unwarrantable liberty of introducing him as a spy into the house. To communicate this explanation to Lady Lydiard would, in her present humor, be simply to produce the dismissal of the steward from her service. The only other alternative was to ask leave to interrogate Moody privately, and, after duly reproving him, to insist on the departure of Old Sharon as the one condition on which Mr. Troy would consent to keep Lady Lydiard in ignorance of the truth.

"I think I shall manage better with Moody if your ladyship will permit me to see him in private," the lawyer said. "Shall I go downstairs and speak to him in his own room?"

"Why should you trouble yourself to do that?" said her ladyship. "See him here, and I will go into the boudoir."

As she made that reply the footman appeared at the drawing-room door.

"Send Moody here," said Lady Lydiard.

The footman's answer, delivered at that moment, assumed an importance which was not expressed in the footman's words. "My lady," he said, "Mr. Moody has gone out."

XIII

While the strange proceedings of the steward were the subject of conversation between Lady Lydiard and Mr. Troy, Moody was alone in his room, occupied in writing to Isabel. Being unwilling that any eyes but his own should see the address, he had himself posted his letter, the time that he had chosen for leaving the house proving, unfortunately, to be also the time proposed by her ladyship for his interview with the lawyer. In ten minutes after the footman had reported his absence, Moody returned. It was then too late to present himself in the drawing-room. In the interval Mr. Troy had taken his leave, and Moody's position had dropped a degree lower in Lady Lydiard's estimation.

Isabel received her letter by the next morning's post. If any justification of Mr. Troy's suspicions had been needed, the terms in which Moody wrote would have amply supplied it.

"DEAR ISABEL (I hope I may call you 'Isabel' without offending you in your present trouble),—I have a proposal to make, which, whether you accept it or not, I beg you will keep a secret from every living creature but ourselves. You will understand my request when I add that these lines relate to the matter of tracing the stolen bank-note.

"I have been privately in communication with a person in London who is, as I believe, the one person competent to help us in gaining our end. He has already made many inquiries in private. With some of them I am acquainted; the rest he has thus far kept to himself. The person to whom I allude particularly wishes to have half an hour's private conversation with you—in my presence. I am bound to warn you that he is a very strange and very ugly old man, and I can only hope that you will look over his personal appearance in consideration of what he is likely to do for you.

"Can you conveniently meet us at the further end of the row of villas in which your aunt lives, the day after to-morrow, at four o'clock? Let me have one line to say if you will keep the appointment, and if the hour named will suit you. And believe me your devoted friend and servant,   ROBERT MOODY."

The lawyer's warning to her to be careful how she yielded too readily to any proposal of Moody's recurred to Isabel's mind while she read those lines. Being pledged to secrecy she could not consult Mr. Troy—she was left to decide for herself.

No obstacle stood in the way of her free choice of alternatives. After their early dinner at three o'clock, Miss Pink habitually retired to her own room "to meditate," as she expressed it. Her "meditations" invariably ended in a sound sleep of some hours; and during that interval Isabel was at liberty to do as she pleased. After considerable hesitation, her implicit belief in Moody's truth and devotion, assisted by a strong feeling of curiosity to see the companion with whom the steward had associated himself, decided Isabel on consenting to keep the appointment.

Taking up her position beyond the houses, on the day and at the hour mentioned by Moody, she believed herself to be fully prepared for the most unfavorable impression which the most disagreeable of all possible strangers could produce.

But the first appearance of Old Sharon—as dirty as ever, clothed in a long, frowzy, gray overcoat, with his pug-dog at his heels, and his smoke-blackened pipe in his mouth, with a tall white hat on his head, which looked as if it had been picked up in a gutter, a hideous leer in his eyes, and a jaunty trip in his walk—took her so completely by surprise that she could only return Moody's friendly greeting by silently pressing his hand. As for Moody's companion, to look at him for a second time was more than she had resolution to do. She kept her eyes fixed on the pug-dog, and with good reason; so far as appearances went, he was indisputably the nobler animal of the two.

Under the circumstances, the interview threatened to begin in a very embarrassing manner. Moody, disheartened by Isabel's silence, made no attempt to set the conversation going; he looked as if he meditated a hasty retreat to the railway station which he had just left. Fortunately he had at his side the right man (for once) in the right place. Old Sharon's effrontery was equal to any emergency.

"I am not a nice-looking old man, my dear, am I?" he said, leering at Isabel with cunning, half-closed eyes. "Bless your heart! you'll soon get used to me. You see, I am the sort of color, as they say at the linen-drapers', that doesn't wash well. It's all through love; upon my life it is! Early in this present century I had my young affections blighted, and I've neglected myself ever since. Disappointment takes different forms, miss, in different men. I don't think I have had heart enough to brush my hair for the last fifty years. She was a magnificent woman, Mr. Moody, and she dropped me like a hot potato. Dreadful! dreadful! Let us pursue this painful subject no further. Ha! here's a pretty country! Here's a nice blue sky! I admire the country, miss; I see so little of it, you know. Have you any objection to walk along in the fields? The fields, my dear, bring out all the poetry of my nature. Where's the dog? Here, Puggy! Puggy! hunt about, my man, and find some dog-grass. Does his inside good, you know, after a meat diet in London. Lord! how I feel my spirits rising in this fine air! Does my complexion look any brighter, miss? Will you run a race with me, Mr. Moody, or will you oblige me with a back at leap-frog? I'm not mad, my dear young lady; I'm only merry. I live, you see, in the London stink, and the smell of the hedges and the wild-flowers is too much for me at first. It gets into my head, it does. I'm drunk! As I live by bread, I'm drunk on fresh air! Oh! what a jolly day! Oh! How young and innocent I do feel!" Here his innocence got the better of him, and he began to sing, " 'I wish I was a little fly, in my love's bosom for to lie!' Hullo! here we are on the nice soft grass! and, oh, my gracious! there's a bank running down into a hollow! I can't stand that, you know. Mr. Moody, hold my hat, and take the greatest care of it. Here goes for a roll down the bank!"

He handed his horrible hat to the astonished Moody, laid himself flat on the top of the bank and deliberately rolled down it, exactly as he might have done when he was a boy. The tails of his long gray coat flew madly in the wind; the dog pursued him, jumping over him, and barking with delight; he shouted and screamed in answer to the dog, as he rolled over and over faster and faster; and when he got up on the level ground, and called out cheerfully to his companions standing above him, "I say, you two, I feel twenty years younger already!" human gravity could hold out no longer. The sad and silent Moody smiled, and Isabel burst into fits of laughter.

"There," he said, "didn't I tell you you would get used to me, miss? There's a great deal of life left in the old man yet—isn't there?

Shy me down my hat, Mr. Moody. And now we'll get to business!"
He turned round to the dog still barking at his heels. "Business,
Puggy!" he called out, sharply, and Puggy instantly shut his mouth,
and said no more.

"Well, now," Old Sharon resumed, when he had joined his
friends and had got his breath again, "let's have a little talk about
yourself, miss. Has Mr. Moody told you who I am, and what I want
with you? Very good. May I offer you my arm? No! You like to be
independent, don't you? All right—I don't object. I am an amiable
old man, I am. About this Lady Lydiard, now? Suppose you tell me
how you first got acquainted with her."

In some surprise at this question, Isabel told her little story.
Observing Sharon's face while she was speaking, Moody saw that he
was not paying the smallest attention to the narrative. His sharp,
shameless black eyes watched the girl's face absently; his gross lips
curled upward in a sardonic and self-satisfied smile. He was evidently setting a trap for her of some kind. Without a word of
warning—while Isabel was in the middle of a sentence—the trap
opened, with the opening of Old Sharon's lips.

"I say!" he burst out, "how came *you* to seal her ladyship's
letter—eh?"

The question bore no sort of relation, direct or indirect, to what
Isabel happened to be saying at the moment. In the sudden surprise
of hearing it, she started and fixed her eyes in astonishment on
Sharon's face. The old vagabond chuckled to himself. "Did you see
that?" he whispered to Moody. "I beg your pardon, miss," he went
on; "I won't interrupt you again. Lord, how interesting it is!—ain't
it, Mr. Moody? Please to go on, miss."

But Isabel, though she spoke with perfect sweetness and temper,
declined to go on. "I had better tell you, sir, how I came to seal her
ladyship's letter," she said. "If I may venture on giving my opinion,
that part of my story seems to be the only part of it which relates to
your business with me to-day."

Without further preface she described the circumstances which
had led to her assuming the perilous responsibility of sealing the
letter. Old Sharon's wandering attention began to wander again; he
was evidently occupied in setting another trap. For the second time
he interrupted Isabel in the middle of a sentence. Suddenly stopping
short, he pointed to some sheep at the further end of the field
through which they happened to be passing at the moment.

"There's a pretty sight!" he said. "There are the innocent sheep a-feeding—all following each other as usual; and there's the sly dog waiting behind the gate till the sheep want his services. Reminds me of Old Sharon and the public." He chuckled over his discovery of the remarkable similarity between the sheepdog and himself, and the sheep and the public, and then burst upon Isabel with a second question. "I say! didn't you look at the letter before you sealed it?"

"Certainly not," Isabel answered.

"Not even at the address?"

"No."

"Thinking of something else—eh?"

"Very likely," said Isabel.

"Was it your new bonnet, my dear?"

Isabel laughed. "Women are not always thinking of their new bonnets," she answered.

Old Sharon, to all appearance, dropped the subject there. He lifted his lean, brown forefinger and pointed again, this time to a house at a short distance from them. "That's a farm-house, surely," he said. "I'm thirsty, after my roll down the hill. Do you think, miss, they would give me a drink of milk?"

"I am sure they would," said Isabel. "I know the people. Shall I go and ask them?"

"Thank you, my dear. One word more before you go. About the sealing of that letter: what *could* you have been thinking of while you were doing it?" He looked hard at her, and took her suddenly by the arm. "Was it your sweetheart?" he asked, in a whisper.

The question instantly reminded Isabel that she had been thinking of Hardyman while she sealed the letter. She blushed as the remembrance crossed her mind. Robert, noticing her embarrassment, spoke sharply to Old Sharon. "You have no right to put such a question to a young lady," he said. "Be a little more careful for the future."

"There! there! don't be hard on me," pleaded the old rogue. "An ugly old man like me may make his innocent little joke—eh, miss? I'm sure you're too sweet-tempered to be angry when I meant no offense. Show me that you bear no malice. Go, like a forgiving young angel, and ask for the milk."

Nobody appealed to Isabel's sweetness of temper in vain. "I will do it with pleasure," she said, and hastened away to the farm-house.

XIV

The instant Isabel was out of hearing, Old Sharon slapped Moody on the shoulder to rouse his attention. "I've got her out of the way," he said; "now listen to me. My business with the young angel is done; I may go back to London."

Moody looked at him in astonishment.

"Lord! how little you know of thieves!" exclaimed Old Sharon. "Why, man alive, I have tried her with two plain tests. If you wanted a proof of her innocence, there it was, as plain as the nose on your face. Did you hear me ask her how she came to seal the letter, just when her mind was running on something else?"

"I heard you," said Moody.

"Did you see how she started and stared at me?"

"I did."

"Well, I can tell you this: if she *had* stolen the money, she would neither have started nor stared. She would have had her answer ready beforehand in her own mind, in case of accidents. There's only one thing, in my experience, that you can never do with a thief, when the thief happens to be a woman—you can never take her by surprise. Put that remark by in your mind; one day you may find a use for remembering it. Did you see her blush, and look quite hurt in her feelings, pretty dear, when I asked about her sweetheart? Do you think a thief, in her place, would have shown such a face as that? Not she! The thief would have been relieved. The thief would have said to herself, 'All right; the more the old fool talks about sweethearts, the further he is from tracing the robbery to me.' Yes! yes! the ground's cleared now, Master Moody. I've reckoned up the servants; I've questioned Miss Isabel; I've made my inquiries in all the other quarters that may be useful to us—and what's the result? The advice I gave when you and the lawyer first came to me—I hate that fellow!—remains as sound and good advice as ever. I have got the thief in my mind," said Old Sharon, closing his cunning eyes and then opening them again, "as plain as I've got you in my eye at this minute. No more of that now," he went on, looking round sharply at the path that led to the farm-house; "I've something particular to say to you, and there's barely time to say it before that nice girl comes back. Look here! do you happen to be acquainted with Mr. Honorable Hardyman's valet?"

Moody's eyes rested on Old Sharon with a searching and doubtful look.

"Mr. Hardyman's valet?" he repeated. "I wasn't prepared to hear Mr. Hardyman's name."

Old Sharon looked at Moody, in his turn, with a flash of sardonic triumph.

"Oho!" he said; "has my good boy learned his lesson? Do you see the thief through my spectacles already?"

"I began to see him," Moody answered, "when you gave us the guinea opinion at your lodgings."

"Will you whisper his name?" asked Old Sharon.

"Not yet. I distrust my own judgment. I'll wait till time proves you're right."

Old Sharon knitted his shaggy brows and shook his head. "If you only had a little more dash and go in you," he said, "you would be a clever fellow. As it is——" He finished the sentence by snapping his fingers with a grin of contempt. "Let's get to business. Are you going back by the next train along with me, or are you going to stop with the young lady?"

"I will follow you by a later train," Moody answered.

"Then I must give you your instructions at once," Sharon continued. "You get better acquainted with Hardyman's valet. Lend him money if he wants it; stick at nothing to make a bosom-friend of him. I can't do that part of it; my appearance would be against me. *You* are the man; you are respectable from the top of your hat to the tips of your boots; nobody would suspect you. Don't make objections! Can you fix the valet? Or can't you?"

"I can try," said Moody. "And what then?"

Old Sharon put his gross lips disagreeably close to Moody's ear.

"Your friend the valet can tell you who his master's bankers are," he said; "and he can supply you with a specimen of his master's handwriting."

Moody drew back as suddenly as if his vagabond companion put a knife at his throat. "You old villain!" he said, "are you tempting me to forgery?"

"You infernal fool!" retorted Old Sharon. "*Will* you hold that long tongue of yours, and hear what I have to say? You go to Hardyman's bankers, with a note in Hardyman's handwriting (exactly imitated by me) to this effect: 'Mr. H. presents his compliments to Messrs. So-and-So, and is not quite certain whether a payment of five hundred pounds has been made within the last week to his account. He will be much obliged if Messrs. So-and-So will inform him by a line in reply whether there is such an entry to his credit in their books, and by whom the payment has been made.' You wait for the bankers' answer, and bring it to me. It's just possible that the name you're afraid to whisper may appear in the letter. If it does, we've caught our man. Is *that* forgery, Mr. Muddlehead Moody? I'll tell you what—if I had lived to be your age, and knew no more of the world than you do, I'd go and hang myself. Steady! here's our charming friend with the milk. Remember your instructions, and don't lose heart if my notion of the payment to the bankers comes to nothing. I know what to do next, in that case— and, what's more, I'll take all the risk and trouble on my own shoulders. Oh, Lord! I'm afraid I shall be obliged to drink the milk, now it's come."

With this apprehension in his mind, he advanced to relieve Isabel of the jug she carried.

"Here's a treat!" he burst out, with an affectation of joy which was completely belied by the expression of his dirty face. "Here's a kind and dear young lady, to help an old man to a drink with her own pretty hands." He paused, and looked at the milk very much as he might have looked at a dose of physic. "Will any one take a drink first?" he asked, offering the jug piteously to Isabel and Moody. "You see, I'm not used to genuine milk; I'm used to chalk and water. I don't know what effect the unadulterated cow might have on my poor old inside." He tasted the milk with the greatest caution. "Upon my soul, this is too rich for me! The unadulterated cow is a deal too strong to be drunk alone. If you'll allow me, I'll qualify it with a drop of gin. Here, Puggy! Puggy!" He set the milk down before the dog, and taking a flask out of his pocket, emptied it in a draught. "That's something like!" he said, smacking his lips with an air of infinite relief. "So sorry, miss, to have given you all your trouble for nothing; it's my ignorance that's to blame, not me. I couldn't know I was unworthy of genuine milk till I tried—could I? And do you know," he proceeded, with his eye directed slyly on the way back to the station, "I begin to think I'm not worthy of the fresh air either. A kind of longing seems to come over me for the London stink. I'm homesick already for the soot of my happy childhood and my own dear native mud. The air is too thin for me, and the sky's too clean; and—Oh, Lord!—when you're used to the roar of the traffic—the busses and the cabs and what not—the silence in these parts is downright awful. I'll wish you good-evening, miss, and get back to London."

Isabel turned to Moody with disappointment plainly expressed in her face and manner.

"Is that all he has to say?" she asked. "You told me he could help us. You led me to suppose he could find the guilty person."

Sharon heard her. "I could name the guilty person," he answered, "as easily, miss, as I could name you."

"Why don't you do it then?" Isabel inquired, not very patiently.

"Because the time's not ripe for it yet, miss—that's one reason. Because, if I mentioned the thief's name, as things are now, you, Miss Isabel, would think me mad; and you would tell Mr. Moody I had cheated him out of his money—that's another reason. The matter's in train, if you will only wait a little longer."

"So you say," Isabel rejoined. "If you really could name the thief, I believe you would do it now."

She turned away with a frown on her pretty face. Old Sharon followed her. Even his coarse sensibilities appeared to feel the irresistible ascendency of beauty and youth.

"I say!" he began, "we must part friends, you know, or I shall break my heart over it. They have got milk at the farm-house. Do you think they have got pen, ink, and paper, too?"

Isabel answered, without turning to look at him, "Of course they have."

"And a bit of sealing-wax?"

"I dare say."

Old Sharon laid his dirty claws on her shoulder, and forced her to face him as the best means of shaking them off.

"Come along!" he said. "I am going to pacify you with some information in writing."

"Why should you write it?" Isabel asked, suspiciously.

"Because I mean to make my own conditions, my dear, before I let you into the secret."

In ten minutes more they were all three in the farm-house parlor. Nobody but the farmer's wife was at home. The good woman trembled from head to foot at the sight of Old Sharon. In all her harmless life she had never yet seen humanity under the aspect in which it was now presented to her. "Mercy preserve us, miss!" she whispered to Isabel, "how come you to be in such company as *that?*"

Instructed by Isabel, she produced the necessary materials for writing and sealing, and, that done, she shrunk away to the door. "Please to excuse me, miss," she said, with a last horrified look at her venerable visitor; "I really can't stand the sight of such a blot of dirt as that in my nice clean parlor." With those words she disappeared, and was seen no more.

Perfectly indifferent to his reception, Old Sharon wrote, inclosed what he had written in an envelope, and sealed it (in the absence of anything better fitted for his purpose) with the mouthpiece of his pipe.

"Now, miss," he said, "you give me your word of honor"—he stopped and looked round at Moody, with a grin—"and you give me yours, that you won't either of you break the seal on this envelope till the expiration of one week from the present day. There are the conditions, Miss Isabel, on which I'll give you your information. If you stop to dispute with me, the candle's alight, and I'll burn the letter."

It was useless to contend with him. Isabel and Moody gave him the promise that he required. He handed the sealed envelope to Isabel with a low bow. "When the week's out," he said, "you will own I'm a cleverer fellow than you think me now. Wish you good-evening, miss. Come along, Puggy! Farewell to the horrid, clean country, and back again to the nice London stink!"

He nodded to Moody—he leered at Isabel—he chuckled to himself—he left the farm-house.

XV

Isabel looked down at the letter in her hand, considered it in silence, and turned to Moody. "I feel tempted to open it already," she said.

"After giving your promise?" Moody gently remonstrated.

Isabel met that objection with a woman's logic.

"Does a promise matter," she asked, "when one gives it to a dirty, disreputable, presuming old wretch like Mr. Sharon? It's a wonder to me that you trust such a creature. *I* wouldn't!"

"I doubted him just as you do," Moody answered, "when I first saw him in company with Mr. Troy. But there was something in the advice he gave us at that first consultation which altered my opinion of him for the better. I dislike his appearance and his manners as much as you do—I may even say I felt ashamed of bringing such a person to see you. And yet I can't think that I have acted unwisely in employing Mr. Sharon."

Isabel listened absently. She had something more to say, and she was considering how she should say it. "May I ask you a bold question?" she began.

"Any question you like."

"Have you——" She hesitated and looked embarrassed. "Have you paid Mr. Sharon much money?" she resumed, suddenly rallying her courage. Instead of answering, Moody suggested that it was time to think of returning to Miss Pink's villa. "Your aunt may be getting anxious about you," he said.

Isabel led the way out of the farm-house in silence. She reverted to Mr. Sharon and the money, however, as they returned by the path across the fields.

"I am sure you will not be offended with me," she said, gently, "if I own that I am uneasy about the expenses. I am allowing you to use your purse as if it were mine, and I have hardly any savings of my own."

Moody entreated her not to speak of it. "How can I put my money to a better use than in serving your interests?" he asked. "My one object in life is to relieve you of your present anxieties. I shall be the happiest man living if you only owe a moment's happiness to my exertions."

Isabel took his hand, and looked at him with grateful tears in her eyes.

"How good you are to me, Mr. Moody!" she said. "I wish I could tell you how deeply I feel your kindness."

"You can do it easily," he answered, with a smile. "Call me 'Robert,' don't call me 'Mr. Moody.' "

She took his arm with a sudden familiarity that charmed him. "If you had been my brother I should have called you 'Robert,' " she said; "and no brother could have been more devoted to me than you are."

He looked eagerly at her bright face turned up to his. "May I never hope to be something nearer and dearer to you than a brother?" he asked, timidly.

She hung her head and said nothing. Moody's memory recalled

Sharon's coarse reference to her "sweetheart." She had blushed when he put the question. What had she done when Moody put *his* question? Her face answered for her—she had turned pale; she was looking more serious than usual. Ignorant as he was of the ways of women, his instinct told him that this was a bad sign. Surely her rising color would have confessed it, if time and gratitude together were teaching her to love him? He sighed as the inevitable conclusion forced itself on his mind.

"I hope I had not offended you?" he said, sadly.

"Oh, no."

"I wish I had not spoken. Pray don't think that I am serving you with any selfish motive."

"I don't think that, Robert. I never could think it of *you*."

He was not quite satisfied yet. "Even if you were to marry some other man," he went on, earnestly, "it would make no difference in what I am trying to do for you. No matter what I might suffer, I should still go on—for your sake."

"Why do you talk so?" she burst out, passionately. "No other man has such a claim as yours to my gratitude and regard. How can you let such thoughts come to you? I have done nothing in secret. I have no friends who are not known to you. Be satisfied with that, Robert, and let us drop the subject."

"Never to take it up again?" he asked, with the infatuated pertinacity of a man clinging to his last hope.

At other times and under other circumstances Isabel might have answered him sharply. She spoke with perfect gentleness now.

"Not for the present," she said. "I don't know my own heart. Give me time."

His gratitude caught at those words, as the drowning man is said to catch at the proverbial straw. He lifted her hand, and suddenly and fondly pressed his lips on it. She showed no confusion. Was she sorry for him, poor wretch?—and was that all?

They walked on, arm in arm, in silence.

Crossing the last field, they entered again on the highroad leading to the row of villas in which Miss Pink lived. The minds of both were preoccupied. Neither of them noticed a gentleman approaching on horseback, followed by a mounted groom. He was advancing slowly, at the walking pace of his horse, and he only observed the two foot-passengers when he was close to them.

"Miss Isabel!"

She started, looked up, and discovered—Alfred Hardyman.

He was dressed in a perfectly made traveling suit of light brown, with a peaked felt hat of a darker shade of the same color, which, in a picturesque sense, greatly improved his personal appearance. His pleasure at discovering Isabel gave the animation to his features which they wanted on ordinary occasions. He sat his horse, a superb hunter, easily and gracefully. His light, amber-colored gloves fitted him perfectly. His obedient servant, on another magnificent horse, waited behind him. He looked the impersonation of rank and breeding, of wealth and prosperity. What a contrast, in a woman's eyes, to the shy, pale, melancholy man in the ill-fitting black clothes, with the wandering, uneasy glances, who stood beneath him, and felt, and showed that he felt, his inferior position keenly! In spite of herself, the treacherous blush flew over Isabel's face, in Moody's presence, and with Moody's eyes distrustfully watching her.

"This is a piece of good fortune that I hardly hoped for," said Hardyman, his cool, quiet, dreary way of speaking quickened, as usual, in Isabel's presence. "I only got back from France this morning, and I called on Lady Lydiard in the hope of seeing you. She was not at home, and you were in the country, and the servants didn't know the address. I could get nothing out of them except that you were on a visit to a relation." He looked at Moody while he was speaking. "Haven't I seen you before?" he said, carelessly. "Yes, at Lady Lydiard's. You're her steward, are you not? How d'ye do?" Moody, with his eyes on the ground, answered silently by a bow. Hardyman, perfectly indifferent whether Lady Lydiard's steward spoke or not, turned on his saddle and looked admiringly at Isabel. "I begin to think my luck has turned at last," he went on, with a smile. "I was jogging along to my farm, and despairing of ever seeing Miss Isabel again—and Miss Isabel herself meets me at the road-side! I wonder whether you are as glad to see me as I am to see you? You won't tell me, eh? May I ask you something else?—are you staying in our neighborhood?"

There was no alternative before Isabel but to answer this last question. Hardyman had met her out walking, and had no doubt drawn the inevitable inference, although he was too polite to say so in plain words.

"Yes, sir," she answered, shyly, "I am staying in this neighborhood."

"And who is your relation?" Hardyman proceeded, in his easy, matter-of-course way. "Lady Lydiard told me, when I had the pleasure of meeting you at her house, that you had an aunt living in the country. I have a good memory, Miss Isabel, for anything that I hear about you. It's your aunt, isn't it? Yes? I know everybody about here. What is your aunt's name?"

Isabel, still resting her hand on Robert's arm, felt it tremble a little as Hardyman made this last inquiry. If she had been speaking to one of her equals, she would have known how to dispose of the question without directly answering it. But what could she say to the magnificent gentleman on the stately horse? He had only to send his servant into the village to ask who the young lady from London was staying with, and the answer, in a dozen mouths at least, would direct him to her aunt. She cast one appealing look at Moody, and pronounced the distinguished name of Miss Pink.

"Miss Pink?" Hardyman repeated. "Surely I know Miss Pink." (He had not the faintest remembrance of her.) "Where did I meet her last?" (He ran over in his memory the different local festivals at which strangers had been introduced to him.) "Was it at the archery meeting? or at the grammar school, when the prizes were given? No? It must have been at the flower-show, then, surely?"

It *had* been at the flower-show. Isabel had heard it from Miss Pink fifty times at least, and was obliged to admit it now.

"I am quite ashamed of never having called," Hardyman proceeded. "The fact is, I have so much to do. I am a bad one at paying visits. Are you on your way home? Let me follow you and make my apologies personally to Miss Pink."

Moody looked at Isabel. It was only a momentary glance, but she perfectly understood it.

"I am afraid, sir, my aunt cannot have the honor of seeing you today," she said.

Hardyman was all compliance. He smiled and patted his horse's neck. "To-morrow, then," he said. "My compliments, and I will call in the afternoon. Let me see, Miss Pink lives at——" He waited, as if he expected Isabel to assist his treacherous memory once more. She hesitated again. Hardyman looked round at his groom. The groom could find out the address, even if he did not happen to know it already. Besides, there was the little row of houses visible at the further end of the road. Isabel pointed to the villas, as a necessary concession to good manners, before the groom could anticipate her. "My aunt lives there, sir, at the house called The Lawn."

"Ah! to be sure," said Hardyman. "I oughtn't to have wanted reminding; but I have so many things to think of at the farm. And I am afraid I must be getting old; my memory isn't as good as it was. I am so glad to have seen you, Miss Isabel. You and your aunt must come and look at my horses. Do you like horses? Are you fond of riding? I have a quiet roan mare that is used to carrying ladies; she would be just the thing for you. Did I beg you to give my best compliments to your aunt? Yes? How well you are looking! our air here agrees with you. I hope I haven't kept you standing too long? I didn't think of it in the pleasure of meeting you. Good-bye, Miss Isabel—good-bye till tomorrow."

He took off his hat to Isabel, nodded to Moody, and pursued his way to the farm.

Isabel looked at her companion. His eyes were still on the ground. Pale, silent, motionless, he waited by her like a dog, until she gave the signal of walking on again toward the house.

"You are not angry with me for speaking to Mr. Hardyman?" she asked, anxiously.

He lifted his head at the sound of her voice. "Angry with you, my dear! Why should I be angry?"

"You seemed so changed, Robert, since we met Mr. Hardyman. I couldn't help speaking to him, could I?"

"Certainly not."

They moved on toward the villa. Isabel was still uneasy. There was something in Moody's silent submission to all that she said and all that she did which pained and humiliated her. "You're not jealous?" she said, smiling timidly.

He tried to speak lightly, on his side. "I have no time to be jealous while I have your affairs to look after," he answered.

She pressed his arm tenderly. "Never fear, Robert, that new friends will make me forget the best and dearest friend who is now at my side." She paused, and looked up at him with a compassionate fondness that was very pretty to see. "I can keep out of the way to-morrow, when Mr. Hardyman calls," she said. "It is my aunt he is coming to see, not me."

It was generously meant. But while her mind was only occupied with the present time, Moody's mind was looking into the future. He was learning the hard lesson of self-sacrifice already. "Do what you think right," he said, quietly; "don't think of me."

They reached the gate of the villa. He held out his hand to say good-bye.

"Won't you come in?" she asked. "Do come in."

"Not now, my dear. I must get back to London as soon as I can. There is some more work to be done for you, and the sooner I do it the better."

She heard his excuse without heeding it.

"You are not like yourself, Robert," she said. "Why is it? What are you thinking of?"

He was thinking of the bright blush that overspread her face when Hardyman first spoke to her; he was thinking of the invitation to her to see the stud-farm, and to ride the roan mare; he was thinking of the utterly powerless position in which he stood toward Isabel and toward the highly born gentleman who admired her. But he kept his doubts and fears to himself. "The train won't wait for me," he said, and held out his hand once more.

She was not only perplexed, she was really distressed. "Don't take leave of me in that cold way!" she pleaded. Her eyes dropped before his, and her lips trembled a little. "Give me a kiss, Robert, at parting." She said those words softly and sadly, out of the depth of her pity for him; he started; his face brightened suddenly; his sinking hope rose again. In another moment the change came; in another moment he understood her. As he touched her cheek with his lips he turned pale again. "Don't quite forget me," he said, in low, faltering tones, and left her.

Miss Pink met Isabel in the hall. Refreshed by unbroken repose, the ex-school-mistress was in the happiest frame of mind for the reception of her niece's news.

Informed that Moody had traveled to South Morden to personally report the progress of the inquiries, Miss Pink highly approved of him as a substitute for Mr. Troy. "Mr. Moody, as a banker's son, is a gentleman by birth," she remarked; "he has condescended in becoming Lady Lydiard's steward. What I saw of him, when he came here with you, prepossessed me in his favor. He has my confidence, Isabel, as well as yours; he is in every respect a superior person to Mr. Troy. Did you meet any friends, my dear, when you were out walking?"

The answer to this question produced a species of transformation in Miss Pink. The rapturous rank-worship of her nation feasted, so to speak, on Hardyman's message. She looked taller and younger than usual; she was all smiles and sweetness. "At last, Isabel, you have seen birth and breeding under your right aspect," she said. "In the society of Lady Lydiard you can not possibly have formed correct ideas of the English aristocracy. Observe Mr. Hardyman when he does me the honor to call to-morrow, and you will see the difference."

"Mr. Hardyman is your visitor, aunt, not mine. I was going to ask you to let me remain up-stairs in my room."

Miss Pink was unaffectedly shocked. "This is what you learn at Lady Lydiard's," she observed. "No, Isabel, your absence would be a breach of good manners; I can not possibly permit it. You will be present to receive our distinguished friend with me. And mind this," added Miss Pink, in her most impressive manner, "if Mr. Hardyman should by any chance ask why you have left Lady Lydiard, not one word about those disgraceful circumstances which connect you with the loss of the bank-note! I should sink into the earth if the smallest hint of what has really happened should reach Mr. Hardyman's ears. My child, I stand toward you in the place of your lamented mother. I have the right to command your silence on this horrible subject, and I do imperatively command it."

In these words foolish Miss Pink sowed the seed for the harvest of trouble that was soon to come.

XVI

Paying his court to the ex-school-mistress on the next day, Hardyman made such excellent use of his opportunities that the visit to the stud-farm took place on the day after. His own carriage was placed at the disposal of Isabel and her aunt, and his own sister was present to confer special distinction on the reception of Miss Pink.

In a country like England, which annually suspends the sitting of its legislature in honor of a horse-race, it is only natural and proper that the comfort of the horses should be the first object of consideration at a stud-farm. Nine tenths of the land at Hardyman's farm were devoted, in one way or another, to the noble quadruped with the low forehead and the long nose. Poor humanity was satisfied with second-rate and third-rate accommodation. The ornamental grounds, very poorly laid out, were also very limited in extent; and as for the dwelling-house, it was literally a cottage. A parlor and a kitchen, a smoking-room, a bedroom, and a spare chamber for a friend, all scantily furnished, sufficed for the modest wants of the owner of the property. If you wished to feast your eyes on luxury, you went to the stables.

The stud-farm being described, the introduction of Hardyman's sister follows in due course.

The Honorable Lavinia Hardyman was, as all persons in society know, married rather late in life to General Drumblade. It is saying a great deal, but it is not saying too much, to describe Mrs. Drumblade as the most mischievous woman of her age in all England. Scandal was the breath of her life; to place people in false positions, to divulge secrets and destroy characters, to undermine friendships and aggravate enmities—these were the sources of enjoyment from which this dangerous woman drew the inexhaustible fund of good spirits that made her a brilliant light in the social sphere. She was one of the privileged sinners of modern society. The worst mischief that she could work was ascribed to her "exuberant vitality." She had that ready familiarity of manner which is (in her class) so rarely discovered to be insolence in disguise. Her power of easy self-assertion found people ready to accept her on her own terms wherever she went. She was one of those big, overpowering women with blunt manners, voluble tongues, and goggle eyes, who carry everything before them. The highest society modestly considered itself in danger of being dull in the absence of Mrs. Drumblade. Even Hardyman himself—who saw as little of her as possible, whose frankly straightforward nature recoiled by instinct from contact with his sister—could think of no fitter person to make Miss Pink's reception agreeable to her while he was devoting his own attentions to her niece. Mrs. Drumblade accepted the position thus offered with the most amiable readiness. In her own private mind she placed an interpretation on her brother's motives which did him the grossest injustice. She believed that Hardyman's designs on Isabel contemplated the most profligate result. To assist this purpose, while the girl's nearest relative was supposed to be taking care of her, was Mrs. Drumblade's idea of "fun." Her worst enemies admitted that the Honorable Lavinia had redeeming qualities, and owned that a keen sense of humor was one of her merits.

Was Miss Pink a likely person to resist the fascinations of Mrs. Drumblade? Alas for the ex-school-mistress! before she had been five minutes at the farm Hardyman's sister had fished for her, caught her, landed her. Poor Miss Pink!

Mrs. Drumblade could assume a grave dignity of manner when

the occasion called for it. She was grave, she was dignified, when Hardyman performed the ceremonies of introduction. She would not say she was charmed to meet Miss Pink—the ordinary slang of society was not for Miss Pink's ears—she would say she felt this introduction as a privilege. It was so seldom that one met with persons of trained intellect in society. Mrs. Drumblade was already informed of Miss Pink's earlier triumphs in the instruction of youth. Mrs. Drumblade had not been blessed with children herself, but she had nephews and nieces, and she was anxious about their education, especially the nieces. What a sweet, modest girl Miss Isabel was! The fondest wish she could form for her nieces would be that they should resemble Miss Isabel when they grew up. The question was as to the best method of education. She would own that she had selfish motives in becoming acquainted with Miss Pink. They were at the farm, no doubt, to see Alfred's horses. Mrs. Drumblade did not understand horses; her interest was in the question of education. She might even confess that she had accepted Alfred's invitation in the hope of hearing Miss Pink's views. There would be opportunities, she trusted, for a little instructive conversation on that subject. It was, perhaps, ridiculous to talk, at her age, of feeling as if she were Miss Pink's pupil, and yet it exactly expressed the nature of the aspiration which was then in her mind. In these terms, feeling her way with the utmost nicety, Mrs. Drumblade wound the net of flattery round and round Miss Pink until her hold on that innocent lady was, in every sense of the word, secure. Before half the horses had been passed under review Hardyman and Isabel were out of sight, and Mrs. Drumblade and Miss Pink were lost in the intricacies of the stables. "Excessively stupid of me! We had better go back and establish ourselves comfortably in the parlor. When my brother misses us he and your charming niece will return to look for us in the cottage." Under cover of this arrangement the separation became complete. Miss Pink held forth on education to Mrs. Drumblade in the parlor, while Hardyman and Isabel were on their way to a paddock at the furthest limits of the property.

"I am afraid you are getting a little tired," said Hardyman. "Won't you take my arm?"

Isabel was on her guard; she had not forgotten what Lady Lydiard had said to her. "No, thank you, Mr. Hardyman; I am a better walker than you think."

Hardyman continued the conversation in his blunt, resolute way.

"I wonder whether you will believe me," he asked, "if I tell you that this is one of the happiest days of my life?"

"I should think you were always happy," Isabel cautiously replied, "having such a pretty place to live in as this."

Hardyman met that answer with one of his quietly positive denials. "A man is never happy by himself," he said. "He is happy with a companion. For instance, I am happy with you."

Isabel stopped and looked back. Hardyman's language was becoming a little too explicit. "Surely we have lost Mrs. Drumblade and my aunt?" she said. "I don't see them anywhere."

"You will see them directly; they are only a long way behind." With this assurance, he returned, in his own obstinate way, to his one object in view. "Miss Isabel, I want to ask you a question. I'm not a ladies' man. I speak my mind plainly to everybody—women included. Do you like being here to-day?"

Isabel's gravity was not proof against this very downright question. "I should be hard to please," she said, laughing, "if I didn't enjoy my visit to the farm."

Hardyman pushed steadily forward through the obstacle of the farm to the question of the farm's master. "You like being here," he repeated. "Do you like me?"

This was serious. Isabel drew back a little and looked at him. He waited with the most impenetrable gravity for her reply.

"I think you can hardly expect me to answer that question," she said.

"Why not?"

"Our acquaintance has been a very short one, Mr. Hardyman. And if *you* are so good as to forget the difference between us, I think *I* ought to remember it."

"What difference?"

"The difference in rank."

Hardyman suddenly stood still, and emphasized his next words by digging his stick into the grass.

"If anything I have said has vexed you," he began, "tell me so plainly, Miss Isabel, and I'll ask your pardon. But don't throw my rank in my face. I cut adrift from all that nonsense when I took this farm and got my living out of the horses. What has a man's rank to do with a man's feelings?" he went on, with another emphatic dig of his stick. "I am quite serious in asking if you like me, for this good reason, that I like you. Yes, I do. You remember that day when I bled the old lady's dog. Well, I have found out since then that there's a sort of incompleteness in my life which I never suspected before. It's you who have put that idea into my head. You didn't mean it, I dare say, but you have done it all the same. I sat alone here yesterday evening smoking my pipe—and I didn't enjoy it. I breakfasted alone this morning—and I didn't enjoy *that*. I said to myself, She's coming to lunch, that's one comfort—I shall enjoy lunch. That's what I feel, roughly described. I don't suppose I've been five minutes together without thinking of you, now in one way and now in another, since the day when I first saw you. When a man comes to my time of life, and has had my experience, he knows what that means. It means, in plain English, that his heart is set on a woman. You're the woman."

Isabel had thus far made several attempts to interrupt him, without success. But when Hardyman's confession attained its culminating point, she insisted on being heard.

"If you will excuse me, sir," she interposed, gravely, "I think I had better go back to the cottage. My aunt is a stranger here, and she doesn't know where to look for us."

"We don't want your aunt," Hardyman remarked, in his most positive manner.

"We do want her," Isabel rejoined. "I won't venture to say it's wrong in you, Mr. Hardyman, to talk to me as you have just done, but I am quite sure it's wrong in me to listen."

He looked at her with such unaffected surprise and distress that she stopped, on the point of leaving him, and tried to make herself better understood.

"I had no intention of offending you, sir," she said, a little confusedly. "I only wanted to remind you that there are some things which a gentleman in your position——" She stopped, tried to finish the sentence, failed, and began another. "If I had been a young lady in your own rank of life," she went on, "I might have thanked you for paying me a compliment, and have given you a serious answer. As it is, I am afraid I must say that you have surprised and disappointed me. I can claim very little for myself, I know; but I did imagine—so long as there was nothing unbecoming in my conduct —that I had some right to your respect."

Listening more and more impatiently, Hardyman took her by the hand, and burst out with another of his abrupt questions.

"What can you possibly be thinking of?" he asked.

She gave him no answer; she only looked at him reproachfully, and tried to release herself.

Hardyman held her hand faster than ever.

"I believe you think me an infernal scoundrel," he said. "I can stand a good deal, Miss Isabel, but I can't stand *that*. How have I failed in respect toward you, if you please? I have told you you're the woman my heart is set on. Well? Isn't it plain what I want of you when I say that? Isabel Miller, I want you to be my wife!"

Isabel's only reply to this extraordinary proposal of marriage was a faint cry of astonishment, followed by a sudden trembling that shook her from head to foot.

Hardyman put his arm round her with a gentleness which his oldest friend would have been surprised to see in him.

"Take your time to think of it," he said, dropping back again into his usual quiet tone. "If you had known me a little better, you wouldn't have mistaken me, and you wouldn't be looking at me now as if you were afraid to believe your own ears. What is there so very wonderful in my wanting to marry you? I don't set up for being a saint. When I was a young man I was no better (and no worse) than other young men. I'm getting on now to middle life. I don't want romances and adventures; I want an easy existence with a nice, lovable woman who will make me a good wife. You're the woman, I tell you again. I know it by what I've seen of you myself, and by what I have heard of you from Lady Lydiard. She said you were prudent and sweet-tempered and affectionate; to which I wish to add that you have just the face and figure that I like, and the modest manners and the blessed absence of all slang in your talk which I don't find in the young women I meet with in the present day. That's my view of it: I think for myself. What does it matter to me whether you're the daughter of a duke or the daughter of a dairyman? It isn't your father I want to marry; it's you. Listen to reason, there's a dear! We only have one question to settle before we go back to your aunt. You wouldn't answer me when I asked it a little while since. Will you answer now? *Do* you like me?"

Isabel looked at him timidly.

"In my position, sir," she asked, "have I any right to like you? What would your relations and friends think if I said Yes?"

Hardyman gave her waist a little admonitory squeeze with his arm.

"What! You're at it again? A nice way to answer a man, to call him 'sir,' and to get behind his rank as if it were a place of refuge from him! I hate talking of myself, but you force me to it. Here is my position in the world: I have got an elder brother; he is married and has a son to succeed him in the title and the property. You understand, so far? Very well! Years ago I shifted my share of the rank (whatever it may be) on to my brother's shoulders. He's a thorough good fellow, and he has carried my dignity for me, without once dropping it, ever since. As to what people may say, they have said it already, from my father and mother downward, in the time when I took to the horses and the farm. If they're the wise people I take them for, they won't be at the trouble of saying it all over again. No, no. Twist it how you may, Miss Isabel, whether I'm single, or whether I'm married, I'm plain Alfred Hardyman; and everybody who knows me knows that I go on my own way, and please myself. If you don't like me, it will be the bitterest disappointment I ever had in my life; but say so honestly, all the same."

Where is the woman in Isabel's place whose capacity for resistance would not have yielded a little to such an appeal as this?

"I should be an insensible wretch," she replied, warmly, "if I didn't feel the honor you have done me, and feel it gratefully."

"Does that mean that you will have me for a husband?" asked downright Hardyman.

She was fairly driven into a corner; but (being a woman) she tried to slip through his fingers at the last moment.

"Will you forgive me," she said, "if I ask for a little more time? I am so bewildered, I hardly know what to say or do for the best. You see, Mr. Hardyman, it would be a dreadful thing for me to be the cause of your giving offense to your family. I am obliged to think of that. It would be so distressing for you (I will say nothing of myself) if your friends closed their doors on me. They might say I was a designing girl, who had taken advantage of your good opinion to raise herself in the world. Lady Lydiard warned me long since not to be ambitious about myself, and not to forget my station in life, because she treated me like her adopted daughter. Indeed—indeed, I can't tell you how I feel your goodness, and the compliment—the very great compliment—you pay me. My heart is free; and if I followed my own inclinations——" She checked herself, conscious that she was on the brink of saying too much. "Will you give me a few days," she pleaded, "to try if I can think composedly of all this? I am only a girl, and I feel quite dazzled by the prospect that you set before me."

Hardyman seized on these words as offering all the encouragement that he desired to his suit.

"Have your own way in this thing, and in everything!" he said, with an unaccustomed fervor of language and manner. "I am so glad to hear that your heart is open to me, and that all your inclinations take my part."

Isabel instantly protested against this misrepresentation of what she had really said. "Oh, Mr. Hardyman, you quite mistake me!"

He answered her very much as he had answered Lady Lydiard when she had tried to make him understand his proper relations toward Isabel.

"No, no; I don't mistake you. I agree to every word you say. How can I expect you to marry me, as you very properly remark, unless I give you a day or two to make up your mind? It's quite enough for me that you like the prospect. If Lady Lydiard treated you as her daughter, why shouldn't you be my wife? It stands to reason that you're quite right to marry a man who can raise you in the world. I like you to be ambitious, though heaven knows it isn't much I can do for you, except to love you with all my heart. Still, it's a great encouragement to hear that her ladyship's views agree with mine——"

"They don't agree, Mr. Hardyman," protested poor Isabel. "You are entirely misrepresenting——"

Hardyman cordially concurred in this view of the matter. "Yes! yes! I can't pretend to represent her ladyship's language, or yours either; I am obliged to take my words as they come to me. Don't disturb yourself: it's all right—I understand. You have made me the happiest man living. I shall ride over to-morrow to your aunt's house and hear what you have to say to me. Mind you're at home! Not a day must pass now without my seeing you. I do love you, Isabel—I do indeed!" He stooped, and kissed her heartily. "Only to reward me," he explained, "for giving you time to think."

She drew herself away from him—resolutely, not angrily. Before she could make a third attempt to place the subject in its right light before him, the luncheon-bell rang at the cottage, and a servant appeared, evidently sent to look for them.

"Don't forget to-morrow," Hardyman whispered, confidentially. "I'll call early, and then go on to London and get the ring."

XVII

Events succeeded each other rapidly after the memorable day, to Isabel, of the luncheon at the farm.

On the next day (the 9th of the month) Lady Lydiard sent for her steward, and requested him to explain his conduct in repeatedly leaving the house without assigning any reason for his absence. She did not dispute his claims to a freedom of action which would not be permitted to an ordinary servant. Her objection to his present course of proceeding related entirely to the mystery in which it was involved, and to the uncertainty in which the household was left as to the hour of his return. On those grounds she thought herself entitled to an explanation. Moody's habitual reserve—strengthened on this occasion by his dread of ridicule if his efforts to serve Isabel ended in failure—disinclined him to take Lady Lydiard into his confidence while his inquiries were still beset with obstacles and doubts. He respectfully entreated her ladyship to grant him a delay of a few weeks before he entered on his explanation. Lady Lydiard's quick temper resented this request. She told Moody plainly that he was guilty of an act of presumption in making his own conditions with his employer. He received the reproof with exemplary resignation, but he held to his conditions nevertheless. From that moment the result of the interview was no longer in doubt. Moody was directed to send in his accounts. The accounts having been examined, and found to be scrupulously correct, he declined accepting the balance of salary that was offered to him. The next day he left Lady Lydiard's service.

On the 10th of the month her ladyship received a letter from her nephew.

The health of Felix had not improved. He had made up his mind to go abroad again toward the end of the month. In the meantime he had written to his friend at Paris, and he had the pleasure of forwarding an answer. The letter inclosed announced that the lost five-hundred-pound note had been made the subject of careful inquiry in Paris. It had not been traced. The French police offered to send to London one of their best men, well acquainted with the English language, if Lady Lydiard was desirous of employing him. He would be perfectly willing to act with an English officer in conducting the investigation, should it be thought necessary. Mr. Troy, being consulted as to the expediency of accepting this proposal, objected to the pecuniary terms demanded as being extravagantly high. He suggested waiting a little before any reply was sent to Paris; and he engaged meanwhile to consult a London solicitor who had great experience in cases of theft, and whose advice might enable them to dispense entirely with the services of the French police.

Being now a free man again, Moody was able to follow his own inclinations in regard to the instructions which he had received from Old Sharon.

The course that had been recommended to him was repellent to the self-respect and the sense of delicacy which were among the inbred virtues of Moody's character. He shrank from forcing himself as a friend on Hardyman's valet; he recoiled from the idea of tempting the man to steal a specimen of his master's handwriting. After some consideration, he decided on applying to the agent who collected the rents at Hardyman's London chambers. Being an old acquaintance of Moody's, this person would certainly not hesitate to communicate the address of Hardyman's bankers, if he knew it. The experiment, tried under these favoring circumstances, proved perfectly successful. Moody proceeded to Sharon's lodgings the same day, with the address of the bankers in his pocket-book. The old vagabond, greatly amused by Moody's scruples, saw plainly enough that so long as he wrote the supposed letter from Hardyman in the third person, it mattered little what handwriting was employed, seeing that no signature would be necessary. The letter was at once composed, on the model which Sharon had already suggested to Moody, and a respectable messenger (so far as outward appearance went) was employed to take it to the bank. In half an hour the answer came back. It added one more to the difficulties which beset the inquiry after the lost money. No such sum as five hundred pounds had been paid, within the dates mentioned, to the credit of Hardyman's account.

Old Sharon was not in the least discomposed by this fresh check. "Give my love to the dear young lady," he said, with his customary impudence, "and tell her we are one degree nearer to finding the thief."

Moody looked at him, doubting whether he was in jest or in earnest.

"Must I squeeze a little more information into that thick head of yours?" asked Sharon. With this question he produced a weekly newspaper, and pointed to a paragraph which reported, among the items of sporting news, Hardyman's recent visit to a sale of horses at a town in the north of France. "We know he didn't pay the bank-note in to his account," Sharon remarked. "What else did he do with it? Took it to pay for the horses that he bought in France! Do you see your way a little plainer now? Very good. Let's try next if the money holds out. Somebody must cross the Channel in search of the note. Which of us two is to sit in the steam-boat with a white basin on his lap? Old Sharon, of course." He stopped to count the money still left out of the sum deposited by Moody to defray the cost of the inquiry. "All right!" he went on. "I've got enough to pay my ex-penses there and back. Don't stir out of London till you hear from me. I can't tell how soon I may want you. If there's any difficulty in tracing the note, your hand will have to go into your pocket again. Can't you get the lawyer to join you? Lord! how I should enjoy squandering *his* money! It's a downright disgrace to me to have only got one guinea out of him. I could tear my flesh off my bones when I think of it."

The same night Old Sharon started for France, by way of Dover and Calais.

Two days elapsed, and brought no news from Moody's agent. On the third day he received some information relating to Sharon—not from the man himself, but in a letter from Isabel Miller:

"For once, dear Robert" [she wrote], "my judgment has turned out to be sounder than yours. That hateful old man has confirmed my worst opinion of him. Pray have him punished. Take him before a magistrate and charge him with cheating you out of your money. I inclose the sealed letter which he gave me at the farmhouse. The week's time before I was to open it expired yesterday. Was there ever anything so impudent and so inhuman? I am too vexed and angry about the money you have wasted on this old wretch to write more.

"Yours, gratefully and affectionately, ISABEL."

The letter in which Old Sharon had undertaken (by way of paci-fying Isabel) to write the name of the thief, contained these lines:

"You are a charming girl, my dear; but you still want one thing to make you perfect, and that is a lesson in patience. I am proud and happy to teach you. The name of the thief remains, for the present, Mr. ———— (Blank)."

From Moody's point of view, there was but one thing to be said of this: it was just like Old Sharon! Isabel's letter was of infinitely greater interest to him. He feasted his eyes on the words above the signature; she signed herself, "Yours, gratefully and affectionately." Did the last word mean that she was really beginning to be fond of him? After kissing the word, he wrote a comforting letter to her, in which he pledged himself to keep a watchful eye on Sharon, and to trust him with no more money until he had honestly earned it first.

A week passed. Moody (longing to see Isabel) still waited in vain for news from France. He had just decided to delay his visit to South Morden no longer, when the errand-boy employed by Sharon brought him this message: "The old 'un's at home, and waitin' to see yer."

XVIII

Sharon's news was not of an encouraging character. He had met with serious difficulties, and had spent the last farthing of Moody's money in attempting to overcome them.

One discovery of importance he had certainly made. A horse withdrawn from the sale was the only horse that had met with Hardyman's approval. He had secured the animal at the high reserved price of twelve thousand francs—being four hundred and eighty pounds in English money—and he had paid with an English bank-note. The seller (a French horse-dealer resident in Brussels) had returned to Belgium immediately on completing the negotiation. Sharon had ascertained his address, and had written to him at Brussels, inclosing the number of the lost bank-note. In two days he had received an answer informing him that the horse-dealer had been called to England by the illness of a relative and that he had hitherto failed to send any address to which his letters could be forwarded. Hearing this, and having exhausted his funds, Sharon had returned to London. It now rested with Moody to decide whether the course of the inquiry should follow the horse-dealer next. There was the cash-account, showing how the money had been spent. And there was Sharon, with his pipe in his mouth and his dog on his lap, waiting for orders.

Moody wisely took time to consider before he committed himself to a decision. In the meanwhile he ventured to recommend a new course of proceeding which Sharon's report had suggested to his mind.

"It seems to me," he said, "that we have taken the roundabout way of getting to our end in view, when the straight road lay before us. If Mr. Hardyman has passed the stolen note, you know as well as I do that he has passed it innocently. Instead of wasting time and money in trying to trace a stranger, why not tell Mr. Hardyman what has happened, and ask him to give us the number of the note? You can't think of everything, I know; but it does seem strange that this idea didn't occur to you before you went to France."

"Mr. Moody," said Old Sharon, "I shall have to cut your acquaintance. You.are a man without faith; I don't like you. As if I hadn't thought of Hardyman weeks since!" he exclaimed, contemptuously. "Are you really soft enough to suppose that a gentleman in his position would talk about his money affairs to me? You know mighty little of him if you do. A fortnight since I sent one of my men (most respectfully dressed), to hang about his farm, and see what information he could pick up. My man became painfully acquainted with the toe of a boot. It was thick, sir; and it was Hardyman's."

"I will run the risk of the boot," Moody replied, in his quiet way.

"And put the question to Hardyman?"

"Yes."

"Very good," said Sharon. "If you get your answer from his tongue instead of his boot, the case is at an end—unless I have made a complete mess of it. Look here, Moody! If you want to do me a good turn, tell the lawyer that the guinea opinion was the right one. Let him know that *he* was the fool, not you, when he buttoned up his pockets and refused to trust me. And, I say!" pursued Old Sharon, relapsing into his customary impudence, "you're in love, you know, with that nice girl. I like her myself. When you marry her, invite me to the wedding. I'll make a sacrifice; I'll brush my hair and wash my face in honor of the occasion."

Returning to his lodgings, Moody found two letters waiting on the table. One of them bore the South Morden postmark. He opened that letter first.

It was written by Miss Pink. The first lines contained an urgent entreaty to keep the circumstances connected with the loss of the five hundred pounds the strictest secret from everyone in general, and from Hardyman in particular. The reasons assigned for making the strange request were next expressed in these terms: "My niece Isabel is, I am happy to inform you, engaged to be married to Mr. Hardyman. If the slightest hint reached him of her having been associated, no matter how cruelly and unjustly, with a suspicion of theft, the marriage would be broken off, and the result to herself and to everybody connected with her would be disgrace for the rest of our lives."

On the blank space at the foot of the page a few words were added in Isabel's writing: "Whatever changes there may be in my life, your place in my heart is one that no other person can fill; it is the place of my dearest friend. Pray write and tell me that you are not distressed and not angry. My one anxiety is that you should remember what I have always told you about the state of my own feelings. My one wish is that you will still let me love you and value you as I might have loved and valued a brother."

The letter dropped from Moody's hand. Not a word, not even a sigh, passed his lips. In tearless silence he submitted to the pang that wrung him—in tearless silence he contemplated the wreck of his life.

XIX

The narrative returns to South Morden and follows the events which attended Isabel's marriage engagement.

To say that Miss Pink, inflated by triumph, rose, morally speaking, from the earth, and floated among the clouds, is to indicate faintly the effect produced on the ex-school-mistress when her niece first informed her of what had happened at the farm. Attacked on one side by her aunt, and on the other by Hardyman, and feebly defended, at the best, by her own doubts and misgivings, Isabel ended in surrendering at discretion. Like thousands of other women in a similar position, she was in the last degree uncertain as to the state of her own heart. To what extent she was insensibly influenced by Hardyman's commanding position in believing herself to be sincerely attached to him, it was beyond her power of self-examination to discover. He doubly dazzled her by his birth and by his celebrity.

Not in England only, but throughout Europe, he was a recognized authority on his own subject. How could she—how could any woman—resist the influence of his steady mind, his firmness of purpose, his manly resolution to owe everything to himself, and nothing to his rank, set off, as these attractive qualities were, by the outward and personal advantages which exercise an ascendency of their own? Isabel was fascinated, and yet Isabel was not at ease. In her lonely moments she was troubled by regretful thoughts of Moody, which perplexed and irritated her. She had always behaved honestly to him; she had never encouraged him to hope that his love for her had the faintest prospect of being returned. Yet, knowing, as she did, that her conduct was blameless so far, there were, nevertheless, perverse sympathies in her which took his part. In the wakeful hours of the night there were whispering voices in her which said: Think of Moody! Had there been a growing kindness toward this good friend in her heart of which she was herself not aware? She tried to detect it—to weigh it for what it was really worth. But it lay too deep to be discovered and estimated, if it did really exist—if it had any sounder origin than her own morbid fancy. In the broad light of day, in the little bustling duties of life, she forgot it again. She could think of what she ought to wear on the wedding-day; she could even try privately how her new signature, "Isabel Hardyman," would look when she had the right to use it. On the whole, it may be said that the time passed smoothly, with some occasional checks and drawbacks, which were the more easily endured seeing that they took their rise in Isabel's own conduct. Compliant as she was in general, there were two instances, among others, in which her resolution to take her own way was not to be overcome. She refused to write either to Moody or to Lady Lydiard informing them of her engagement; and she steadily disapproved of Miss Pink's policy of concealment in the matter of the robbery at Lady Lydiard's house. Her aunt could only secure her as a passive accomplice by stating family considerations in the strongest possible terms. "If the disgrace was confined to you, my dear, I might leave you to decide. But I am involved in it, as your nearest relative; and, what is more, even the sacred memories of your father and mother might feel the slur cast on them." This exaggerated language—like all exaggerated language, a mischievous weapon in the arsenal of weakness and prejudice—had its effect on Isabel. Reluctantly and sadly she consented to be silent.

Miss Pink wrote word of the engagement to Moody first, reserving to a later day the superior pleasure of informing Lady Lydiard of the very event which that audacious woman had declared to be impossible. To her aunt's surprise, just as she was about to close the envelope, Isabel stepped forward, and inconsistently requested leave to add a postscript to the very letter which she had refused to write! Miss Pink was not even permitted to see the postscript. Isabel secured the envelope the moment she laid down her pen, and retired to her room with a headache (which was heart-ache in disguise) for the rest of the day.

While the question of the marriage was still in debate, an event occurred which exercised a serious influence on Hardyman's future plans.

He received a letter from the Continent which claimed his immediate attention. One of the sovereigns of Europe had decided on making some radical changes in the mounting and equipment of a cavalry regiment, and he required the assistance of Hardyman in that important part of the contemplated reform which was connected with the choice and purchase of horses. Setting his own interests out of the question, Hardyman owed obligations to the kindness of his illustrious correspondent which made it impossible for him to send an excuse. In a fortnight's time, at the latest, it would be necessary for him to leave England, and a month or more might elapse before it would be possible for him to return.

Under these circumstances, he proposed, in his own precipitate way, to hasten the date of the marriage. The necessary legal delay would permit the ceremony to be performed on that day fortnight. Isabel might then accompany him on his journey, and spend a brilliant honeymoon at the foreign court. She at once refused not only to accept this proposal, but even to take it into consideration. While Miss Pink dwelt eloquently on the shortness of the notice, Miss Pink's niece based her resolution on far more important grounds. Hardyman had not yet announced the contemplated marriage to his parents and friends, and Isabel was determined not to become his wife until she could be first assured of a courteous and tolerant reception by the family, if she could hope for no warmer welcome at their hands.

Hardyman was not a man who yielded easily, even in trifles. In the present case his dearest interests were concerned in inducing Isabel to reconsider her decision. He was still vainly trying to shake her resolution when the afternoon post brought a letter for Miss Pink, which introduced a new element of disturbance into the discussion. The letter was nothing less than Lady Lydiard's reply to the written announcement of Isabel's engagement, dispatched on the previous day by Miss Pink.

Her ladyship's answer was a surprising short one. It only contained these lines:

"Lady Lydiard begs to acknowledge the receipt of Miss Pink's letter requesting that she will say nothing to Mr. Hardyman of the loss of a bank-note in her house, and assigning as a reason that Miss Isabel Miller is engaged to be married to Mr. Hardyman, and might be prejudiced in his estimation if the facts were made known. Miss Pink may make her mind easy. Lady Lydiard has not the slightest intention of taking Mr. Hardyman into her confidence on the subject of her domestic affairs. With regard to the proposed marriage, Lady Lydiard casts no doubt on Miss Pink's perfect sincerity and good faith; but, at the same time, she positively declines to believe that Mr. Hardyman means to make Miss Isabel Miller his wife. Lady L. will yield to the evidence of a properly attested certificate—and to nothing else."

A folded piece of paper, directed to Isabel, dropped out of this characteristic letter as Miss Pink turned from the first page to the second. Lady Lydiard addressed her adopted daughter in these words:

"I was on the point of leaving home to visit you again, when I received your aunt's letter. My poor deluded child, no words can tell how distressed I am about you. You are already sacrificed to the folly of the most foolish woman living. For God's sake take care you do not fall a victim next to the designs of a profligate man! Come to me instantly, Isabel, and I promise to take care of you."

Fortified by these letters, and aided by Miss Pink's indignation, Hardyman pressed his proposal on Isabel with renewed resolution. She made no attempt to combat his arguments—she only held firmly by her decision. Without some encouragement from Hardyman's father and mother she still steadily refused to become his wife. Irritated already by Lady Lydiard's letters, he lost the self-command which so eminently distinguished him in the ordinary affairs of life, and showed the domineering and despotic temper which was an inbred part of his disposition. Isabel's high spirit at once resented the harsh terms in which he spoke to her. In the plainest words she released him from his engagement, and, without waiting for his excuses, quitted the room.

Left together, Hardyman and Miss Pink devised an arrangement which paid due respect to Isabel's scruples, and at the same time met Lady Lydiard's insulting assertion of disbelief in Hardyman's honor, by a formal and public announcement of the marriage.

It was proposed to give a garden party at the farm in a week's time, for the express purpose of introducing Isabel to Hardyman's family and friends in the character of his betrothed wife. If his father and mother accepted the invitation, Isabel's only objection to hastening their union would fall to the ground. Hardyman might in that case plead with his imperial correspondent for a delay in his departure of a few days more; and the marriage might still take place before he left England. Isabel, at Miss Pink's intercession, was induced to accept her lover's excuses, and, in the event of her favorable reception by Hardyman's parents at the farm, to give her consent (not very willingly even yet) to hastening the ceremony which was to make her Hardyman's wife.

On the next morning the whole of the invitations was sent out, excepting the invitation to Hardyman's father and mother. Without mentioning it to Isabel, Hardyman decided on personally appealing to his mother before he ventured on taking the head of the family into his confidence.

The result of the interview was partially successful—and no more. Lord Rotherfield declined to see his youngest son; and he had engagements which would, under any circumstances, prevent his being present at the garden-party. But, at the express request of Lady Rotherfield, he was willing to make certain concessions.

"I have always regarded Alfred as a barely sane person," said his lordship, "since he turned his back on his prospects to become a horse-dealer. If we decline altogether to sanction this new act—I won't say of insanity, I will say of absurdity—on his part, it is impossible to predict to what discreditable extremities he may not proceed. We must temporize with Alfred. In the meantime I shall endeavor to obtain some information respecting this young person —named Miller, I think you said, and now resident at South

Morden. If I am satisfied that she is a woman of reputable character, possessing an average education and presentable manners, we
may as well let Alfred take his own way. He is out of the pale of
society, as it is; and Miss Miller has no father and mother to com-
plicate matters, which is distinctly a merit on her part—and, in
short, if the marriage is not absolutely disgraceful, the wisest way
(as we have no power to prevent it) will be to submit. You will say
nothing to Alfred about what I propose to do. I tell you plainly I
don't trust him. You will simply inform him from me that I want
time to consider, and that, unless he hears to the contrary in the
interval, he may expect to have the sanction of your presence at his
breakfast, or luncheon, or whatever it is. I must go to town in a day
or two, and I shall ascertain what Alfred's friends know about this
last of his many follies, if I meet any of them at the club."

Returning to South Morden in no serene frame of mind, Hardyman found Isabel in a state of depression which perplexed and
alarmed him.

The news that his mother might be expected to be present at the
garden-party failed entirely to raise her spirits. The only explanation
she gave of the change in her was that the dull, heavy weather of the
last few days made her feel a little languid and nervous. Naturally
dissatisfied with this reply to his inquiries, Hardyman asked for Miss
Pink. He was informed that Miss Pink could not see him. She was
constitutionally subject to asthma, and having warnings of a return
of the malady, she was (by the doctor's advice) keeping her room.
Hardyman returned to the farm in a temper which was felt by
everybody in his employment, from the trainer to the stable-boys.

While the apology made for Miss Pink stated no more than the
plain truth, it must be confessed that Hardyman was right in declin-
ing to be satisfied with Isabel's excuse for the melancholy that op-
pressed her. She had that morning received Moody's answer to the
lines which she had addressed to him at the end of her aunt's letter,
and she had not yet recovered from the effect which it had produced
on her spirits.

"It is impossible for me to say honestly that I am not distressed"
[Moody wrote] "by the news of your marriage engagement. The
blow has fallen very heavily on me. When I look at the future now, I
see only a dreary blank. This is not your fault; you are in no way to
blame. I remember the time when I should have been too angry to

own this—when I might have said or done things which I should have bitterly repented afterward. That time is past. My temper has been softened since I have befriended you in your troubles. That good at least has come out of my foolish hopes, and perhaps also out of the true sympathy which I have felt for you. I can honestly ask you to accept my heart's dearest wishes for your happiness, and I can keep the rest to myself.

"Let me say a word now relating to the efforts that I have made to help you since that sad day when you left Lady Lydiard's house.

"I had hoped (for reasons which it is needless to mention here) to interest Mr. Hardyman himself in aiding our inquiry. But your aunt's wishes, as expressed in her letter to me, close my lips. I will only ask you, at some convenient time, to let me mention the last discoveries that we have made; leaving it to your discretion, when Mr. Hardyman has become your husband, to ask him the questions which, under other circumstances, I should have put to him myself.

"It is, of course, possible that the view I take of Mr. Hardyman's capacity to help us may be a mistaken one. In this case, if you still wish the investigation to be privately carried on, I beg of you to let me continue to direct it, as the greatest favor you can confer on your devoted friend.

"You need be under no apprehension about the expense to which you are likely to put me. I have unexpectedly inherited what is to me a handsome fortune.

"The same post which brought your aunt's letter brought a line from a lawyer, asking me to see him on the subject of my late father's affairs. I waited a day or two before I could summon heart enough to see him, or to see anybody; and then I went to his office. You have heard that my father's bank stopped payment, at a time of commercial panic. His failure was mainly attributable to the treachery of a friend to whom he had lent a large sum of money, and who paid him the yearly interest without acknowledging that every farthing of it had been lost in unsuccessful speculations. The son of this man has prospered in business, and he has honorably devoted a part of his wealth to the payment of his father's creditors. Half the sum due to *my* father has thus passed into my hands as his next of kin, and the other half is to follow in course of time. If my hopes had been fulfilled, how gladly I should have shared my prosperity with you! As it is, I have far more than enough for my wants as a lonely man, and plenty left to spend in your service.

"God bless and prosper you, my dear. I shall ask you to accept a little present from me, among the other offerings that are made to you before the wedding-day.

R. M."

The studiously considerate and delicate tone in which these lines were written had an effect on Isabel which was exactly the opposite of the effect intended by the writer. She burst into a passionate fit of tears, and in the safe solitude of her room the despairing words escaped her, "I wish I had died before I met with Alfred Hardyman!"

As the days wore on, disappointments and difficulties seemed, by a kind of fatality, to beset the contemplated announcement of the marriage.

Miss Pink's asthma, developed by the unfavorable weather, set the doctor's art at defiance, and threatened to keep that unfortunate lady a prisoner in her room on the day of the party. Hardyman's invitations were in some cases refused, and in others accepted by husbands, with excuses for the absence of their wives. His elder brother made an apology for himself as well as for his wife. Felix Sweetsir wrote, "With pleasure, dear Alfred, if my health permits me to leave the house." Lady Lydiard, invited at Miss Pink's special request, sent no reply. The one encouraging circumstance was the silence of Lady Rotherfield. So long as her son received no intimation to the contrary, it was a sign that Lord Rotherfield permitted his wife to sanction the marriage by her presence.

Hardyman wrote to his imperial correspondent, engaging to leave England on the earliest possible day, and asking to be pardoned if he failed to express himself more definitely, in consideration of domestic affairs which it was necessary to settle before he started for the Continent. If there should not be time enough to write again, he promised to send a telegraphic announcement of his departure. Long afterward Hardyman remembered the misgivings that had troubled him when he wrote that letter. In the rough draft of it he had mentioned, as his excuse for not being yet certain of his own movements, that he expected to be immediately married. In the fair copy the vague foreboding of some accident to come was so painfully present to his mind that he struck out the words which referred to his marriage and substituted the designedly indefinite phrase, "domestic affairs."

XX

The day of the garden-party arrived. There was no rain, but the air was heavy, and the sky was overcast by lowering clouds.

Some hours before the guests were expected Isabel arrived alone at the farm, bearing the apologies of unfortunate Miss Pink, still kept a prisoner in her bed-chamber by the asthma. In the confusion produced at the cottage by the preparations for entertaining the company, the one room in which Hardyman could receive Isabel with the certainty of not being interrupted was the smoking-room. To this haven of refuge he led her—still reserved and silent, still not restored to her customary spirits. "If any visitors come before the time," Hardyman said to his servant, "tell them I am engaged at the stables—I must have an hour's quiet talk with you," he continued, turning to Isabel, "or I shall be in too bad a temper to receive my guests with common politeness. The worry of giving this party is not to be told in words. I almost wish I had been content with presenting you to my mother, and had let the rest of my acquaintance go to the devil."

A quiet half hour passed, and the first visitor, a stranger to the servants, appeared at the cottage gate. He was a middle-aged man, and he had no wish to disturb Mr. Hardyman. "I will wait in the grounds," he said, "and trouble nobody." The middle-aged man who expressed himself in these modest terms was Robert Moody.

Five minutes later a carriage drove up to the gate. An elderly lady got out ot it, followed by a fat white Scotch terrier that growled at every stranger within his reach. It is needless to introduce Lady Lydiard and Tommie.

Informed that Mr. Hardyman was at the stables, Lady Lydiard gave the servant her card. "Take that to your master, and say I won't detain him five minutes." With these words her ladyship sauntered into the grounds. She looked about her with observant eyes, not only noticing the tent which had been set up on the grass to accommodate the expected guests, but entering it, and looking at the waiters who were engaged in placing the luncheon on the table. Returning to the outer world, she next remarked that Mr. Hardyman's lawn was in very bad order. Barren, sun-dried patches, and little holes and crevices opened here and there by the action of the summer heat, announced that the lawn, like everything else at the farm, had been neglected in the exclusive attention paid to the claims of the horses. Reaching a shrubbery which bounded one side of the grounds next, her ladyship became aware of a man slowly approaching her, to all appearance absorbed in thought. The man drew a little nearer. She lifted her glasses to her eyes, and recognized—Moody.

No embarrassment was produced on either side by this unexpected meeting. Lady Lydiard had, not long since, sent to ask her former steward to visit her, regretting in her warm-hearted way the terms on which they had separated, and wishing to atone for the harsh language that had escaped her at their parting interview. In the friendly talk which followed the reconciliation, Lady Lydiard not only heard the news of Moody's pecuniary inheritance, but, noticing the change in his appearance for the worse, contrived to extract from him the confession of his ill-starred passion for Isabel. To discover him now, after all that he had acknowledged, walking about the grounds at Hardyman's farm, took her ladyship completely by surprise. "Good heavens!" she exclaimed, in her loudest tones, "what are *you* doing here?"

"You mentioned Mr. Hardyman's garden-party, my lady, when I had the honor of waiting on you," Moody answered. "Thinking over it, afterward, it seemed the fittest occasion I could find for making a little wedding-present to Miss Isabel. Is there any harm in my asking Mr. Hardyman to let me put the present on her plate, so that she may see it when she sits down to luncheon? If your ladyship thinks so I will go away directly, and send the gift by post."

Lady Lydiard looked at him attentively. "You don't despise the girl," she asked, "for selling herself for rank and money? I do, I can tell you."

Moody's worn white face flushed a little. "No, my lady, I can't hear you say that. Isabel would not have engaged herself to Mr. Hardyman unless she had been fond of him—as fond, I dare say, as I once hoped she might be of me. It's a hard thing to confess that; but I do confess it, in justice to her—God bless her!"

The generosity that spoke in those simple words touched the finest sympathies in Lady Lydiard's nature. "Give me your hand," she said, with her own generous spirit kindling in her eyes. "You have a good heart, Moody. Isabel Miller is a fool for not marrying *you*—and one day she will know it."

Before a word more could pass between them, Hardyman's voice was audible on the other side of the shrubbery, calling irritably to his servant to find Lady Lydiard.

Moody retired to the further end of the walk, while Lady Lydiard advanced in the opposite direction, so as to meet Hardyman at the entrance to the shrubbery. He bowed stiffly, and begged to know why her ladyship had honored him with a visit.

Lady Lydiard replied, without noticing the coldness of her reception:

"I have not been very well, Mr. Hardyman, or you would have seen me before this. My only object in presenting myself here is to make my excuses personally for having written of you in terms which expressed a doubt of your honor. I have done you an injustice, and I beg you to forgive me."

Hardyman acknowledged this frank apology as unreservedly as it had been offered to him. "Say no more, Lady Lydiard. And let me hope, now you are here, that you will honor my little party with your presence."

Lady Lydiard gravely stated her reasons for not accepting the invitation.

"I disapprove so strongly of unequal marriages," she said, walking on slowly toward the cottage, "that I can not, in common consistency, become one of your guests. I shall always feel interested in Isabel Miller's welfare; and I can honestly say I shall be glad if your married life proves that my old-fashioned prejudices are without justification in your case. Accept my thanks for your invitation, and let me hope that my plain-speaking has not offended you."

She bowed and looked about her for Tommie before she advanced to the carriage waiting for her at the gate. In the surprise of seeing Moody, she had forgotten to look back for the dog when she entered the shrubbery. She now called to him, and blew the whistle at her watch-chain. Not a sign of Tommie was to be seen. Hardyman instantly directed the servants to search in the cottage and out of the cottage for the dog. The order was obeyed with all needful activity and intelligence, and entirely without success. For the time being, at any rate, Tommie was lost.

Hardyman promised to have the dog looked for in every part of the farm, and to send him back in the care of one of his own men. With these polite assurances Lady Lydiard was obliged to be satisfied. She drove away in a very despondent frame of mind. "First

Isabel, and now Tommie," thought her ladyship. "I am losing the only companions who made life tolerable to me."

Returning from the garden-gate, after taking leave of his visitor, Hardyman received from his servant a handful of letters which had just arrived for him. Walking slowly over the lawn as he opened them, he found nothing but excuses for the absence of guests who had already accepted their invitations. He had just thrust the letters into his pocket, when he heard footsteps behind him, and, looking round, found himself confronted by Moody.

"Halloo! have you come here to lunch?" Hardyman asked, roughly.

"I have come here, sir, with a little gift for Miss Isabel, in honor of her marriage," Moody answered, quietly. "And I ask your permission to put it on the table, so that she may see it when your guests sit down to luncheon."

He opened a jeweler's case as he spoke, containing a plain gold bracelet with an inscription engraved on the inner side: "To Miss Isabel Miller, with the sincere good wishes of Robert Moody."

Plain as it was, the design of the bracelet was unusually beautiful. Hardyman had noticed Moody's agitation on the day when he had met Isabel near her aunt's house, and had drawn his own conclusions from it. His face darkened with a momentary jealousy, as he looked at the bracelet. "All right, old fellow!" he said, with contemptuous familiarity. "Don't be modest. Wait and give it to her with your own hand."

"No, sir," said Moody. "I would rather leave it, if you please, to speak for itself."

Hardyman understood the delicacy of feeling which dictated those words, and, without well knowing why, resented it. He was on the point of speaking, under the influence of this unworthy feeling, when Isabel's voice reached his ears, calling to him from the cottage.

Moody's face contracted with a sudden expression of pain as he, too, recognized the voice. "Don't let me detain you, sir," he said, sadly. "Good-morning!"

Hardyman left him without ceremony. Moody, slowly following, entered the tent. All the preparations for the luncheon had been completed; nobody was there. The places to be occupied by the guests were indicated by cards bearing their names. Moody found Isabel's card, and put his bracelet inside the folded napkin on her plate. For a while he stood with his hand on the table, thinking. The temptation to communicate once more with Isabel before he lost her forever was fast getting the better of his powers of resistance. "If I could persuade her to write a word to say she liked her bracelet," he thought, "it would be a comfort when I go back to my solitary life." He tore a leaf out of his pocket-book, and wrote on it: "One line to say you accept my gift and my good wishes. Put it under the cushion of your chair, and I shall find it when the company have left the tent." He slipped the paper into the case which held the bracelet, and instead of leaving the farm as he had intended, turned back to the shelter of the shrubbery.

XXI

Hardyman went on to the cottage. He found Isabel in some agitation. And there by her side, with his tail wagging slowly, and his eye on Hardyman in expectation of a possible kick—there was the lost Tommie!

"Has Lady Lydiard gone?" Isabel asked, eagerly.

"Yes," said Hardyman. "Where did you find the dog?"

As events had ordered it, the dog had found Isabel—under these circumstances.

The appearance of Lady Lydiard's card in the smoking-room had been an alarming event for Lady Lydiard's adopted daughter. She was guiltily conscious of not having answered her ladyship's note, inclosed in Miss Pink's letter, and of not having taken her ladyship's advice in resisting the advances of Hardyman. As he rose to leave the room and receive his visitor in the grounds, Isabel entreated him to say nothing of her presence at the farm, unless Lady Lydiard exhibited a forgiving turn of mind by asking to see her. Left by herself in the smoking-room, she suddenly heard a bark in the passage which had a familiar sound in her ears. She opened the door and in rushed Tommie, with one of his shrieks of delight. Curiosity had taken him into the house. He had heard the voices in the smoking-room, had recognized Isabel's voice, and had waited, with his customary cunning and his customary distrust of strangers, until Hardyman was out of the way. Isabel kissed and caressed him, and then drove him out again to the lawn, fearing that Lady Lydiard might return to look for him. Going back to the smoking-room, she stood at the window watching for Hardyman's return. When the servants came in to look for the dog, she could only tell them that she had last seen him in the grounds, not far from the cottage. The useless search being abandoned, and the carriage having left the gate, who should crawl out from the back of a cupboard in which some empty hampers were placed but Tommie himself! How he had contrived to get back to the smoking-room (unless she had omitted to completely close the door on her return) it was impossible to say. But there he was, determined this time to stay with Isabel, and keeping in his hiding-place until he heard the movement of the carriage-wheels, which informed him that his lawful mistress had left the cottage. Isabel had at once called to Hardyman, on the chance that the carriage might yet be stopped. It was already out of sight, and nobody knew which of two roads it had taken, both leading to London. In this emergency Isabel could only look at Hardyman and ask what was to be done.

"I can't spare a servant till after the party," he answered. "The dog must be tied up at the stables."

Isabel shook her head. Tommie was not accustomed to be tied up. He would make a disturbance, and he would be beaten by the grooms. "I will take care of him," she said. "He won't leave me."

"There's something else to think of besides the dog," Hardyman rejoined, irritably. "Look at these letters!" He pulled them out of his pocket as he spoke. "Here are no less than seven men, all calling themselves my friends, who accepted my invitation, and who write to excuse themselves on the very day of the party! Do you know why? They're all afraid of my father: I forgot to tell you he's a cabinet minister as well as a lord. Cowards and cads! They have heard he isn't coming, and they wish to curry favor with the great man by stopping away. Come along, Isabel! Let's take their names off the luncheon-table. Not a man of them shall ever darken my doors again!"

"I am to blame for what has happened," Isabel answered, sadly. "I am estranging you from your friends. There is still time, Alfred, to alter your mind and let me go."

He put his arm round her with rough fondness. "I would sacrifice every friend I have in the world rather than lose you. Come along!"

They left the cottage. At the entrance of the tent Hardyman noticed the dog at Isabel's heels, and vented his ill-temper, as usual with male humanity, on the nearest unoffending creature that he could find. "Be off, you mongrel brute!" he shouted. The tail of Tommie relaxed from its customary tight curve over the small of his back, and the legs of Tommie (with his tail between them) took him at full gallop to the friendly shelter of the cupboard in the smoking-room. It was one of those trifling circumstances which women notice seriously. Isabel said nothing; she only thought to herself, "I wish he had shown his temper when I first knew him!"

They entered the tent.

"I'll read the names," said Hardyman, "and you find the cards and tear them up. Stop! I'll keep the cards. You're just the sort of woman my father likes. He'll be reconciled to me when he sees you, after we are married. If one of those men ever asks him for a place, I'll take care, if it's years hence, to put an obstacle in his way. Here, take my pencil, and make a mark on the cards to remind me; the same mark I set against a horse in my book when I don't like him—a cross enclosed in a circle." He produced his pocket-book. His hands trembled with anger as he gave the pencil to Isabel and laid the book on the table. He had just read the name of the first false friend, and Isabel had just found the card, when a servant appeared with a message: "Mrs. Drumblade has arrived, sir, and wishes to see you on a matter of the greatest importance."

Hardyman left the tent, not very willingly. "Wait here," he said to Isabel; "I'll be back directly."

She was standing near her own place at the table. Moody had left one end of the jeweler's case visible above the napkin to attract her attention. In a minute more the bracelet and the note were in her hands. She dropped on her chair, overwhelmed by the conflicting emotions that rose in her at the sight of the bracelet, at the reading of the note. Her head drooped, and the tears filled her eyes. "Are all women as blind as I have been to what is good and noble in the men who love them?" she wondered, sadly. "Better as it is," she thought, with a bitter sigh; "I am not worthy of him."

As she took up the pencil to write her answer to Moody on the back of her dinner-card, the servant appeared again at the door of the tent.

"My master wants you at the cottage, miss, immediately."

Isabel rose, putting the bracelet and the note in the silver-mounted leather pocket (a present from Hardyman) which hung at her belt. In the hurry of passing round the table to get out she never noticed that her dress touched Hardyman's pocket-book, placed close to the edge, and threw it down on the grass below. The book fell into one of the heat-cracks which Lady Lydiard had noticed as evidence of the neglected condition of the cottage-lawn.

"You ought to hear the pleasant news my sister has just brought me," said Hardyman when Isabel joined him in the parlor. "Mrs. Drumblade has been told, on the best authority, that my mother is not coming to the party."

"There must be some reason, of course, dear Isabel," added Mrs. Drumblade. "Have you any idea of what it can be? I haven't seen my mother myself, and all my inquiries have failed to find it out."

She looked searchingly at Isabel as she spoke. The mask of sympathy on her face was admirably worn. Nobody who possessed only a superficial acquaintance with Mrs. Drumblade's character would have suspected how thoroughly she was enjoying in secret the position of embarrassment in which her news had placed her brother. Instinctively doubting whether Mrs. Drumblade's friendly behavior was quite so sincere as it appeared to be, Isabel answered that she was a stranger to Lady Rotherfield, and was therefore quite at a loss to explain the cause of her ladyship's absence. As she spoke, the guests began to arrive in quick succession, and the subject was dropped, as a matter of course.

It was not a merry party. Hardyman's approaching marriage had been made the topic of much malicious gossip, and Isabel's character had, as usual in such cases, become the object of all the false reports that scandal could invent. Lady Rotherfield's absence confirmed the general conviction that Hardyman was disgracing himself. The men were all more or less uneasy. The women resented the discovery that Isabel was, personally speaking at least, beyond the reach of hostile criticism. Her beauty was viewed as a downright offense; her refined and modest manners were set down as perfect acting—"Really disgusting my dear, in so young a girl." General Drumblade—a large and moldy veteran, in a state of chronic astonishment (after his own matrimonial experience) at Hardyman's folly at marrying at all—diffused a wide circle of gloom wherever he went and whatever he did. His accomplished wife, forcing her high spirits on everybody's attention with a sort of kittenish playfulness, intensified the depressing effect of the general dullness by all the force of the strongest contrast. After waiting half an hour for his mother, and waiting in vain, Hardyman led the way to the tent in despair. "The sooner I fill their stomachs and get rid of them," he thought, savagely, "the better I shall be pleased."

The luncheon was attacked by the company with a certain silent ferocity, which the waiters noticed as remarkable, even in their large experience. The men drank deeply, but with wonderfully little effect in raising their spirits; the women, with the exception of amiable Mrs. Drumblade, kept Isabel deliberatly out of the conversation that went on among them. General Drumblade, sitting next to her in one of the places of honor, discoursed to Isabel privately on "my brother-in-law Hardyman's infernal temper." A young marquis, on the other side—a mere lad, chosen to make the necessary speech in acknowledgment of his superior rank—rose, in a state of nervous trepidation, to propose Isabel's health as the chosen bride of their host. Pale and trembling, conscious of having forgotten the words he learned beforehand, this unhappy young nobleman began, "Ladies and gentlemen, I haven't an idea——" He stopped, put his hand to his head, stared wildly, and sat down again, having contrived to state his own case with masterly brevity and perfect truth in a speech of seven words.

While the dismay in some cases and the amusement in others was still at its height, Hardyman's valet made his appearance, and approaching his master, said, in a whisper, "Could I speak to you, sir, for a moment outside?"

"What the devil do you want?" Hardyman asked, irritably. "Is that a letter in your hand? Give it to me."

The valet was a Frenchman. In other words, he had a sense of what was due to himself. His master had forgotten this. He gave up the letter with a certain dignity of manner, and left the tent. Hardyman opened the letter. He turned pale as he read it, crumpled it in his hands, and threw it down on the table. "By G—d, it's a lie!" he exclaimed, furiously.

The guests rose in confusion. Mrs. Drumblade, finding the letter within her reach, coolly possessed herself of it, recognized her mother's handwriting, and read these lines:

"I have only now succeeded in persuading your father to let me write to you. For God's sake, break off your marriage at any sacrifice. Your father has heard, on unanswerable authority, that Miss Isabel Miller left her situation in Lady Lydiard's house on suspicion of theft."

While his sister was reading this letter, Hardyman had made his way to Isabel's chair. "I must speak to you directly," he whispered.

"Come away with me." He turned, as he took her arm, and looked at the table. "Where is my letter?" he asked. Mrs. Drumblade handed it to him, dexterously crumpled up again, as she had found it.

"No bad news, dear Alfred, I hope?" she said, in her most affectionate manner. Hardyman snatched the letter from her, without answering, and led Isabel out of the tent.

"Read that!" he said, when they were alone. "And tell me at once whether it's true or false."

Isabel read the letter. For a moment the shock of the discovery held her speechless. She recovered herself, and returned the letter.

"It is true," she answered.

Hardyman staggered back as if she had shot him.

"True that you are guilty?" he asked.

"No; I am innocent. Everybody who knows me believes in my innocence. It is true that the appearances were against me. They are against me still." Having said this, she waited, quietly and firmly, for his next words.

He passed his hand over his forehead with a sigh of relief. "It's bad enough as it is," he said, speaking quietly on his side. "But the remedy for it is plain enough. Come back to the tent."

She never moved. "Why?" she asked.

"Do you suppose I don't believe in your innocence, too?" he answered. "The one way of setting you right with the world is for me to make you my wife, in spite of the appearances that point to you. I'm too fond of you, Isabel, to give you up. Come back with me, and I will announce our marriage to my friends."

She took his hand and kissed it. "It is generous and good of you," she said; "but it must not be."

He took a step nearer to her. "What do you mean?" he asked.

"It was against my will," she pursued, "that my aunt concealed the truth from you. I did wrong to consent to it; I will do wrong no more. Your mother is right, Alfred. After what has happened, I am not fit to be your wife until my innocence is proved. It is not proved yet."

The angry color began to rise in his face once more. "Take care," he said; "I am not in a humor to be trifled with."

"I am not trifling with you," she answered, in low, sad tones.

"You really mean what you say?"

"I mean it."

"Don't be obstinate, Isabel. Take time to consider."

"You are very kind, Alfred. My duty is plain to me. I will marry you—if you still wish it—when my good name is restored to me—not before."

He laid one hand on her arm, and pointed with the other to the guests in the distance, all leaving the tent on the way to their carriages.

"Your good name will be restored to you," he said, "on the day when I make you my wife. The worst enemy you have can not associate *my* name with a suspicion of theft. Remember that, and think a little before you decide. You see those people there. If you don't change your mind by the time they have got to the cottage, it's good-bye between us, and good-bye forever. I refuse to wait for you; I refuse to accept a conditional engagement. Wait, and think. They're walking slowly; you have got some minutes more."

He still held her arm, watching the guests as they gradually receded from view. It was not until they had all collected in a group outside the cottage door that he spoke himself, or that he permitted Isabel to speak again.

"Now," he said, "you have had your time to get cool. Will you take my arm and join those people with me, or will you say good-bye forever?"

"Forgive me, Alfred," she began, gently. "I can not consent, in justice to you, to shelter myself behind your name. It is the name of your family, and they have a right to expect that you will not degrade it——"

"I want a plain answer," he interposed, sternly. "Which is it? Yes or no?"

She looked at him with sad, compassionate eyes. Her voice was firm as she answered him in the one word he had desired. The word was—"No!"

Without speaking to her, without even looking at her, he turned and walked back to the cottage.

Making his way silently through the group of visitors—every one of whom had been informed of what had happened by his sister—with his head down and his lips fast closed, he entered the parlor, and rang the bell which communicated with his foreman's room at the stables.

"You know that I am going abroad on business?" he said, when the man appeared.

"Yes, sir."

"I am going to-day—going by the night train to Dover. Order the horse to be put to instantly in the dog-cart. Is there anything wanted before I am off?"

The inexorable necessities of business asserted their claims through the obedient medium of the foreman. Chafing at the delay, Hardyman was obliged to sit at his desk, signing checks and passing accounts, with the dog-cart waiting in the stable-yard.

A knock at the door startled him in the middle of his work. "Come in!" he called out, sharply.

He looked up, expecting to see one of the guests or one of the servants. It was Moody who entered the room. Hardyman laid down his pen, and fixed his eyes sternly on the man who had dared to interrupt him.

"What the devil do *you* want?" he asked.

"I have seen Miss Isabel, and spoken with her," Moody replied. "Mr. Hardyman, I believe it is in your power to set this matter right. For the young lady's sake, sir, you must not leave England without doing it."

Hardyman turned to his foreman. "Is this fellow mad or drunk?" he asked.

Moody proceeded as calmly and as resolutely as if those words had not been spoken. "I apologize for my intrusion, sir. I will trouble you with no explanations; I will only ask one question. Have you a memorandum of the number of that five-hundred-pound note which you paid away in France?"

Hardyman lost all control over himself.

"You scoundrel!" he cried; "have you been prying into my private affairs? Is it *your* business to know what I did in France?"

"Is it *your* vengeance on a woman to refuse to tell her the number of a bank-note?" Moody rejoined, firmly.

That answer forced its way through Hardyman's anger to Hardyman's sense of honor. He rose and advanced to Moody. For a moment the two men faced each other in silence. "You're a bold fellow," said Hardyman, with a sudden change from anger to irony. "I'll do the lady justice. I'll look at my pocket-book."

He put his hand into the breast-pocket of his coat; he searched his other pockets; he turned over the objects on his writing-table. The book was gone.

Moody watched him with a feeling of despair. "Oh, Mr. Hardyman, don't say you have lost your pocket-book!"

He sat down again at his desk, with sullen submission to the new disaster. "All I can say is, you're at liberty to look for it," he replied. "I must have dropped it somewhere." He turned impatiently to the foreman. "Now, then, what is the next check wanted? I shall go mad if I wait in this d——d place much longer."

Moody left him, and found his way to the servants' offices. "Mr. Hardyman has lost his pocket-book," he said. "Look for it, in-doors and out, on the lawn and in the tent. Ten pounds reward for the man who finds it!"

Servants and waiters instantly dispersed, eager for the promised reward. The men who pursued the search outside the cottage divided their forces. Some of them examined the lawn and the flower beds; others went straight to the empty tent. These last were too completely absorbed in pursuing the object in view to notice that they disturbed a dog eating a stolen lunch of his own from the morsels left on the plates. The dog slunk away under the canvas when the men came in, waiting in hiding until they had gone, then returned to the tent and went on with his luncheon.

Moody hastened back to the part of the grounds (close to the shrubbery) in which Isabel was waiting his return.

She looked at him, while he was telling her of his interview with Hardyman, with an expression in her eyes which he had never seen in them before—an expression which set his heart beating wildly, and made him break off in his narrative before he had reached the end.

"I understand," she said, quietly, as he stopped in confusion. "You have made one more sacrifice to my welfare. Robert, I believe you are the noblest man that ever breathed the breath of life!"

His eyes sunk before hers; he blushed like a boy. "I have done nothing for you yet," he said. "Don't despair of the future if the pocket-book should not be found. I know who the man is who received the bank-note, and I have only to find him to decide the question whether it *is* the stolen note or not."

She smiled sadly at his enthusiasm. "Are you going back to Mr. Sharon to help you?" she asked. "That trick he played me has destroyed *my* belief in him. He no more knows than I do who the thief really is."

"You are mistaken, Isabel. He knows, and I know." He stopped there, and made a sign to her to be silent. One of the servants was approaching them.

"Is the pocket-book found?" Moody asked.

"No, sir."

"Has Mr. Hardyman left the cottage?"

"He has just gone, sir. Have you any further instructions to give us?"

"No. There is my address in London if the pocket-book should be found."

The man took the card that was handed to him, and retired. Moody offered his arm to Isabel. "I am at your service," he said, "when you wish to return to your aunt."

They had advanced nearly as far as the tent, on their way out of the grounds, when they were met by a gentleman walking toward them from the cottage. He was a stranger to Isabel. Moody immediately recognized him as Mr. Felix Sweetsir.

"Ha! our good Moody!" cried Felix. "Enviable man! you look younger than ever." He took off his hat to Isabel; his bright, restless eyes suddenly became quiet as they rested on her. "Have I the honor of addressing the future Mrs. Hardyman? May I offer my best congratulations? What has become of our friend Alfred?"

Moody answered for Isabel. "If you will make inquiries at the cottage, sir," he said, "you will find that you are mistaken, to say the least of it, in addressing your questions to this young lady."

Felix took off his hat again with the most becoming appearance of surprise and distress.

"Something wrong, I fear," he said, addressing Isabel. "I am indeed ashamed if I have ignorantly given you a moment's pain. Pray accept my most sincere apologies. I have only this instant arrived; my health would not allow me to be present at the luncheon. Permit me to express the earnest hope that matters may be set right, to the satisfaction of all parties. Good-afternoon."

He bowed with elaborate courtesy, and turned back to the cottage.

"Who is that?" Isabel asked.

"Lady Lydiard's nephew, Mr. Felix Sweetsir," Moody answered, with a sudden sternness of tone and a sudden coldness of manner which surprised Isabel.

"You don't like him?" she said.

As she spoke, Felix stopped to give audience to one of the grooms, who had, apparently, been sent with a message to him. He turned so that his face was once more visible to Isabel. Moody pressed her hand significantly as it rested on his arm.

"Look well at that man," he whispered. "It's time to warn you. Mr. Felix Sweetsir is the worst enemy you have!"

Isabel heard him in speechless astonishment. He went on in tones that trembled with suppressed emotion.

"You doubt if Sharon knows the thief. You doubt if I know the thief. Isabel, as certainly as the heaven is above us, there stands the wretch who stole the bank-note!"

She drew her hand out of his arm with a cry of terror. She looked at him as if she doubted whether he was in his right mind.

He took her hand, and waited a moment, trying to compose himself.

"Listen to me," he said. "At the first consultation I had with Sharon he gave this advice to Mr. Troy and to me. He said, 'Suspect the very last person on whom suspicion could possibly fall.' Those words, taken with the questions he had asked before he pronounced his opinion, struck through me as if he had struck me with a knife. I instantly suspected Lady Lydiard's nephew. Wait! From that time to this I have said nothing of my suspicion to any living soul. I knew in my own heart that it took its rise in the inveterate dislike that I have always felt for Mr. Sweetsir, and I distrusted it accordingly. But I went back to Sharon, for all that, and put the case into his hands. His investigations informed me that Mr. Sweetsir owed 'debts of honor' (as gentlemen call them), incurred through lost bets, to a large number of persons, and among them a bet of five hundred pounds lost to Mr. Hardyman. Further inquiries showed that Mr. Hardyman had taken the lead in declaring that he would post Mr. Sweetsir as a defaulter, and have him turned out of his clubs, and turned out of the betting-ring. Ruin stared him in the face if he failed to pay his debt to Mr. Hardyman on the last day left to him—the day after the note was lost. On that very morning Lady Lydiard, speaking to me of her nephew's visit to her, said, 'If I had given him an opportunity of speaking, Felix would have borrowed money of me; I saw it in his face.' One moment more, Isabel. I am not only certain that Mr. Sweetsir took the five-hundred-pound note out of the open letter, I am firmly persuaded that he is the man who told Lord Rotherfield of the circumstances under which you left Lady Lydiard's house. Your marriage to Mr. Hardyman might have put you in a position to detect the theft. You, not I, might in that case have discovered from your husband that the stolen note was the note with which Mr. Sweetsir paid his debt. He came here, you may depend on it, to make sure that he had succeeded in destroying your prospects. A more depraved villain at heart than that man never swung from a gallows!"

He checked himself at those words. The shock of the disclosure, the passion and vehemence with which he spoke, overwhelmed Isabel. She trembled like a frightened child.

While he was still trying to soothe and reassure her a low whining made itself heard at their feet. They looked down, and saw Tommie. Finding himself noticed at last, he expressed his sense of relief by a bark. Something dropped out of his mouth. As Moody stooped to pick it up, the dog ran to Isabel and pushed his head against her feet, as his way was when he expected to have the handkerchief thrown over him preparatory to one of those games at hide-and-seek which have been already mentioned. Isabel put out her hand to caress him, when she was stopped by a cry from Moody. It was *his* turn to tremble now. His voice faltered as he said the words, "The dog has found the pocket-book!"

He opened the book with shaking hands. A betting-book was bound up in it with the customary calendar. He turned to the date of the day after the robbery.

There was the entry: "Felix Sweetsir. Paid £500. Note numbered N 8, 70,564; dated 15th May, 1875."

Moody took from his waistcoat-pocket his own memorandum of the number of the lost bank-note. "Read it, Isabel," he said. "I won't trust my memory."

She read it. The number and date of the note entered in the pocket-book exactly corresponded with the number and date of the note that Lady Lydiard had placed in her letter.

Moody handed the pocket-book to Isabel. "There is the proof of your innocence," he said, "thanks to the dog. Will you write and tell Mr. Hardyman what has happened?" he asked, with his head down and his eyes on the ground.

She answered him, with the bright color suddenly flowing over her face.

"*You* shall write to him," she said, "when the time comes."

"What time?" he asked.

She threw her arms round his neck, and hid her face on his bosom. "The time," she whispered, "when I am your wife."

A low growl from Tommie reminded them that he too had some claim to be noticed.

Isabel dropped on her knees, and saluted her old play-fellow with the heartiest kisses she had ever given him since the day when their acquaintance began. "You darling!" she said, as she put him down again, "what can I do to reward you?"

Tommie rolled over on his back—more slowly than usual, in consequence of his luncheon in the tent. He elevated his four paws in the air, and looked lazily at Isabel out of his bright brown eyes. If ever a dog's look spoke yet, Tommie's look said, "I have eaten too much; rub my stomach."

POSTSCRIPT

Persons of a speculative turn of mind are informed that the following document is for sale, and are requested to mention what sum they will give for it:

"I O U, Lady Lydiard, five hundred pounds (£ 500).
                                        Felix Sweetsir."

Her ladyship became possessed of this pecuniary remittance under circumstances that surround it with a halo of romantic interest. It was the last communication she was destined to receive from her accomplished nephew; and there was a note attached to it, which can not fail to enhance its value in the estimation of all right-minded persons who assist the circulation of paper-money.

The lines that follow are strictly confidential:

"*Note.*—Our excellent Moody informs me, my dear aunt, that you have decided (against his advice) on 'refusing to prosecute.' I have not the slightest idea of what he means; but I am very much obliged to him, nevertheless, for reminding me of a circumstance which is of some interest to yourself personally.

"I am on the point of retiring to the Continent in search of health. One generally forgets something important when one starts on a journey. Before Moody called, I had entirely forgotten to mention that I had the pleasure of borrowing five hundred pounds of you some little time since.

"On the occasion to which I refer, your language and manner suggested that you would not lend me the money if I asked for it.

Obviously, the only course left was to take it without asking. I took it while Moody was gone to get me some Curaçoa; and I returned it to the picture-gallery in time to receive that delicious liqueur from the footman's hands.

"You will naturally ask why I found it necessary to supply myself (if I may borrow an expression from the language of State finance) with this 'forced loan.' I was actuated by motives which I think do me honor. My position at the time was critical in the extreme. My credit with the money-lenders was at an end; my friends had all turned their backs on me. I must either take the money or disgrace my family. If there is a man living who is sincerely attached to his family, I am that man. I took the money.

"Conceive your position as my aunt (I say nothing of myself), if I had adopted the other alternative. Turned out of the Jockey Club, turned out of Tattersalls', turned out of the betting-ring; in short, posted publicly as a defaulter before the noblest institution in England—the Turf; and all for want of five hundred pounds to stop the mouth of the greatest brute I know of—Alfred Hardyman! Let me not harrow your feelings (and mine) by dwelling on it. Dear and admirable woman! To you belongs the honor of saving the credit of the family. I can claim nothing but the inferior merit of having offered you the opportunity.

"My I O U, it is needless to say, accompanies these lines. Can I do anything for you abroad?   F.S."

To this it is only necessary to add, first, that Moody was perfectly right in believing F. S. to be the person who informed Hardyman's father of Isabel's position when she left Lady Lydiard's house; and, secondly, that Felix did really forward Mr. Troy's narrative of the theft to the French police, altering nothing in it but the number of the lost bank-note.

What is there left to write about? Nothing is left but to say good-bye (very sorrowfully on the writer's part) to the Persons of the Story.

Good-bye to Miss Pink—who will regret to her dying day that Isabel's answer to Hardyman was No.

Good-bye to Lady Lydiard—who differs with Miss Pink and would have regretted it to *her* dying day if the answer had been Yes.

Good-bye to Moody and Isabel—whose history has closed with the closing of the clergyman's book on their wedding-day.

Good-bye to Old Sharon—who, a martyr to his promise, brushed his hair and washed his face in honor of Moody's marriage; and catching a severe cold as the necessary consequence, declared in the intervals of sneezing, that he would "never do it again."

And last, not least, good-bye to Tommie. No. The writer gave Tommie his dinner not half an hour since, and is too fond of him to say good-bye.

The Big Bow Mystery

by

ISRAEL ZANGWILL

INTRODUCTION:
OF MURDERS AND MYSTERIES

As this little book was written some four years ago, I feel able to review it without prejudice. A new book just hot from the brain is naturally apt to appear faulty to its begetter, but an old book has got into the proper perspective and may be praised by him without fear or favor. "The Big Bow Mystery" seems to me an excellent murder story, as murder stories go, for, while as sensational as the most of them, it contains more humor and character creation than the best. Indeed, the humor is too abundant. Mysteries should be sedate and sober. There should be a pervasive atmosphere of horror and awe such as Poe manages to create. Humor is out of tone; it would be more artistic to preserve a somber note throughout. But I was a realist in those days, and in real life mysteries occur to real persons with their individual humors, and mysterious circumstances are apt to be complicated by comic. The indispensable condition of a good mystery is that it should be able and unable to be solved by the reader, and that the writer's solution should satisfy. Many a mystery runs on breathlessly enough till the dénouement is reached, only to leave the reader with the sense of having been robbed of his breath under false pretenses. And not only must the solution be adequate, but all its data must be given in the body of the story. The author must not suddenly spring a new person or a new circumstance upon his reader at the end. Thus, if a friend were to ask me to guess who dined with him yesterday, it would be fatuous if he had in mind somebody of whom he knew I had never heard. The only person who has ever solved "The Big Bow Mystery" is myself. This is not paradox but plain fact. For long before the book was written, I said to myself one night that no mystery-monger had ever murdered a man in a room to which there was no possible access. The puzzle was scarcely propounded ere the solution flew up and the idea lay stored in my mind till, years later, during the silly season, the editor of a popular London evening paper, anxious to let the sea-serpent have a year off, asked me to provide him with a more original piece of fiction. I might have refused, but there was murder in my soul, and here was the opportunity. I went to work seriously, though the *Morning Post* subsequently said the skit was too labored, and I succeeded at least in exciting my readers, so many of whom sent in unsolicited testimonials in the shape of solutions during the run of the story that, when it ended, the editor asked me to say something by way of acknowledgement. Thereupon I wrote a letter to the paper, thanking the would-be solvers for their kindly attempts to help me out of the mess into which I had got the plot. I did not like to wound their feelings by saying straight out that they had failed, one and all, to hit on the real murderer, just like real police, so I tried to break the truth to them in a roundabout, mendacious fashion, as thus:

To the Editor of "The Star."

SIR: Now that "The Big Bow Mystery" is solved to the satisfaction of at least one person, will you allow that person the use of your invaluable columns to enable him to thank the hundreds of your readers who have favored him with their kind suggestions and solutions while his tale was running and they were reading? I ask this more especially because great credit is due to them for enabling me to end the story in a manner so satisfactory to myself. When I started it, I had, of course, no idea who had done the murder, but I was determined no one should guess it. Accordingly, as each correspondent sent in the name of a suspect, I determined he or she should not be the guilty party. By degrees every one of the characters got ticked off as innocent—all except one, and I had no option but to make that character the murderer. I was very sorry to do this, as I rather liked that particular person, but when one has such ingenious readers, what can one do? You can't let anybody boast that he guessed aright, and, in spite of the trouble of altering the plot five or six times, I feel that I have chosen the course most consistent with the dignity of my profession. Had I not been impelled by this consideration I should certainly have brought in a verdict against

Mrs. Drabdump, as recommended by the reader who said that, judging by the illustration in the "Star," she must be at least seven feet high, and, therefore, could easily have got on the roof and put her (proportionately) long arm down the chimney to effect the cut. I am not responsible for the artist's conception of the character. When I last saw the good lady she was under six feet, but your artist may have had later information. The "Star" is always so frightfully up to date. I ought not to omit the humorous remark of a correspondent, who said: "Mortlake might have swung in some wild way from one window to another, *at any rate in a story.*" I hope my fellow-writers thus satirically prodded will not demand his name, as I object to murders, "at any rate in real life." Finally, a word with the legions who have taken me to task for allowing Mr. Gladstone to write over 170 words on a postcard. It is all owing to you, sir, who announced my story as containing humorous elements. I tried to put in some, and this gentle dig at the grand old correspondent's habits was intended to be one of them. However, if I *am* to be taken "at the foot of the letter" (or rather of the postcard), I must say that only to-day I received a postcard containing about 250 words. But this was not from Mr. Gladstone. At any rate, till Mr. Gladstone himself repudiates this postcard, I shall consider myself justified in allowing it to stand in the book.

Again thanking your readers for their valuable assistance,
    Yours, etc.

One would have imagined that nobody could take this seriously, for it is obvious that the mystery-story is just the one species of story that can not be told impromptu or altered at the last moment, seeing that it demands the most careful piecing together and the most elaborate dove-tailing. Nevertheless, if you cast your joke upon the waters, you shall find it no joke after many days. This is what I read in the *Lyttelton Times*, New Zealand: "The chain of circumstantial evidence seems fairly irrefragable. From all accounts, Mr. Zangwill himself was puzzled, after carefully forging every link, how to break it. The method ultimately adopted I consider more ingenious than convincing." After that I made up my mind never to joke again, but this good intention now helps to pave the beaten path.

LONDON, September, 1895.   I. ZANGWILL.

NOTE

The Mystery which the author will always associate with this story is how he got through the task of writing it. It was written in a fortnight—day by day—to meet a sudden demand from the "Star," which made "a new departure" with it.

The said fortnight was further disturbed by an extraordinary combined attack of other troubles and tasks. This is no excuse for the shortcomings of the book, as it was always open to the writer to revise or suppress it. The latter function may safely be left to the public, while if the work stands—almost to a letter—as it appeared in the "Star," it is because the author cannot tell a story more than once.

The introduction of Mr. Gladstone into a fictitious scene is defended on the ground that he is largely mythical.

I. Z.

I

On a memorable morning of early December London opened its eyes on a frigid grey mist. There are mornings when King Fog masses his molecules of carbon in serried squadrons in the city, while he scatters them tenuously in the suburbs; so that your morning train may bear you from twilight to darkness. But to-day the enemy's manœuvring was more monotonous. From Bow even unto Hammersmith there draggled a dull, wretched vapour, like the wraith of an impecunious suicide come into a fortune immediately after the fatal deed. The barometers and thermometers had sympathetically shared its depression, and their spirits (when they had any) were low. The cold cut like a many-bladed knife.

Mrs. Drabdump, of 11 Glover Street, Bow, was one of the few persons in London whom fog did not depress. She went about her work quite as cheerlessly as usual. She had been among the earliest to be aware of the enemy's advent, picking out the strands of fog from the coils of darkness the moment she rolled up her bedroom blind and unveiled the sombre picture of the winter morning. She knew that the fog had come to stay for the day at least, and that the gas-bill for the quarter was going to beat the record in high-jumping. She also knew that this was because she had allowed her new gentleman lodger, Mr. Arthur Constant, to pay a fixed sum of a shilling a week for gas, instead of charging him a proportion of the actual account for the whole house. The meteorologists might have saved the credit of their science if they had reckoned with Mrs. Drabdump's next gas-bill when they predicted the weather and made "Snow" the favourite, and said that "Fog" would be nowhere. Fog was everywhere, yet Mrs. Drabdump took no credit to herself for her prescience.

Mrs. Drabdump indeed took no credit for anything, paying her way along doggedly, and struggling through life like a wearied swimmer trying to touch the horizon. That things always went as badly as she had foreseen did not exhilarate her in the least.

Mrs. Drabdump was a widow. Widows are not born but made, else you might have fancied Mrs. Drabdump had always been a widow. Nature had given her that tall, spare form, and that pale, thin-lipped, elongated, hard-eyed visage, and that painfully precise hair, which are always associated with widowhood in low life. It is only in higher circles that women can lose their husbands and yet remain bewitching. The late Mr. Drabdump had scratched the base of his thumb with a rusty nail, and Mrs. Drabdump's foreboding that he would die of lockjaw had not prevented her wrestling day and night with the shadow of Death, as she had wrestled with it vainly twice before, when Katie died of diphtheria and little Johnny of scarlet fever. Perhaps it is from overwork among the poor that Death has been reduced to a shadow.

Mrs. Drabdump was lighting the kitchen fire. She did it very scientifically, as knowing the contrariety of coal and the anxiety of flaming sticks to end in smoke unless rigidly kept up to the mark. Science was a success as usual; and Mrs. Drabdump rose from her knees content, like a Parsee priestess who had duly paid her morning devotions to her deity. Then she started violently, and nearly lost her balance. Her eye had caught the hands of the clock on the mantel. They pointed to fifteen minutes to seven. Mrs. Drabdump's devotion to the kitchen fire invariably terminated at fifteen minutes past six. What was the matter with the clock?

Mrs. Drabdump had an immediate vision of Snoppet, the neighbouring horologist, keeping the clock in hand for weeks and then returning it only superficially repaired and secretly injured more vitally "for the good of the trade." The evil vision vanished as quickly as it came, exorcised by the deep boom of St. Dunstan's bells chiming the three-quarters. In its place a greater horror surged. Instinct had failed; Mrs. Drabdump had risen at half-past six instead of six. Now she understood why she had been feeling so dazed and strange and sleepy. She had overslept herself.

Chagrined and puzzled, she hastily set the kettle over the crackling coal, discovering a second later that she had overslept herself because Mr. Constant wished to be woke three-quarters of an hour earlier than usual, and to have his breakfast at seven, having to speak at an early meeting of discontented tram-men. She ran at once, candle in hand, to his bedroom. It was upstairs. All "upstairs" was Arthur Constant's domain, for it consisted of but two mutually independent rooms. Mrs. Drabdump knocked viciously at the door of the one he used for a bedroom, crying, "Seven o'clock, sir. You'll be late, sir. You must get up at once." The usual slumberous "All right" was not forthcoming; but, as she herself had varied her morning salute, her ear was less expectant of the echo. She went downstairs, with no foreboding save that the kettle would come off second best in the race between its boiling and her lodger's dressing.

For she knew there was no fear of Arthur Constant's lying deaf to the call of Duty—temporarily represented by Mrs. Drabdump. He was a light sleeper, and the tram conductors' bells were probably ringing in his ears, summoning him to the meeting. Why Arthur Constant, B.A.—white-handed and white-shirted, and gentleman to the very purse of him—should concern himself with tram-men, when fortune had confined his necessary relations with drivers to cabmen at the least, Mrs. Drabdump could not quite make out. He probably aspired to represent Bow in Parliament; but then it would surely have been wiser to lodge with a landlady who possessed a vote by having a husband alive. Nor was there much practical wisdom in his wish to black his own boots (an occupation in which he shone but little), and to live in every way like a Bow working man. Bow working men were not so lavish in their patronage of water, whether existing in drinking glasses, morning tubs, or laundress's establishments. Nor did they eat the delicacies with which Mrs. Drabdump supplied him, with the assurance that they were the artisan's appanage. She could not bear to see him eat things unbefitting his station. Arthur Constant opened his mouth and ate what his landlady gave him, not first deliberately shutting his eyes according to the formula, but rather pluming himself on keeping them very wide open. But it is difficult for saints to see through their own haloes; and in practice an aureola about the head is often indistinguishable from a mist.

The tea to be scalded in Mr. Constant's pot, when that cantankerous kettle should boil, was not the coarse mixture of black and green sacred to herself and Mr. Mortlake, of whom the thoughts of breakfast now reminded her. Poor Mr. Mortlake, gone off without any to Devonport, somewhere about four in the fog-thickened darkness of a winter night! Well, she hoped his journey would be duly rewarded, that his perks would be heavy, and that he would make as good a thing out of the "travelling expenses" as rival labour leaders roundly accused him of to other people's faces. She did not grudge him his gains, nor was it her business if, as they alleged, in introducing Mr. Constant to her vacant rooms, his idea was not merely to benefit his landlady. He had done her an uncommon good turn, queer as was the lodger thus introduced. His own apostleship to the sons of toil gave Mrs. Drabdump no twinges of perplexity. Tom Mortlake had been a compositor; and apostleship was obviously a profession better paid and of a higher social status. Tom Mortlake— the hero of a hundred strikes—set up in print on a poster, was unmistakably superior to Tom Mortlake setting up other men's names at a case. Still, the work was not all beer and skittles, and Mrs. Drabdump felt that Tom's latest job was not enviable.

She shook his door as she passed it on her way back to the kitchen, but there was no response. The street door was only a few feet off down the passage, and a glance at it dispelled the last hope that Tom had abandoned the journey. The door was unbolted and unchained, and the only security was the latchkey lock. Mrs. Drabdump felt a whit uneasy, though, to give her her due, she never suffered as much as most good housewives do from criminals who never come. Not quite opposite, but still only a few doors off, on the other side of the street, lived the celebrated ex-detective Grodman, and, illogically enough, his presence in the street gave Mrs. Drabdump a curious sense of security, as of a believer living under the shadow of the fane. That any human being of ill-odour should consciously come within a mile of the scent of so famous a sleuth-hound seemed to her highly improbable. Grodman had retired (with a competence) and was only a sleeping dog now; still, even criminals would have sense enough to let him lie.

So Mrs. Drabdump did not really feel that there had been any danger, especially as a second glance at the street door showed that Mortlake had been thoughtful enough to slip the loop that held back the bolt of the big lock. She allowed herself another throb of sympathy for the labour leader whirling on his dreary way towards Devonport Dockyard. Not that he had told her anything of his journey, beyond the town; but she knew Devonport had a Dockyard because Jessie Dymond—Tom's sweetheart—once mentioned that her aunt lived near there, and it lay on the surface that Tom had gone to help the dockers, who were imitating their London brethren. Mrs. Drabdump did not need to be told things to be aware of them. She went back to prepare Mr. Constant's superfine tea, vaguely wondering why people were so discontented nowadays. But when she brought up the tea and the toast and the eggs to Mr. Constant's sitting-room (which adjoined his bedroom, though without communicating with it), Mr. Constant was not sitting in it. She lit the gas, and laid the cloth; then she returned to the landing and beat at the bedroom door with an imperative palm. Silence alone answered her. She called him by name and told him the hour, but hers was the only voice she heard, and it sounded strangely to her in the shadows of the staircase. Then, muttering, "Poor gentleman, he had the toothache last night; and p'r'haps he's only just got a wink o' sleep. Pity to disturb him for the sake of them grizzling conductors. I'll let him sleep his usual time," she bore the tea-pot downstairs with a mournful, almost poetic, consciousness that soft boiled eggs (like love) must grow cold.

Half-past seven came—and she knocked again. But Constant slept on.

His letters, always a strange assortment, arrived at eight, and a telegram came soon after. Mrs. Drabdump rattled his door, shouted, and at last put the wire under it. Her heart was beating fast enough now, though there seemed to be a cold, clammy snake curling round it. She went downstairs again and turned the handle of Mortlake's room, and went in without knowing why. The coverlet of the bed showed that the occupant had only laid down in his clothes, as if fearing to miss the early train. She had not for a moment expected to find him in the room; yet somehow the consciousness that she was alone in the house with the sleeping Constant seemed to flash for the first time upon her, and the clammy snake tightened its folds round her heart.

She opened the street door, and her eye wandered nervously up and down. It was half-past eight. The little street stretched cold and still in the grey mist, blinking bleary eyes at either end, where the street lamps smouldered on. No one was visible for the moment, though smoke was rising from many of the chimneys to greet its sister mist. At the house of the detective across the way the blinds were still down and the shutters up. Yet the familiar, prosaic aspect of the street calmed her. The bleak air set her coughing; she slammed the door to, and returned to the kitchen to make fresh tea for Constant, who could only be in a deep sleep. But the canister trembled in her grasp. She did not know whether she dropped it or threw it down, but there was nothing in the hand that battered again a moment later at the bedroom door. No sound within answered the clamour without. She rained blow upon blow in a sort of spasm of frenzy, scarce remembering that her object was merely to wake her lodger, and almost staving in the lower panels with her kicks. Then she turned the handle and tried to open the door, but it was locked. The resistance recalled her to herself—she had a moment of shocked decency at the thought that she had been about to enter Constant's bedroom. Then the terror came over her afresh. She felt that she was alone in the house with a corpse. She sank to the floor, cowering; with difficulty stifling a desire to scream. Then she rose with a jerk and raced down the stairs without looking behind her, and threw open the door and ran out into the street, only pulling up with her left hand violently agitating Grodman's door-knocker. In a moment the first-floor window was raised—the little house was of the same pattern as her own—and Grodman's full fleshy face loomed through the fog in sleepy irritation from under a nightcap. Despite its scowl the ex-detective's face dawned upon her like the sun upon an occupant of the haunted chamber.

"What in the devil's the matter?" he growled. Grodman was not an early bird, now that he had no worms to catch. He could afford to despise proverbs now, for the house in which he lived was his, and he lived in it because several other houses in the street were also his, and it is well for the landlord to be about his own estate in Bow, where poachers often shoot the moon. Perhaps the desire to enjoy his greatness among his early cronies counted for something, too, for he had been born and bred at Bow, receiving when a youth his first engagement from the local police quarters, whence he had drawn a few shillings a week as an amateur detective in his leisure hours.

Grodman was still a bachelor. In the celestial matrimonial bureau a partner might have been selected for him, but he had never been able to discover her. It was his one failure as a detective. He was a self-sufficing person, who preferred a gas stove to a domestic; but in deference to Glover Street opinion he admitted a female factotum between ten A.M and ten P.M., and equally in deference to Glover Street opinion, excluded her between ten P.M. and ten A.M.

"I want you to come across at once," Mrs. Drabdump gasped, "something has happened to Mr. Constant."

"What! Not bludgeoned by the police at the meeting this morning, I hope?"

"No, no! He didn't go. He is dead."

"Dead?" Grodman's face grew very serious now.

"Yes. Murdered!"

"What?" almost shouted the ex-detective. "How? When? Where? Who?"

"I don't know. I can't get to him. I have beaten at his door. He does not answer."

Grodman's face lit up with relief.

"You silly woman! Is that all? I shall have a cold in my head. Bitter weather. He's dog-tired after yesterday—processions, three speeches, kindergarten, lecture on 'the moon,' article on co-opera-tion. That's his style." It was also Grodman's style. He never wasted words.

"No," Mrs. Drabdump breathed up at him solemnly, "he's dead."

"All right; go back. Don't alarm the neighbourhood unnecessarily. Wait for me. Down in five minutes." Grodman did not take this Cassandra of the kitchen too seriously. Probably he knew his woman. His small, bead-like eyes glittered with an almost amused smile as he withdrew them from Mrs. Drabdump's ken, and shut down the sash with a bang. The poor woman ran back across the road and through her door, which she would not close behind her. It seemed to shut her in with the dead. She waited in the passage. After an age—seven minutes by any honest clock—Grodman made his appearance, looking as dressed as usual, but with unkempt hair and with dis-consolate side-whisker. He was not quite used to that side-whisker yet, for it had only recently come within the margin of cultivation. In active service Grodman had been clean-shaven, like all members of *the* profession—for surely your detective is the most versatile of actors. Mrs. Drabdump closed the street-door quietly, and pointed to the stairs, fear operating like a polite desire to give him precedence. Grodman ascended, amusement still glimmering in his eyes. Arrived on the landing he knocked peremptorily at the door, crying, "Nine o' clock, Mr. Constant; nine o' clock?" When he ceased there was no other sound or movement. His face grew more serious. He waited, then knocked, and cried louder. He turned the handle, but the door was fast. He tried to peer through the keyhole, but it was blocked. He shook the upper panels, but the door seem bolted as well as locked. He stood still, his face set and rigid, for he liked and esteemed the man.

"Ay, knock your loudest," whispered the pale-faced woman. "You'll not wake him now."

The grey mist had followed them through the street-door, and hovered about the staircase, charging the air with a moist sepulchral odour.

"Locked and bolted," muttered Grodman, shaking the door afresh.

"Burst it open," breathed the woman, trembling violently all over,

and holding her hands before her as if to ward off the dreadful vision.
Without another word, Grodman applied his shoulder to the door,
and made a violent muscular effort. He had been an athlete in his
time, and the sap was yet in him. The door creaked, little by little it
began to give, the woodwork enclosing the bolt of the lock splintered,
the panels bent inwards, the large upper bolt tore off its iron staple:
the door flew back with a crash. Grodman rushed in.

"My God!" he cried. The woman shrieked. The sight was too
terrible.

. . . .

Within a few hours the jubilant newsboys were shrieking "Horrible
Suicide in Bow," and *The Moon* poster added, for the satisfaction of
those too poor to purchase: "A Philanthropist Cuts His Throat."

II

But the newspapers were premature. Scotland Yard refused to
prejudice the case despite the penny-a-liners. Several arrests were
made, so that later editions were compelled to soften "Suicide" into
"Mystery." The people arrested were a nondescript collection of
tramps. Most of them had committed other offences for which the
police had not arrested them. One bewildered-looking gentleman
gave himself up (as if he were a riddle), but the police would have
none of him, and restored him forthwith to his friends and keepers.
The number of candidates for each new opening in Newgate is
astonishing.

The full significance of this tragedy of a noble young life cut short
had hardly time to filter into the public mind, when a fresh sensation
absorbed it. Tom Mortlake had been arrested the same day at
Liverpool on suspicion of being concerned in the death of his fellow-
lodger. The news fell like a bombshell upon a land in which Tom
Mortlake's name was a household word. That the gifted artisan
orator, who had never shrunk upon occasion from launching red
rhetoric at society, should actually have shed blood seemed too
startling, especially as the blood shed was not blue, but the property
of a lovable young middle-class idealist, who had now literally given
his life to the Cause. But this supplementary sensation did not grow
to a head, and everybody (save a few labour leaders) was relieved to
hear that Tom had been released almost immediately, being merely
subpœnaed to appear at the inquest. In an interview which he

accorded to the representative of a Liverpool paper the same afternoon, he stated that he put his arrest down entirely to the enmity and
rancour entertained towards him by the police throughout the
country. He had come to Liverpool to trace the movements of a
friend about whom he was very uneasy, and he was making anxious
inquiries at the docks to discover at what times steamers left for
America, when the detectives stationed there had, in accordance with
instructions from headquarters, arrested him as a suspicious-looking
character. "Though," said Tom, "they must very well have known my
phiz, as I have been sketched and caricatured all over the shop. When
I told them who I was they had the decency to let me go. They thought
they'd scored off me enough, I reckon. Yes, it certainly *is* a strange
coincidence that I might actually have had something to do with the
poor fellow's death, which has cut me up as much as anybody; though
if they had known I had just come from the 'scene of the crime,'
and actually lived in the house, they would probably have—let me
alone." He laughed sarcastically. "They are a queer lot of muddle-
heads are the police. Their motto is, 'First catch your man, then cook
the evidence.' If you're on the spot you're guilty because you're
there, and if you're elsewhere you're guilty because you have
gone away. Oh, I know them! If they could have seen their way to
clap me in quod, they'd ha' done it. Luckily I know the number of
the cabman who took me to Euston before five this morning."

"If they clapped you in quod," the interviewer reported himself
as facetiously observing, "the prisoners would be on strike in a week."

"Yes, but there would be so many blacklegs ready to take their
places," Mortlake flashed back, "that I'm afraid it 'ould be no go.
But do excuse me. I am so upset about my friend. I'm afraid he has
left England, and I have to make inquiries; and now there's poor
Constant gone—horrible! horrible! and I'm due in London at the
inquest. I must really run away. Good-bye. Tell your readers it's all
a police grudge."

"One last word, Mr. Mortlake, if you please. Is it true that you
were billed to preside at a great meeting of clerks at St. James's
Hall between one and two to-day to protest against the German
invasion?"

"Whew! so I was. But the beggars arrested me just before one,
when I was going to wire, and then the news of poor Constant's end
drove it out of my head. What a nuisance! Lord, how troubles do
come together! Well, good-bye, send me a copy of the paper."

Tom Mortlake's evidence at the inquest added little beyond this to the public knowledge of his movements on the morning of the Mystery. The cabman who drove him to Euston had written indignantly to the papers to say that he picked up his celebrated fare at Bow Railway Station at about half-past four A.M., and the arrest was a deliberate insult to democracy, and he offered to make an affidavit to that effect, leaving it dubious to which effect. But Scotland Yard betrayed no itch for the affidavit in question, and No. 2138 subsided again into the obscurity of his rank. Mortlake—whose face was very pale below the black mane brushed back from his fine forehead—gave his evidence in low, sympathetic tones. He had known the deceased for over a year, coming constantly across him in their common political and social work, and had found the furnished rooms for him in Glover Street at his own request, they just being to let when Constant resolved to leave his rooms at Oxford House in Bethnal Green, and to share the actual life of the people. The locality suited the deceased, as being near the People's Palace. He respected and admired the deceased, whose genuine goodness had won all hearts. The deceased was an untiring worker; never grumbled, was always in fair spirits, regarded his life and wealth as a sacred trust to be used for the benefit of humanity. He had last seen him at a quarter past nine P.M., on the day preceding his death. He (witness) had received a letter by the last post which made him uneasy about a friend. He went up to consult deceased about it. Deceased was evidently suffering from toothache, and was fixing a piece of cotton-wool in a hollow tooth, but he did not complain. Deceased seemed rather upset by the news he brought, and they both discussed it rather excitedly.

By a JURYMAN: Did the news concern him?

MORTLAKE: Only impersonally. He knew my friend, and was keenly sympathetic when one was in trouble.

CORONER: Could you show the jury the letter you received?

MORTLAKE: I have mislaid it, and cannot make out where it has got to. If you think it relevant or essential, I will state what the trouble was.

CORONER: Was the toothache very violent?

MORTLAKE: I cannot tell. I think not, though he told me it had disturbed his rest the night before.

CORONER: What time did you leave him?

MORTLAKE: About twenty to ten.

CORONER: And what did you do then?

MORTLAKE: I went out for an hour or so to make some inquiries.

Then I returned, and told my landlady I should be leaving by an early train for—for the country.

CORONER: And that was the last you saw of the deceased?

MORTLAKE: (with emotion): The last.

CORONER: How was he when you left him?

MORTLAKE: Mainly concerned about my trouble.

CORONER: Otherwise you saw nothing unusual about him?

MORTLAKE: Nothing.

CORONER: What time did you leave the house on Tuesday morning?

MORTLAKE: At about five-and-twenty minutes past four.

CORONER: Are you sure that you shut the street door?

MORTLAKE: Quite sure. Knowing my landlady was rather a timid person, I even slipped the bolt of the big lock, which was usually tied back. It was impossible for anyone to get in, even with a latchkey.

Mrs. Drabdump's evidence (which, of course, preceded his) was more important, and occupied a considerable time, unduly eked out by Drabdumpian padding. Thus she not only deposed that Mr. Constant had the toothache, but that it was going to last about a week; in tragi-comic indifference to the radical cure that had been effected. Her account of the last hours of the deceased tallied with Mortlake's, only that she feared Mortlake was quarrelling with him over something in a letter that came by the nine o'clock post. Deceased had left the house a little after Mortlake, but had returned before him, and had gone straight to his bedroom. She had not actually seen him come in, having been in the kitchen, but she heard his latchkey, followed by his light step up the stairs.

A JURYMAN: How do you know it was not somebody else? (*Sensation, of which the juryman tries to look unconscious.*)

WITNESS: He called down to me over the banisters, and says in his sweetest voice, "Be hextra sure to wake me at a quarter to seven, Mrs. Drabdump, or else I shan't get to my tram meeting."

(*Juryman collapses.*)

CORONER: And did you wake him?

MRS. DRABDUMP (breaking down): Oh, my lud, how can you ask?

CORONER: There, there, compose yourself. I mean did you try to wake him?

MRS. DRABDUMP: I have taken in and done for lodgers this seventeen years, my lud, and have always gave satisfaction; and Mr. Mortlake, he wouldn't ha' recommended me otherwise, though I wish to Heaven the poor gentleman had never——

CORONER: Yes, yes, of course. You tried to rouse him?

But it was some time before Mrs. Drabdump was sufficiently calm
to explain that, though she had overslept herself, and though it would
have been all the same anyhow, she *had* come up to time. Bit by bit
the tragic story was forced from her lips—a tragedy that even her
telling could not make tawdry. She told with superfluous detail how—
when Mr. Grodman broke in the door—she saw her unhappy gentle-
man-lodger lying on his back in bed, stone dead, with a gaping red
wound in his throat; how her stronger-minded companion calmed her
a little by spreading a handkerchief over the distorted face; how they
then looked vainly about and under the bed for any instrument by
which the deed could have been done, the veteran detective carefully
making a rapid inventory of the contents of the room, and taking
notes of the precise position and condition of the body before anything was disturbed by the arrival of gapers or bunglers; how she had
pointed out to him that both the windows were firmly bolted to keep
out the cold night air; how, having noted this down with a puzzled
pitying shake of the head, he had opened the window to summon the
police, and espied in the fog one Denzil Cantercot, whom he called,
and told to run to the nearest police-station and ask them to send on
an inspector and a surgeon. How they both remained in the room till
the police arrived, Grodman pondering deeply the while and making
notes every now and again, as fresh points occurred to him, and asking her questions about the poor, weak-headed young man. Pressed
as to what she meant by calling the deceased "weak-headed," she
replied that some of her neighbours wrote him begging letters, though,
Heaven knew, they were better off than herself, who had to scrape
her fingers to the bone for every penny she earned. Under further
pressure from Mr. Talbot, who was watching the inquiry on behalf of
Arthur Constant's family, Mrs. Drabdump admitted that the deceased had behaved like a human being, nor was there anything externally eccentric or queer in his conduct. He was always cheerful and
pleasant spoken, though certainly soft—God rest his soul. No; he
never shaved, but wore all the hair that Heaven had given him.

By a JURYMAN: She thought deceased was in the habit of locking
his door when he went to bed. Of course, she couldn't say for certain.
(Laughter.) There was no need to bolt the door as well. The bolt
slid upwards, and was at the top of the door. When she first let
lodgings, her reasons for which she seemed anxious to publish, there
had only been a bolt, but a suspicious lodger, she would not call him
a gentleman, had complained that he could not fasten his door behind him, and so she had been put to the expense of having a lock

made. The complaining lodger went off soon after without paying his rent. (Laughter.) She had always known he would.

The CORONER: Was deceased at all nervous?

WITNESS: No, he was a very nice gentleman. (A laugh.)

CORONER: I mean did he seem afraid of being robbed?

WITNESS: No, he was always goin' to demonstrations. (Laughter.) I told him to be careful. I told him I lost a purse with 3s. 2d. myself on Jubilee Day.

Mrs. Drabdump resumed her seat, weeping vaguely.

The CORONER: Gentlemen, we shall have an opportunity of viewing the room shortly.

The story of the discovery of the body was retold, though more scientifically, by Mr. George Grodman, whose unexpected resurgence into the realm of his early exploits excited as keen a curiosity as the reappearance "for this occasion only" of a retired prima donna. His book, *Criminals I Have Caught,* passed from the twenty-third to the twenty-fourth edition merely on the strength of it. Mr. Grodman stated that the body was still warm when he found it. He thought that death was quite recent. The door he had had to burst was bolted as well as locked. He confirmed Mrs. Drabdump's statement about the windows; the chimney was very narrow. The cut looked as if done by a razor. There was no instrument lying about the room. He had known the deceased about a month. He seemed a very earnest, simple-minded young fellow, who spoke a great deal about the brotherhood of man. (The hardened old man-hunter's voice was not free from a tremor as he spoke jerkily of the dead man's enthusiasms.) He should have thought the deceased the last man in the world to commit suicide.

Mr. DENZIL CANTERCOT was next called: He was a poet. (Laughter.) He was on his way to Mr. Grodman's house to tell him he had been unable to do some writing for him because he was suffering from writer's cramp, when Mr. Grodman called to him from the window of No. 11 and asked him to run for the police. No, he did not run; he was a philosopher. (Laughter.) He returned with them to the door, but did not go up. He had no stomach for crude sensations. (Laughter.) The grey fog was sufficiently unbeautiful for him for one morning. (Laughter.)

Inspector HOWLETT said: About 9:45 on the morning of Tuesday, 4th December, from information received, he went to 11 Glover Street, Bow, and there found the dead body of a young man, lying on his back with his throat cut. The door of the room had been smashed in, and the lock and the bolt evidently forced. The room was tidy. There were no marks of blood on the floor. A purse full of gold was on the dressing-table beside a big book. A hip-bath, with cold water, stood beside the bed, over which was a hanging book-case. There was a large wardrobe against the wall next to the door. The chimney was very narrow. There were two windows, one bolted. It was about eighteen feet to the pavement. There was no way of climbing up. No one could possibly have got out of the room, and then bolted the doors and windows behind him; and he had searched all parts of the room in which anyone might have been concealed. He had been unable to find any instrument in the room in spite of exhaustive search, there being not even a penknife in the pockets of the clothes of the deceased, which lay on a chair. The house and the backyard, and the adjacent pavement, had also been fruitlessly searched.

Sergeant RUNNYMEDE made an identical statement, saving only that *he* had gone with Dr. Robinson and Inspector Howlett.

Dr. ROBINSON, divisional surgeon, said: The deceased was lying on his back, with his throat cut. The body was not yet cold, the abdominal region being quite warm. Rigor mortis had set in in the lower jaw, neck, and upper extremities. The muscles contracted when beaten. I inferred that life had been extinct some two or three hours, probably not longer, it might have been less. The bed-clothes would keep the lower part warm for some time. The wound, which was a deep one, was five and a half inches right to left across the throat to a point under the left ear. The upper portion of the windpipe was severed, and likewise the jugular vein. The muscular coating of the carotid artery was divided. There was a slight cut, as if in continuation of the wound, on the thumb of the left hand. The hands were clasped underneath the head. There was no blood on the right hand. The wound could not have been self-inflicted. A sharp instrument had been used, such as a razor. The cut might have been made by a left-handed person. No doubt death was practically instantaneous. I saw no signs of a struggle about the body or the room. I noticed a purse on the dressing-table, lying next to Madame Blavatsky's big book on Theosophy. Sergeant Runnymede drew my attention to the fact that the door had evidently been locked and bolted from within.

By a JURYMAN: I do not say the cuts could not have been made by a right-handed person. I can offer no suggestion as to how the inflictor of the wound got in or out. Extremely improbable that the cut was self-inflicted. There was little trace of the outside fog in the room.

Police-constable WILLIAMS said he was on duty in the early hours of the morning of the 4th inst. Glover Street lay within his beat. He saw or heard nothing suspicious. The fog was never very dense, though nasty to the throat. He had passed through Glover Street about half-past four. He had not seen Mr. Mortlake or anybody else leave the house.

The Court here adjourned, the Coroner and the jury repairing in a body to 11 Glover Street, to view the house and the bedroom of the deceased. And the evening posters announced "The Bow Mystery Thickens."

III

Before the inquiry was resumed, all the poor wretches in custody had been released on suspicion that they were innocent; there was not a single case even for a magistrate. Clues, which at such seasons are gathered by the police like blackberries off the hedges, were scanty and unripe. Inferior specimens were offered them by bushels, but there was not a good one among the lot. The police could not even manufacture a clue.

Arthur Constant's death was already the theme of every hearth, railway-carriage and public-house. The dead idealist had points of contact with so many spheres. The East-end and the West-end alike were moved and excited, the Democratic Leagues and the Churches, the Doss-houses and the Universities. The pity of it! And then the impenetrable mystery of it!

The evidence given in the concluding portion of the investigation was necessarily less sensational. There were no more witnesses to bring the scent of blood over the coroner's table; those who had yet to be heard were merely relatives and friends of the deceased, who spoke of him as he had been in life. His parents were dead, perhaps happily for them; his relatives had seen little of him, and had scarce heard as much about him as the outside world. No man is a prophet in his own country, and, even if he migrates, it is advisable for him to leave his family at home. His friends were a motley crew; friends of the same friend are not necessarily friends of one another. But their diversity only made the congruity of the tale they had to tell more striking. It was tale of a man who had never made an enemy even by benefiting him, nor lost a friend even by refusing his favours; the tale of a man whose heart overflowed with peace and goodwill

to all men all the year round; of a man to whom Christmas came not once, but three hundred and sixty-five times a year; it was the tale of a brilliant intellect, who gave up to mankind what was meant for himself, and worked as a labourer in the vineyard of humanity, never crying that the grapes were sour; of a man uniformly cheerful and of good courage, living in that forgetfulness of self which is the truest antidote to despair. And yet there was not quite wanting the note of pain to jar the harmony and make it human. Richard Elton, his chum from boyhood, and vicar of Somerton, in Midlandshire, handed to the coroner a letter received from the deceased about ten days before his death, containing some passages which the coroner read aloud:—
"Do you know anything of Schopenhauer? I mean anything beyond the current misconceptions? I have been making his acquaintance lately. He is an agreeable rattle of a pessimist; his essay on 'The Misery of Mankind' is quite lively reading. At first his assimilation of Christianity and Pessimism (it occurs in his essay on 'Suicide') dazzled me as an audacious paradox. But there is truth in it. Verily the whole creation groaneth and travaileth, and man is a degraded monster, and sin is over all. Ah, my friend, I have shed many of my illusions since I came to this seething hive of misery and wrongdoing. What shall one man's life—a million men's lives—avail against the corruption, the vulgarity, and the squalor of civilisation? Sometimes I feel like a farthing rushlight in the Hall of Eblis. Selfishness is so long and life so short. And the worst of it is that everybody is so beastly contented. The poor no more desire comfort than the rich culture. The woman, to whom a penny school fee for her child represents an appreciable slice off her income, is satisfied that the rich we shall always have with us.

"The real old Tories are the paupers in the Workhouse. The Radical working men are jealous of their own leaders, and the leaders are jealous of one another. Schopenhauer must have organised a Labour Party in his salad days. And yet one can't help feeling that he committed suicide as a philosopher by not committing it as a man. He claims kinship with Buddha, too; though Esoteric Buddhism at least seems spheres removed from the philosophy of 'the Will and the Idea.' What a wonderful woman Madame Blavatsky must be! I can't say I follow her, for she is up in the clouds nearly all the time, and I haven't as yet developed an astral body. Shall I send you on her book? It is fascinating. . . . I am becoming quite a fluent orator. One soon gets into the way of it. The horrible thing is that you catch yourself saying things to lead up to 'Cheers' instead of sticking to the plain realities of the business. Lucy is still doing the galleries in

Italy. It used to pain me sometimes to think of my darling's happiness when I came across a flat-chested factory-girl. Now I feel her happiness is as important as a factory-girl's."

Lucy, the witness explained, was Lucy Brent, the betrothed of the deceased. The poor girl had been telegraphed for, and had started for England. The witness stated that the outburst of despondency in this letter was almost a solitary one, most of the letters in his possession being bright, buoyant, and hopeful. Even this letter ended with a humorous statement of the writer's manifold plans and projects for the New Year. The deceased was a good Churchman.

CORONER: Was there any private trouble in his own life to account for the temporary despondency?

WITNESS: Not so far as I am aware. His financial position was exceptionally favourable.

CORONER: There had been no quarrel with Miss Brent?

WITNESS: I have the best authority for saying that no shadow of difference had ever come between them.

CORONER: Was the deceased left-handed?

WITNESS: Certainly not. He was not even ambidexter.

A JURYMAN: Isn't Shoppinhour one of the infidel writers, published by the Freethought Publication Society?

WITNESS: I do not know who publishes his books.

The JURYMAN (a small grocer and big raw-boned Scotchman, rejoicing in the name of Sandy Sanderson and the dignities of deaconry and membership of the committee of the Bow Conservative Association): No equeevocation, sir. Is he not a secularist, who has lectured at the Hall of Science?

WITNESS: No, he is a foreign writer—(Mr. Sanderson was heard to thank Heaven for this small mercy)—who believes that life is not worth living.

The JURYMAN: Were you not shocked to find the friend of a meenister reading such impure leeterature?

WITNESS: The deceased read everything. Schopenhauer is the author of a system of philosophy, and not what you seem to imagine. Perhaps you would like to inspect the book? (Laughter.)

The JURYMAN: I would na' touch it with a pitchfork. Such books should be burnt. And this Madame Blavatsky's book—what is that? Is that also pheelosophy?

WITNESS: No. It is Theosophy. (Laughter.)

MR. ALLAN SMITH, secretary of the Tram-men's Union, stated that he had had an interview with the deceased on the day before his death, when he (the deceased) spoke hopefully of the prospects of the movement, and wrote him out a cheque for ten guineas for his Union. Deceased promised to speak at a meeting called for a quarter past seven A.M. the next day.

Mr. EDWARD WIMP, of the Scotland Yard Detective Department, said that the letters and papers of the deceased threw no light upon the manner of his death, and they would be handed back to the family. His Department had not formed any theory on the subject.

The Coroner proceeded to sum up the evidence. "We have to deal, gentlemen," he said, "with a most incomprehensible and mysterious case, the details of which are yet astonishingly simple. On the morning of Tuesday, the 4th inst., Mrs. Drabdump, a worthy hard-working widow, who lets lodgings at 11 Glover Street, Bow, was unable to arouse the deceased, who occupied the entire upper floor of the house. Becoming alarmed, she went across to fetch Mr. George Grodman, a gentleman known to us all by reputation, and to whose clear and scientific evidence we are much indebted, and got him to batter in the door. They found the deceased lying back in bed with a deep wound in his throat. Life had only recently become extinct. There was no trace of any instrument by which the cut could have been effected: there was no trace of any person who could have effected the cut. No person could apparently have got in or out. The medical evidence goes to show that the deceased could not have inflicted the wound himself. And yet, gentlemen, there are, in the nature of things, two—only two—alternative explanations of his death. Either the wound was inflicted by his own hand, or it was inflicted by another's. I shall take each of these possibilities separately. First, did the deceased commit suicide? The medical evidence says deceased was lying with his hands clasped behind his head. Now the wound was made from right to left, and terminated by a cut on the left thumb. If the deceased had made it he would have had to do it with his right hand, while his left hand remained under his head—a most peculiar and unnatural position to assume. Moreover, in making a cut with the right hand, one would naturally move the hand from left to right. It is unlikely that the deceased would move his right hand so awkwardly and unnaturally, unless, of course, his object was to baffle suspicion. Another point is that on this hypothesis, the deceased would have had to replace his right hand beneath his head. But Dr. Robinson believes that death was instantaneous. If so, deceased could have had no time to pose so neatly. It is just possible the cut was made with the left hand, but then the deceased was right-handed. The absence of any signs of a possible weapon undoubtedly goes to corroborate the medical evidence. The police have made an exhaustive search in all places where the razor or other weapon or instrument might by any possibility have been concealed, including the bed-clothes, the mattress, the pillow, and the street into which it might have been dropped. But all theories involving the wilful concealment of the fatal instrument have to reckon with the fact or probability that death was instantaneous, also with the fact that there was no blood about the floor. Finally, the instrument used was in all likelihood a razor, and the deceased did not shave, and was never known to be in possession of any such instrument. If, then, we were to confine ourselves to the medical and police evidence, there would, I think, be little hesitation in dismissing the idea of suicide. Nevertheless, it is well to forget the physical aspect of the case for a moment and to apply our minds to an unprejudiced inquiry into the mental aspect of it. Was there any reason why the deceased should wish to take his own life? He was young, wealthy, and popular, loving and loved; life stretched fair before him. He had no vices. Plain living, high thinking, and noble doing were the three guiding stars of his life. If he had had ambition, an illustrious public career was within his reach. He was an orator of no mean power, a brilliant and industrious man. His outlook was always on the future—he was always sketching out ways in which he could be useful to his fellow-men. His purse and his time were ever at the command of whosoever could show fair claim upon them. If such a man were likely to end his own life, the science of human nature would be at an end. Still, some of the shadows of the picture have been presented to us. The man had his moments of despondency —as which of us has not? But they seem to have been few and passing. Anyhow, he was cheerful enough on the day before his death. He was suffering, too, from toothache. But it does not seem to have been violent, nor did he complain. Possibly, of course, the pain became very acute in the night. Nor must we forget that he may have overworked himself, and got his nerves into a morbid state. He worked very hard, never rising later than half-past seven, and doing far more than the professional 'labor leader.' He taught, and wrote, as well as spoke and organised. But on the other hand all witnesses agreed that he was looking forward eagerly to the meeting of the tram-men on the morning of the 4th inst. His whole heart was in the movement. Is it likely that this was the night he would choose for quitting the scene of his usefulness? Is it likely that if he had chosen it, he would not have left letters and a statement behind, or made a last will and testament? Mr. Wimp has found no possible clue to such conduct in his papers. Or is it likely he would have concealed the instrument? The only positive sign of intention is the bolting of his door in addition to the usual locking of it, but one cannot lay much stress on that. Regarding the mental aspects alone, the balance is largely against suicide; looking at the physical aspects, suicide is well-nigh impossible. Putting the two together, the case against suicide is all but mathematically complete. The answer, then, to our first question, Did the deceased commit suicide? is, that he did not."

The Coroner paused, and everybody drew a long breath. The lucid exposition had been followed with admiration. If the Coroner had stopped now, the jury would have unhesitatingly returned a verdict of "murder." But the Coroner swallowed a mouthful of water and went on:—

"We now come to the second alternative—was the deceased the victim of homicide? In order to answer that question in the affirmative it is essential that we should be able to form some conception of the *modus operandi*. It is all very well for Dr. Robinson to say the cut was made by another hand; but in the absence of any theory as to how the cut could possibly have been made by that other hand, we should be driven back to the theory of self-infliction, however improbable it may seem to medical gentlemen. Now, what are the facts? When Mrs. Drabdump and Mr. Grodman found the body it was yet warm, and Mr. Grodman, a witness fortunately qualified by special experience, states that death had been quite recent. This tallies closely enough with the view of Dr. Robinson, who, examining the body about an hour later, put the time of death at two or three hours before, say seven o'clock. Mrs. Drabdump had attempted to wake the deceased at a quarter to seven, which would put back the act to a little earlier. As I understand from Dr. Robinson, that it is impossible to fix the time very precisely, death may have very well taken place several hours before Mrs. Drabdump's first attempt to wake deceased. Of course, it may have taken place between the first and second calls, as he may merely have been sound asleep at first; it may also not impossibly have taken place considerably earlier than the first call, for all the physical data seem to prove. Nevertheless, on the whole, I think we shall be least likely to err if we assume the time of death to be half-past six. Gentlemen, let us picture to ourselves No. 11 Glover Street, at half-past six. We have seen the house; we know exactly how it is constructed. On the ground floor a front room tenanted by Mr. Mortlake, with two windows giving on the street, both securely bolted; a back room occupied by the landlady; and the kitchen. Mrs. Drabdump did not leave her bedroom till half-past six, so that we may be sure all the various doors and windows have not yet been unfastened; while the season of the year is a guarantee that nothing had been left open. The front door, through which Mr. Mortlake has gone out before half-past four, is guarded by the latchkey and the big lock. On the upper floor are two rooms—a front room used by deceased for a bedroom, and a back room which he used as a sitting-room. The back room has been left open, with the key inside, but the window is fastened. The door of the front room is not only locked, but bolted. We have seen the splintered mortice and the staple of the upper bolt violently forced from the woodwork and resting on the pin. The windows are bolted, the fasteners being firmly fixed in the catches. The chimney is too narrow to admit of the passage of even a child. This room, in fact, is as firmly barred in as if beseiged. It has no communication with any other part of the house. It is as absolutely self-centred and isolated as if it were a fort in the sea or a log-hut in the forest. Even if any strange person is in the house, nay, in the very sitting-room of the deceased, he cannot get into the bedroom, for the house is one built for the poor, with no communication between the different rooms, so that separate families, if need be, may inhabit each. Now, however, let us grant that some person has achieved the miracle of getting into the front room, first floor, 18 feet from the ground. At half-past six, or thereabouts, he cuts the throat of the sleeping occupant. How is he then to get out without attracting the attention of the now roused landlady? But let us concede him that miracle, too. How is he to go away and yet leave the doors and windows locked and bolted from within? This is a degree of miracle at which my credulity must draw the line. No, the room had been closed all night—there is scarce a trace of fog in it. No one could get in or out. Finally, murders do not take place without motive. Robbery and revenge are the only conceivable motives. The deceased had not an enemy in the world; his money and valuables were left untouched. Everything was in order. There were no signs of a struggle. The answer, then, to our second inquiry—was the deceased killed by another person?—is that he was not.

"Gentlemen, I am aware that this sounds impossible and contradictory. But it is the facts that contradict themselves. It seems clear that the deceased did not commit suicide. It seems equally clear that the deceased was not murdered. There is nothing for it, therefore, gentlemen, but to return a verdict tantamount to an acknowledgement of our incompetence to come to any adequately grounded conviction whatever as to the means or the manner by which the deceased met his death. It is the most inexplicable mystery in all my experience." (Sensation.)

The FOREMAN (after a colloquy with Mr. Sandy Sanderson): We are not agreed, sir. One of the jurors insists on a verdict of "Death from visitation by the act of God."

IV

But Sandy Sanderson's burning solicitude to fix the crime flickered out in the face of opposition, and in the end he bowed his head to the inevitable "open verdict." Then the floodgates of inkland were opened, and the deluge pattered for nine days on the deaf coffin where the poor idealist mouldered. The tongues of the Press were loosened, and the leader-writers revelled in recapitulating the circumstances of "The Big Bow Mystery," though they could contribute nothing but adjectives to the solution. The papers teemed with letters—it was a kind of Indian summer of the silly season. But the editors could not keep them out, nor cared to. The mystery was the one topic of conversation everywhere—it was on the carpet and the bare boards alike, in the kitchen and the drawing-room. It was discussed with science or stupidity, with aspirates or without. It came up for breakfast with the rolls, and was swept off the supper-table with the last crumbs.

No. 11 Glover Street, Bow, remained for days a shrine of pilgrimage. The once sleepy little street buzzed from morning till night. From all parts of the town people came to stare up at the bedroom window and wonder with a foolish face of horror. The pavement was often blocked for hours together, and itinerant vendors of refreshment made it a new market centre, while vocalists hastened thither to sing the delectable ditty of the deed without having any voice in the matter. It was a pity the Government did not erect a toll-gate at either end of the street. But Chancellors of the Exchequer rarely avail themselves of the more obvious expedients for paying off the National Debt.

Finally, familiarity bred contempt, and the wits grew facetious at the expense of the Mystery. Jokes on the subject appeared even in the comic papers.

To the proverb, "You must not say Bo to a goose," one added: "or else she will explain you the Mystery." The name of the gentleman who asked whether the Bow Mystery was not 'arrowing shall not be divulged. There was more point in "Dagonet's" remark that, if he had been one of the unhappy jurymen, he would have been driven to "suicide." A professional paradox-monger pointed triumphantly to the somewhat similar situation in "The Murder in the Rue Morgue," and said that Nature had been plagiarising again—like the monkey she was—and he recommended Poe's publishers to apply for an injunction. More seriously, Poe's solution was re-suggested by "Constant Reader" as an original idea. He thought that a small organ-grinder's monkey might have got down the chimney with its master's razor, and, after attempting to shave the occupant of the bed, had returned the way it came. This idea created considerable sensation, but a correspondent with a long train of letters draggling after his name pointed out that a monkey small enough to get down so narrow a flue would not be strong enough to inflict so deep a wound. This was disputed by a third writer, and the contest raged so keenly about the power of monkey's muscles that it was almost taken for granted that a monkey was the guilty party. The bubble was pricked by the pen of "Common Sense," who laconically remarked that no traces of soot or blood had been discovered on the floor, or on the nightshirt, or the counterpane. The *Lancet's* leader on the Mystery was awaited with interest. It said: "We cannot join in the praises that have been showered upon the coroner's summing up. It shows again the evils resulting from having coroners who are not medical men. He seems to have appreciated but inadequately the significance of the medical evidence. He should certainly have directed the jury to return a verdict of murder on that. What was it to do with him that he could see no way by which the wound could have been inflicted by an outside agency? It was for the police to find how that was done. Enough that it was impossible for the unhappy young man to have inflicted such a wound, and then to have had strength and will power enough to hide the instrument and to remove perfectly every trace of his having left the bed for the purpose." It is impossible to enumerate all the theories propounded by the amateur detectives, while Scotland Yard religiously held its tongue. Ultimately the interest on the subject became confined to a few papers which had received the best letters. Those papers that couldn't get interesting letters stopped the correspondence and sneered at the "sensationalism" of those that could. Among the mass of fantasy there were not a few notable solutions, which failed brilliantly, like rockets posing as fixed stars. One was that in the obscurity of the fog the murderer had ascended to the window of the bedroom by means of a ladder from the pavement. He had then with a diamond cut one of the panes away, and effected an entry through the aperture. On leaving he fixed in the pane of glass again (or another which he had brought with him) and thus the room remained with its bolts and locks untouched. On its being pointed out that the panes were too small, a third correspondent showed that that didn't matter, as it was only necessary to insert the hand and undo the fastening, when the entire window could be opened, the process being reversed by the murderer on leaving. This pretty edifice of glass was smashed by a glazier, who wrote to say that a pane could hardly be fixed in from only one side of a window frame, that it would fall out when touched, and that in any case the wet putty could not have escaped detection. A door panel sliced out and replaced was alsb put forward, and as many trap-doors and secret passages were ascribed to No. 11 Glover Street, as if it were a mediæval castle. Another of these clever theories was that the murderer was in the room the whole time the police were there—hidden in the wardrobe. Or he had got behind the door when Grodman broke it open, so that he was not noticed in the excitement of the discovery, and escaped with his weapon at the moment when Grodman and Mrs. Drabdump were examining the window fastenings.

Scientific explanations also were to hand to explain how the assassin locked and bolted the door behind him. Powerful magnets outside the door had been used to turn the key and push the bolt within. Murderers armed with magnets loomed on the popular imagination like a new microbe. There was only one defect in this ingenious theory—the thing could not be done. A physiologist recalled the conjurors who swallow swords—by an anatomical peculiarity of the throat—and said that the deceased might have swallowed the weapon after cutting his own throat. This was too much for the public to swallow. As for the idea that the suicide had been effected with a penknife or its blade, or a bit of steel, which had then got buried in the wound, not even the quotation of Shelley's line:

"Makes such a wound, the knife is lost in it."

could secure it a moment's acceptance. The same reception was accorded to the idea that the cut had been made with a candle-stick (or other harmless necessary bedroom article) constructed like a sword-stick. Theories of this sort caused a humorist to explain that the deceased had hidden the razor in his hollow tooth! Some kind friend of Messrs. Maskelyne and Cook suggested that they were the only persons who could have done the deed, as no one else could get out of a locked cabinet. But perhaps the most brilliant of these flashes of false fire was the facetious, yet probably half seriously meant letter that appeared in the *Pell Mell Press* under the heading of

"THE BIG BOW MYSTERY SOLVED.

"SIR,—You will remember that when the Whitechapel murders were agitating the universe, I suggested that the district coroner was the assassin. My suggestion has been disregarded. The coroner is still at large. So is the Whitechapel murderer. Perhaps this suggestive coincidence will incline the authorities to pay more attention to me this time. The problem seems to be this. The deceased could not have cut his own throat. The deceased could not have had his throat cut for him. As one of the two must have happened, this is obvious nonsense. As this is obvious nonsense I am justified in disbelieving it. As this obvious nonsense was primarily put in circulation by Mrs. Drabdump and Mr. Grodman, I am justified in disbelieving *them*. In short, sir, what guarantee have we that the whole tale is not a cock-and-bull story, invented by the two persons who first found the body? What proof is there that the deed was not done by these persons themselves, who then went to work to smash the door and break the locks and the bolts, and fasten up all windows before they called the police in?—I enclose my card, and am, sir, yours truly,

"ONE WHO LOOKS THROUGH
HIS OWN SPECTACLES."

"[Our correspondent's theory is not so audaciously original as he seems to imagine. Has he not looked through the spectacles of the people who persistently suggested that the Whitechapel murderer was invariably the policeman who found the body? *Somebody* must find the body, if it is to be found at all.—ED. *P.M.P.*]"

The editor had reason to be pleased that he inserted this letter, for it drew the following interesting communication from the great detective himself:—

"THE BIG BOW MYSTERY SOLVED.

"SIR,—I do not agree with you that your correspondent's theory lacks originality. On the contrary, I think it is delightfully original. In fact it has given me an idea. What that idea is I do not yet propose to say, but if 'One Who Looks Through His Own Spectacles' will favour me with his name and address I shall be happy to inform him a little before the rest of the world whether his germ has borne any fruit. I feel he is a kindred spirit, and take this opportunity of saying publicly that I was extremely disappointed at the unsatisfactory verdict. The thing was a palpable assassination; an open verdict has a tendency to relax the exertions of Scotland Yard. I hope I shall not be accused of immodesty, or of making personal reflections, when I say that the Department has had several notorious failures of late. It is not what it used to be. Crime is becoming impertinent. It no longer knows its place, so to speak. It throws down the gauntlet where once it used to cower in its fastnesses. I repeat, I make these remarks solely in the interest of law and order. I do not for one moment believe that Arthur Constant killed himself, and if Scotland Yard satisfies itself with that explanation, and turns on its other side and goes to sleep again, then, sir, one of the foulest and most horrible crimes of the century will for ever go unpunished. My acquaintance with the unhappy victim was but recent; still, I saw and knew enough of the man to be certain (and I hope I have seen and known enough of other men to judge) that he was a man constitutionally incapable of committing an act of violence, whether against himself or anybody else. He would not hurt a fly, as the saying goes. And a man of that gentle stamp always lacks the active energy to lay hands on himself. He was a man to be esteemed in no common degree, and I feel proud to be able to say that he considered me a friend. I am hardly at the time of life at which a man cares to put on his harness again; but, sir, it is impossible that I should ever know a day's rest till the perpetrator of this foul deed is discovered. I have already put myself in communication with the family of the victim, who, I am pleased to say, have every confidence in me, and look to me to clear the name of their unhappy relative from the semi-imputation of suicide. I shall be pleased if anyone who shares my distrust of the authorities, and who has any clue whatever to this terrible mystery or any plausible suggestion to offer, if, in brief, any 'One who looks through his own spectacles' will communicate with me. If I were asked to indicate the direction in which new clues might be most usefully sought, I should say, in the first instance, anything is valuable that helps us to piece together a complete picture of the manifold activities of the man in the East-end. He entered one way or another into the lives of a good many people; is it true that he nowhere made enemies? With the best intentions a man may wound or offend; his interference may be resented; he may even excite jealousy. A young man like the late Mr. Constant could not have had as much practical sagacity as he had goodness. Whose corns did he tread on? The more we know of the last few months of his life the more we shall know of the manner of death. Thanking you by anticipation for the insertion of this letter in your valuable columns, I am, sir, yours truly,

"GEORGE GRODMAN.

"*46 Glover Street, Bow.*"

"*P.S.*—Since writing the above lines, I have, by the kindness of Miss Brent, been placed in possession of a most valuable letter, probably the last letter written by the unhappy gentleman. It is dated Monday, 3 December, the very eve of the murder, and was addressed to her at Florence, and has now, after some delay, followed her back to London where the sad news unexpectedly brought her. It is a letter couched, on the whole, in the most hopeful spirit, and speaks in detail of his schemes. Of course there are things in it not meant for the ears of the public, but there can be no harm in transcribing an important passage:—

"'You seem to have imbibed the idea that the East-end is a kind of Golgotha, and this despite that the books out of which you probably got it are carefully labelled "Fiction." Lamb says somewhere that we think of the "Dark Ages" as literally without sunlight, and so I fancy people like you, dear, think of the "East-end" as a mixture of mire, misery, and murder. How's that for alliteration? Why, within five minutes' walk of me there are the loveliest houses, with gardens back and front, inhabited by very fine people and furniture. Many of my university friends' mouths would water if they knew the income of some of the shopkeepers in the High Road.

"'The rich people about here may not be so fashionable as those in Kensington and Bayswater, but they are every bit as stupid and materialistic. I don't deny, Lucy, I *do* have my black moments, and I do sometimes pine to get away from all this to the lands of sun and lotus-eating. But, on the whole, I am too busy even to dream of dreaming. My real black moments are when I doubt if I am really doing any good. But yet on the whole my conscience or my self-conceit tells me that I am. If one cannot do much with the mass, there is at least the consolation of doing good to the individual. And, after all, is it not enough to have been an influence for good over one or two human souls? There are quite fine characters hereabout—especially in the women—natures capable not only of self-sacrifice, but of delicacy of sentiment. To have learnt to know of such, to have been of services to one or two of such—is not this ample return? I could not get to St. James's Hall to hear your friend's symphony at the Henschel concert. I have been reading Mme. Blavatsky's latest book, and getting quite interested in occult philosophy. Unfortunately I have to do all my reading in bed, and I don't find the book as soothing a soporific as most new books. For keeping one awake I find Theosophy as bad as toothache. . . .' "

"THE BIG BOW MYSTERY SOLVED.

"SIR,—I wonder if any one besides myself has been struck by the incredible bad taste of Mr. Grodman's letter in your last issue. That he, a former servant of the Department, should publicly insult and run it down can only be charitably explained by the supposition that his judgment is failing him in his old age. In view of this letter, are the relatives of the deceased justified in entrusting him with any private documents? It is, no doubt, very good of him to undertake to avenge one whom he seems snobbishly anxious to claim as a friend; but, all things considered, should not his letter have been headed, 'The Big Bow Mystery Shelved?'—I enclose my card, and am, sir, your obedient servant,

"SCOTLAND YARD."

George Grodman read this letter with annoyance, and crumpling up the paper, murmured scornfully, "Edward Wimp!"

V

"Yes, but what will become of the Beautiful?" said Denzil Cantercot.

"Hang the Beautiful!" said Peter Crowl, as if he were on the committee of the Academy. "Give me the True."

Denzil did nothing of the sort. He didn't happen to have it about him.

Denzil Cantercot stood smoking a cigarette in his landlord's shop, and imparting an air of distinction and an agreeable aroma to the close leathery atmosphere. Crowl cobbled away, talking to his tenant without raising his eyes. He was a small, big-headed, sallow, sad-eyed man, with a greasy apron. Denzil was wearing a heavy overcoat with a fur collar. He was never seen without it in public during the winter. In private he removed it and sat in his shirt sleeves. Crowl was a thinker, or thought he was—which seems to involve original thinking anyway. His hair was thinning rapidly at the top, as if his brain were struggling to get as near as possible to the realities of things. He prided himself on having no fads. Few men are without some foible or hobby; Crowl felt almost lonely at times in his superiority. He was a Vegetarian, a Secularist, a Blue Ribbonite, a Republican, and an Anti-tobacconist. Meat was a fad. Drink was a fad. Religion was a fad. Monarchy was a fad. Tobacco was a fad. "A plain man like me," Crowl used to say, "can live without fads." "A plain man" was Crowl's catchword. When of a Sunday morning he stood on Mile End Waste, which was opposite his shop—and held forth to the crowd on the evils of kings, priests, and mutton chops, the "plain man" turned up at intervals like the "theme" of a symphonic movement. "I am only a plain man and I want to know." It was a phrase that sabred the spider-webs of logical refinement, and held them up scornfully on the point. When Crowl went for a little recreation in Victoria Park on Sunday afternoons, it was with this phrase that he invariably routed the supernaturalists. Crowl knew his Bible better than most ministers, and always carried a minutely-printed copy in his pocket, dog-eared to mark contradictions in the text. The second chapter of Jeremiah says one thing; the first chapter of Corinthians says another. Two contradictory statements *may* both be true, but "I am only a plain man, and I want to know." Crowl spent a large part of his time in setting "the word against the word." Cock-fighting affords its votaries no acuter pleasure than Crowl derived from setting two texts by the ears. Crowl had a metaphysical genius which sent his Sunday morning disciples frantic with admiration, and struck the enemy dumb with dismay. He had discovered, for instance, that the Deity could not *move,* owing to already filling all space. He was also the first to invent, for the confusion of the clerical, the crucial case of a saint dying at the Antipodes contemporaneously with another in London. Both went skyward to Heaven, yet the two travelled in directly opposite directions. In all eternity they would never meet. Which, then, got to Heaven? Or was there no such place? "I am only a plain man, and I want to know."

Preserve us our open spaces; they exist to testify to the incurable interest of humanity in the Unknown and the Misunderstood. Even 'Arry is capable of five minutes' attention to speculative theology, if 'Arriet isn't in a 'urry.

Peter Crowl was not sorry to have a lodger like Denzil Cantercot, who, though a man of parts and thus worth powder and shot, was so hopelessly wrong on all subjects under the sun. In only one point did Peter Crowl agree with Denzil Cantercot—he admired Denzil Cantercot secretly. When he asked him for the True—which was about twice a day on the average—he didn't really expect to get it from him. He knew that Denzil was a poet.

"The Beautiful," he went on, "is a thing that only appeals to men like you. The True is for all men. The majority have the first claim. Till then you poets must stand aside. The True and the Useful—that's what we want. The Good of Society is the only test of things. Everything stands or falls by the Good of Society."

"The Good of Society!" echoed Denzil scornfully. "What's the good of Society? The Individual is before all. The mass must be sacrificed to the Great Man. Otherwise the Great Man will be sacrificed to the mass. Without great men there would be no art. Without art life would be a blank."

"Ah, but we should fill it up with bread and butter," said Peter Crowl.

"Yes, it is bread and butter that kills the Beautiful," said Denzil Cantercot bitterly. "Many of us start by following the butterfly through the verdant meadows, but we turn aside—"

"To get the grub," chuckled Peter, cobbling away.

"Peter, if you make a jest of everything, I'll not waste my time on you."

Denzil's wild eyes flashed angrily. He shook his long hair. Life was very serious to him. He never wrote comic verse intentionally.

There are three reasons why men of genius have long hair. One is, that they forget it is growing. The second is, that they like it. The third is, that it comes cheaper; they wear it long for the same reason that they wear their hats long.

Owing to this peculiarity of genius, you may get quite a reputation for lack of twopence. The economic reason did not apply to Denzil, who could always get credit with the profession on the strength of his appearance. Therefore, when street arabs vocally commanded him to get his hair cut, they were doing no service to barbers. Why does all the world watch over barbers and conspire to promote their interests? Denzil would have told you it was not to serve the barbers, but to gratify the crowd's instinctive resentment of originality. In his palmy days Denzil had been an editor, but he no more thought of turning his scissors against himself than of swallowing his paste. The efficacy of hair has changed since the days of Samson, otherwise Denzil would have been a Hercules instead of a long, thin, nervous man, looking too brittle and delicate to be used even for a pipe-cleaner. The narrow oval of his face sloped to a pointed, untrimmed beard. His linen was reproachable, his dingy boots were down at heel, and his cocked hat was drab with dust. Such are the effects of a love for the Beautiful.

Peter Crowl was impressed with Denzil's condemnation of flip-pancy, and he hastened to turn off the joke.

"I'm quite serious," he said. "Butterflies are no good to nothing or nobody; caterpillars at least save the birds from starving."

"Just like your view of things, Peter," said Denzil. "Good morning, madam." This to Mrs. Crowl, to whom he removed his hat with elaborate courtesy. Mrs. Crowl grunted and looked at her husband with a note of interrogation in each eye. For some seconds Crowl stuck to his last, endeavouring not to see the question. He shifted uneasily on his stool. His wife coughed grimly. He looked up, saw her towering over him, and helplessly shook his head in a horizontal direction. It was wonderful how Mrs. Crowl towered over Mr. Crowl, even when he stood up in his shoes. She measured half an inch less. It was quite an optical illusion.

"Mr. Crowl," said Mrs. Crowl, "then I'll tell him."

"No, no, my dear, not yet," faltered Peter, helplessly; "leave it to me."

"I've left it to you long enough. You'll never do nothing. If it was a question of provin' to a lot of chuckleheads that Jollygee and Genesis, or some other dead and gone Scripture folk that don't consarn no mortal soul, used to contradict each other, your tongue 'ud run thirteen to the dozen. But when it's a matter of takin' the bread out o' the mouths o' your own children, you ain't got no more to say for yourself than a lamppost. Here's a man stayin' with you for weeks and weeks—eatin' and drinkin' the flesh off your bones—without payin' a far——"

"Hush, hush, mother; it's all right," said poor Crowl, red as fire.

Denzil looked at her dreamily. "It is possible you are alluding to me, Mrs. Crowl?" he said.

"Who then should I be alludin' to, Mr. Cantercot? Here's seven weeks come and gone, and not a blessed 'aypenny have I——"

"My dear Mrs. Crowl," said Denzil, removing his cigarette from his mouth with a pained air, "why reproach *me* for *your* neglect?"

"*My* neglect! I like that!"

"I don't," said Denzil more sharply. "If you had sent me in the bill you would have had the money long ago. How do you expect me to think of these details?"

"We ain't so grand down here. People pays their way—they don't get no *bills*," said Mrs. Crowl, accentuating the word with infinite scorn.

Peter hammered away at a nail, as though to drown his spouse's voice.

"It's three pounds fourteen and eightpence, if you're so anxious to know," Mrs. Crowl resumed. "And there ain't a woman in the Mile End Road as 'ud a-done it cheaper, with bread at fourpence three-farden a quartern and landlords clamourin' for rent every Monday morning almost afore the sun's up and folks draggin' and slidderin' on till their shoes is only fit to throw after brides and Christmas comin' and sevenpence a week for schoolin'!"

Peter winced under the last item. He had felt it coming—like Christmas. His wife and he parted company on the question of Free Education. Peter felt that having brought nine children into the world, it was only fair he should pay a penny a week for each of those old enough to bear educating. His better half argued that, having so many children, they ought in reason to be exempted. Only people who had few children could spare the penny. But the one point on which the cobbler-sceptic of the Mile End Road got his way was this of the fees. It was a question of conscience, and Mrs. Crowl had never made application for their remission, though she often slapped her children in vexation instead. They were used to slapping, and when nobody else slapped them they slapped one another. They were bright, ill-mannered brats, who pestered their parents and worried their teachers, and were as happy as the Road was long.

"Bother the school fees!" Peter retorted, vexed. "Mr. Cantercot's not responsible for your children."

"I should hope not, indeed, Mr. Crowl," Mrs. Crowl said sternly. "I'm ashamed of you." And with that she flounced out of the shop into the back parlour.

"It's all right," Peter called after her soothingly. "The money'll be all right, mother."

In lower circles it is customary to call your wife your mother; in somewhat superior circles it is the fashion to speak of her as "the wife," as you speak of "the Stock Exchange," or "the Thames," without claiming any peculiar property. Instinctively men are ashamed of being moral and domesticated.

Denzil puffed his cigarette, unembarrassed. Peter bent attentively over his work, making nervous stabs with his awl. There was a long silence. An organ-grinder played a waltz outside, unregarded; and, failing to annoy anybody, moved on. Denzil lit another cigarette. The dirty-faced clock on the wall chimed twelve.

"What do you think," said Crowl, "of Republics?"

"They are low," Denzil replied. "Without a Monarch there is no visible incarnation of Authority."

"What! do you call Queen Victoria visible?"

"Peter, do you want to drive me from the house? Leave frivolousness to women, whose minds are only large enough for domestic difficulties. Republics are low. Plato mercifully kept the poets out of his. Republics are not congenial soil for poetry."

"What nonsense! If England dropped its fad of Monarchy and became a Republic to-morrow, do you mean to say that—?"

"I mean to say there would be no Poet Laureate to begin with."

"Who's fribbling now, you or me, Cantercot? But I don't care a button-hook about poets, present company always excepted. I'm only a plain man, and I want to know where's the sense of givin' any one person authority over everybody else?"

"Ah, that's what Tom Mortlake used to say. Wait till you're in power, Peter, with trade-union money to control, and working men bursting to give you flying angels and to carry you aloft, like a banner, huzzahing."

"Ah, that's because he's head and shoulders above 'em already," said Crowl, with a flash in his sad grey eyes. "Still, it don't prove that I'd talk any different. And I think you're quite wrong about his being spoilt. Tom's a fine fellow—a man every inch of him, and that's a good many. I don't deny he has his weaknesses, and there was a time when he stood in this very shop and denounced that poor dead Constant. 'Crowl,' said he, 'that man'll do mischief. I don't like these kid-glove philanthropists mixing themselves up in practical labour disputes they don't understand.' "

Denzil whistled involuntarily. It was a piece of news.

"I dare say," continued Crowl, "he's a bit jealous of anybody's interference with his influence. But in this case the jealousy did wear off, you see, for the poor fellow and he got quite pals, as everybody knows. Tom's not the man to hug a prejudice. However, all that don't prove nothing against Republics. Look at the Czar and the Jews. I'm only a plain man, but I wouldn't live in Russia for—not for all the leather in it! An Englishman, taxed as he is to keep up his Fad of Monarchy, is at least king in his own castle, whoever bosses it at Windsor. Excuse me a minute, the missus is callin'.'"

"Excuse *me* a minute. I'm going, and I want to say before I go—
I feel it only right you should know at once—that after what has
passed to-day I can never be on the same footing here as in the—
shall I say pleasant?—days of yore."

"Oh, no, Cantercot. Don't say that; don't say that!" pleaded the
little cobbler.

"Well, shall I say unpleasant, then?"

"No, no, Cantercot. Don't misunderstand me. Mother has been
very much put to it lately to rub along. You see she has such a growing family. It grows—daily. But never mind her. You pay whenever
you've got the money."

Denzil shook his head. "It cannot be. You know when I came here
first I rented your top room and boarded myself. Then I learnt to
know you. We talked together. Of the Beautiful. And the Useful. I
found you had no soul. But you were honest, and I liked you. I went
so far as to take my meals with your family. I made myself at home
in your back parlour. But the vase has been shattered (I do not refer
to that on the mantelpiece), and though the scent of the roses may
cling to it still, it can be pieced together—nevermore." He shook his
hair sadly and shambled out of the shop. Crowl would have gone
after him, but Mrs. Crowl was still calling, and ladies must have
the precedence in all polite societies.

Cantercot went straight—or as straight as his loose gait permitted
—to 46 Glover Street, and knocked at the door. Grodman's factotum
opened it. She was a pock-marked person, with a brickdust complexion and a coquettish manner.

"Oh! here we are again!" she said vivaciously.

"Don't talk like a clown," Cantercot snapped. "Is Mr. Grodman
in?"

"No, you've put him out," growled the gentleman himself, suddenly appearing in his slippers. "Come in. What the devil have you
been doing with yourself since the inquest? Drinking again?"

"I've sworn off. Haven't touched a drop since—"

"The murder?"

"Eh?" said Denzil Cantercot, startled. "What do you mean?"

"What I say. Since December 4. I reckon everything from that
murder, now, as they reckon longitude from Greenwich."

"Oh," said Denzil Cantercot.

"Let me see. Nearly a fortnight. What a long time to keep away
from Drink—and Me."

"I don't know which is worse," said Denzil, irritated. "You both steal away my brains."

"Indeed?" said Grodman, with an amused smile. "Well, it's only petty pilfering, after all. What's put salt on your wounds?"

"The twenty-fourth edition of my book."

"*Whose* book?"

"Well, *your* book. You must be making piles of money out of *Criminals I Have Caught.*"

" 'Criminals *I* Have Caught,' " corrected Grodman. "My dear Denzil, how often am I to point out that *I* went through the experiences that make the backbone of my book, not *you*? In each case *I* cooked the criminal's goose. Any journalist could have supplied the dressing."

"The contrary. The journeymen of journalism would have left the truth naked. You yourself could have done that—for there is no man to beat you at cold, lucid, scientific statement. But I idealised the bare facts and lifted them into the realm of poetry and literature. The twenty-fourth edition of the book attests my success."

"Rot! The twenty-fourth edition was all owing to the murder. Did you do that?"

"You take one up so sharply, Mr. Grodman," said Denzil, changing his tone.

"No—I've retired," laughed Grodman.

Denzil did not reprove the ex-detective's flippancy. He even laughed a little.

"Well, give me another fiver, and I'll cry 'quits.' I'm in debt."

"Not a penny. Why haven't you been to see me since the murder? I had to write that letter to the *Pell Mell Press* myself. You might have earned a crown."

"I've had writer's cramp, and couldn't do your last job. I was coming to tell you so on the morning of the—"

"Murder. So you said at the inquest."

"It's true."

"Of course. Weren't you on your oath? It was very zealous of you to get up so early to tell me. In which hand did you have the cramp?"

"Why, in the right, of course."

"And you couldn't write with your left?"

"I don't think I could even hold a pen."

"Or any other instrument, mayhap. What had you been doing to bring it on?"

"Writing too much. That is the only possible cause."

"Oh! I didn't know. Writing what?"

Denzil hesitated. "An epic poem."

"No wonder you're in debt. Will a sovereign get you out of it?"

"No; it wouldn't be in the least use to me."

"Here it is, then."

Denzil took the coin and his hat.

"Aren't you going to earn it, you beggar? Sit down and write something for me."

Denzil got pen and paper, and took his place.

"What do you want me to write?"

"Your Epic Poem."

Denzil started and flushed. But he set to work. Grodman leaned back in his arm-chair and laughed, studying the poet's grave face.

Denzil wrote three lines and paused.

"Can't remember any more? Well, read me the start."

Denzil read:

"Of man's first disobedience and the fruit
Of that forbidden tree whose mortal taste
   Brought death into the world—"

"Hold on!" cried Grodman. "What morbid subjects you choose, to be sure."

"Morbid! Why, Milton chose the same subject!"

"Blow Milton. Take yourself off—you and your Epics."

Denzil went. The pock-marked person opened the street door for him.

"When am I to have that new dress, dear?" she whispered coquettishly.

"I have no money, Jane," he said shortly.

"You have a sovereign."

Denzil gave her the sovereign, and slammed the door viciously. Grodman overheard their whispers, and laughed silently. His hearing was acute. Jane had first introduced Denzil to his acquaintance about two years ago, when he spoke of getting an amanuensis, and the poet had been doing odd jobs for him ever since. Grodman argued that Jane had her reasons. Without knowing them, he got a hold over both. There was no one, he felt, he could not get a hold over. All men —and women—have something to conceal, and you have only to pretend to know what it is. Thus Grodman, who was nothing if not scientific.

Denzil Cantercot shambled home thoughtfully, and abstractedly took his place at the Crowl dinner-table.

VI

Mrs. Crowl surveyed Denzil Cantercot so stonily and cut him his beef so savagely that he said grace when the dinner was over. Peter fed his metaphysical genius on tomatoes. He was tolerant enough to allow his family to follow their Fads; but no savoury smells ever tempted him to be false to his vegetable loves. Besides, meat might have reminded him too much of his work. There is nothing like leather, but Bow beefsteaks occasionally come very near it.

After dinner Denzil usually indulged in poetic reverie. But to-day he did not take his nap. He went out at once to "raise the wind." But there was a dead calm everywhere. In vain he asked for an advance at the office of the *Mile End Mirror,* to which he contributed scathing leaderettes about vestrymen. In vain he trudged to the City and offered to write the *Ham and Eggs Gazette* an essay on the modern methods of bacon-curing. Denzil knew a great deal about the breeding and slaughtering of pigs, smoke-lofts and drying processes, having for years dictated the policy of the *New Pork Herald* in these momentous matters. Denzil also knew a great deal about many other esoteric matters, including weaving machines, the manufacture of cabbage leaves and snuff, and the inner economy of drain-pipes. He had written for the trade papers since boyhood. But there is great competition on these papers. So many men of literary gifts know all about the intricate technicalities of manufactures and markets, and are eager to set the trade right. Grodman perhaps hardly allowed sufficiently for the step backwards that Denzil made when he devoted his whole time for months to *Criminals I Have Caught.* It was as damaging as a debauch. For when your rivals are pushing forwards, to stand still is to go back.

In despair Denzil shambled toilsomely to Bethnal Green. He paused before a window of a little tobacconist's shop, wherein was displayed a placard announcing

"PLOTS FOR SALE."

The announcement went on to state that a large stock of plots was to be obtained on the premises—embracing sensational plots, humorous plots, love plots, religious plots, and poetic plots; also complete manuscripts, original novels, poems, and tales. Apply within.

It was a very dirty-looking shop, with begrimed bricks and blackened woodwork. The window contained some musty old books, an assortment of pipes and tobacco, and a large number of the vilest daubs unhung, painted in oil on Academy boards, and unframed. These were intended for landscapes, as you could tell from the titles. The most expensive was "Chingford Church," and it was marked 1s. 9d. The others ran from 6d. to 1s. 3d., and were mostly representations of Scottish scenery—a loch with mountains in the background, with solid reflections in the water and a tree in the foreground. Sometimes the tree would be in the background. Then the loch would be in the foreground. Sky and water were intensely blue in all. The name of the collection was "Original oil-paintings done by hand." Dust lay thick upon everything, as if carefully shovelled on; and the proprietor looked as if he slept in his shop-window at night without taking his clothes off. He was a gaunt man with a red nose, long but scanty black locks covered by a smoking cap, and a luxuriant black moustache. He smoked a long clay pipe, and had the air of a broken-down operatic villain.

"Ah, good afternoon, Mr. Cantercot," he said, rubbing his hands, half from cold, half from usage; "what have you brought me?"

"Nothing," said Denzil, "but if you will lend me a sovereign I'll do you a stunner."

The operatic villain shook his locks, his eyes full of pawky cunning. "If you did it after that, it *would* be a stunner."

What the operatic villain did with these plots, and who bought them, Cantercot never knew nor cared to know. Brains are cheap to-day, and Denzil was glad enough to find a customer.

"Surely you've known me long enough to trust me," he cried.

"Trust is dead," said the operatic villain, puffing away.

"So is Queen Anne," cried the irritated poet. His eyes took a dangerous hunted look. Money he must have. But the operatic villain was inflexible. No plot, no supper.

Poor Denzil went out flaming. He knew not where to turn. Temporarily he turned on his heel again and stared despairingly at the shop-window. Again he read the legend

"PLOTS FOR SALE."

He stared so long at this that it lost its meaning. When the sense of the words suddenly flashed upon him again, they bore a new significance. He went in meekly, and borrowed fourpence of the operatic villain. Then he took the 'bus for Scotland Yard. There was a not ill-looking servant girl in the 'bus. The rhythm of the vehicle shaped itself into rhymes in his brain. He forgot all about his situation and his object. He had never really written an epic—except "Paradise Lost" —but he composed lyrics about wine and women and often wept to think how miserable he was. But nobody ever bought anything of him, except articles on bacon-curing or attacks on vestrymen. He was a strange, wild creature, and the wench felt quite pretty under his ardent gaze. It almost hypnotised her, though, and she looked down at her new French kid boots to escape it.

At Scotland Yard Denzil asked for Edward Wimp. Edward Wimp was not on view. Like kings and editors, detectives are difficult of approach—unless you are a criminal, when you cannot see anything of them at all. Denzil knew of Edward Wimp, principally because of Grodman's contempt for his successor. Wimp was a man of taste and culture. Grodman's interests were entirely concentrated on the problems of logic and evidence. Books about these formed his sole reading; for *belles lettres* he cared not a straw. Wimp, with his flexible intellect, had a great contempt for Grodman and his slow, laborious, ponderous, almost Teutonic methods. Worse, he almost threatened to eclipse the radiant tradition of Grodman by some wonderfully ingenious bits of workmanship. Wimp was at his greatest in collecting circumstantial evidence; in putting two and two together to make five. He would collect together a number of dark and disconnected data and flash across them the electric light of some unifying hypothesis in a way which would have done credit to a Darwin or a Faraday. An intellect which might have served to unveil the secret workings of nature was subverted to the protection of a capitalistic civilisation.

By the assistance of a friendly policeman, whom the poet magnetised into the belief that his business was a matter of life and death, Denzil obtained the great detective's private address. It was near King's Cross. By a miracle Wimp was at home in the afternoon. He was writing when Denzil was ushered up three pairs of stairs into his presence, but he got up and flashed the bull's-eye of his glance upon the visitor.

"Mr. Denzil Cantercot, I believe," said Wimp.

Denzil started. He had not sent up his name, merely describing himself as a gentleman.

"That is my name," he murmured.

"You were one of the witnesses at the inquest on the body of the late Arthur Constant. I have your evidence there." He pointed to a file. "Why have you come to give fresh evidence?"

Again Denzil started, flushing in addition this time. "I want money," he said, almost involuntarily.

"Sit down." Denzil sat. Wimp stood.

Wimp was young and fresh-coloured. He had a Roman nose, and was smartly dressed. He had beaten Grodman by discovering the wife Heaven meant for him. He had a bouncing boy, who stole jam out of the pantry without anyone being the wiser. Wimp did what work he could do at home in a secluded study at the top of the house. Outside his chamber of horrors he was the ordinary husband of commerce. He adored his wife, who thought poorly of his intellect but highly of his heart. In domestic difficulties Wimp was helpless. He could not tell even whether the servant's "character" was forged or genuine. Probably he could not level himself to such petty problems. He was like the senior wrangler who has forgotten how to do quadratics, and has to solve equations of the second degree by the calculus.

"How much money do you want?" he asked.

"I do not make bargains," Denzil replied, his calm come back by this time. "I came here to tender you a suggestion. It struck me that you might offer me a fiver for my trouble. Should you do so, I shall not refuse it."

"You shall not refuse it—if you deserve it."

"Good. I will come to the point at once. My suggestion concerns —Tom Mortlake."

Denzil threw out the name as if it were a torpedo. Wimp did not move.

"Tom Mortlake," went on Denzil, looking disappointed, "had a sweetheart." He paused impressively.

Wimp said, "Yes?"

"Where is that sweetheart now?"

"Where, indeed?"

"You know about her disappearance?"

"You have just informed me of it."

"Yes, she is gone—without a trace. She went about a fortnight before Mr. Constant's murder."

"Murder? How do you know it was murder?"

"Mr. Grodman says so," said Denzil, startled again.

"H'm! Isn't that rather a proof that it was suicide? Well, go on."

"About a fortnight before the suicide, Jessie Dymond disappeared. So they tell me in Stepney Green, where she lodged and worked."

"What was she?"

"She was a dressmaker. She had a wonderful talent. Quite fashionable ladies got to know of it. One of her dresses was presented at Court.
I think the lady forgot to pay for it; so Jessie's landlady said."

"Did she live alone?"

"She had no parents, but the house was respectable."

"Good-looking, I suppose?"

"As a poet's dream."

"As yours, for instance?"

"I am a poet; I dream."

"You dream you are a poet. Well, well! She was engaged to Mortlake?"

"Oh yes! They made no secret of it. The engagement was an old
one. When he was earning 36s. a week as a compositor, they were
saving up to buy a home. He worked at Railton and Hockes' who
print the *New Pork Herald*. I used to take my 'copy' into the comps'
room, and one day the Father of the Chapel told me all about 'Mortlake and his young woman.' Ye gods! How times are changed! Two
years ago Mortlake had to struggle with my caligraphy—now he is
in with all the nobs, and goes to the 'At Homes' of the aristocracy."

"Radical M.P.'s," murmured Wimp, smiling.

"While I am still barred from the dazzling drawing-rooms, where
beauty and intellect forgather. A mere artisan! A manual labourer!"
Denzil's eyes flashed angrily. He rose with excitement. "They say he
always *was* a jabberer in the composing room, and he has jabbered
himself right out of it and into a pretty good thing. He didn't have
much to say about the crimes of capital when he was set up to second
the toast of 'Railton and Hockes' at the beanfeast."

"Toast and butter, toast and butter," said Wimp genially. "I
shouldn't blame a man for serving the two together, Mr. Cantercot."

Denzil forced a laugh. "Yes; but consistency's *my* motto. I like to
see the royal soul immaculate, unchanging, immovable by fortune.
Anyhow, when better times came for Mortlake the engagement still
dragged on. He did not visit her so much. This last autumn he saw
very little of her."

"How do you know?"

"I—I was often in Stepney Green. My business took me past the
house of an evening. Sometimes there was no light in her room. That
meant she was downstairs gossiping with the landlady."

"She might have been out with Tom?"

"No, sir; I knew Tom was on the platform somewhere or other. He was working up to all hours organising the eight hours working movement."

"A very good reason for relaxing his sweethearting."

"It was. He never went to Stepney Green on a week night."

"But you always did."

"No—not every night."

"You didn't go in?"

"Never. She wouldn't permit my visits. She was a girl of strong character. She always reminded me of Flora Macdonald."

"Another lady of your acquaintance?"

"A lady I know better than the shadows who surround me, who is more real to me than the women who pester me for the price of apartments. Jessie Dymond, too, was of the race of heroines. Her eyes were clear blue, two wells with Truth at the bottom of each. When I looked into those eyes my own were dazzled. They were the only eyes I could never make dreamy." He waved his hand as if making a pass with it. "It was she who had the influence over me."

"You knew her, then?"

"Oh, yes. I knew Tom from the old *New Pork Herald* days, and when I first met him with Jessie hanging on his arm he was quite proud to introduce her to a poet. When he got on he tried to shake me off."

"You should have repaid him what you borrowed."

"It—it—was only a trifle," stammered Denzil.

"Yes, but the world turns on trifles," said the wise Wimp.

"The world is itself a trifle," said the pensive poet. "The Beautiful alone is deserving of our regard."

"And when the Beautiful was not gossiping with her landlady, did she gossip with you as you passed the door?"

"Alas, no! She sat in her room reading, and cast a shadow—"

"On your life?"

"No; on the blind."

"Always one shadow?"

"No, sir. Once or twice, two."

"Ah, you had been drinking."

"On my life, not. I have sworn off the treacherous wine-cup."

"That's right. Beer is bad for poets. It makes their feet shaky. Whose was the second shadow?"

"A man's."

"Naturally. Mortlake's, perhaps."

"Impossible. He was still striking eight hours."

"You found out whose shadow? You didn't leave a shadow of doubt?"

"No; I waited till the substance came out."

"It was Arthur Constant."

"You are a magician! You—you terrify me. Yes, it was he."

"Only once or twice, you say?"

"I didn't keep watch over them."

"No, no, of course not. You only passed casually. I understand you thoroughly."

Denzil did not feel comfortable at the assertion.

"What did he go there for?" Wimp went on.

"I don't know. I'd stake my soul on Jessie's honour."

"You might double your stake without risk."

"Yes, I might! I would! You see her with my eyes."

"For the moment they are the only ones available. When was the last time you saw the two together?"

"About the middle of November."

"Mortlake knew nothing of the meetings?"

"I don't know. Perhaps he did. Mr. Constant had probably enlisted her in his social mission work. I knew she was one of the attendants at the big children's tea in the Great Assembly Hall early in November. He treated her quite like a lady. She was the only attendant who worked with her hands."

"The others carried the cups on their feet, I suppose."

"No; how could that be? My meaning is that all the other attendants were real ladies, and Jessie was only an amateur, so to speak. There was no novelty for her in handing kids cups of tea. I daresay she had helped her landlady often enough at that—there's quite a bushel of brats below stairs. It's almost as bad as at friend Crowl's. Jessie was a real brick. But perhaps Tom didn't know her value. Perhaps he didn't like Constant to call on her, and it led to a quarrel. Anyhow, she's disappeared, like the snowfall on the river. There's not a trace. The landlady, who was such a friend of hers that Jessie used to make up her stuff into dresses for nothing, tells me that she's dreadfully annoyed at not having been left the slightest clue to her late tenant's whereabouts."

"You have been making inquiries on your own account apparently?"

"Only of the landlady. Jessie never even gave her the week's notice, but paid her in lieu of it, and left immediately. The landlady told me I could have knocked her down with a feather. Unfortunately, I wasn't there to do it, or I should certainly have knocked her down for not keeping her eyes open better. She says if she had only had the least suspicion beforehand that the minx (she dared to call Jessie a minx) was going, she'd have known where, or her name would have been somebody else's. And yet she admits that Jessie was looking ill and worried. Stupid old hag!"

"A woman of character," murmured the detective.

"Didn't I tell you so?" cried Denzil eagerly. "Another girl would have let it out that she was going. But no, not a word. She plumped down the money and walked out. The landlady ran upstairs. None of Jessie's things were there. She must have quietly sold them off, or transferred them to the new place. I never in my life met a girl who so thoroughly knew her own mind or had a mind so worth knowing. She always reminded me of the Maid of Saragossa."

"Indeed! And when did she leave?"

"On the 19th of November."

"Mortlake of course knows where she is?"

"I can't say. Last time I was at the house to inquire—it was at the end of November—he hadn't been seen there for six weeks. He wrote to her, of course, sometimes—the landlady knew his writing."

Wimp looked Denzil straight in the eyes, and said, "You mean, of course, to accuse Mortlake of the murder of Mr. Constant?"

"N-n-no, not at all," stammered Denzil, "only you know what Mr. Grodman wrote to the *Pell Mell*. The more we know about Mr. Constant's life the more we shall know about the manner of his death. I thought my information would be valuable to you, and I brought it."

"And why didn't you take it to Mr. Grodman?"

"Because I thought it wouldn't be valuable to *me*."

"You wrote *Criminals I Have Caught*?"

"How—how do you know that?" Wimp was startling him to-day with a vengeance.

"Your style, my dear Mr. Cantercot. The unique noble style."

"Yes, I was afraid it would betray me," said Denzil. "And since you know, I may tell you that Grodman's a mean curmudgeon. What does he want with all that money and those houses—a man with no sense of the Beautiful? He'd have taken my information, and given me more kicks than ha'pence for it, so to speak."

"Yes, he is a shrewd man after all. I don't see anything valuable in your evidence against Mortlake."

"No!" said Denzil in a disappointed tone, and fearing he was going to be robbed. "Not when Mortlake was already jealous of Mr. Constant, who was a sort of rival organiser, unpaid! A kind of blackleg doing the work cheaper—nay, for nothing."

"Did Mortlake tell you he was jealous?" said Wimp, a shade of sarcastic contempt piercing through his tones.

"Oh, yes! He said to me, 'That man will work mischief. I don't like your kid-glove philanthropists meddling in matters they don't understand.' "

"Those were his very words?"

"His *ipsissima verba*."

"Very well. I have your address in my files. Here is a sovereign for you."

"Only one sovereign! It's not the least use to me."

"Very well. It's of great use to me. I have a wife to keep."

"I haven't," said Denzil with a sickly smile, "so perhaps I can manage on it after all." He took his hat and the sovereign.

Outside the door he met a rather pretty servant just bringing in some tea to her master. He nearly upset her tray at sight of her. She seemed more amused at the *rencontre* than he.

"Good afternoon, dear," she said coquettishly. "You might let me have that sovereign. I do so want a new Sunday bonnet."

Denzil gave her the sovereign, and slammed the hall-door viciously when he got to the bottom of the stairs. He seemed to be walking arm-in-arm with the long arm of coincidence. Wimp did not hear the duologue. He was already busy on his evening's report to head-quarters. The next day Denzil had a body-guard wherever he went. It might have gratified his vanity had he known it. But to-night he was yet unattended, so no one noted that he went to 46 Glover Street, after the early Crowl supper. He could not help going. He wanted to get another sovereign. He also itched to taunt Grodman. Not succeeding in the former object, he felt the road open for the second.

"Do you still hope to discover the Bow murderer?" he asked the old bloodhound.

"I can lay my hand on him now," Grodman announced curtly.

Denzil hitched his chair back involuntarily. He found conversation with detectives as lively as playing at skittles with bombshells. They got on his nerves terribly, these undemonstrative gentlemen with no sense of the Beautiful.

"But why don't you give him up to justice?" he murmured.

"Ah—it has to be proved yet. But it is only a matter of time."

"Oh!" said Denzil, "and shall I write the story for you?"

"No. You will not live long enough."

Denzil turned white. "Nonsense! I am years younger than you," he gasped.

"Yes," said Grodman, "but you drink so much."

VII

When Wimp invited Grodman to eat his Christmas plum-pudding at King's Cross, Grodman was only a little surprised. The two men were always overwhelmingly cordial when they met, in order to disguise their mutual detestation. When people really like each other, they make no concealment of their mutual contempt. In his letter to Grodman, Wimp said that he thought it might be nicer for him to keep Christmas in company than in solitary state. There seems to be a general prejudice in favour of Christmas numbers, and Grodman yielded to it. Besides, he thought that a peep at the Wimp domestic interior would be as good as a pantomime. He quite enjoyed the fun that was coming, for he knew that Wimp had not invited him out of mere "peace and goodwill."

There was only one other guest at the festive board. This was Wimp's wife's mother's mother, a lady of sweet seventy. Only a minority of mankind can obtain a grandmother-in-law by marrying, but Wimp was not unduly conceited. The old lady suffered from delusions. One of them was that she was a centenarian. She dressed for the part. It is extraordinary what pains ladies will take to conceal their age. Another of Wimp's grandmother-in-law's delusions was that Wimp had married to get her into the family. Not to frustrate his design, she always gave him her company on high-days and holidays. Wilfred Wimp—the little boy who stole the jam—was in great form at the Christmas dinner. The only drawback to his enjoyment was that its sweets needed no stealing. His mother presided over the platters, and thought how much cleverer Grodman was than her husband. When the pretty servant who waited on them was momentarily out of the room, Grodman had remarked that she seemed very inquisitive. This coincided with Mrs. Wimp's own convictions, though Mr. Wimp could never be brought to see anything unsatisfactory or suspicious about the girl, not even though there were faults in spelling in the "character" with which her last mistress had supplied her.

It was true that the puss had pricked up her ears when Denzil Cantercot's name was mentioned. Grodman saw it, and watched her,

and fooled Wimp to the top of his bent. It was, of course, Wimp who
introduced the poet's name, and he did it so casually that Grodman
perceived at once that he wished to pump him. The idea that the
rival bloodhound should come to him for confirmation of suspicions
against his pet jackal was too funny. It was almost as funny to
Grodman that evidence of some sort should be obviously lying
to hand in the bosom of Wimp's hand-maiden; so obviously that
Wimp could not see it. Grodman enjoyed his Christmas dinner,
secure that he had not found a successor after all. Wimp, for
his part, contemptuously wondered at the way Grodman's thought
hovered about Denzil without grazing the truth. A man constantly
about him, too!

"Denzil is a man of genius," said Grodman. "And as such comes
under the heading of Suspicious Characters. He has written an Epic
Poem and read it to me. It is morbid from start to finish. There is
'death' in the third line. I daresay you know he polished up my
book?" Grodman's artlessness was perfect.

"No. You surprise me," Wimp replied. "I'm sure he couldn't have
done much to it. Look at your letter in the *Pell Mell*. Who wants
more polish and refinement than that showed?"

"Ah, I didn't know you did me the honour of reading that."

"Oh, yes; we both read it," put in Mrs. Wimp. "I told Mr. Wimp
it was very clever and cogent. After that quotation from the letter to
the poor fellow's *fiancée* there could be no more doubt but that it was
murder. Mr. Wimp was convinced by it too, weren't you, Edward?"

Edward coughed uneasily. It was a true statement, and therefore
an indiscreet. Grodman would plume himself terribly. At this moment Wimp felt that Grodman had been right in remaining a bachelor.
Grodman perceived the humour of the situation, and wore a curious,
sub-mocking smile.

"On the day I was born," said Wimp's grandmother-in-law, "over
a hundred years ago, there was a babe murdered"—Wimp found
himself wishing it had been she. He was anxious to get back to Cantercot. "Don't let us talk shop on Christmas Day," he said, smiling at
Grodman. "Besides, murder isn't a very appropriate subject."

"No, it ain't," said Grodman. "How did we get on to it? Oh, yes
—Denzil Cantercot. Ha! ha! ha! That's curious, for since Denzil re-
vised *Criminals I Have Caught,* his mind's running on nothing but
murders. A poet's brain is easily turned."

Wimp's eye glittered with excitement and contempt for Grodman's blindness. In Grodman's eye there danced an amused scorn of Wimp; to the outsider his amusement appeared at the expense of the poet.

Having wrought his rival up to the highest pitch, Grodman slyly and suddenly unstrung him.

"How lucky for Denzil!" he said, still in the same naïve, facetious Christmasy tone, "that he can prove an alibi in this Constant affair."

"An alibi!" gasped Wimp. "Really?"

"Oh, yes. He was with his wife, you know. She's my woman of all work, Jane. She happened to mention his being with her."

Jane had done nothing of the kind. After the colloquy he had overheard, Grodman had set himself to find out the relation between his two employees. By casually referring to Denzil as "your husband," he so startled the poor woman that she did not attempt to deny the bond. Only once did he use the two words, but he was satisfied. As to the alibi, he had not yet troubled her; but to take its existence for granted would upset and discomfort Wimp. For the moment that was triumph enough for Wimp's guest.

"Par," said Wilfred Wimp, "what's a alleybi? A marble?"

"No, my lad," said Grodman, "it means being somewhere else when you're supposed to be somewhere."

"Ah, playing truant," said Wilfred self-consciously; his schoolmaster had often proved an alibi against him. "Then Denzil will be hanged."

Was it a prophecy? Wimp accepted it as such; as an oracle from the gods bidding him mistrust Grodman. Out of the mouths of little children issueth wisdom; sometimes even when they are not saying their lessons.

"When I was in my cradle, a century ago," said Wimp's grandmother-in-law, "men were hanged for stealing horses."

They silenced her with snapdragon performances.

Wimp was busy thinking how to get at Grodman's factotum.

Grodman was busy thinking how to get at Wimp's domestic.

Neither received any of the usual messages from the Christmas Bells.

.   .   .   .   .   .

The next day was sloppy and uncertain. A thin rain drizzled languidly. One can stand that sort of thing on a summer Bank Holiday; one expects it. But to have a bad December Bank Holiday is too much of a bad thing. Some steps should surely be taken to confuse the weather clerk's chronology. Once let him know that Bank

Holiday is coming, and he writes to the company for more water. To-day his stock seemed low, and he was dribbling it out; at times the wintry sun would shine in a feeble, diluted way, and though the holiday-makers would have preferred to take their sunshine neat, they swarmed forth in their myriads whenever there was a ray of hope. But it was only dodging the raindrops; up went the umbrellas again, and the streets became meadows of ambulating mushrooms.

Denzil Cantercot sat in his fur overcoat at the open window, looking at the landscape in water-colours. He smoked an after-dinner cigarette, and spoke of the Beautiful. Crowl was with him. They were in the first-floor front, Crowl's bedroom, which, from its view of the Mile End Road, was livelier than the parlour with its outlook on the backyard. Mrs. Crowl was an anti-tobacconist as regards the best bedroom; but Peter did not like to put the poet or his cigarette out. He felt there was something in common between smoke and poetry, over and above their being both Fads. Besides, Mrs. Crowl was sulking in the kitchen. She had been arranging for an excursion with Peter and the children to Victoria Park. (She had dreamed of the Crystal Palace, but Santa Claus had put no gifts in the cobbler's shoes.) Now she could not risk spoiling the feather in her bonnet. The nine brats expressed their disappointment by slapping one another on the staircases. Peter felt that Mrs. Crowl connected him in some way with the rainfall, and was unhappy. Was it not enough that he had been deprived of the pleasure of pointing out to the superstitious majority the mutual contradictions of Leviticus and the Song of Solomon? It was not often that Crowl could count on such an audience.

"And you still call Nature Beautiful?" he said to Denzil, pointing to the ragged sky and the dripping eaves. "Ugly old scarecrow!"

"Ugly she seems to-day," admitted Denzil. "But what is Ugliness but a higher form of Beauty? You have to look deeper into it to see it; such vision is the priceless gift of the few. To me this wan desolation of sighing rain is lovely as the sea-washed ruins of cities."

"Ah, but you wouldn't like to go out into it," said Peter Crowl. As he spoke the drizzle suddenly thickened into a torrent.

"We do not always kiss the woman we love."

"Speak for yourself, Denzil. I'm only a plain man, and I want to know if Nature isn't a Fad. Hallo, there goes Mortlake! Lord, a minute of this will soak him to the skin."

The labour leader was walking along with bowed head. He did not seem to mind the shower. It was some seconds before he even heard Crowl's invitation to him to take shelter. When he did hear it he shook his head.

"I know I can't offer you a drawing-room with duchesses stuck about it," said Peter, vexed.

Tom turned the handle of the shop door and went in. There was nothing in the world which now galled him more than the suspicion that he was stuck-up and wished to cut old friends. He picked his way through the nine brats who clung affectionately to his wet knees, dispersing them finally by a jet of coppers to scramble for. Peter met him on the stairs and shook his hand lovingly and admiringly, and took him into Mrs. Crowl's bedroom.

"Don't mind what I say, Tom. I'm only a plain man, and my tongue will say what comes uppermost! But it ain't from the soul, Tom, it ain't from the soul," said Peter, punning feebly, and letting a mirthless smile play over his sallow features. "You know Mr. Cantercot, I suppose? The poet."

"Oh, yes; how do you do, Tom?" cried the Poet. "Seen the *New Pork Herald* lately? Not bad, those old times, eh?"

"No," said Tom, "I wish I was back in them."

"Nonsense, nonsense," said Peter, in much concern. "Look at the good you are doing to the working man. Look how you are sweeping away the Fads. Ah, it's a grand thing to be gifted, Tom. The idea of your chuckin' yourself away on a composin' room! Manual labour is all very well for plain men like me, with no gift but just enough brains to see into the realities of things—to understand that we've got no soul and no immortality, and all that—and too selfish to look after anybody's comfort but my own and mother's and the kids'. But men like you and Cantercot—it ain't right that you should be peggin' away at low material things. Not that I think Cantercot's gospel any value to the masses. The Beautiful is all very well for folks who've got nothing else to think of, but give me the True. You're the man for my money, Mortlake. No reference to the funds, Tom, to which I contribute little enough, Heaven knows; though how a *place* can know anything, Heaven alone knows. *You* give us the Useful, Tom; that's what the world wants more than the Beautiful."

"Socrates said that the Useful *is* the Beautiful," said Denzil.

"That may be," said Peter, "but the Beautiful ain't the Useful."

"Nonsense!" said Denzil. "What about Jessie—I mean Miss Dymond? There's a combination for you. She always reminds me of Grace Darling. How *is* she, Tom?"

"She's dead!" snapped Tom.

"What?" Denzil turned as white as a Christmas ghost.

"It was in the papers," said Tom; "all about her and the lifeboat."

"Oh, you mean Grace Darling," said Denzil, visibly relieved. "I meant Miss Dymond."

"You needn't be so interested in her," said Tom surlily. "She don't appreciate it. Ah, the shower is over. I must be going."

"No, stay a little longer, Tom," pleaded Peter. "I see a lot about you in the papers, but very little of your dear old phiz now. I can't spare the time to go and hear you. But I really must give myself a treat. When's your next show?"

"Oh, I am always giving shows," said Tom, smiling a little. "But my next big performance is on the twenty-first of January, when that picture of poor Mr. Constant is to be unveiled at the Bow Break o' Day Club. They have written to Gladstone and other big pots to come down. I do hope the old man accepts. A non-political gathering like this is the only occasion we could both speak at, and I have never been on the same platform with Gladstone."

He forgot his depression and ill-temper in the prospect, and spoke with more animation.

"No, I should hope not, Tom," said Peter. "What with his Fads about the Bible being a Rock, and Monarchy being the right thing, he is a most dangerous man to lead the Radicals. He never lays his axe to the root of anything—except oak trees."

"Mr. Cantercot!" It was Mrs. Crowl's voice that broke in upon the tirade. "There's a *gentleman* to see you." The astonishment Mrs. Crowl put into the "gentleman" was delightful. It was almost as good as a week's rent to her to give vent to her feelings. The controversial couple had moved away from the window when Tom entered, and had not noticed the immediate advent of another visitor who had spent his time profitably in listening to Mrs. Crowl before asking to see the presumable object of his visit.

"Ask him up if it's a friend of yours, Cantercot," said Peter. It was Wimp. Denzil was rather dubious as to the friendship, but he preferred to take Wimp diluted. "Mortlake's upstairs," he said; "will you come up and see him?"

Wimp had intended a duologue, but he made no objection, so he, too, stumbled through the nine brats to Mrs. Crowl's bedroom. It was a queer quartette. Wimp had hardly expected to find anybody at the house on Boxing Day, but he did not care to waste a day. Was not Grodman, too, on the track? How lucky it was that Denzil had made the first overtures, so that he could approach him without exciting his suspicion.

Mortlake scowled when he saw the detective. He objected to the police—on principle. But Crowl had no idea who the visitor was, even when told his name. He was rather pleased to meet one of Denzil's high-class friends, and welcomed him warmly. Probably he was some famous editor, which would account for his name stirring vague recollections. He summoned the eldest brat and sent him for beer (people would have their Fads), and not without trepidation called down to "Mother" for glasses. "Mother" observed at night (in the same apartment) that the beer money might have paid the week's school fees for half the family.

"We were just talking of poor Mr. Constant's portrait, Mr. Wimp," said the unconscious Crowl; "they're going to unveil it, Mortlake tells me, on the twenty-first of next month at the Bow Break o' Day Club."

"Ah," said Wimp, elated at being spared the trouble of manœuvring the conversation. "Mysterious affair that, Mr. Crowl."

"No; it's the right thing," said Peter. "There ought to be some memorial of the man in the district where he worked and where he died, poor chap." The cobbler brushed away a tear.

"Yes, it's only right," echoed Mortlake a whit eagerly. "He was a noble fellow, a true philanthropist. The only thoroughly unselfish worker I've ever met."

"He was that," said Peter: "and it's a rare pattern is unselfishness. Poor fellow, poor fellow. He preached the Useful, too. I've never met his like. Ah, I wish there was a Heaven for him to go to!" He blew his nose violently with a red pocket-handkerchief.

"Well, he's there, if there *is*," said Tom.

"I hope he is," added Wimp fervently; "but I shouldn't like to go there the way he did."

"You were the last person to see him, Tom, weren't you?" said Denzil.

"Oh, no," answered Tom quickly. "You remember he went out after me; at least, so Mrs. Drabdump said at the inquest."

"That last conversation he had with you, Tom," said Denzil. "He didn't say anything to you that would lead you to suppose—"

"No, of course not!" interrupted Mortlake impatiently.

"Do you really think he was murdered, Tom?" said Denzil.

"Mr. Wimp's opinion on that point is more valuable than mine," replied Tom testily. "It may have been suicide. Men often get sick of life—especially if they are bored," he added meaningly.

"Ah, but you were the last person known to be with him," said Denzil.

Crowl laughed. "Had you there, Tom."

But they did not have Tom there much longer, for he departed, looking even worse-tempered than when he came. Wimp went soon after, and Crowl and Denzil were left to their interminable argumentation concerning the Useful and the Beautiful.

Wimp went West. He had several strings (or cords) to his bow, and he ultimately found himself at Kensal Green Cemetery. Being there, he went down the avenues of the dead to a grave to note down the exact date of a death. It was a day on which the dead seemed enviable. The dull, sodden sky, the dripping, leafless trees, the wet spongy soil, the reeking grass—everything combined to make one long to be in a warm, comfortable grave away from the leaden *ennuis* of life. Suddenly the detective's keen eye caught sight of a figure that made his heart throb with sudden excitement. It was that of a woman in a grey shawl and a brown bonnet standing before a railed-in grave. She had no umbrella. The rain plashed mournfully upon her, but left no trace on her soaking garments. Wimp crept up behind her, but she paid no heed to him. Her eyes were lowered to the grave, which seemed to be drawing them towards it by some strange morbid fascination. His eyes followed hers. The simple headstone bore the name: "Arthur Constant."

Wimp tapped her suddenly on the shoulder.

"How do you do, Mrs. Drabdump?"

Mrs. Drabdump went deadly white. She turned round, staring at Wimp without any recognition.

"You remember me, surely," he said, "I've been down once or twice to your place about that poor gentleman's papers." His eye indicated the grave.

"Lor! I remember you now," said Mrs. Drabdump.

"Won't you come under my umbrella? You must be drenched to the skin."

"It don't matter, sir. I can't take no hurt. I've had the rheumatics this twenty year."

Mrs. Drabdump shrank from accepting Wimp's attentions, not so much perhaps because he was a man as because he was a gentleman. Mrs. Drabdump liked to see the fine folks keep their place, and not contaminate their skirts by contact with the lower castes. "It's set wet, it'll rain right into the new year," she announced. "And they say a bad beginnin' makes a worse endin'." Mrs. Drabdump was one of those persons who give you the idea that they just missed being born barometers.

"But what are you doing in this miserable spot, so far from home?" queried the detective.

"It's Bank Holiday," Mrs. Drabdump reminded him in tones of acute surprise. "I always make a hexcursion on Bank Holiday."

VIII

The New Year brought Mrs. Drabdump a new lodger. He was an old gentleman with a long grey beard. He rented the rooms of the late Mr. Constant, and lived a very retired life. Haunted rooms or rooms that ought to be haunted if the ghosts of those murdered in them had any self-respect—are supposed to fetch a lower rent in the market. The whole Irish problem might be solved if the spirits of "Mr. Balfour's victims" would only depreciate the value of property to a point consistent with the support of an agricultural population. But Mrs. Drabdump's new lodger paid so much for his rooms that he laid himself open to a suspicion of a special interest in ghosts. Perhaps he was a member of the Psychical Society. The neighbourhood imagined him another mad philanthropist, but as he did not appear to be doing any good to anybody it relented and conceded his sanity. Mortlake, who occasionally stumbled across him in the passage, did not trouble himself to think about him at all. He was too full of other troubles and cares. Though he worked harder than ever, the spirit seemed to have gone out of him. Sometimes he forgot himself in a fine rapture of eloquence—lashing himself up into a divine resentment of injustice or a passion of sympathy with the sufferings of his brethren—but mostly he plodded on in dull, mechanical fashion. He still made brief provincial tours, starring a day here and a day there, and everywhere his admirers remarked how jaded and overworked he looked. There was talk of starting a subscription to give him a holiday on the Continent—a luxury obviously unobtainable on the few pounds allowed him per week. The new lodger would doubtless have been pleased to subscribe, for he seemed quite to like occupying Mortlake's chamber the nights he was absent, though he was thoughtful enough not to disturb that hard-worked landlady in the adjoining room by unseemly noise. Wimp was always a quiet man.

Meantime the 21st of the month approached, and the East End

was in excitement. Mr. Gladstone had consented to be present at the
ceremony of unveiling the portrait of Arthur Constant, presented by
an unknown donor to the Bow Break o' Day Club, and it was to be a
great function. The whole affair was outside the lines of party politics,
so that even Conservatives and Socialists considered themselves
justified in pestering the committee for tickets. To say nothing of
ladies. As the committee desired to be present themselves, nine-
tenths of the applications for admission had to be refused, as is usual
on these occasions. The committee agreed among themselves to exclude the fair sex altogether as the only way of disposing of their
womankind, who were making speeches as long as Mr. Gladstone's.
Each committeeman told his sisters, female cousins and aunts, that
the other committeemen had insisted on divesting the function of
all grace; and what could a man do when he was in a minority of one?

Crowl, who was not a member of the Break o' Day Club, was
particularly anxious to hear the great orator whom he despised;
fortunately Mortlake remembered the cobbler's anxiety to hear himself, and on the eve of the ceremony sent him a ticket. Crowl was in
the first flush of possession when Denzil Cantercot returned, after a
sudden and unannounced absence of three days. His clothes were
muddy and tattered, his cocked hat was deformed, his cavalier beard
was matted, and his eyes were bloodshot. The cobbler nearly dropped
the ticket at the sight of him. "Hullo, Cantercot!" he gasped. "Why,
where have you been all these days?"

"Terribly busy!" said Denzil. "Here, give me a glass of water. I'm
dry as the Sahara."

Crowl ran inside and got the water, trying hard not to inform
Mrs. Crowl of their lodger's return. "Mother" had expressed herself
freely on the subject of the poet during his absence, and not in terms
which would have commended themselves to the poet's fastidious
literary sense. Indeed, she did not hesitate to call him a sponger and
a low swindler, who had run away to avoid paying the piper. Her
fool of a husband might be quite sure he would never set eyes on the
scoundrel again. However, Mrs. Crowl was wrong. Here was Denzil
back again. And yet Mr. Crowl felt no sense of victory. He had no
desire to crow over his partner and to utter that "See! didn't I tell
you so?" which is a greater consolation than religion in most of the
misfortunes of life. Unfortunately, to get the water, Crowl had to go
to the kitchen; and as he was usually such a temperate man, this
desire for drink in the middle of the day attracted the attention of

the lady in possession. Crowl had to explain the situation. Mrs. Crowl ran into the shop to improve it. Mr. Crowl followed in dismay, leaving a trail of spilt water in his wake.

"You good-for-nothing, disreputable scarecrow, where have—"

"Hush, mother. Let him drink. Mr. Cantercot is thirsty."

"Does he care if my children are hungry?"

Denzil tossed the water greedily down his throat almost at a gulp, as if it were brandy.

"Madam," he said, smacking his lips, "I do care. I care intensely. Few things in life would grieve me more deeply than to hear that a child, a dear little child—the Beautiful in a nutshell—had suffered hunger. You wrong me." His voice was tremulous with the sense of injury. Tears stood in his eyes.

"Wrong you? I've no wish to *wrong* you," said Mrs. Crowl. "I should like to *hang* you."

"Don't talk of such ugly things," said Denzil, touching his throat nervously.

"Well, what have you been doin' all this time?"

"Why, what should I be doing?"

"How should I know what became of you? I thought it was another murder."

"What!" Denzil's glass dashed to fragments on the floor. "What do you mean?"

But Mrs. Crowl was glaring too viciously at Mr. Crowl to reply. He understood the message as if it were printed. It ran: "You have broken one of my best glasses. You have annihilated threepence, or a week's school fees for half the family." Peter wished she would turn the lightning upon Denzil, a conductor down whom it would run innocuously. He stooped down and picked up the pieces as carefully as if they were cuttings from the Koh-i-noor. Thus the lightning passed harmlessly over his head and flew towards Cantercot.

"What do I mean?" Mrs. Crowl echoed, as if there had been no interval. "I mean that it would be a good thing if you *had* been murdered."

"What beautiful ideas you have, to be sure!" murmured Denzil.

"Yes; but they'd be useful," said Mrs. Crowl, who had not lived with Peter all these years for nothing. "And if you haven't been murdered what *have* you been doing?"

"My dear, my dear," put in Crowl, deprecatingly, looking up from his quadrupedal position like a sad dog, "you are not Cantercot's keeper."

"Oh, ain't I?" flashed his spouse. "Who else keeps him, I should like to know?"

Peter went on picking up the pieces of the Koh-i-noor.

"I have no secrets from Mrs. Crowl," Denzil explained courteously. "I have been working day and night bringing out a new paper. Haven't had a wink of sleep for three nights."

Peter looked up at his bloodshot eyes with respectful interest.

"The capitalist met me in the street—an old friend of mine—I was overjoyed at the *rencontre* and told him the idea I'd been brooding over for months, and he promised to stand all the racket."

"What sort of a paper?" said Peter.

"Can you ask? To what do you think I've been devoting my days and nights but to the cultivation of the Beautiful?"

"Is that what the paper will be devoted to?"

"Yes. To the Beautiful."

"I know," snorted Mrs. Crowl, "with portraits of actresses."

"Portraits? Oh, no!" said Denzil. "That would be the True. Not the Beautiful."

"And what's the name of the paper?" asked Crowl.

"Ah, that's a secret, Peter. Like Scott, I prefer to remain anonymous."

"Just like your Fads. I'm only a plain man, and I want to know where the fun of anonymity comes in? If I had any gifts, I should like to get the credit. It's a right and natural feeling, to my thinking."

"Unnatural, Peter; unnatural. We're all born anonymous, and I'm for sticking close to Nature. Enough for me that I disseminate the Beautiful. Any letters come during my absence, Mrs. Crowl?"

"No," she snapped. "But a gent named Grodman called. He said you hadn't been to see him for some time, and looked annoyed to hear you'd disappeared. How much have you let *him* in for?"

"The man's in *my* debt," said Denzil, annoyed. "I wrote a book for him and he's taken all the credit for it, the rogue! My name doesn't appear even in the Preface. What's that ticket you're looking so lovingly at, Peter?"

"That's for to-night—the unveiling of Constant's portrait. Gladstone speaks. Awful demand for places."

"Gladstone!" sneered Denzil. "Who wants to hear Gladstone! A man who's devoted his life to pulling down the pillars of Church and State."

"A man who's devoted his whole life to propping up the crumbling

Fads of Religion and Monarchy. But, for all that, the man has his gifts, and I'm burnin' to hear him."

"I wouldn't go out of my way an inch to hear him," said Denzil; and went up to his room, and when Mrs. Crowl sent him up a cup of nice strong tea at tea-time, the brat who bore it found him lying dressed on the bed, snoring unbeautifully.

The evening wore on. It was fine frosty weather. The Whitechapel Road swarmed with noisy life, as though it were a Saturday night. The stars flared in the sky like the lights of celestial costermongers. Everybody was on the alert for the advent of Mr. Gladstone. He must surely come through the Road on his journey from the West Bow-wards. But nobody saw him or his carriage, except those about the Hall. Probably he went by tram most of the way. He would have caught cold in an open carriage, or bobbing his head out of the window of a closed.

"If he had only been a German prince, or a cannibal king," said Crowl bitterly, as he plodded towards the Club, "we should have disguised Mile End in bunting and blue fire. But perhaps it's a compliment. He knows his London, and it's no use trying to hide the facts from him. They must have queer notions of cities, those monarchs. They must fancy everybody lives in a flutter of flags and walks about under triumphal arches, like as if I were to stitch shoes in my Sunday clothes." By a defiance of chronology Crowl had them on to-day, and they seemed to accentuate the simile.

"And why shouldn't life be fuller of the Beautiful?" said Denzil. The poet had brushed the reluctant mud off his garments to the extent it was willing to go, and had washed his face, but his eyes were still bloodshot from the cultivation of the Beautiful. Denzil was accompanying Crowl to the door of the Club out of good fellowship. Denzil was himself accompanied by Grodman, though less obtrusively. Least obtrusively was he accompanied by his usual Scotland Yard shadows, Wimp's agents. There was a surging nondescript crowd about the Club, so that the police, and the doorkeeper, and the stewards could with difficulty keep out the tide of the ticketless, through which the current of the privileged had equal difficulty in permeating. The streets all around were thronged with people longing for a glimpse of Gladstone. Mortlake drove up in a hansom (his head a self-conscious pendulum of popularity, swaying and bowing to right and left) and received all the pent-up enthusiasm.

"Well, good-bye, Cantercot," said Crowl.

"No, I'll see you to the door, Peter."

They fought their way shoulder to shoulder.

Now that Grodman had found Denzil he was not going to lose him again. He had only found him by accident, for he was himself bound to the unveiling ceremony, to which he had been invited in view of his known devotion to the task of unveiling the Mystery. He spoke to one of the policemen about, who said, "Ay, ay, sir," and he was prepared to follow Denzil, if necessary, and to give up the pleasure of hearing Gladstone for an acuter thrill. The arrest must be delayed no longer.

But Denzil seemed as if he were going in on the heels of Crowl. This would suit Grodman better. He could then have the two pleasures. But Denzil was stopped half-way through the door.

"Ticket, sir!"

Denzil drew himself up to his full height.

"Press," he said majestically. All the glories and grandeurs of the Fourth Estate were concentrated in that haughty monosyllable. Heaven itself is full of journalists who have overawed St. Peter. But the doorkeeper was a veritable dragon.

"What paper, sir?"

"*New Pork Herald,*" said Denzil sharply. He did not relish his word being distrusted.

"*New York Herald,*" said one of the bystanding stewards, scarce catching the sounds. "Pass him in."

And in the twinkling of an eye Denzil had eagerly slipt inside.

But during the brief altercation Wimp had come up. Even he could not make his face quite impassive, and there was a suppressed intensity in the eyes and a quiver about the mouth. He went in on Denzil's heels, blocking up the doorway with Grodman. The two men were so full of their coming *coups* that they struggled for some seconds, side by side, before they recognised each other. Then they shook hands heartily.

"That was Cantercot just went in, wasn't it, Grodman?" said Wimp.

"I didn't notice," said Grodman, in tones of utter indifference.

At bottom Wimp was terribly excited. He felt that his *coup* was going to be executed under very sensational circumstances. Everything would combine to turn the eyes of the country upon him—nay, of the world, for had not the Big Bow Mystery been discussed in every language under the sun? In these electric times the criminal receives a cosmopolitan reputation. It is a privilege he shares with few other artists. This time Wimp would be one of them. And, he felt, deservedly so. If the criminal had been cunning to the point of genius in planning the murder, he had been acute to the point of divination in detecting it. Never before had he pieced together so broken a chain. He could not resist the unique opportunity of setting a sensational scheme in a sensational framework. The dramatic instinct was strong in him; he felt like a playwright who has constructed a strong melodramatic plot, and has the Drury Lane stage suddenly offered him to present it on. It would be folly to deny himself the luxury, though the presence of Mr. Gladstone and the nature of the ceremony should perhaps have given him pause. Yet, on the other hand, these were the very factors of the temptation. Wimp went in and took a seat behind Denzil. All the seats were numbered, so that everybody might have the satisfaction of occupying somebody else's. Denzil was in the special reserved places in the front row just by the central gangway; Crowl was squeezed into a corner behind a pillar near the back of the hall. Grodman had been honoured with a seat on the platform, which was accessible by steps on the right and left, but he kept his eye on Denzil. The picture of the poor idealist hung on the wall behind Grodman's head, covered by its curtain of brown holland. There was a subdued buzz of excitement about the hall, which swelled into cheers every now and again as some gentleman known to fame or Bow took his place upon the platform. It was occupied by several local M.P.'s of varying politics, a number of other Parliamentary satellites of the great man, three or four labour leaders, a peer or two of philanthropic pretensions, a sprinkling of Toynbee and Oxford Hall men, the president and other honorary officials, some of the family and friends of the deceased, together with the inevitable percentage of persons who had no claim to be there save cheek. Gladstone was late—later than Mortlake, who was cheered to the echo when he arrived, someone starting, "For He's a Jolly Good Fellow," as if it were a political meeting. Gladstone came in just in time to acknowledge the compliment. The noise of the song, trolled out from iron lungs, had drowned the huzzahs heralding the old man's advent. The convivial chorus went to Mortlake's head, as if champagne had really preceded it. His eyes grew moist and dim. He saw himself swimming to the Millennium on waves of enthusiasm. Ah, how his brother toilers should be rewarded for their trust in him!

With his usual courtesy and consideration, Mr. Gladstone had refused to perform the actual unveiling of Arthur Constant's portrait. "That," he said in his postcard, "will fall most appropriately to Mr.

Mortlake, a gentleman who has, I am given to understand, enjoyed the personal friendship of the late Mr. Constant, and has co-operated with him in various schemes for the organisation of skilled and un-skilled classes of labour, as well as for the diffusion of better ideals— ideals of self-culture and self-restraint—among the working men of Bow, who have been fortunate, so far as I can perceive, in the possession (if in one case unhappily only temporary possession) of two such men of undoubted ability and honesty to direct their divided counsels and to lead them along a road, which, though I cannot pledge myself to approve of it in all its turnings and windings, is yet not unfitted to bring them somewhat nearer to goals to which there are few of us but would extend some measure of hope that the working-classes of this great Empire may in due course, yet with no unnecessary delay, be enabled to arrive."

Mr. Gladstone's speech was an expansion of his postcard, punctu-ated by cheers. The only new thing in it was the graceful and touching way in which he revealed what had been a secret up till then—that the portrait had been painted and presented to the Bow Break o' Day Club, by Lucy Brent, who in the fullness of time would have been Arthur Constant's wife. It was a painting for which he had sat to her while alive, and she had stifled yet pampered her grief by working hard at it since his death. The fact added the last touch of pathos to the occasion. Crowl's face was hidden behind his red handkerchief; even the fire of excitement in Wimp's eye was quenched for a moment by a tear-drop, as he thought of Mrs. Wimp and Wilfred. As for Grodman, there was almost a lump in his throat. Denzil Cantercot was the only unmoved man in the room. He thought the episode quite too Beautiful, and was already weaving it into rhyme.

At the conclusion of his speech Mr. Gladstone called upon Tom Mortlake to unveil the portrait. Tom rose, pale and excited. His hand faltered as he touched the cord. He seemed overcome with emotion. Was it the mention of Lucy Brent that had moved him to his depths?

The brown holland fell away—the dead stood revealed as he had been in life. Every feature, painted by the hand of Love, was instinct with vitality: the fine, earnest face, the sad kindly eyes, the noble brow seeming still a-throb with the thought of Humanity. A thrill ran through the room—there was a low, undefinable murmur. Oh, the pathos and the tragedy of it! Every eye was fixed, misty with emotion, upon the dead man in the picture and the living man who stood, pale and agitated, and visibly unable to commence his speech, at the side of the canvas. Suddenly a hand was laid upon the labour leader's shoulder, and there rang through the hall in Wimp's clear decisive tones the words—"Tom Mortlake, I arrest you for the murder of Arthur Constant!"

IX

For a moment there was an acute, terrible silence. Mortlake's face was that of a corpse; the face of the dead man at his side was flushed with the hues of life. To the overstrung nerves of the onlookers, the brooding eyes of the picture seemed sad and stern with menace, and charged with the lightnings of doom.

It was a horrible contrast. For Wimp, alone, the painted face had fuller, more tragical meanings. The audience seemed turned to stone. They sat or stood—in every variety of attitude—frozen, rigid. Arthur Constant's picture dominated the scene, the only living thing in a hall of the dead.

But only for a moment. Mortlake shook off the detective's hand.

"Boys!" he cried, in accents of infinite indignation, "this is a police conspiracy."

His words relaxed the tension. The stony figures were agitated. A dull excited hubbub answered him. The little cobbler darted from behind his pillar, and leapt up on a bench. The cords of his brow were swollen with excitement. He seemed a giant overshadowing the hall.

"Boys!" he roared, in his best Victoria Park voice, "listen to me. This charge is a foul and damnable lie."

"Bravo!" "Hear, hear!" "Horray!" "It is!" was roared back at him from all parts of the room. Everybody rose and stood in tentative attitudes, excited to the last degree.

"Boys!" Peter roared on, "you all know me. I'm a plain man, and I want to know if it's likely a man would murder his best friend."

"No," in a mighty volume of sound.

Wimp had scarcely calculated upon Mortlake's popularity. He stood on the platform, pale and anxious as his prisoner.

"And if he did, why didn't they prove it the first time?"

"Hear, Hear!"

"And if they want to arrest him, why couldn't they leave it till the ceremony was over? Tom Mortlake's not the man to run away."

"Tom Mortlake! Tom Mortlake! Three cheers for Tom Mortlake! Hip, hip, hip, hooray!"

"Three groans for the police!" "Hoo! Oo! Oo!"

Wimp's melodrama was not going well. He felt like the author to whose ears is borne the ominous sibilance of the pit. He almost wished he had not followed the curtain-raiser with his own stronger drama. Unconsciously the police, scattered about the hall, drew together. The people on the platform knew not what to do. They had all risen and stood in a densely-packed mass. Even Mr. Gladstone's speech failed him in circumstances so novel. The groans died away; the cheers for Mortlake rose and swelled and fell and rose again. Sticks and umbrellas were banged and rattled, handkerchiefs were waved, the thunder deepened. The motley crowd still surging about the hall took up the cheers, and for hundreds of yards around people were going black in the face out of mere irresponsible enthusiasm. At last Tom waved his hand—the thunder dwindled, died. The prisoner was master of the situation.

Grodman stood on the platform, grasping the back of his chair, a curious mocking Mephistophelian glitter about his eyes, his lips wreathed into a half smile. There was no hurry for him to get Denzil Cantercot arrested now. Wimp had made an egregious, a colossal blunder. In Grodman's heart there was a great glad calm as of a man who has strained his sinews to win in a famous match, and has heard the judge's word. He felt almost kindly to Denzil now.

Tom Mortlake spoke. His face was set and stony. His tall figure was drawn up haughtily to its full height. He pushed the black mane back from his forehead with a characteristic gesture. The fevered audience hung upon his lips—the men at the back leaned eagerly forward—the reporters were breathless with fear lest they should miss a word. What would the great labour leader have to say at this supreme moment?

"Mr. Chairman and gentlemen—It is to me a melancholy pleasure to have been honoured with the task of unveiling to-night this portrait of a great benefactor to Bow and a true friend to the labouring-classes. Except that he honoured me with his friendship while living, and that the aspirations of my life have, in my small and restricted way, been identical with his, there is little reason why this honourable duty should have fallen upon me. Gentlemen, I trust that we shall all find an inspiring influence in the daily vision of the dead, who yet liveth in our hearts and in this noble work of art—wrought, as Mr. Gladstone has told us, by the hand of one who loved him." The speaker paused a moment, his low vibrant tones faltering into silence. "If we humble working men of Bow can never hope to exert individually a tithe of the beneficial influence wielded by Arthur Constant, it is yet possible for each of us to walk in the light he has kindled in our midst—a perpetual lamp of self-sacrifice and brotherhood."

That was all. The room rang with cheers. Tom Mortlake resumed his seat. To Wimp the man's audacity verged on the Sublime; to Denzil on the Beautiful. Again there was a breathless hush. Mr. Gladstone's mobile face was working with excitement. No such extraordinary scene had occurred in the whole of his extraordinary experience. He seemed about to rise. The cheering subsided to a painful stillness. Wimp cut the situation by laying his hand again upon Tom's shoulder.

"Come quietly with me," he said. The words were almost a whisper, but in the supreme silence they travelled to the ends of the hall.

"Don't you go, Tom!" The trumpet tones were Peter's. The call thrilled an answering chord of defiance in every breast, and a low ominous murmur swept through the hall.

Tom rose, and there was silence again. "Boys," he said, "let me go. Don't make any noise about it. I shall be with you again to-morrow."

But the blood of the Break o' Day boys was at fever heat. A hurtling mass of men struggled confusedly from their seats. In a moment all was chaos. Tom did not move. Half a dozen men, headed by Peter, scaled the platform. Wimp was thrown to one side, and the invaders formed a ring round Tom's chair. The platform people scampered like mice from the centre. Some huddled together in the corners, others slipped out at the rear. The committee congratulated themselves on having had the self-denial to exclude ladies. Mr. Gladstone's satellites hurried the old man off and into his carriage; though the fight promised to become Homeric. Grodman stood at the side of the platform secretly more amused than ever, concerning himself no more with Denzil Cantercot, who was already strengthening his nerves at the bar upstairs. The police about the hall blew their whistles, and policemen came rushing in from outside and the neighbourhood. An Irish M.P. on the platform was waving his gingham like a shillelagh in sheer excitement, forgetting his new-found respectability and dreaming himself back at Donnybrook Fair. Him a conscientious constable floored with a truncheon. But a shower of fists fell on the zealot's face, and he tottered back bleeding. Then the storm broke in all its fury. The upper air was black with staves, sticks, and umbrellas, mingled with the pallid hailstones of knobby fists. Yells, and groans, and hoots, and battle-cries blent in grotesque chorus, like one of Dvořák's weird diabolical movements. Mortlake stood impassive, with arms folded, making no further effort, and the battle raged round him as the water swirls round some steadfast rock. A posse of police from the back fought their way steadily towards him, and charged up the heights of the platform steps, only to be sent tumbling backwards, as their leader was hurled at them like a battering-ram. Upon the top of the heap he fell, surmounting the strata of policemen. But others clambered upon them, escalading the platform. A moment more and Mortlake would have been taken. Then the miracle happened.

As when of old a reputable goddess *ex machinâ* saw her favourite hero in dire peril, straightway she drew down a cloud from the celestial stores of Jupiter and enveloped her fondling in kindly night, so that his adversary strove with the darkness, so did Crowl, the cunning cobbler, the much-daring, essay to ensure his friend's safety. He turned off the gas at the meter.

An Arctic night—unpreceded by twilight—fell, and there dawned the sabbath of the witches. The darkness could be felt—and it left blood and bruises behind it. When the lights were turned on again, Mortlake was gone. But several of the rioters were arrested, triumphantly.

And through all, and over all, the face of the dead man who had sought to bring peace on earth, brooded.

. . . . . .

Crowl sat meekly eating his supper of bread and cheese, with his head bandaged, while Denzil Cantercot told him the story of how he had rescued Tom Mortlake. He had been among the first to scale the height, and had never budged from Tom's side or from the forefront of the battle till he had seen him safely outside and into a by-street.

"I am so glad you saw that he got away safely," said Crowl, "I wasn't quite sure he would."

"Yes; but I wish some cowardly fool hadn't turned off the gas. I like men to *see* that they are beaten."

"But it seemed—easier," faltered Crowl.

"Easier!" echoed Denzil, taking a deep draught of bitter. "Really, Peter, I'm sorry to find you always will take such low views. It may be easier, but it's shabby. It shocks one's sense of the Beautiful."

Crowl ate his bread and cheese shamefacedly.

"But what was the use of breaking your head to save him?" said Mrs. Crowl with an unconscious pun. "He must be caught."

"Ah, I don't see how the Useful *does* come in, now," said Peter, thoughfully. "But I didn't think of that at the time."

He swallowed his water quickly, and it went the wrong way and added to his confusion. It also began to dawn upon him that he might be called to account. Let it be said that he wasn't. He had taken too prominent a part.

Meantime, Mrs. Wimp was bathing Mr. Wimp's eye, and rubbing him generally with arnica. Wimp's melodrama had been, indeed, a sight for the gods. Only, virtue was vanquished and vice triumphant. The villain had escaped, and without striking a blow.

X

There was matter and to spare for the papers the next day. The striking ceremony—Mr. Gladstone's speech—the sensational arrest—these would of themselves have made excellent themes for reports and leaders. But the personality of the man arrested, and the Big Bow Mystery Battle—as it came to be called—gave additional piquancy to the paragraphs and the posters. The behaviour of Mortlake put the last touch to the picturesqueness of the position. He left the hall when the lights went out, and walked unnoticed and unmolested through pleiads of policemen to the nearest police station, where the superintendent was almost too excited to take any notice of his demand to be arrested. But to do him justice, the official yielded as soon as he understood the situation. It seems inconceivable that he did not violate some red-tape regulation in so doing. To some this self-surrender was limpid proof of innocence; to others it was the damning token of despairing guilt.

The morning papers were pleasant reading for Grodman, who chuckled as continuously over his morning egg, as if he had laid it. Jane was alarmed for the sanity of her saturnine master. As her husband would have said, Grodman's grins were not Beautiful. But he made no effort to suppress them. Not only had Wimp perpetrated a grotesque blunder, but the journalists to a man were down on his great sensation tableau, though their denunciations did not appear in the dramatic columns. The Liberal papers said that he had endangered Mr. Gladstone's life; the Conservative that he had unloosed the raging elements of Bow blackguardism, and set in motion forces which might have easily swelled to a riot, involving severe destruction of property. But "Tom Mortlake" was, after all, the thought swamping every other. It was, in a sense, a triumph for the man.

But Wimp's turn came when Mortlake, who reserved his defence, was brought up before a magistrate, and by force of the new evidence, fully committed for trial on the charge of murdering Arthur Constant. Then men's thoughts centred again on the Mystery, and the solution of the inexplicable problem agitated mankind from China to Peru.

In the middle of February, the great trial befell. It was another of the opportunities which the Chancellor of the Exchequer neglects. So stirring a drama might have easily cleared its expenses—despite the length of the cast, the salaries of the stars, and the rent of the house— in mere advance booking. For it was a drama which (by the rights of Magna Charta) could never be repeated; a drama which ladies of fashion would have given their earrings to witness, even with the central figure not a woman. And there *was* a woman in it anyhow, to judge by the little that had transpired at the magisterial examination, and the fact that the country was placarded with bills offering a reward for information concerning a Miss Jessie Dymond. Mortlake was defended by Sir Charles Brown-Harland, Q.C., retained at the expense of the Mortlake Defence Fund (subscriptions to which came also from Australia and the Continent), and set on his mettle by the fact that he was the accepted labour candidate for an East-end constituency. Their Majesties, Victoria and the Law, were represented by Mr. Robert Spigot, Q.C.

Mr. SPIGOT, Q.C., in presenting his case, said: "I propose to show that the prisoner murdered his friend and fellow-lodger, Mr. Arthur Constant, in cold blood, and with the most careful premeditation; premeditation so studied, as to leave the circumstances of the death an impenetrable mystery for weeks to all the world, though, fortunately, without altogether baffling the almost superhuman ingenuity of Mr. Edward Wimp, of the Scotland Yard Detective Department. I propose to show that the motives of the prisoner were jealousy and revenge; jealousy, not only of his friend's superior influence over the working men he himself aspired to lead, but the more commonplace animosity engendered by the disturbing element of a woman having relations to both. If, before my case is complete, it will be my painful duty to show that the murdered man was not the saint the world had agreed to paint him, I shall not shrink from unveiling the truer picture, in the interests of justice, which cannot say *nil nisi bonum* even of the dead. I propose to show that the murder was committed by the prisoner shortly before half-past six on the morning of December 4th, and that the prisoner having, with the remarkable ingenuity which he has shown throughout, attempted to prepare an alibi by feigning to leave London by the *first* train to Liverpool, returned home, got in with his latchkey through the street-door, which he had left on the latch, unlocked his victim's bedroom with a key which he possessed, cut the sleeping man's throat, pocketed the razor, locked the door again, and gave it the appearance of being bolted, went downstairs, unslipped the bolt of the big lock, closed the door behind him, and got to Euston in time for the *second* train to Liverpool. The fog helped his proceedings throughout." Such was in sum the theory of the prosecution. The pale, defiant figure in the dock winced perceptibly under parts of it.

Mrs. Drabdump was the first witness called for the prosecution. She was quite used to legal inquisitiveness by this time, but did not appear in good spirits.

"On the night of December 3rd, you gave the prisoner a letter?"

"Yes, your ludship."

"How did he behave when he read it?"

"He turned very pale and excited. He went up to the poor gentleman's room, and I'm afraid he quarrelled with him. He might have left his last hours peaceful." (Amusement.)

"What happened then?"

"Mr. Mortlake went out in a passion, and came in again in about an hour."

"He told you he was going away to Liverpool very early the next morning?"

"No, your ludship, he said he was going to Devonport." (Sensation.)

"What time did you get up the next morning?"

"Half-past six."

"That is not your usual time?"

"No, I always get up at six."

"How do you account for the extra sleepiness?"

"Misfortunes will happen."

"It wasn't the dull, foggy weather?"

"No, my lud, else I should never get up early." (Laughter.)

"You drink something before going to bed?"

"I like my cup o' tea. I take it strong, without sugar. It always steadies my nerves."

"Quite so. Where were you when the prisoner told you he was going to Devonport?"

"Drinkin' my tea in the kitchen."

"What should you say if prisoner dropped something in it to make you sleep late?"

WITNESS (startled): "He ought to be shot."

"He might have done it without your noticing it, I suppose?"

"If he was clever enough to murder the poor gentleman, he was clever enough to try and poison me."

The JUDGE: "The witness in her replies must confine herself to the evidence."

Mr. SPIGOT, Q.C.: "I must submit to your lordship that it is a very logical answer, and exactly illustrates the interdependence of the probabilities. Now, Mrs. Drabdump, let us know what happened when you awoke at half-past six the next morning."

Thereupon Mrs. Drabdump recapitulated the evidence (with new redundancies, but slight variations) given by her at the inquest. How she became alarmed—how she found the street-door locked by the big lock—how she roused Grodman, and got him to burst open the door—how they found the body—all this with which the public was already familiar *ad nauseam* was extorted from her afresh.

"Look at this key (key passed to witness). Do you recognise it?"

"Yes; how did you get it? It's the key of my first-floor front. I am sure I left it sticking in the door."

"Did you know a Miss Dymond?"

"Yes, Mr. Mortlake's sweetheart. But I knew he would never marry her, poor thing." (Sensation.)

"Why not?"

"He was getting too grand for her." (Amusement.)

"You don't mean anything more than that?"

"I don't know; she only came to my place once or twice. The last time I set eyes on her must have been in October."

"How did she appear?"

"She was very miserable, but she wouldn't let you see it." (Laughter.)

"How has the prisoner behaved since the murder?"

"He always seemed very glum and sorry for it."

Cross-examined: "Did not the prisoner once occupy the bedroom of Mr. Constant, and give it up to him, so that Mr. Constant might have the two rooms on the same floor?"

"Yes, but he didn't pay as much."

"And, while occupying this front bedroom, did not the prisoner once lose his key and have another made?"

"He did; he was very careless."

"Do you know what the prisoner and Mr. Constant spoke about on the night of December 3rd?"

"No; I couldn't hear."

"Then how did you know they were quarrelling?"

"They were talkin' so loud."

Sir CHARLES BROWN-HARLAND, Q.C. (sharply): "But I'm talking loudly to you now. Should you say I was quarrelling?"

"It takes two to make a quarrel." (Laughter.)

"Was prisoner the sort of man who, in your opinion, would commit a murder?"

"No, I never should ha' guessed it was him."

"He always struck you as a thorough gentleman?"

"No, my lud. I knew he was only a comp."

"You say the prisoner has seemed depressed since the murder. Might not that have been due to the disappearance of his sweetheart?"

"No, he'd more likely be glad to get rid of her."

"Then he wouldn't be jealous if Mr. Constant took her off his hands?" (Sensation.)

"Men are dog-in-the-mangers."

"Never mind about men, Mrs. Drabdump. Had the prisoner ceased to care for Miss Dymond?"

"He didn't seem to think of her, my lud. When he got a letter in her handwriting among his heap he used to throw it aside till he'd torn open the others."

BROWN-HARLAND, Q.C. (with a triumphant ring in his voice): "Thank you, Mrs. Drabdump. You may sit down."

SPIGOT, Q.C.: "One moment, Mrs. Drabdump. You say the prisoner had ceased to care for Miss Dymond. Might not this have been in consequence of his suspecting for some time that she had relations with Mr. Constant?"

The JUDGE: "That is not a fair question."

SPIGOT, Q.C.: "That will do, thank you, Mrs. Drabdump."

BROWN-HARLAND, Q.C.: "No; one question more, Mrs. Drabdump. Did you ever see anything—say, when Miss Dymond came to your house—to make you suspect anything between Mr. Constant and the prisoner's sweetheart?"

"She did meet him once when Mr. Mortlake was out. (Sensation.)

"Where did she meet him?"

"In the passage. He was going out when she knocked and he opened the door." (Amusement.)

"You didn't hear what they said?"

"I ain't a eavesdropper. They spoke friendly and went away together."

Mr. GEORGE RODMAN was called, and repeated his evidence at the inquest. Cross-examined, he testified to the warm friendship between Mr. Constant and the prisoner. He knew very little about Miss Dymond, having scarcely seen her. Prisoner had never spoken to him much about her. He should not think she was much in prisoner's thoughts. Naturally the prisoner had been depressed by the death of his friend. Besides, he was overworked. Witness thought highly of Mortlake's character. It was incredible that Constant had had improper relations of any kind with his friend's promised wife. Grodman's evidence made a very favourable impression on the jury; the prisoner looked his gratitude; and the prosecution felt sorry it had been necessary to call this witness.

Inspector HOWLETT and Sergeant RUNNYMEDE had also to repeat their evidence. Dr. ROBINSON, police surgeon, likewise re-tendered his evidence as to the nature of the wound, and the approximate hour of death. But this time he was much more severely examined. He would not bind himself down to state the time within an hour or two. He thought life had been extinct two or three hours when he arrived, so that the deed had been committed between seven and eight. Under gentle pressure from the prosecuting counsel, he admitted that it might possibly have been between six and seven. Cross-examined, he reiterated his impression in favour of the later hour.

Supplementary evidence from medical experts proved as dubious and uncertain as if the court had confined itself to the original witness. It seemed to be generally agreed that the data for determining the time of death of any body were too complex and variable to admit of very precise inference; rigor mortis and other symptoms setting in within very wide limits and differing largely in different persons. All agreed that death from such a cut must have been practically instantaneous, and the theory of suicide was rejected by all. As a whole the medical evidence tended to fix the time of death, with a high degree of probability, between the hours of six and half-past eight. The efforts of the prosecution were bent upon throwing back the time of death to as early as possible after about half-past five. The defence spent all its strength upon pinning the experts to the conclusion that death could not have been earlier than seven. Evidently the prosecution was going to fight hard for the hypothesis that Mortlake had committed the crime in the interval between the first and second trains for Liverpool; while the defence was concentrating itself on an alibi, showing that the prisoner had travelled by the second train, which left Euston Station at a quarter-past seven, so that there could have been no possible time for the passage between Bow and Euston. It was an exciting struggle. As yet the contending forces seemed equally matched. The evidence had gone as much for as against the prisoner. But everybody knew that worse lay behind.

"Call Edward Wimp."

The story EDWARD WIMP had to tell began tamely enough with thrice-threshed-out facts. But at last the new facts came.

"In consequence of suspicions that had formed in your mind you took up your quarters, disguised, in the late Mr. Constant's rooms?"

"I did; at the commencement of the year. My suspicions had gradually gathered against the occupants of No. 11 Glover Street, and I resolved to quash or confirm these suspicions once for all."

"Will you tell the jury what followed?"

"Whenever the prisoner was away for the night I searched his room. I found the key of Mr. Constant's bedroom buried deeply in the side of prisoner's leather sofa. I found what I imagine to be the letter he received on December 3rd, in the pages of a 'Bradshaw' lying under the same sofa. There were two razors about."

Mr. SPIGOT, Q.C., said:—"The key has already been identified by Mrs. Drabdump. The letter I now propose to read."

It was undated, and ran as follows:—

"DEAR TOM,—This is to bid you farewell. It is best for us all. I am going a long way, dearest. Do not seek to find me, for it will be useless. Think of me as one swallowed up by the waters, and be assured that it is only to spare you shame and humiliation in the future that I tear myself from you and all the sweetness of life. Darling, there is no other way. I feel you could never marry me now. I have felt it for months. Dear Tom, you will understand what I mean. We must look facts in the face. I hope you will always be friends with Mr. Constant. Good-bye, dear. God bless you! May you always be happy, and find a worthier wife than I. Perhaps when you are great, and rich, and famous, as you deserve, you will sometimes think not unkindly of one who, however faulty and unworthy of you, will at least love you till the end.—Yours, till death,

JESSIE."

By the time this letter was finished numerous old gentlemen, with wigs or without, were observed to be polishing their glasses. Mr. Wimp's examination was resumed.

"After making these discoveries what did you do?"

"I made inquiries about Miss Dymond, and found Mr. Constant had visited her once or twice in the evening. I imagined there would be some traces of a pecuniary connection. I was allowed by the family to inspect Mr. Constant's cheque-book, and found a paid cheque made out for £25 in the name of Miss Dymond. By inquiry at the Bank, I found it had been cashed on November 12th of last year. I then applied for a warrant against the prisoner."

Cross-examined: "Do you suggest that the prisoner opened Mr. Constant's bedroom with the key you found?"

"Certainly."

BROWN-HARLAND, Q.C. (sarcastically): "And locked the door from within with it on leaving?"

"Certainly."

"Will you have the goodness to explain how the trick was done?"

"It wasn't done. (Laughter.) The prisoner probably locked the door from the outside. Those who broke it open naturally imagined it had been locked from the inside when they found the key inside. The key would, on this theory, be on the floor, as the outside locking could not have been effected if it had been in the lock. The first persons to enter the room would naturally believe it had been thrown down in the bursting of the door. Or it might have been left sticking very loosely inside the lock so as not to interfere with the turning of the outside key, in which case it would also probably have been thrown to the ground."

"Indeed. Very ingenious. And can you also explain how the prisoner could have bolted the door within from the outside?"

"I can. (Renewed sensation.) There is only one way in which it was possible—and that was, of course, a mere conjuror's illusion. To cause a locked door to appear bolted in addition, it would only be necessary for the person on the inside of the door to wrest the staple containing the bolt from the woodwork. The bolt in Mr. Constant's bedroom worked perpendicularly. When the staple was torn off, it

would simply remain at rest on the pin of the bolt instead of supporting it or keeping it fixed. A person bursting open the door and finding the staple resting on the pin and torn away from the lintel of the
door, would, of course, imagine he had torn it away, never dreaming
the wresting off had been done beforehand." (Applause in court,
which was instantly checked by the ushers.) The counsel for the defence felt he had been entrapped in attempting to be sarcastic with
the redoubtable detective. Grodman seemed green with envy. It was
the one thing he had not thought of.

Mrs. Drabdump, Grodman, Inspector Howlett, and Sergeant
Runnymede were recalled and re-examined by the embarrassed Sir
Charles Brown-Harland as to the exact condition of the lock and
the bolt and the position of the key. It turned out as Wimp had suggested; so prepossessed were the witnesses with the conviction that
the door was locked and bolted from the inside when it was burst
open that they were a little hazy about the exact details. The damage
had been repaired, so that it was all a question of precise past observation. The inspector and the sergeant testified that the key was in the
lock when they saw it, though both the mortice and the bolt were
broken. They were not prepared to say that Wimp's theory was impossible; they would even admit it was quite possible that the staple
of the bolt had been torn off beforehand. Mrs. Drabdump could give
no clear account of such petty facts in view of her immediate engrossing interest in the horrible sight of the corpse. Grodman alone
was positive that the key was in the door when he burst it open. No,
he did not remember picking it up from the floor and putting it in.
And he was certain that the staple of the bolt was *not* broken, from
the resistance he experienced in trying to shake the upper panels of
the door.

By the Prosecution: "Don't you think, from the comparative ease
with which the door yielded to your onslaught, that it is highly probable that the pin of the bolt was not in a firmly fixed staple, but in
one already detached from the woodwork of the lintel?"

"The door did not yield so easily."

"But you must be a Hercules."

"Not quite; the bolt was old, and the woodwork crumbling; the
lock was new and shoddy. But I have always been a strong man."

"Very well, Mr. Grodman. I hope you will never appear at the
music-halls." (Laughter.)

Jessie Dymond's landlady was the next witness for the prosecution.
She corroborated Wimp's statements as to Constant's occasional visits,

and narrated how the girl had been enlisted by the dead philanthropist as a collaborator in some of his enterprises. But the most telling portion of her evidence was the story of how, late at night, on December 3rd, the prisoner called upon her and inquired wildly about the whereabouts of his sweetheart. He said he had just received a mysterious letter from Miss Dymond saying she was gone. She (the landlady) replied that she could have told him that weeks ago, as her ungrateful lodger was gone now some three weeks without leaving a hint behind her. In answer to his most ungentlemanly raging and raving, she told him it served him right, as he should have looked after her better, and not kept away for so long. She reminded him that there were as good fish in the sea as ever came out, and a girl of Jessie's attractions need not pine away (as she had seemed to be pining away) for lack of appreciation. He then called her a liar and left her, and she hoped never to see his face again, though she was not surprised to see it in the dock.

Mr. FITZJAMES MONTGOMERY, a bank clerk, remembered cashing the cheque produced. He particularly remembered it, because he paid the money to a very pretty girl. She took the entire amount in gold. At this point the case was adjourned.

DENZIL CANTERCOT was the first witness called for the prosecution on the resumption of the trial. Pressed as to whether he had not told Mr. Wimp that he had overheard the prisoner denouncing Mr. Constant, he could not say. He had not actually heard the prisoner's denunciations; he might have given Mr. Wimp a false impression, but then Mr. Wimp was so prosaically literal. (Laughter.) Mr. Crowl had told him something of the kind. Cross-examined, he said Jessie Dymond was a rare spirit and she always reminded him of Joan of Arc.

Mr. CROWL, being called, was extremely agitated. He refused to take the oath, and informed the court that the Bible was a Fad. He could not swear by anything so self-contradictory. He would affirm. He could not deny—though he looked like wishing to—that the prisoner had at first been rather mistrustful of Mr. Constant, but he was certain that the feeling had quickly worn off. Yes, he was a great friend of the prisoner, but he didn't see why that should invalidate his testimony especially as he had not taken an oath. Certainly the prisoner seemed rather depressed when he saw him on Bank Holiday, but it was overwork on behalf of the people and for the demolition of the Fads.

Several other familiars of the prisoner gave more or less reluctant testimony as to his sometimes prejudice against the amateur rival labour leader. His expressions of dislike had been strong and bitter. The prosecution also produced a poster announcing that the prisoner would preside at a great meeting of clerks on December 4th. He had not turned up at this meeting nor sent any explanation. Finally, there was the evidence of the detectives who originally arrested him at Liverpool Docks in view of his suspicious demeanour. This completed the case for the prosecution.

Sir CHARLES BROWN-HARLAND, Q.C., rose with a swagger and a rustle of his silk gown, and proceeded to set forth the theory of the defence. He said he did not purpose to call many witnesses. The hypothesis of the prosecution was so inherently childish and inconsequential, and so dependent upon a bundle of interdependent probabilities that it crumbled away at the merest touch. The prisoner's character was of unblemished integrity, his last public appearance had been made on the same platform with Mr. Gladstone, and his honesty and highmindedness had been vouched for by statesmen of the highest standing. His movements could be accounted for from hour to hour —and those with which the prosecution credited him rested on no tangible evidence whatever. He was also credited with superhuman ingenuity and diabolical cunning of which he had shown no previous symptom. Hypothesis was piled on hypothesis, as in the old Oriental legend, where the world rested on the elephant and the elephant on the tortoise. It might be worth while, however, to point out that it was at least quite likely that the death of Mr. Constant had not taken place before seven, and as the prisoner left Euston Station at 7.15 A.M. for Liverpool, he could certainly not have got there from Bow in the time; also that it was hardly possible for the prisoner, who could prove being at Euston Station at 5.25 A.M., to travel backwards and forwards to Glover Street and commit the crime all within less than two hours. "The real facts," said Sir Charles impressively, "are most simple. The prisoner, partly from pressure of work, partly (he had no wish to conceal) from worldly ambition, had begun to neglect Miss Dymond, to whom he was engaged to be married. The man was but human, and his head was a little turned by his growing importance. Nevertheless, at heart he was still deeply attached to Miss Dymond. She, however, appears to have jumped to the conclusion that he had ceased to love her, that she was unworthy of him, unfitted by education to take her place side by side with him in the new spheres to which he was mounting—that, in short, she was a drag on his career. Being, by all accounts, a girl of remarkable force of character, she resolved to cut the Gordian knot by leaving London, and, fearing lest her affianced husband's conscientiousness should induce him to sacrifice himself to her; dreading also, perhaps, her own weakness, she made the parting absolute, and the place of her refuge a mystery. A theory has been suggested which drags an honoured name in the mire—a theory so superfluous that I shall only allude to it. That Arthur Constant could have seduced, or had any improper relations with, his friend's betrothed, is a hypothesis to which the lives of both give the lie. Before leaving London—or England—Miss Dymond wrote to her aunt in Devonport—her only living relative in this country—asking her as a great favour to forward an addressed letter to the prisoner, a fortnight after receipt. The aunt obeyed implicitly. This was the letter which fell like a thunderbolt on the prisoner on the night of December 3rd. All his old love returned—he was full of self-reproach and pity for the poor girl. The letter read ominously. Perhaps she was going to put an end to herself. His first thought was to rush up to his friend, Constant, to seek his advice. Perhaps Constant knew something of the affair. The prisoner knew the two were in not infrequent communication. It is possible—my lord and gentlemen of the jury, I do not wish to follow the methods of the prosecution and confuse theory with fact, so I say it is possible—that Mr. Constant had supplied her with the £25 to leave the country. He was like a brother to her, perhaps even acted imprudently in calling upon her, though neither dreamed of evil. It is possible that he may have encouraged her in her abnegation and in her altruistic aspirations, perhaps even without knowing their exact drift, for does he not speak in his very last letter of the fine female characters he was meeting, and the influence for good he had over individual human souls? Still, this we can now never know, unless the dead speak or the absent return. It is also not impossible that Miss Dymond was entrusted with the £25 for charitable purposes. But to come back to certainties. The prisoner consulted Mr. Constant about the letter. He then ran to Miss Dymond's lodgings in Stepney Green, knowing beforehand his trouble would be futile. The letter bore the postmark of Devonport. He knew the girl had an aunt there; possibly she might have gone to her. He could not telegraph, for he was ignorant of the address. He consulted his 'Bradshaw,' and resolved to leave by the 5.30 A.M. from Paddington, and told his landlady so. He left the letter in the 'Bradshaw,' which ultimately got thrust among a pile of papers under the sofa, so that he had to get another. He was careless and disorderly, and the key

found by Mr. Wimp in his sofa, which he was absurdly supposed
to have hidden there after the murder, must have lain there for some
years, having been lost there in the days when he occupied the bedroom afterwards rented by Mr. Constant. For it was his own sofa, removed from that room, and the suction of sofas was well known.
Afraid to miss his train, he did not undress on that distressful night.
Meantime the thought occurred to him that Jessie was too clever a
girl to leave so easy a trail, and he jumped to the conclusion that
she would be going to her married brother in America, and had gone
to Devonport merely to bid her aunt farewell. He determined therefore to get to Liverpool, without wasting time at Devonport, to in-
stitute inquiries. Not suspecting the delay in the transit of the letter,
he thought he might yet stop her, even at the landing-stage or on the
tender. Unfortunately his cab went slowly in the fog, he missed the
first train, and wandered about brooding disconsolately in the mist
till the second. At Liverpool his suspicious, excited demeanour procured his momentary arrest. Since then the thought of the lost girl
has haunted and broken him. That is the whole, the plain, and the
sufficing story."

The effective witnesses for the defence were, indeed, few. It is so
hard to prove a negative. There was Jessie's aunt, who bore out the
statement of the counsel for the defence. There were the porters who
saw him leave Euston by the 7.15 train for Liverpool, and arrive just
too late for the 5.15; there was the cabman (2138), who drove
him to Euston just in time, he (witness) thought, to catch the 5.15
A.M. Under cross-examination, the cabman got a little confused; he
was asked whether, if he really picked up the prisoner at Bow Railway Station at about 4.30, he ought not to have caught the first
train at Euston. He said the fog made him drive rather slowly, but
admitted the mist was transparent enough to warrant full speed.
He also admitted being a strong trade unionist, SPIGOT, Q.C. artfully
extorting the admission as if it were of the utmost significance. Finally,
there were numerous witnesses—of all sorts and conditions—to the
prisoner's high character, as well as to Arthur Constant's blameless
and moral life.

In his closing speech on the third day of the trial, Sir CHARLES
pointed out with great exhaustiveness and cogency the flimsiness of
the case for the prosecution, the number of hypotheses it involved,
and their mutual interdependence. Mrs. Drabdump was a witness
whose evidence must be accepted with extreme caution. The jury
must remember that she was unable to dissociate her observations

from her inferences, and thought that the prisoner and Mr. Constant
were quarrelling merely because they were agitated. He dissected
her evidence, and showed that it entirely bore out the story of the
defence. He asked the jury to bear in mind that no positive evidence
(whether of cabmen or others) had been given of the various and
complicated movements attributed to the prisoner on the morning
of December 4th, between the hours of 5.25 and 7.15 A.M., and that
the most important witness on the theory of the prosecution—he
meant, of course, Miss Dymond—had not been produced. Even if
she were dead, and her body were found, no countenance would be
given to the theory of the prosecution, for the mere conviction that
her lover had deserted her would be a sufficient explanation of her
suicide. Beyond the ambiguous letter, no tittle of evidence of her
dishonour—on which the bulk of the case against the prisoner rested
—had been adduced. As for the motive of political jealousy, that had
been a mere passing cloud. The two men had become fast friends.
As to the circumstances of the alleged crime, the medical evidence
was on the whole in favour of the time of death being late; and the
prisoner had left London at a quarter-past seven. The drugging theory
was absurd, and as for the too clever bolt and lock theories, Mr.
Grodman, a trained scientific observer, had pooh-poohed them. He
would solemnly exhort the jury to remember that if they condemned
the prisoner they would not only send an innocent man to an ig-
nominious death on the flimsiest circumstantial evidence, but they
would deprive the working men of this country of one of their truest
friends and their ablest leader.

The conclusion of Sir Charles's vigorous speech was greeted with
irrepressible applause.

Mr. SPIGOT, Q.C., in closing the case for the prosecution, asked
the jury to return a verdict against the prisoner for as malicious and
premeditated a crime as ever disgraced the annals of any civilised
country. His cleverness and education had only been utilised for the
devil's ends, while his reputation had been used as a cloak. Everything
pointed strongly to the prisoner's guilt. On receiving Miss Dymond's
letter announcing her shame, and (probably) her intention to commit suicide, he had hastened upstairs to denounce Constant. He had
then rushed to the girl's lodgings, and, finding his worst fears confirmed, planned at once his diabolically ingenious scheme of revenge.
He told his landlady he was going to Devonport, so that if he bungled,
the police would be put temporarily off his track. His real destination
was Liverpool, for he intended to leave the country. Lest, however,

his plan should break down here, too, he arranged an ingenious alibi by being driven to Euston for the 5.15 train to Liverpool. The cabman would not know he did not intend to go by it, but meant to return to 11 Glover Street, there to perpetrate this foul crime, interruption to which he had possibly barred by drugging his landlady. His presence at Liverpool (whither he really went by the second train) would corroborate the cabman's story. That night he had not undressed nor gone to bed; he had plotted out his devilish scheme till it was perfect; the fog came as an unexpected ally to cover his movements. Jealousy, outraged affection, the desire for revenge, the lust for political power—these were human. They might pity the criminal, they could not find him innocent of the crime.

Mr. Justice CROGIE, summing up, began dead against the prisoner. Reviewing the evidence, he pointed out that plausible hypotheses neatly dovetailed did not necessarily weaken one another, the fitting so well together of the whole rather making for the truth of the parts. Besides, the case for the prosecution was as far from being all hypothesis as the case for the defence was from excluding hypotheses. The key, the letter, the reluctance to produce the letter, the heated interview with Constant, the mis-statement about the prisoner's destination, the flight to Liverpool, the false tale about searching for a "him," the denunciations of Constant, all these were facts. On the other hand, there were various lacunæ and hypotheses in the case for the defence. Even conceding the somewhat dubious alibi afforded by the prisoner's presence at Euston at 5.25 A.M., there was no attempt to account for his movements between that and 7.15 A.M. It was as possible that he returned to Bow as that he lingered about Euston. There was nothing in the medical evidence to make his guilt impossible. Nor was there anything inherently impossible in Constant's yielding to the sudden temptation of a beautiful girl, nor in a working girl deeming herself deserted, temporarily succumbing to the fascinations of a gentleman and regretting it bitterly afterwards. What had become of the girl was a mystery. Hers might have been one of those nameless corpses which the tide swirls up on slimy river banks. The jury must remember, too, that the relation might not have actually passed into dishonour, it might have been just grave enough to smite the girl's conscience, and to induce her to behave as she had done. It was enough that her letter should have excited the jealousy of the prisoner. There was one other point which he would like to impress on the jury, and which the counsel for the prosecution had not sufficiently insisted upon. This was that the prisoner's guiltiness was the

only plausible solution that had ever been advanced of the Bow
Mystery. The medical evidence agreed that Mr. Constant did not die
by his own hand. Someone must therefore have murdered him. The
number of people who could have had any possible reason or opportunity to murder him was extremely small. The prisoner had both
reason and opportunity. By what logicians called the method of ex-
clusion, suspicion would attach to him on even slight evidence. The
actual evidence was strong and plausible, and now that Mr. Wimp's
ingenious theory had enabled them to understand how the door could
have been apparently locked and bolted from within, the last difficulty
and the last argument for suicide had been removed. The prisoner's
guilt was as clear as circumstantial evidence could make it. If they let
him go free, the Bow Mystery might henceforward be placed among
the archives of unavenged assassinations. Having thus well-nigh hung
the prisoner, the judge wound up by insisting on the high probability
of the story for the defence, though that, too, was dependent in important details upon the prisoner's mere private statements to his
counsel. The jury, being by this time sufficiently muddled by his im-
partiality, were dismissed, with the exhortation to allow due weight
to every fact and probability in determining their righteous verdict.

The minutes ran into hours, but the jury did not return. The shadows of night fell across the reeking fevered court before they announced their verdict—

"Guilty."

The judge put on his black cap.

The great reception arranged outside was a fiasco; the evening
banquet was indefinitely postponed. Wimp had won; Grodman felt
like a whipped cur.

XI

"So you were right," Denzil could not help saying as he greeted
Grodman a week afterwards. "I shall *not* live to tell the story of how
you discovered the Bow murderer."

"Sit down," growled Grodman; "perhaps you will, after all." There
was a dangerous gleam in his eyes. Denzil was sorry he had spoken.

"I sent for you," Grodman said, "to tell you that on the night Wimp
arrested Mortlake I had made preparations for your arrest."

Denzil gasped, "What for?"

"My dear Denzil, there is a little law in this country invented for the confusion of the poetic. The greatest exponent of the Beautiful is only allowed the same number of wives as the greengrocer. I do not blame you for not being satisfied with Jane—she is a good servant but a bad mistress—but it was cruel to Kitty not to inform her that Jane had a prior right to you, and unjust to Jane to let her know of the contract with Kitty."

"They both know it now well enough, curse 'em," said the poet.

"Yes; your secrets are like your situations—you can't keep 'em long. My poor poet, I pity you—betwixt the devil and the deep sea."

"They're a pair of harpies, each holding over me the Damocles sword of an arrest for bigamy. Neither loves me."

"I should think they would come in very useful to you. You plant one in my house to tell my secrets to Wimp, and you plant one in Wimp's house to tell Wimp's secrets to me, I suppose. Out with some, then."

"Upon my honour you wrong me. Jane brought *me* here, not I Jane. As for Kitty, I never had such a shock in my life as at finding her installed in Wimp's house."

"She thought it safer to have the law handy for your arrest. Besides, she probably desired to occupy a parallel position to Jane's. She must do something for a living; *you* wouldn't do anything for hers. And so you couldn't go anywhere without meeting a wife! Ha! ha! ha! Serves you right, my polygamous poet."

"But why should *you* arrest me?"

"Revenge, Denzil. I have been the best friend you ever had in this cold, prosaic world. You have eaten my bread, drunk my claret, written my book, smoked my cigars, and pocketed my money. And yet, when you have an important piece of information bearing on a mystery about which I am thinking day and night, you calmly go and sell it to Wimp."

"I did-didn't," stammered Denzil.

"Liar! Do you think Kitty has any secrets from me? As soon as I discovered your two marriages I determined to have you arrested for—your treachery. But when I found you had, as I thought, put Wimp on the wrong scent, when I felt sure that by arresting Mortlake he was going to make a greater ass of himself than even nature had been able to do, then I forgave you. I let you walk about the earth—and drink—freely. Now it is Wimp who crows—everybody pats him on the back—they call him the mystery man of the Scotland

Yard tribe. Poor Tom Mortlake will be hanged, and all through your telling Wimp about Jessie Dymond!"

"It was you yourself," said Denzil sullenly. "Everybody was giving it up. But you said 'Let us find out all that Arthur Constant did in the last few months of his life.' Wimp couldn't miss stumbling on Jessie sooner or later. I'd have throttled Constant, if I had known he'd touched her," he wound up with irrelevant indignation.

Grodman winced at the idea that he himself had worked *ad majorem gloriam* of Wimp. And yet, had not Mrs. Wimp let out as much at the Christmas dinner?

"What's past is past," he said gruffly. "But if Tom Mortlake hangs, you go to Portland."

"How can I help Tom hanging?"

"Help the agitation as much as you can. Write letters under all sorts of names to all the papers. Get everybody you know to sign the great petition. Find out where Jessie Dymond is—the girl who holds the proof of Mortlake's innocence."

"You really believe him innocent?"

"Don't be satirical, Denzil. Haven't I taken the chair at all the meetings? Am I not the most copious correspondent of the Press?"

"I thought it was only to spite Wimp."

"Rubbish. It's to save poor Tom. He no more murdered Arthur Constant than—you did!" He laughed an unpleasant laugh.

Denzil bade him farewell, frigid with fear.

Grodman was up to his ears in letters and telegrams. Somehow he had become the leader of the rescue party—suggestions, subscriptions came from all sides. The suggestions were burnt, the subscriptions acknowledged in the papers and used for hunting up the missing girl. Lucy Brent headed the list with a hundred pounds. It was a fine testimony to her faith in her dead lover's honour.

The release of the Jury had unloosed "The Greater Jury," which always now sits upon the smaller. Every means was taken to nullify the value of the "palladium of British liberty." The foreman and the jurors were interviewed, the judge was judged, and by those who were no judges. The Home Secretary (who had done nothing beyond accepting office under the Crown) was vituperated, and sundry provincial persons wrote confidentially to the Queen. Arthur Constant's backsliding cheered many by convincing them that others were as bad as themselves; and well-to-do tradesmen saw in Mortlake's wickedness the pernicious effects of Socialism. A dozen new theories were afloat. Constant had committed suicide by Esoteric Buddhism, as witness his devotion to Madame Blavatsky, or he had been murdered by his Mahatma or victimised by Hypnotism, Mesmerism, Somnambulism, and other weird abstractions. Grodman's great point was— Jessie Dymond must be produced, dead or alive. The electric current scoured the civilised world in search of her. What wonder if the shrewder sort divined that the indomitable detective had fixed his last hope on the girl's guilt? If Jessie had wrongs why should she not have avenged them herself? Did she not always remind the poet of Joan of Arc?

Another week passed; the shadow of the gallows crept over the days; on, on, remorselessly drawing nearer, as the last ray of hope sank below the horizon. The Home Secretary remained inflexible; the great petitions discharged their signatures at him in vain. He was a Conservative, sternly conscientious; and the mere insinuation that his obstinacy was due to the politics of the condemned only hardened him against the temptation of a cheap reputation for magnanimity. He would not even grant a respite, to increase the chances of the discovery of Jessie Dymond. In the last of the three weeks there was a final monster meeting of protest. Grodman again took the chair, and several distinguished faddists were present, as well as numerous respectable members of society. The Home Secretary acknowledged the receipt of their resolutions. The Trade Unions were divided in their allegiance; some whispered of faith and hope, others of financial defalcations. The former essayed to organise a procession and an indignation meeting on the Sunday preceding the Tuesday fixed for the execution, but it fell through on a rumour of confession. The Monday papers contained a last masterly letter from Grodman exposing the weakness of the evidence, but they knew nothing of a confession. The prisoner was mute and disdainful, professing little regard for a life empty of love and burdened with self-reproach. He refused to see clergymen. He was accorded an interview with Miss Brent in the presence of a gaoler, and solemnly asseverated his respect for her dead lover's memory. Monday buzzed with rumours; the evening papers chronicled them hour by hour. A poignant anxiety was abroad. The girl would be found. Some miracle would happen. A reprieve would arrive. The sentence would be commuted. But the short day darkened into night even as Mortlake's short day was darkening. And the shadow of the gallows crept on and on, and seemed to mingle with the twilight.

Crowl stood at the door of his shop, unable to work. His big grey eyes were heavy with unshed tears. The dingy wintry road seemed one vast cemetery; the street lamps twinkled like corpse-lights. The confused sounds of the street-life reached his ear as from another world. He did not see the people who flitted to and fro amid the gathering shadows of the cold, dreary night. One ghastly vision flashed and faded and flashed upon the background of the duskiness.

Denzil stood beside him, smoking in silence. A cold fear was at his heart. That terrible Grodman! As the hangman's cord was tightening round Mortlake, he felt the convict's chains tightening round himself. And yet there was one gleam of hope, feeble as the yellow flicker of the gas-lamp across the way. Grodman had obtained an interview with the condemned late that afternoon, and the parting had been painful, but the evening paper, that in its turn had obtained an interview with the ex-detective, announced on its placard

"GRODMAN STILL CONFIDENT,"

and the thousands who yet pinned their faith on this extraordinary man refused to extinguish the last sparks of hope. Denzil had bought the paper and scanned it eagerly, but there was nothing save the vague assurance that the indefatigable Grodman was still almost pathetically expectant of the miracle. Denzil did not share the expectation; he meditated flight.

"Peter," he said at last, "I'm afraid it's all over."

Crowl nodded, heart-broken. "All over!" he repeated, "and to think that he dies—and it is—all over!"

He looked despairingly at the blank wintry sky, where leaden clouds shut out the stars. "Poor, poor young fellow! To-night alive and thinking. To-morrow night a clod, with no more sense or motion than a bit of leather! No compensation nowhere for being cut off innocent in the pride of youth and strength! A man who has always preached the Useful day and night, and toiled and suffered for his fellows. Where's the justice of it, where's the justice of it?" he demanded fiercely. Again his wet eyes wandered upwards towards Heaven, that Heaven away from which the soul of a dead saint at the Antipodes was speeding into infinite space.

"Well, where was the justice for Arthur Constant if he, too, was innocent?" said Denzil. "Really, Peter, I don't see why you should take it for granted that Tom is so dreadfully injured. Your horny-handed labour leaders are, after all, men of no æsthetic refinement, with no sense of the Beautiful; you cannot expect them to be exempt from the coarser forms of crime. Humanity must look for other leaders—to the seers and the poets!"

"Cantercot, if you say Tom's guilty I'll knock you down." The little cobbler turned upon his tall friend like a roused lion. Then he added, "I beg your pardon, Cantercot, I don't mean that. After all, I've no grounds. The judge is an honest man, and with gifts I can't lay claim to. But I believe in Tom with all my heart. And if Tom is guilty I believe in the Cause of the People with all my heart all the same. The Fads are doomed to death, they may be reprieved, but they must die at last."

He drew a deep sigh, and looked along the dreary Road. It was quite dark now, but by the light of the lamps and the gas in the shop windows the dull, monotonous Road lay revealed in all its sordid, familiar outlines; with its long stretches of chill pavement, its unlovely architecture, and its endless stream of prosaic pedestrians.

A sudden consciousness of the futility of his existence pierced the little cobbler like an icy wind. He saw his own life, and a hundred million lives like his, swelling and breaking like bubbles on a dark ocean, unheeded, uncared for.

A newsboy passed along, clamouring "The Bow murderer, preparations for the hexecution!"

A terrible shudder shook the cobbler's frame. His eyes ranged sightlessly after the boy; the merciful tears filled them at last.

"The Cause of the People," he murmured, brokenly, "I believe in the Cause of the People. There is nothing else."

"Peter, come in to tea, you'll catch cold," said Mrs. Crowl.

Denzil went in to tea and Peter followed.

Meantime, round the house of the Home Secretary, who was in town, an ever-augmenting crowd was gathered, eager to catch the first whisper of a reprieve.

The house was guarded by a cordon of police, for there was no inconsiderable danger of a popular riot. At times a section of the crowd groaned and hooted. Once a volley of stones was discharged at the windows. The newsboys were busy vending their special editions, and the reporters struggled through the crowd, clutching descriptive pencils, and ready to rush off to telegraph offices should anything "extra special" occur. Telegraph boys were coming up every now and again with threats, messages, petitions, and exhortations from all parts of the country to the unfortunate Home Secretary, who was striving to keep his aching head cool as he went through the voluminous evidence for the last time and pondered over the more important letters which "The Greater Jury" had contributed to the obscuration of the problem. Grodman's letters in that morning's paper shook him most; under his scientific analysis the circumstantial chain seemed forged of painted cardboard. Then the poor man read the judge's summing up, and the chain became tempered steel. The noise of the crowd outside broke upon his ear in his study like the roar of a distant ocean. The more the rabble hooted him, the more he essayed to hold scrupulously the scales of life and death. And the crowd grew and grew, as men came away from their work. There were many that loved the man who lay in the jaws of death, and a spirit of mad revolt surged in their breasts. And the sky was grey, and the bleak night deepened, and the shadow of the gallows crept on.

Suddenly a strange inarticulate murmur spread through the crowd, a vague whisper of no one knew what. Something had happened. Somebody was coming. A second later and one of the outskirts of the throng was agitated, and a convulsive cheer went up from it, and was taken up infectiously all along the street. The crowd parted—a hansom dashed through the centre. "Grodman! Grodman!" shouted those who recognised the occupant. "Grodman! Hurrah!" Grodman was outwardly calm and pale, but his eyes glittered; he waved his hand encouragingly as the hansom dashed up to the door, cleaving the turbulent crowd as a canoe cleaves the waters. Grodman sprang out, the constables at the portal made way for him respectfully. He knocked imperatively, the door was opened cautiously; a boy rushed up and delivered a telegram; Grodman forced his way in, gave his name, and insisted on seeing the Home Secretary on a matter of life and death. Those near the door heard his words and cheered, and the crowd divined the good omen, and the air throbbed with cannonades of joyous sound. The cheers rang in Grodman's ears as the door slammed behind him. The reporters struggled to the front. An excited knot of working men pressed round the arrested hansom, they took the horse out. A dozen enthusiasts struggled for the honour of placing themselves between the shafts. And the crowd awaited Grodman.

XII

Grodman was ushered into the conscientious Minister's study. The doughty chief of the agitation was, perhaps, the one man who could not be denied. As he entered, the Home Secretary's face seemed lit up with relief. At a sign from his master, the amanuensis who had brought in the last telegram took it back with him into the outer room where he worked. Needless to say, not a tithe of the Minister's correspondence ever came under his own eyes.

"You have a valid reason for troubling me, I suppose, Mr. Grodman?" said the Home Secretary, almost cheerfully. "Of course it is about Mortlake?"

"It is; and I have the best of all reasons."

"Take a seat. Proceed."

"Pray do not consider me impertinent, but have you ever given any attention to the science of evidence?"

"How do you mean?" asked the Home Secretary, rather puzzled, adding, with a melancholy smile, "I have had to do so, lately. Of course, I've never been a criminal lawyer, like some of my predecessors. But I should hardly speak of it as a science; I look upon it as a question of common-sense."

"Pardon me, sir. It is the most subtle and difficult of all the sciences. It is, indeed, rather the science of the sciences. What is the whole of Inductive Logic, as laid down, say, by Bacon and Mill, but an attempt to appraise the value of evidence, the said evidence being the trails left by the Creator, so to speak? The Creator has—I say it in all reverence—drawn a myriad red herrings across the track, but the true scientist refuses to be baffled by superficial appearances in detecting the secrets of Nature. The vulgar herd catches at the gross apparent fact, but the man of insight knows that what lies on the surface does lie."

"Very interesting, Mr. Grodman, but really—"

"Bear with me, sir. The science of evidence being thus so extremely subtle, and demanding the most acute and trained observation of facts, the most comprehensive understanding of human psychology, is naturally given over to professors who have not the remotest idea that 'things are not what they seem,' and that everything is other than it appears; to professors, most of whom by their year-long devotion to the shop-counter or the desk, have acquired an intimate acquaintance with all the infinite shades and complexities of things and human nature. When twelve of these professors are put in a box, it is called a jury. When one of these professors is put in a box by himself, he is called a witness. The retailing of evidence—the observation of the facts—is given over to people who go through their lives without eyes; the appreciation of evidence—the judging of these facts—is surrendered to people who may possibly be adepts in weighing out pounds of sugar. Apart from their sheer inability to fulfil either function—to observe, or to judge—their observation and their judgment alike are vitiated by all sorts of irrelevant prejudices."

"You are attacking trial by jury."

"Not necessarily. I am prepared to accept that scientifically, on the ground that, as there are, as a rule, only two alternatives, the balance of probability is slightly in favour of the true decision being come to. Then, in cases where experts like myself have got up the evidence, the jury can be made to see through trained eyes."

The Home Secretary tapped impatiently with his foot.

"I can't listen to abstract theorising," he said. "Have you any fresh concrete evidence?"

"Sir, everything depends on our getting down to the root of the matter. What percentage of average evidence should you think is thorough, plain, simple, unvarnished fact, 'the truth, the whole truth, and nothing but the truth'?"

"Fifty?" said the Minister, humouring him a little.

"Not five. I say nothing of lapses of memory, of inborn defects of observational power—though the suspiciously precise recollection of dates and events possessed by ordinary witnesses in important trials taking place years after the occurrences involved, is one of the most amazing things in the curiosities of modern jurisprudence. I defy you, sir, to tell me what you had for dinner last Monday, or what exactly you were saying and doing at five o'clock last Tuesday afternoon. Nobody whose life does not run in mechanical grooves can do anything of the sort; unless, of course, the facts have been very impressive. But this by the way. The great obstacle to veracious observation is the element of prepossession in all vision. Has it ever struck you, sir, that we never *see* anyone more than once, if that? The first time we meet a man we may possibly see him as he is; the second time our vision is coloured and modified by the memory of the first. Do our friends appear to us as they appear to strangers? Do our rooms, our furniture, our pipes strike our eye as they would strike the eye of an outsider, looking on them for the first time? Can a mother see her babe's ugliness, or a lover his mistress's short-comings, though they stare everybody else in the face? Can we see ourselves as others see us? No; habit, prepossession changes all. The mind is a large factor of every so-called external fact. The eye sees, sometimes, what it wishes to see, more often what it expects to see. You follow me, sir?"

The Home Secretary nodded his head less impatiently. He was beginning to be interested. The hubbub from without broke faintly upon their ears.

"To give you a definite example. Mr. Wimp says that when I burst open the door of Mr. Constant's room on the morning of December 4th, and saw that the staple of the bolt had been wrested by the pin from the lintel, I jumped at once to the conclusion that I had broken the bolt. Now I admit that this was so; only in things like this you do not seem to *conclude,* you jump so fast that you *see,* or seem to see. On the other hand, when you *see* a *standing* ring of fire produced by whirling a burning stick, you do *not* believe in its continuous existence. It is the same when witnessing a legerdemain performance. Seeing is not always believing, despite the proverb; but believing is often seeing. It is not to the point that in that little matter of the door Wimp was as hopelessly and incurably wrong as he has been in everything all along. The door *was* securely bolted. Still, I confess that I should have seen that I had broken the bolt in forcing the door, even if it had been broken beforehand. Never once since December 4th did this possibility occur to me till Wimp with perverted ingenuity suggested it. If this is the case with a trained observer, one moreover fully conscious of this ineradicable tendency of the human mind, how must it be with an untrained observer?"

"Come to the point, come to the point," said the Home Secretary, putting out his hand as if it itched to touch the bell on the writing-table.

"Such as," went on Grodman imperturbably, "such as—Mrs. Drabdump. That worthy person is unable, by repeated violent knocking, to arouse her lodger who yet desires to be aroused; she becomes alarmed, she rushes across to get my assistance; I burst open the door—what do you think the good lady expected to see?"

"Mr. Constant murdered, I suppose," murmured the Home Secretary wonderingly.

"Exactly. And so she saw it. And what should you think was the condition of Arthur Constant when the door yielded to my violent exertions and flew open?"

"Why, was he not dead?" gasped the Home Secretary, his heart fluttering violently.

"Dead? A young, healthy fellow like that! When the door flew open, Arthur Constant was sleeping the sleep of the just. It was a deep, a very deep sleep, of course, else the blows at his door would long since have awakened him. But all the while Mrs. Drabdump's fancy was picturing her lodger cold and stark, the poor young fellow was lying in bed in a nice warm sleep."

"You mean to say you found Arthur Constant alive?"

"As you were last night."

The Minister was silent, striving confusedly to take in the situation. Outside the crowd was cheering again. It was probably to pass the time.

"Then, when was he murdered?"

"Immediately afterwards."

"By whom?"

"Well, that is, if you will pardon me, not a very intelligent question. Science and common-sense are in accord for once. Try the method of exhaustion. It must have been either by Mrs. Drabdump or myself."

"You mean to say that Mrs. Drabdump—!"

"Poor dear Mrs. Drabdump, you don't deserve this of your Home Secretary! The idea of that good lady!"

"It was *you! !*"

"Calm yourself, my dear Home Secretary. There is nothing to be alarmed at. It was a solitary experiment, and I intend it to remain so." The noise without grew louder. "Three cheers for Grodman! Hip, hip, hip, horray," fell faintly on their ears.

But the Minister, pallid and deeply moved, touched the bell. The Home Secretary's home secretary appeared. He looked at the great man's agitated face with suppressed surprise.

"Thank you for calling in your amanuensis," said Grodman. "I intended to ask you to lend me his services. I suppose he can write shorthand."

The Minister nodded, speechless.

"That is well. I intend this statement to form the basis of an appendix to the twenty-fifth edition—sort of silver wedding—of my book, *Criminals I Have Caught*. Mr. Denzil Cantercot, who, by the will I have made to-day, is appointed my literary executor, will have the task of working it up with literary and dramatic touches after the model of the other chapters of my book. I have every confidence he will be able to do me as much justice, from a literary point of view, as you, sir, no doubt will from a legal. I feel certain he will succeed in catching the style of the other chapters to perfection."

"Templeton," whispered the Home Secretary, "this man may be a lunatic. The effort to solve the Big Bow Mystery may have addled his brain. Still," he added aloud, "it will be as well for you to take down his statement in shorthand."

"Thank you, sir," said Grodman, heartily. "Ready, Mr. Templeton? Here goes. My career till I left the Scotland Yard Detective Department is known to all the world. Is that too fast for you, Mr. Templeton? A little? Well, I'll go slower; but pull me up if I forget to keep the brake on. When I retired, I discovered that I was a bachelor. But it was too late to marry. Time hung heavy on my hands. The preparation of my book, *Criminals I Have Caught,* kept me occupied for some months. When it was published, I had nothing more to do but think. I had plenty of money, and it was safely invested; there was no call for speculation. The future was meaningless to me; I regretted I had not elected to die in harness. As idle old men must, I lived in the past. I went over and over again my ancient exploits; I re-read my book. And as I thought and thought, away from the excitement of the actual hunt, and seeing the facts in a truer perspective, so it grew daily clearer to me that criminals were more fools than rogues. Every crime I had traced, however cleverly perpetrated, was from the point of view of penetrability a weak failure. Traces and trails were left on all sides—ragged edges, rough-hewn corners; in short, the job was botched, artistic completeness unattained. To the vulgar, my feats might seem marvellous—the average man is mystified to grasp how you detect the letter 'e' in a simple cryptogram—to myself they were as commonplace as the crimes they unveiled. To me now, with my lifelong study of the science of evidence, it seemed possible to commit not merely one but a thousand crimes that should be absolutely undiscoverable. And yet criminals would go on sinning, and giving themselves away, in the same old grooves—no originality, no dash, no individual insight, no fresh conception! One would imagine there were an Academy of crime with forty thousand armchairs. And gradually, as I pondered and brooded over the thought, there came upon me the desire to commit a crime that should baffle detection. I could invent hundreds of such crimes, and please myself by imagining them done; but would they really work out in practice? Evidently the sole performer of my experiment must be myself; the subject—whom or what? Accident should determine. I itched to commence with murder—to tackle the stiffest problems first, and I burned to startle and baffle the world—especially the world of which I had ceased to be. Outwardly I was calm, and spoke to the people about me as usual. Inwardly I was on fire with a consuming scientific passion. I sported with my pet theories, and fitted them mentally on everyone I met. Every friend or acquaintance I sat and gossiped with, I was plotting how to murder without leaving a clue. There is not one of my friends or acquaintances I have not done away with in thought. There is no public man—have no fear, my dear Home Secretary—I have not planned to assassinate secretly, mysteriously, unintelligibly, undiscoverably. Ah, how I could give the stock criminals points—with their second-hand motives, their conventional conceptions, their commonplace details, their lack of artistic feeling and restraint."

The crowd had again started cheering. Impatient as the watchers were, they felt that no news was good news. The longer the interview accorded by the Home Secretary to the chairman of the Defence Committee, the greater the hope his obduracy was melting. The idol of the people would be saved, and "Grodman" and "Tom Mortlake" were mingled in the exultant plaudits.

"The late Arthur Constant," continued the great criminologist, "came to live nearly opposite me. I cultivated his acquaintance—he was a lovable young fellow, an excellent subject for experiment. I do not know when I have ever taken to a man more. From the moment I first set eyes on him, there was a peculiar sympathy between us. We were drawn to each other. I felt instinctively he would be the man. I loved to hear him speak enthusiastically of the Brotherhood of Man—I, who knew the brotherhood of man was to the ape, the serpent, and the tiger—and he seemed to find a pleasure in stealing a moment's chat with me from his engrossing self-appointed duties. It is a pity humanity should have been robbed of so valuable a life. But it had to be. At a quarter to ten on the night of December 3rd he came to me. Naturally I said nothing about this visit at the inquest or the trial. His object was to consult me mysteriously about some girl. He said he had privately lent her money—which she was to repay at her convenience. What the money was for he did not know, except that it was somehow connected with an act of abnegation in which he had vaguely encouraged her. The girl had since disappeared, and he was in distress about her. He would not tell me who it was— of course now, sir, you know as well as I it was Jessie Dymond—but asked for advice as to how to set about finding her. He mentioned that Mortlake was leaving for Devonport by the first train on the next day. Of old I should have connected these two facts and sought the thread: now, as he spoke, all my thoughts were dyed red. He was suffering perceptibly from toothache, and in answer to my sympathetic inquiries told me it had been allowing him very little sleep. Everything

combined to invite the trial of one of my favourite theories. I spoke
to him in a fatherly way, and when I had tendered some vague advice
about the girl, I made him promise to secure a night's rest (before he
faced the arduous tram-men's meeting in the morning) by taking a
sleeping draught. I gave him a quantity of sulphonal in a phial. It is
a new drug, which produces protracted sleep without disturbing
digestion, and which I use myself. He promised faithfully to take
the draught; and I also exhorted him earnestly to bolt and bar and
lock himself in, so as to stop up every chink or aperture by which
the cold air of the winter's night might creep into the room. I remonstrated with him on the careless manner he treated his body, and he
laughed in his good-humoured, gentle way, and promised to obey
me in all things. And he did. That Mrs. Drabdump, failing to rouse
him, would cry 'Murder!' I took for certain. She is built that way.
As even Sir Charles Brown-Harland remarked, she habitually takes
her prepossessions for facts, her inferences for observations. She
forecasts the future in grey. Most women of Mrs. Drabdump's class
would have behaved as she did. She happened to be a peculiarly favourable specimen for working on by 'suggestion,' but I would have
undertaken to produce the same effect on almost any woman. The
Key to the Big Bow Mystery is feminine psychology. The only uncertain link in the chain was, Would Mrs. Drabdump rush across to
get *me* to break open the door? Women always rush for a man. I was
well-nigh the nearest, and certainly the most authoritative man in the
street, and I took it for granted she would."

"But suppose she hadn't?" the Home Secretary could not help
asking.

"Then the murder wouldn't have happened, that's all. In due
course Arthur Constant would have awoke, or somebody else breaking open the door would have found him sleeping; no harm done,
nobody any the wiser. I could hardly sleep myself that night. The
thought of the extraordinary crime I was about to commit—a burning curiosity to know whether Wimp would detect the *modus operandi*—the prospect of sharing the feeling of murderers with whom
I had been in contact all my life without being in touch with
the terrible joys of their inner life—the fear lest I should be too fast
asleep to hear Mrs. Drabdump's knock—these things agitated me
and disturbed my rest. I lay tossing on my bed, planning every detail
of poor Constant's end. The hours dragged slowly and wretchedly on
towards the misty dawn. I was racked with suspense. Was I to be
disappointed after all? At last the welcome sound came—the rat-

tat-tat of murder. The echoes of that knock are yet in my ears. 'Come over and kill him!' I put my nightcapped head out of the window and told her to wait for me. I dressed hurriedly, took my razor, and went across to 11 Glover Street. As I broke open the door of the bedroom in which Arthur Constant lay sleeping, his head resting on his hands, I cried, 'My God!' as if I saw some awful vision. A mist as of blood swam before Mrs. Drabdump's eyes. She cowered back, for an instant (I divined rather than saw the action) she shut off the dreaded sight with her hands. In that instant I had made my cut—precisely, scientifically—made so deep a cut and drawn out the weapon so sharply that there was scarce a drop of blood on it; then there came from the throat a jet of blood which Mrs. Drabdump, conscious only of the horrid gash, saw but vaguely. I covered up the face quickly with a handkerchief to hide any convulsive distortion. But as the medical evidence (in this detail accurate) testified, death was instantaneous. I pocketed the razor and the empty sulphonal phial. With a woman like Mrs. Drabdump to watch me, I could do anything I pleased. I got her to draw my attention to the fact that both the windows were fastened. Some fool, by the by, thought there was a discrepancy in the evidence because the police found only one window fastened, forgetting that, in my innocence, I took care not to refasten the window I had opened to call for aid. Naturally I did not call for aid before a considerable time had elapsed. There was Mrs. Drabdump to quiet, and the excuse of making notes—as an old hand. My object was to gain time. I wanted the body to be fairly cold and stiff before being discovered, though there was not much danger here; for, as you saw by the medical evidence, there is no telling the time of death to an hour or two. The frank way in which I said the death was very recent disarmed all suspicion, and even Dr. Robinson was unconsciously worked upon, in adjudging the time of death, by the knowledge (query here, Mr. Templeton) that it had preceded my advent on the scene.

"Before leaving Mrs. Drabdump, there is just one point I should like to say a word about. You have listened so patiently, sir, to my lectures on the science of sciences that you will not refuse to hear the last. A good deal of importance has been attached to Mrs. Drabdump's oversleeping herself by half an hour. It happens that this (like the innocent fog which has also been made responsible for much) is a purely accidental and irrelevant circumstance. In all works on inductive logic it is thoroughly recognised that only some of the circumstances of a phenomenon are of its essence and casually interconnected; there is always a certain proportion of heterogeneous accompaniments which have no intimate relation whatever with the phenomenon. Yet, so crude is as yet the comprehension of the science of evidence, that *every* feature of the phenomenon under investigation is made equally important, and sought to be linked with the chain of evidence. To attempt to explain everything is always the mark of the tiro. The fog and Mrs. Drabdump's oversleeping herself were mere accidents. There are always these irrelevant accompaniments, and the true scientist allows for this element of (so to speak) chemically unrelated detail. Even I never counted on the unfortunate series of accidental phenomena which have led to Mortlake's implication in a net-work of suspicion. On the other hand, the fact that my servant, Jane, who usually goes about ten, left a few minutes earlier on the night of December 3rd, so that she didn't know of Constant's visit, was a relevant accident. In fact, just as the art of the artist or the editor consists largely in knowing what to leave out, so does the art of the scientific detector of crime consist in knowing what details to ignore. In short, to explain everything is to explain too much. And too much is worse than too little.

"To return to my experiment. My success exceeded my wildest dreams. None had an inkling of the truth. The insolubility of the Big Bow Mystery teased the acutest minds in Europe and the civilised world. That a man could have been murdered in a thoroughly inaccessible room savoured of the ages of magic. The redoubtable Wimp, who had been blazoned as my successor, fell back on the theory of suicide. The mystery would have slept till my death, but— I fear—for my own ingenuity. I tried to stand outside myself, and to look at the crime with the eyes of another, or of my old self. I found the work of art so perfect as to leave only one sublimely simple solution. The very terms of the problem were so inconceivable that, had I not been the murderer, I should have suspected myself, in conjunction, of course, with Mrs. Drabdump. The first persons to enter the room would have seemed to me guilty. I wrote at once (in a disguised hand and over the signature of 'One Who Looks Through His Own Spectacles') to the *Pell Mell Press* to suggest this. By associating myself thus with Mrs. Drabdump I made it difficult for people to dissociate the two who entered the room together. To dash a half-truth in the world's eyes is the surest way of blinding it altogether. This pseudonymous letter of mine I contradicted (in my own name) the next day, and in the course of the long letter which I was tempted to write, I adduced fresh evidence against the theory of suicide. I was disgusted with the open verdict, and wanted men to be up and doing and trying to find me out. I enjoyed the hunt more.

"Unfortunately, Wimp, set on the chase again by my own letter, by dint of persistent blundering, blundered into a track which—by a devilish tissue of coincidences I had neither foreseen nor dreamt of— seemed to the world the true. Mortlake was arrested and condemned. Wimp had apparently crowned his reputation. This was too much. I had taken all this trouble merely to put a feather in Wimp's cap, whereas I had expected to shake his reputation by it. It was bad enough that an innocent man should suffer; but that Wimp should achieve a reputation he did not deserve, and overshadow all his predecessors by dint of a colossal mistake, this seemed to me intoler- able. I have moved Heaven and earth to get the verdict set aside, and to save the prisoner; I have exposed the weakness of the evidence; I have had the world searched for the missing girl; I have petitioned and agitated. In vain. I have failed. Now I play my last card. As the overweening Wimp could not be allowed to go down to posterity as the solver of this terrible mystery, I decided that the condemned man might just as well profit by his exposure. That is the reason I make the exposure to-night, before it is too late to save Mortlake."

"So that is the reason?" said the Home Secretary with a suspicion of mockery in his tones.

"The sole reason."

Even as he spoke, a deeper roar than ever penetrated the study. "A Reprieve! Hooray! Hooray!" The whole street seemed to rock with earthquake, and the names of Grodman and Mortlake to be thrown up in a fiery jet. "A Reprieve! A Reprieve!" The very windows rattled. And even above the roar rose the shrill voices of the news- boys: "Reprieve of Mortlake! Mortlake reprieved!"

Grodman looked wonderingly towards the street. "How do they know?" he murmured.

"Those evening papers are amazing," said the Minister drily. "But I suppose they had everything ready in type for the contingency." He turned to his secretary. "Templeton, have you got down every word of Mr. Grodman's confession?"

"Every word, sir."

"Then bring in the cable you received just as Mr. Grodman en- tered the house."

Templeton went back into the outer room and brought back the cablegram that had been lying on the Minister's writing-table when Grodman came in. The Home Secretary silently handed it to his visitor. It was from the Chief of Police of Melbourne, announcing that Jessie Dymond had just arrived in that city in a sailing vessel, ignorant of all that had occurred, and had been immediately despatched back to England, having made a statement entirely corroborating the theory of the defence.

"Pending further inquiries into this," said the Home Secretary, not without appreciation of the grim humour of the situation as he glanced at Grodman's ashen cheeks, "I had already reprieved the prisoner. Mr. Templeton went out to despatch the messenger to the governor of Newgate as you entered this room. Mr. Wimp's card-castle would have tumbled to pieces without your assistance. Your still undiscoverable crime would have shaken his reputation as you intended."

A sudden explosion shook the room and blent with the cheers of the populace. Grodman had shot himself—very scientifically—in the heart. He fell at the Home Secretary's feet, stone dead.

Some of the working men who had been standing waiting by the shafts of the hansom helped to bear the stretcher.